YOU MAKE MY HEART STOP

BECKY HUNTER

FOREVER

New York Boston

Forever
Hachette Book Group
1290 Avenue of the Americas, New York, NY 10104
read-forever.com
@readforeverpub

Originally published in 2024 by Corvus, an imprint of Atlantic Books Ltd, London, UK
First U.S. Edition: April 2025

Forever is an imprint of Grand Central Publishing. The Forever name and logo are registered trademarks of Hachette Book Group, Inc.

The publisher is not responsible for websites (or their content) that are not owned by the publisher.

The Hachette Speakers Bureau provides a wide range of authors for speaking events. To find out more, go to hachettespeakersbureau.com or email HachetteSpeakers@hbgusa .com.

Forever books may be purchased in bulk for business, educational, or promotional use. For information, please contact your local bookseller or the Hachette Book Group Special Markets Department at special.markets@hbgusa.com.

Library of Congress Cataloging-in-Publication Data

Names: Hunter, Becky, author.
Title: You make my heart stop / Becky Hunter.
Description: First US edition. | New York : Forever, 2025.
Identifiers: LCCN 2024045049 | ISBN 9781538741818 (trade paperback) | ISBN 9781538741825 (ebook)
Subjects: LCGFT: Romance fiction. | Novels.
Classification: LCC PR6108.U586 Y68 2025 | DDC 823/.92—dc23/eng/20241004
LC record available at https://lccn.loc.gov/2024045049

ISBN: 9781538741818 (trade paperback), 9781538741825 (ebook)

Printed in the United States of America

CW

10 9 8 7 6 5 4 3 2 1

YOU
MAKE MY
HEART
STOP

Also by Becky Hunter

One Moment

Chapter One

The first time Emery dies, she is only five years old. She is playing in what I presume is her garden—a neat sort of garden, well tended, with climbing plants twining their way up the wooden fencing and a stepping-stone path that winds through the grass to the pond at the back, where insects hum around the lilies. The smell of freshly cut grass hangs in the air—not from this garden, which is tastefully overgrown, but from one of the neighbors', hidden from sight in an illusion of privacy. Soft music thrums from the slightly crackly radio inside the kitchen, the back door open wide to tempt a summer breeze.

Emery's father is standing on the patio, tending to a barbecue. The sausages sizzle as he drops them on. Her mother is sitting a few feet away, sun hat pulled down over her face, a full glass of rosé next to her on a table. Condensation beads around the edges, but the glass looks untouched, all her attention instead on a printed-out document on her lap.

There is another girl too, sitting on the edge of the patio, not far from where Emery plays. She's older—maybe around ten—and tall, in a slightly awkward, lanky way. She has similar coloring to

Emery's mum, the same olive skin tone, her hair a warm brown curtain around her face. She is reading, the pages of the book well thumbed: *Are You There, God? It's Me, Margaret*. But she keeps glancing up, toward Emery, like she is checking in on her little sister, even though she can't possibly know what's about to happen.

I turn my attention to Emery reluctantly, unable to put it off any longer. I know it's her I'm here for, of course. But there is a heavier-than-usual dread in my stomach this time around. Because she's only a child.

She is barefoot, crouching in the grass, peering intently at something there. One hand is clutching a stick, the other splayed on the ground, supporting her weight. She's not really moving, just staring, a crease in her little forehead, like she is contemplating a problem she can't solve. Dark curls fall to her shoulders, framing a heart-shaped face. Something in me twinges as I look at that face, at the innocence there. A deep, painful twinge I thought I'd managed to shut down, out of necessity.

She springs to her feet with sudden determination, still clutching her little stick. I see the grass stains on her dungarees, the way she trips over their cuffs, slightly too long for her short legs.

"Emery?" It's the father who is calling, frowning over at her, barbecue tongs in hand. "Where are you going?"

The mother glances up, her face partly obscured in the shadow of her sun hat. "Leave her be, James." She says it on a sigh, and I know why. It shouldn't matter where Emery is going, what she's doing. She should be safe here, in their garden. James glances at his wife, then back to their daughter.

"She hasn't got shoes on," he states.

"She'll be fine."

"There are stinging nettles by the pond."

"Well, she'll learn not to go near them barefoot again if she gets stung, won't she?" Emery's mother is looking back down at her document now, so she doesn't see the way her husband's eyes narrow in silent disapproval at her words.

Emery is already off in any case, sprinting down the garden, toward the pond. The pond—perhaps that is the danger? I never know how, exactly, it will happen, only that it will. Sometimes it's obvious—the hospital bed or the car driving too fast—but often, like today, I'm in the dark. All I know is that it will happen, and imminently. I only ever see the brief moments before someone's death, get an impression of their lives right then. To give context, I think, though I can't be sure—it's not like anyone handed me a rule book.

Even knowing all this, I can't help the lurch toward her. Can't stop myself from trying to grab her, to keep her away from the pond. Because I don't want to see this tiny girl, full of light and energy, fighting for breath as water floods her lungs. But it's fruitless, of course it is. I feel the jerk around my midriff pulling me to immobility. I am not supposed to prevent what is happening here.

In the end, though, it's not drowning I have to worry about.

"Ow!" It's an angry sound, not hurt, not afraid. But as she

frowns down at the thorn in her foot, I see her go pale. It's not even a big thorn, and there is only the smallest pinprick of blood escaping the wound. It's nothing. Something to extract with tweezers, and for Mummy to kiss better.

But in the instant before she falls to the ground, I already know, the way I do every time. It's over, just like that, her heart ceasing to function. Because this tiny thorn, the smallest of pricks—that's all it took for this little girl's heart to stop beating.

She collapses, landing with a soft thump on the summer-dried ground. Her curls splay around her face, and a few centimeters from her limp, chubby fingers, the stick she was playing with rolls to a stop.

"Emery!" The scream comes from the sister first. She is running down the garden, her long legs covering the distance with ease.

There's a clatter, tongs falling to the patio, as James abandons the barbecue, running too, his wife not far behind. Her face is set, almost businesslike, and she pushes past her husband to get there first. "What's happened?" she demands. "Emery?" The word is a little harsh, like she's expecting the child to get up, as if she's playing a prank on them all. But I can hear the panic lacing it.

This might be the worst of it, though I change my mind frequently on that. But hearing them scream, the loved ones who are left behind, hearing them plead or sob, or just go silent, an emptiness descending on them—that is up there with the things I hate the most. Sometimes there is no one around to see it, the moment of passing. That's hard too.

I don't have to watch the rest, though. I see the mother crouch down, her touch soft despite the firm set of her face, hear the whimpering of the sister as she looks over her mum's shoulder, and then I am somewhere else entirely. And so is Emery.

She blinks at me with those big brown eyes. She is in the same dungarees, though these ones do not have grass stains on, nor are they a bit too big for her. She must not have noticed either of those things, in that garden.

I can't help wondering how I look to her. I am me, every time, and there are elements that I know remain constant—they can't imagine me into someone else entirely. My hair will always stay the same color, for instance—tree-bark brown—and I'm always around the same height and weight. But just as subtle things about their appearance can change, in this place, I've gathered, the way they perceive me can be altered too.

"Who are you?" There is no fear in her voice, only a healthy dose of suspicion.

I take a breath. This should be the bit I'm good at, by now. "I'm here to help you." I try to inject calmness and confidence into my voice. Try not to think of how very young she is, how unfair it is that her life has been snatched away by a thorn. Sometimes, this part is quick—with the ones who knew death was coming, who have had time to accept that, to say goodbye. For those, often comfort and reassurance is all that is needed. Some are angry—that can take a little longer. What will it take for Emery? What does she need to help her come to terms with her death? How am I supposed to help a child accept that?

I feel something acid rise in my throat, a bitter taste. Maybe that's why I've never had to help a child before now—because I haven't been ready. Mind you, I don't feel ready now. And it's pointless to try and think of the higher purpose here—I've given up on that. I've *tried* to give up on that.

Emery cocks her head at me. There is something there, in that action. Not familiarity, but a strange sense that it will become familiar, somehow. It's enough to make the back of my neck prickle with unease. "Help me do what?" she asks.

My mouth feels dry. Usually, they are aware that they are dead, on some level. It's not like we stand over their body or anything; they don't have to watch loved ones grieve or panic—that would hardly be conducive to "moving on." Whatever the hell that means. But they seem to come here with an understanding of what's happening, even if they don't want to admit to that.

Is it her age that prevents her from understanding what seems to be implicit for everyone else? She has so little life experience; everything must feel new and strange, all the time. I'm struck then by my inadequacy. By the complete and utter bullshit of all this. That I have been put here, somehow, and now I am supposed to help her when I have absolutely no idea how to do that. How is that fair to her? That I, of all people, should be the last one she sees before she dies? I may have only spent moments in her life, but I know with utter certainty that she deserves better than that.

"Help you come to terms…" She frowns, little bushy

eyebrows pulling together. Right. She is only five. "Um... I'm here to make sure you're okay." She nods slowly.

"Well, I'm Emery."

"Yes," I agree. Her name is the only thing I already know about her.

"And this," she announces with grandeur, "is weird."

I'm half waiting for her to ask whether she's dreaming. That happens a fair amount—people unable to let go, clinging to the possibility that they will return to consciousness. But she doesn't. She looks around instead, and it's only then that our surroundings come into focus, as the memory takes shape around us.

It's a bedroom. The twin beds have matching linen—blue and white striped duvet covers, pillowcases with bright blue and purple flowers, and a white fluffy cushion to set the whole thing off. The room is an odd combination of understated—pale, faded green wallpaper—and over the top; a bright abstract painting with bold colors and shapes takes up half the wall opposite the beds. There's a sink in the corner, with a small mirror and a wooden shelf hanging above it, where two toothbrushes sit in a plastic cup. A faint smell of bacon hovers in the air, coming from outside the closed door.

Emery goes to sit on one of the beds, reaches over to play with the lamp on the bedside table. A dim yellow glow flickers on and off around the room. "Hey, I remember this place," she says.

I perch on the other bed. It creaks under my weight. "Tell me about it."

She glances at me, and I see a flicker of unease there for the first time. Odd; the memory usually makes people feel more comfortable, not less. "Why?"

"Don't you want to?"

She picks up the fluffy cushion from behind her, pulls it to her chest and looks at me over the top of it. I feel it again—that pull of recognition. Like I *know* her. Only that's not quite right. Because that look she's giving me—it feels like an older version of her is peering out at me. Something that can't be possible.

"It's BMB," she says eventually.

Despite the situation, I feel my lips twitch. "Do you mean a B *and* B?"

"Right. That. We went on holiday—Mum, Dad and me and Amber."

"Amber—that's your sister?"

She nods. "My big sister," she qualifies unnecessarily. To be fair, she doesn't realize it's unnecessary. "I was allowed to share a room with her. This room. She would never let me before because she said I would keep her awake. She said I *snore*." She wrinkles her little button nose at the indignity of that. "Which I don't." She hugs the cushion tighter to her, and when she speaks again it's with a frailty that sends a fracture through my heart. "Why are we here?" Her voice is so small. This is the reason I try to treat it all clinically, try not to let myself think too hard about the people themselves, what they are like, what they've lost. It's the only way I stay sane.

"It's a memory. It's *your* memory."

She frowns. "If it's my memory, why isn't Amber here?" She glances at the door, like she's expecting her sister to walk through it. There is something so hopeful about her expression, and there it is again, the horrible twinge, something I wish I didn't have to feel, because it's too damn hard.

"She can't come," I say gently. "I'm sorry, but it's just you and me." Other people are never in the memories. I suppose it's because they can't come here in the same way—or maybe because if they were here, they wouldn't leave room for me and what I have to do. But I think the memory still allows whoever I'm with to remember the people who made it special, and that must be part of the comfort.

Emery looks at me again, and I see some sort of realization settle on her. "I want to go home," she whispers.

I don't know what to say. No, that's not true. I should tell her the truth. *You can't go home.* I can hear the words in my mind, know the right tone to use, apologetic but firm. But they stick in my throat. I take a breath, and it feels shaky. The memory around us seems to tremble too. I think for a moment it's me, that I'm losing my mind—because why not lose that too?—but Emery sits up straighter, her eyes darting around, her fingers turning white as they press into the cushion.

"What was that?" she asks sharply.

"I don't know," I say, before I can think better of it. She gives me a frightened look, and I curse myself inwardly. I'm here to make her feel better—I shouldn't admit to not knowing things. But it's true—I have no idea why the memory feels fragile, like it's not solid enough around us. I want to blame it on her being so young, on the fact that her memories will be fragile because of that, but I'm not quite sure that's it.

"I'm sorry," I say. "I don't mean to scare you."

"I'm not scared of *you*." She says it like it's the most obvious thing in the world. "I know you're a goodie."

It nearly makes me laugh. *Goodie*. As opposed to "baddie," I presume. There's something weirdly satisfying at being classed as good by her, though. "How?" I can't help asking.

She shrugs. "I just do."

"Then why are you scared?" An obvious question, perhaps, but I need to get her talking about it.

She worries at her lip. "I don't think I'm supposed to be here."

Supposed to be here. It's something I've grappled with many times over—the suddenness of death, who is or isn't supposed to die, and when. Who decides that?

I get up, cross to the end of her bed and perch on it. Despite the shakiness of the memory earlier, the carpet feels solid enough underfoot. I wait until she makes eye contact, still curled up with her cushion at the head of the bed. "I can't do much about the fact that you're here," I say, and my voice is almost a whisper. "But I promise you, you're going to be okay." I don't usually promise anything of the sort. I'm very careful about the assurances I give—because I have no fucking clue what happens next. So I shouldn't be promising her. But I can't help it.

She takes a breath, nods. "Can I go back now? They'll be worried about where I am."

I start to open my mouth to speak, not even sure what I'm going to say, but something stops me. Things always feel very real in these memories—there might not be people, but right now I can hear the clatter coming from downstairs, and the smell of coffee has merged with the bacon. The tip of Emery's head is reflected in the little mirror above the sink, and the duvet is soft where my palms rest on it. All of this I expect. What I don't expect is the haze that is now settling around it all, like heat off sun-drenched tarmac. This, like the tremor, is something I've never seen before.

Usually, when they are ready, people fade. I'm not sure where they go or what happens exactly, but it's almost like they recede into the memory itself, becoming a part of it, before everything disappears completely. But right now, Emery is not fading. She is becoming more solid, standing out against the haze of the memory.

"What's happening?" Her voice is higher-pitched now, reflecting the frightened child she is. It brings me back to myself, makes me realize how I've been staring. She looks down at her hands, hands that are standing out in stark contrast to the murkiness of the memory. "What's wrong?" she demands, and I'm reminded of the determination with which she got up from the grass and sprinted across the garden. What was she running toward? I want to ask, but I'm out of time.

"I..." I swallow, the words sticky in my throat. Because it shouldn't be possible. "I think our time here is up."

The tension in her body seems to ease at that, and she nods, like it's an answer that makes perfect sense. She gives me a very considered look, for someone so young. "Will I see you again?"

I don't know what to say. Usually, when I see someone, it is unequivocally the end. But with her, I get the sense that it's all only just beginning.

All at once, she disappears, not with a gradual fade like the others but with a sudden absence, yanked away from this place completely, like she was never supposed to be here. And in the brief moment before I am joined by someone new, I whisper into the darkness, "Yes, I think you just might."

Chapter Two

One minute later (August 1984)

AGE 5

Emery woke to the sound of her mum crying, which struck her as odd, because her mum never cried. Sometimes her face would go red, and her eyes would go all scary and shiny, but she never *sobbed* like she was doing now. It made Emery not want to open her eyes. Because it must be really, really bad if her mum was crying.

She could feel her mum's hands on her chest, knew they were her hands because they smelled of that funny hand stuff she used. She knew she was lying on the ground outside because it was hard and bumpy underneath her back and the grass was tickling her bare feet and she could smell that grassy-earthy smell. She could feel the sun on her face and arms, and it was really warm, but actually she felt kind of cold right then, and as she thought that, she shivered. And that made everything *hurt*. A sharp, horrible pain that she didn't want to feel again. Mostly where her mum's hands were but sort of all over, too.

Her mum's breathing hitched. "Emery?"

Emery opened her eyes, looking up into her mum's blotchy face. She noticed that one of her hands was much hotter and stickier than the other and looked over to see Amber, completely

white, gripping it. Beside Amber was the stick she'd been playing with moments ago. She'd dropped it, she remembered. As
she'd fallen. And ouch, yes, that was why! She could still feel
the thorn in her foot.

"You're hurting my hand, Amber," she said. Her voice
scratched her throat on its way out.

Amber let go, and her mum laughed, though it sounded a
bit like another sob. "James! James, she's okay!"

"Oh my God, oh thank God." Her dad's voice sounded all
breathy and weird. He wasn't on the ground with them, but
she could hear footsteps. "Emery, can I—"

"What are you doing?" her mum screamed. "You're supposed
to be on the phone to the ambulance!"

"Yes, and they're coming," her dad snapped.

"Well get back inside and find out how long they'll be!"
Emery flinched at the harsh tone. "Sorry," her mum said, stroking her hair. "Sorry, darling."

Emery blinked up at her. "What happened?"

"You were..." But her mum broke off. "How long, James?"
she barked instead.

Emery tried to sit up, but her mum pushed her back down.
Emery looked at Amber for help, but Amber was just staring at her, and her eyes looked really, really big, like maybe
she'd start crying too. "Why do we need to go in an ambulance?" Emery asked. She knew about ambulances. They had
lights and they carried very, very sick people to doctors to
make them better. They were for people with broken legs or
who were about to die. Emery looked down at her own legs,

wriggled her toes experimentally. The thorn was still stinging, but otherwise her legs seemed fine.

But her mum was still looking at her weirdly, and Emery felt her lip start to wobble. "What's wrong with me?"

Her mum let out another sob, so that when she said, "Nothing, you're fine, darling," it sounded like a lie.

But Amber was smiling now. "It'll be fun, Little Em." Her voice was croaky, like one of the bad guys in a film. "Maybe they'll put the lights on."

"But why? I'm fine. I think I just fell over. And then there was this man—"

"A man?" her mum asked sharply.

"Yes. A man. He was nice. He said he'd help me." Emery bit her lip. "But I don't think he knew what to do really. We were back in the BMB." She frowned. "The B *and* B." She looked up at her sister. "Remember, Amber? Me and you shared a room."

"Darling," her mum said hesitantly, "you haven't left the garden." She put a hand to Emery's head, like she did when she was checking her temperature.

"He was real," Emery said firmly.

"Well," her mum said, her voice still all choked. "Well, he sounds…" But whatever he sounded like, Emery didn't find out, because her mum trailed off. "James! Can't you tell them to hurry up?"

"Yes, Alice, what do you think I'm doing?"

Emery looked at her sister. "He was real, Amber," she said, sticking out her lip a bit for emphasis. "I saw him."

Amber lifted her hand to brush hair out of her face. Her hand was shaking, Emery noticed. But she nodded. "I know." Emery let out a relieved sigh. "Like Kitty, right?" Amber continued. And Emery's heart sank, because it turned out her sister didn't know. Because Kitty was made up—an imaginary friend—and this wasn't like that at all.

* *

Emery sat on a bed with white sheets, kicking her legs as she looked around the boring room while the doctor talked to her parents. There was nothing to do in here, and it smelled funny, and she could hear weird noises from the room next to them. They'd been here for *ages* while two different people had poked at Emery and put her through a machine, which had been scary, and then while they were waiting, Amber had found a piece of paper and a pen and they'd played tic-tac-toe, but even that had become boring after a while. And the doctor talking to her parents now wasn't even the nice one. The woman had been nice. She'd asked Emery about her favorite things, and they'd found out they liked a lot of the same stuff, like strawberry ice cream, but not vanilla because that was boring, and fizzy cola bottles and *The Aristocats*.

"It's a very rare heart condition," the doctor was saying. He had a long nose and his two front teeth stuck out a bit. Emery looked at Amber, who was sitting on the other side of their mum while their dad paced around the room, and stuck her own front teeth out. Amber grinned but made a flapping gesture to tell her to stop it. She wasn't *that* much older, really, but she did like telling Emery what to do.

"It's a little like reflex anoxic syndrome, where the child stops breathing, only this time, it's Emery's heart that stops beating."

"Stops *beating*?" her dad repeated, and Emery saw the warning look her mum gave him. Saw the glance her mum gave *her*. That was how she knew it was bad. She felt her heart give a little jolt, rested a hand there. She could *feel* it beating. She wanted to tell them that, but no one was looking at her anymore. She reached out for her mum's hand, and her mum took it, squeezed.

"Shock can trigger it," the long-nosed, big-toothed doctor continued, like her dad hadn't said anything at all. "It doesn't have to be something particularly painful or scary, just enough of a surprise to trigger a . . . spasm."

Spasm. Emery had no idea what that was. Was it bad? He made it sound bad.

"The condition is in the very early stages of research, I'm afraid, so I can't tell you an awful lot . . ." her mum muttered something under her breath at that, "but as long as her heart can be started again within four or five minutes, there should be no damage to her brain."

Emery frowned. What did he mean, damage to her brain? Was her *brain* hurt now? She didn't have a headache. Maybe she should tell them that, too.

"How are we supposed to do that?" her dad asked, and his voice sounded too high, all squeaky. He wouldn't stand still.

Emery watched him pace. He was still in the shorts he'd been wearing in the garden—his ugly brown ones—and those sandals he wore even though you could see his hairy big toe, and he looked silly in this white room, she decided.

"CPR training for a start," the doctor was saying, "and you'll need to make sure that any caregivers or teachers are aware of the condition and what to do."

"And what if no one is around?" her dad asked. He said it quietly, like he thought Emery wouldn't be able to hear, even though she was sitting right there. Grown-ups did this all the time—had conversations and thought she wasn't listening. They did it less with Amber—no one really talked *about* Amber in front of Amber, and they didn't talk about things they didn't want overheard. That was why Emery was always the spy if she and Amber played a trick on their mum and dad. Not very often, only when Emery could make Amber play with her, but still.

"Like I said, we're still in the early stages, but if her heart won't restart of its own accord, then…" The doctor broke off, clearing his throat, and glanced at Emery. And fine, she might not understand *everything* he was saying, but she knew it was to do with her heart and her brain, and from the way her parents were reacting, it was all quite bad. She felt a lump in her throat. She was trying not to be a cry-baby, but they were scaring her.

Her mum glanced at her too, then looked at Amber. "Amber, maybe you could take your sister outside. Here." She fumbled in her handbag and brought out two whole pounds. "Go and get something from the vending machine."

Amber nodded, took the money and jumped off the bed, holding her hand out for Emery. Emery frowned. She didn't like them talking about her in front of her, but she also didn't want them talking about her when she wasn't there.

"Come on," Amber said, smiling. "Bet they have Freddos. We can get *loads* of Freddos with this."

Emery took her hand, because she really did want a chocolate frog, and she really was fed up with this room.

She glanced up at her sister as they walked down the corridor. "What did they mean, about my heart? Is it broken?"

"No." But Amber said it really quickly, and she was frowning—and Emery considered the possibility that maybe even *Amber* didn't know, which was crazy, because Amber knew everything.

"I don't want it to be broken," Emery whispered. "And I don't want my brain to be funny either. Why did they keep saying that?"

Amber put an arm around her and squeezed. Amber's arm was all skinny really, like a twig, but right then it felt strong and safe. "It's just the doctor being silly, Little Em. Doctors are very serious, you know that." She said it wisely, in her more usual omniscient tone.

Emery pursed her lips, because she didn't know that, but maybe if Amber thought she should know it then she should pretend she did. So she nodded. And she felt fine, didn't she? She'd fallen over, that was all, and the grown-ups were making it into a big deal.

"Want a piggyback?" Amber asked, bending down so Emery

could clamber on. Amber had such long hair now, Emery thought. It was *way* longer than hers, even though she'd been trying to grow it for *ages*. Their mum said it was because Amber's hair was straight and it would take longer for Emery's to grow, which didn't seem very fair. It wasn't her fault her hair was curly, was it?

Amber took Emery into a big room with loads of people sitting around and Emery saw the vending machine on the other side of it. "So, who was this man you saw?" Amber asked. When Emery said nothing, she prompted, "You said you saw a man? Was he there to look after you when you fell?"

"I suppose so." Though Emery and Amber had had a few babysitters, and he was definitely nothing like them.

"What's his name?"

Emery shook her head. "I don't know." Maybe she should have asked.

"Well, shall we give him one?"

Emery said nothing, just held on to her sister's neck, bobbing slightly as Amber walked.

"Em? We could make one up for him. What did he look like?"

"I don't want to talk about it," Emery said, the way Amber said she didn't want to talk about *loads* of things these days. But Emery didn't want to talk about it because Amber thought he wasn't real—and if he wasn't real it would be okay to give him a fake name, but he *was* real, so it wouldn't be right. What if he didn't like the made-up name? She wouldn't want a made-up name. Sometimes she wanted to be called Rella, because it was a cooler version of Cinderella, but mostly she wanted to be called Emery.

"Okay," Amber said. She was quiet for a minute and then, just as they reached the vending machine and she dropped Emery to her feet, she said, "It'll be okay, Little Em, you know that, right?"

"I know that," Emery said, confidently. She believed it, because Amber wouldn't lie to her. She could trust Amber more than anyone ever. Then she remembered that the man had also told her it would be okay. And somehow, she knew she could trust him too.

Chapter Three

Seven years later (April 1991)

AGE 12

Emery squared her shoulders and marched over to her dad where he was sitting on one of their blue camping chairs in a circle with the other adults, around the embers of last night's fire. They were all cupping steaming mugs of tea or coffee, poured from thermos flasks. Someone had got up super early and been to the bakery and bought some pastries and a stack of newspapers, which were now being handed round. They all looked pretty bleary-eyed to Emery; she knew there had been a lot of wine involved last night. From inside their tent, she and Bonnie had listened to them cackling into the early hours of the morning, clearly overexcited on the first day of the camping trip.

Her dad looked up at her, wearing that ridiculous red bobble hat of his, the one that made him look like a weird, slimmer version of Father Christmas. It wasn't on straight, and on one side some of his black curls, the ones that she had inherited, had broken free. Why they were going camping in April was beyond Emery—hadn't everyone known it would be cold? Her dad had been checking the weather obsessively in the week running up to the trip, until her mum had snapped at him one evening: *It's the New Forest, James, not the bloody Arctic.*

"Me and Bonnie are going to go and explore for a bit," she announced. Her breath steamed out in front of her in the crisp morning air.

Her dad lifted one eyebrow. "Are you now?"

"Yes." She'd figured that telling him rather than asking him was a better strategy. "We're going to take our bikes. We won't go far, just around the campsite."

She watched as her dad frowned, and felt her heart sink. She'd wanted Bonnie to ask him because she thought he might be more likely to say yes to her, but Bonnie was a wimp and had insisted they each ask their own parents. And as Emery's mum was nowhere to be seen yet, that left her dad. She'd been all for just sneaking off, but Bonnie had adamantly refused.

"I don't think that's a good idea," her dad said, not meeting her eye.

Emery dredged up her calm, patient voice. "We'll be perfectly safe."

"Emery, you're only twelve and I'd rather you weren't off on your own." Her age wasn't the reason, and they both knew it. "We're all going to go horse riding soon anyway," he continued. "That will be fun!" Emery doubted it—she had a suspicion her dad wouldn't actually let her get on a horse once they were there, and even if he was persuaded, there would be no chance of her going fast, like she wanted to.

"I don't want to go horse riding—I want to go cycling with Bonnie."

His frown deepened, making the other lines on his face crease in solidarity. His eyebrows were peppered with gray—that probably meant the rest of his hair would go gray soon, too. "It will be a nice activity to do together, as a group. And we'll be getting ready soon, there's not enough time for you to go off on your own."

"Dad! You're being unfair." It was childish, and she regretted the petulant tone as soon as the words were out, but she couldn't help it. It *was* unfair.

Her mum appeared at this point, wearing the thick-rimmed glasses she'd got a few years ago, her hair, the same warm brown color as Amber's, tied up messily on top of her head. She was wearing an oversized shirt over tracksuit bottoms, and she shivered as she pushed the tent flap aside. She'd arrived late last night, Emery knew—she'd had to work, so had missed the first day of the trip. Not that that was anything new—she often worked during their holidays. "What's all this?" she asked.

Emery folded her arms. "Dad won't let me and Bonnie go cycling on our own around the campsite."

A sigh. "Oh James, don't be silly—of course they can go." Emery met her mother's gaze for a moment and felt a flash of solidarity zip through the space between them. Yes, her mum might work all the time, and yes, some of the other parents thought she was a bit "aloof," but at least she got it.

"I don't think it's very safe," her dad said stiffly, turning to look at her mum. Emery could only see the back of his bobble hat, but she could imagine the look he was giving her.

"It's perfectly safe," her mum said with a wave of her hand. "That's why we picked this place—child friendly."

"That's not what I mean, as you well know." There was a

beat of silence, and Emery suddenly felt like all the eyes around the circle were on her. She glanced around, looking for her aunt Helen—another voice of reason she could add to the argument—but she was nowhere to be seen. Probably still in bed, knowing Helen.

"You can't wrap her in cotton wool her whole life, James," Emery's mum said quietly.

Emery shifted from foot to foot, feeling heat rise across her chest. The other adults were pretending not to listen, but she still didn't want everyone knowing about her condition. Although come to think of it, maybe her dad had already told them all so they knew what to do if something happened. She scowled at the thought. She'd told Bonnie because she'd had to explain why her dad was weirdly overprotective, but she'd made it sound like it wasn't a big deal. Which it wasn't. It had only happened once, and she barely remembered it.

"She's going to be a teenager soon," her mum continued. "What are you going to do, stop her from ever leaving the house?" Emery found this ridiculous—the idea that magically turning thirteen would transform her into an entirely different entity who would be entitled to more independence. Then again, if turning thirteen magically *did* grant her more independence, who was she to argue? "Besides," her mum continued, "it might never happen again. We can't live waiting for it, it's not healthy." She raised her voice then, cutting off whatever her dad had been about to say, and looked across to the other side of the circle. "What do you think, Maureen? About Bonnie and Emery going off for a little bike ride while we all get ready?"

Emery glanced over to where Bonnie's mum was sitting with rollers in her red hair—a more vibrant red than Bonnie's "strawberry blonde." She'd literally never seen Maureen look anything other than perfect, so it was a bit like seeing an actor without a costume. Then again, Maureen already had a full face of makeup on. She was who Bonnie and Emery went to if they wanted to try out makeup—she'd already taught them how to do eyeliner. Emery's mum hardly ever wore makeup—she'd told Emery it was frivolous when she'd asked her why not, and that it was pandering to the patriarchy. Emery had had to look up the word "patriarchy" in a dictionary, but she still wasn't sure why wearing eyeliner was such a big deal.

"Oh, I think it's a great idea," Maureen said. "All for it."

Emery saw a muscle jump in the side of her dad's neck, the way it did when he was annoyed but trying to hold it back. "I'm still not sure it's—"

"Colin is going to go too," Maureen said, her voice booming over the ashes. A few of the other adults looked up from their newspapers, wondering what all the fuss was about. Bonnie gave her brother a scathing look, but Emery didn't mind if Colin tagged along. She was trying out the idea of having a crush on him—she figured it was about time she had a crush on *someone*, and Bonnie's older brother seemed like the sensible choice, out of the options available.

Her dad gave Colin, with his floppy blonde hair and Guns N' Roses hoodie, an appraising look. No doubt a fourteen-year-old boy was inherently untrustworthy—though Emery doubted her dad had been anything but trustworthy when *he* was fourteen. He'd been the type of kid to immediately own up to starting an argument, according to Aunt Helen, which, she said, was highly annoying because it had meant their parents never believed her if she told them something was his fault, since he'd tell them himself if it was. Now, he pulled his red bobble hat off his head and ran his hand through his curls. "I'd feel better if Amber could go with you too."

As one, they all looked over to where Amber was curled in one of the nearby camping chairs, pulled back from the circle, her long legs folded under her oversized sweater. She'd had a fringe cut recently—a fringe that categorically did not suit her, as Emery had told her on multiple occasions—and she seemed to be hiding behind it, pretending she couldn't see any of them.

"We don't need a babysitter," Emery huffed. Then she glanced at her sister again, immediately feeling guilty for saying it. But Amber didn't appear to have heard, and was still frowning down at the textbook she was reading. She probably didn't want to hang out with her and Bonnie—that was what she always said if Emery ever asked her these days. She was far too busy making a big deal out of studying for her A levels, and had grown distinctly boring as a result. Emery had already vowed not to be like that at seventeen—where was all the fun, going out to parties and kissing boys, that kind of thing?

"Amber?" their dad prompted. "Will you go with Bonnie and Emery?"

"And Colin!" Maureen called.

Amber looked up at their dad, a slightly wild look in her

eyes—amber eyes, though their parents insisted they hadn't known they would turn out this color when they'd named her. "Dad, I can't, I've got to revise."

"I'm sure you can—"

"I said I can't, okay! I've got mocks when we get back."

Emery glanced over at Bonnie at this, and they exchanged a quick grin before looking away from one another, not wanting to do anything to jeopardize the negotiations. But Amber got so worked up, it was hard not to find her funny at times. Her dad couldn't exactly complain, though—he was the one always telling them to think about their career options and that the grades they got now would affect their whole lives; what did he expect?

"Just go, Emery," her mum said quietly. She followed this up with a small nod, and her lips twitched into a smile. This was why Emery loved her mum. And before her dad could argue any more, she took the permission and ran, gesturing at Bonnie to follow her. They exchanged a victory grin as they unlocked their bikes, Colin just behind.

"Ready?" Emery asked, looking between Colin and Bonnie as she swung her leg over her bike. Without waiting for an answer, she sped off, pedaling as fast as she could, wanting to be away before anyone could call her back. She heard Colin laughing behind her and grinned over her shoulder at him, reveling in the freedom.

She slowed when they reached the edge of the campsite and Colin pulled up next to her, Bonnie a few meters behind. "So where are your grand plans taking you?" he asked.

Emery shrugged. "We were just going to go and explore the site." She frowned around at the tents. "I was expecting there to be something a bit more to actually explore, though."

Colin glanced at the gravel track that led away from the campsite and toward the road. "Let's go into the village."

Bonnie came to a stop on Emery's other side and made a face, clearly about to protest—she wasn't very good at doing things she wasn't supposed to. But Emery spoke before she could. "You're on." And fine, okay, it was partly out of a need to impress Colin, to show that she was as mature as he was, but it was also because she knew her dad would like the thought of her going to the village even less than riding around the campsite, and that made her want to do it even more.

They both started pedaling again, the gravel crunching under their tires, and ignored Bonnie's "Guys!" behind them. She'd follow, Emery knew. She was getting hot in her coat now, the sun warm on her face. Maybe April wasn't *so* bad for camping.

"So, you working hard at school like your sister?" Colin asked, putting on a teasing voice.

Emery rolled her eyes. "My exams don't even *count*, like I have to think about any of that."

"You will soon. They start you early, trust me."

It was said with all the wisdom of a fourteen-year-old, and Emery couldn't help snorting quietly. She glanced at him as they reached the end of the gravel track and headed right, following signs to the village. Colin wasn't *bad*-looking—he was tall-ish, and his skin was pretty clear, and his eyes were a brighter blue than Bonnie's gray-blue, which was a good thing because if their eyes were the same it would be too like kissing her best friend. Not that she was even sure she wanted to kiss him, but she should probably get her first kiss out of the way at some point.

"They'll start you on work experience and everything soon," he continued. "Get you planning your future."

Emery pff'd. "Trust me, I won't be planning my future any time soon."

"Colin wants to be a journalist," Bonnie said from just behind them, her tone almost scathing. "He did his work experience at the *Cambridge Evening News*, didn't you, Colin?"

"Yeah, so?"

"He went on and on about the *news*, when all he did was make tea and bring biscuits."

"That's not true," Colin said with a grunt.

"It is, I heard you telling Mum."

"Shut it, binface," Colin growled. His cheeks were slightly pink now and it made him look younger, more like the boys in Emery's year, even though he made a big deal about being in Year 10.

They raced along the pavement next to the road, swerving around pedestrians, until they reached a cobbled street. Colin braked suddenly so that Emery and Bonnie almost ran into the back of him. Emery peered down the street to see loads of little quaint touristy shops and cafés opening up. And—yes! "Hey, let's get ice cream!" She repositioned her bike and started pedaling toward the gelateria up ahead, complete with a blue and white awning and a fat cardboard Italian man outside.

"You read my mind," Colin said from behind her. Good thing Emery had thought to bring her pocket money, just in case.

The three of them rested their bikes next to one of the metal outdoor tables and headed inside. Bonnie got two scoops of mint choc chip—her go-to—and Colin went for chocolate, which Emery deemed boring, picking the ginger-pineapple just because it sounded the most obscure.

"You really going to eat that?" Colin asked, with a suspicious look at her yellow ice cream.

"Of course."

He made a face. "You're braver than me."

Emery laughed and tried out a casual hair flick. Bonnie gave her a funny look as she did so. Maybe not, then.

The three of them sat on one of the benches outside. Emery looked at Colin over her ice cream. "You seriously want to be a journalist?"

He shrugged. "Well, I mean, yeah. Probably."

It was baffling to her that anyone could know what they wanted to do. Amber was like that too, so convinced she'd be a physiotherapist, a random career plucked from a hat before she'd even left school.

She frowned at Bonnie. "You don't know what you want to do, do you?"

Bonnie shook her head. "No idea." Well, at least someone was with her.

When they'd all finished their ice creams, Emery sighed. "We should probably go back." Maybe if she wasn't gone for ages and proved that she could look after herself, her dad would chill out a bit more for the rest of the trip.

They all clambered onto their bikes, and Colin gave Emery a sly glance. "Race you back?"

She was off before he could say *go*, grinning to herself as she sped away from him, ignoring a woman who shouted at her to watch out and laughing as she careened around the corner, back to the gravel path that led to the campsite. She heard Bonnie's familiar huff of frustration as she left her behind, heard Colin laughing too as he tried to catch up with her.

He overtook her halfway along the gravel path, and Emery felt her legs burn as she tried to get in front again. She glanced quickly over her shoulder, was reassured when she saw Bonnie—a little way back, but still coming.

She was practically neck and neck with Colin as they swerved into the campsite without slowing down. "Hey, guys, wait!" Bonnie called, but they were too caught up in the race to take any notice of her.

They were nearly back now—she was sure their tents were just up there. She pushed a bit harder, her thighs screaming at her, and yes! She was neck and neck with Colin. She could see their group ahead, caught sight of her dad standing up, facing them, though he was too far away for her to make out his features. Seriously? Had he been waiting for them this entire time?

It was that moment of distraction that allowed Colin to get the better of her, and he pulled ahead, grinning back at her, his blonde hair flopping across his eyes. She scowled, tried to pump her legs faster. She didn't see the bump on the track until it was too late. She hit it at speed, a jolt running through her as the bike skidded out from underneath her.

She felt the solid impact when she hit the ground, and even as she threw out her hands to break her fall, pain lanced down her neck as her head was whipped back. Her teeth clashed together, the force of it ricocheting through her skull. A sharp pain seared the inside of her mouth, and she tasted the metallic tang of blood.

Then, for a brief second, there was nothing.

Chapter Four

Emery blinked a few times. There was no pain anymore. No taste of blood in her mouth, no headache, and when she checked her palms, no sign of the dirt that she'd face-planted into.

She was also, as it turned out, not in the campsite anymore. Instead, she was in the middle of a forest. She realized then that she was high up—on a wooden platform, halfway up one of the trees, a light breeze tugging at her curls. She was in the shade, but sunlight filtered through the canopy overhead, creating pockets of light and dark on the forest floor below. She heard laughter somewhere nearby—a child's delighted squeal—and glanced around but couldn't see where it was coming from. There was no one else here.

No one except him.

"I *knew* it," she breathed. He was standing a meter or so away from her, hands tucked into the pockets of his jeans. *Jeans.* For some reason it seemed bizarre that he was wearing jeans, of all things. She looked down at herself, saw she was still in the same coat she'd put on this morning.

"Knew what?" he asked conversationally, as if it was totally normal that they'd be meeting like this. His voice was low, with an accent. Scottish? She was pretty sure that was a Scottish accent—faint, but definitely there. Why on earth did he have a Scottish accent?

"I knew you weren't a figment of my imagination," she clarified.

He was watching her intently. His eyes were a light gray-green color, kind of mysterious-looking. Though to be fair, she was pretty sure *anyone* would look mysterious in this kind of situation. He was tall—she'd thought that might be because she'd been so small last time around, but he really *was* tall, and she reckoned if he pouted, he'd have a face like that actor Bonnie was obsessed with—David someone or other—who had these great cheekbones and an impressive jaw and really good eyebrows, all offset by his dark hair.

"Emery," he said, and it was almost like he was trying out the sound of her name.

She shifted from foot to foot. She wasn't sure where to look. She settled for staring at his chin. "Yes. I thought we'd established that last time." She was speaking too quickly, not quite managing the cool nonchalance she was aiming for. But what was she supposed to say? She'd spent years wondering whether it had really happened. She'd tried to figure out what he might be—an angel, a ghost, a spirit of some kind? In the end, she'd almost convinced herself that she'd made the whole thing up. Yet here he was, in front of her. *Talking* to her.

"Sorry," he was saying. He slipped a hand out of his pocket, ran it through his hair—a nice chestnut-brown color, like the conkers she'd got into the habit of collecting a few years ago. Then she'd found out that they kept spiders away, and actually, she quite liked spiders and the spiders needed somewhere to live too, didn't they? So she'd stopped collecting them. "I suppose I'd wondered if you were a figment of *my* imagination. The girl who went back to life," he mused.

It was all so damn freaky that she decided not to comment on that.

"It looks different," she said instead. "To last time. This place, I mean." She gestured around the forest. She noticed now that there was a zip wire on the platform, heading through the trees. She couldn't make out where it went to—part of the fun had been *not* knowing. And then she remembered there was a little clearing, further ahead, and that the forest wasn't really as big as it seemed. She frowned. "Or—*is* it a place? Is this real?"

"Well," he said, rocking back on his heels, "I'm not sure about it on a metaphysical level, but I'm going to go with yes, it's real, in that it's happening. It doesn't look the same because this place molds to your memory—a memory you feel comforted by. I suppose that changes as you change as a person."

"You *suppose*?"

"Sorry. This is the first time this has happened to me— seeing someone more than once, I mean." He clapped his hands together. "So, where are we this time?"

"You don't know?" Emery asked.

"It's your memory."

She gave him a suspicious look, but his expression stayed neutral as he leaned back against the tree trunk, waiting for her to answer. "It's—*was*—summer camp. After the end of Year 5. Bonnie—she's my friend—"

"The redhead? Behind you, when you were cycling?"

She narrowed her eyes. "Yes. How did you know that? Do you, like, *watch*? Because that's kind of creepy."

He shook his head. "I only see the moments before you die."

She grimaced. "I am dead then." It seemed the only logical conclusion, of course, but it was a bit different hearing it out loud.

He winced, like he shouldn't have said anything. "Yes. Sorry."

Dead. It was the word everyone danced around when they talked about her heart condition. The word that lingered at the edges of so many conversations with doctors, her sister, her parents. Not just conversations *with* her, but *about* her too. "I'll go back, though, right? When they start my heart again."

They. God, her dad would have seen the whole thing, would no doubt be running toward her right now, in utter panic. She swallowed. "That's what happened last time." They'd explained it to her, when she'd been old enough to ask, to understand.

He ran a hand through his hair again. "I...I don't know."

Her dad would bring her back, she thought firmly. He'd get her mum there too, and between them, the two of them would know what to do. That was what all the CPR training had been about, right? They'd been to a training day every year since she was five, in case anything like this happened again. But she felt a rush of guilt. It was her fault—they'd be scared, and if she hadn't insisted on going cycling, this wouldn't be happening.

"I shouldn't have been on the bike," she muttered, looking down at the forest floor.

"It wasn't your fault, Emery," he said, and his voice was calm, soothing. Sympathetic, in a way that made her eyes sting.

No. She didn't want to cry. Didn't want to think about how scared everyone must be—her family, but Bonnie and Colin, too. She didn't want to think about how she could have avoided it, if she'd listened to her dad, and how now she'd proved him right—that she wasn't safe, that she couldn't be allowed the same freedoms as other people her age. She didn't want to think about what she might face if—*when*—she went back.

So she changed the subject. "You said you see the moments before . . . Well, you know. How much before? Did you see the ice cream?" For some reason the thought of him witnessing her brief, ineffective attempt at flirting sat uncomfortably with her.

"No . . . ?" He cocked an eyebrow, like he might be wondering what it was about the ice cream that was making her look awkward.

"But you saw the bike falling and everything?"

"Yes." There was a brief pause, and his expression tightened, just for an instant. But then he smiled a sympathetic smile, and she was sure she'd imagined it. "It looked like it hurt."

She gave a shrug. "Not really," she lied. It was warm, so she stripped off her coat, revealing her stripy pink and green sweater underneath. "But does that mean . . . do you only watch me?" If so, there might be something in the guardian angel theory.

"No. I help people when they—"

"Die," she said bluntly.

"Yes."

"So what are you, an angel of death or something?"

"I'm not sure what you'd call me," he said, thoughtfully.

"You don't *know*?"

"No."

"Well, that's helpful," she muttered. He snorted quietly and she smiled, pleased to have made him laugh. "What's your name?"

"It doesn't matter what my name is."

Emery folded her arms and prepared to stare him out, the way she was practiced at doing. The way that almost always got an answer. But he shook his head firmly.

"I'm not the important one here. You are."

She huffed out a breath and turned away, looking at the zip wire. She reached up to finger the harness that you had to strap yourself into if you wanted to ride it. Then she glanced over her shoulder. He was still leaning against the tree, watching her carefully, like he wasn't quite sure what to make of her.

"Does anyone ever think you're God?"

"Sometimes. It makes for an interesting conversation."

"I'll bet."

She looked down at the forest floor. She'd never been scared of heights—or rather, she'd ignored the unease that came from being so high up—but it was quite a long way down. Then she looked back at him. "You're not, are you? God, I mean."

"No. Definitely not."

She blew out a breath, a bit relieved by that. "Just checking." She paused. "Does he exist?" She frowned, remembering her mum's patriarchy comment. "Or she." She cocked her head. "Them?"

He shook his head. "No idea."

She wrinkled her nose. "You'd think you'd have more answers, wouldn't you?"

"You'd think," he said drily. After a beat, he spoke again. "Shall we just say I'm a guide?"

She made a face, and he raised his eyebrows in question. "Makes me think of Girl Guides," she muttered.

Now those eyebrows pulled together. "That some kind of club? Wait, I know it. Like Scouts?"

"Yeah. My sister tried to make me join—I hated it."

She tried to study him without looking like that was what she was doing. She'd never been able to pull his face into focus afterward, much as she'd tried—and it wasn't like she could bring out a photo to help her. He wasn't as old as she'd thought he was, she decided. Older than her, obviously. Older than Amber too, she reckoned, but younger than her parents. Not the old man full of wisdom she'd been imagining.

"Are you the only one of you? The only *guide*." She dragged out the word, made it sound deliberately stupid.

"No, there are others—I can hardly help everyone."

"No," Emery agreed. "That would be a lot of people, wouldn't it?"

"I've never met any of the others, though," he added after a beat. "We exist . . . separately from one another."

She sniffed. "Sounds boring."

He smiled. "I don't feel bored. I'm always meeting people, even if the encounters are only fleeting."

She reached up to twirl one of her curls around her forefinger. "Sounds lonely, then." He didn't contradict her, but rather looked away, through the forest. She bit her lip. Stupid. Why did she have to say that? "Sorry," she said quickly.

He looked back at her, smiled again—only this time, it seemed a little forced. "Don't be." He pushed away from the tree, came to stand next to her and peered along the zip line. "So, where are we, exactly? Summer camp where?"

"In Wales, somewhere." She reached up again to grab the harness. She could forget the harness, leap off the platform. No one here to stop her. And what would happen, anyway, if she fell? She was already dead, wasn't she? "I don't know where, exactly. Somewhere beginning with A, maybe?" She looked at him to see if he might know a Welsh place with a forest beginning with A, but he shook his head apologetically.

She made a face. "You're really *not* all-knowing, are you?"

"Would it be better if I were? I could pretend, if you like?" There was a hint of a smile behind his polite expression.

She wanted to say something sassy back, like how being all-knowing seemed like the type of qualification that you should have when you applied for a job as a guide for dead people, but she remembered the way he'd looked when she'd brought up the lonely thing and decided against it.

She sat down, swinging her legs over the platform, and

marveled at the freedom of being able to do so without anyone telling her to be careful. "Anyway, me and Bonnie went—everyone in our year did. It was the first time Mum and Dad let me stay somewhere overnight, would you believe?" She rolled her eyes. "They were always such a nightmare about that." But then she *was* dead, wasn't she? The thing they'd been so scared of had happened again. The thought made her feel a bit hot and panicky, so she pushed it aside. "Anyway, this is the zip line," she finished, somewhat lamely.

"So I gather."

She glanced at him, not sure whether he was joking with her. He was hard to read. "I wasn't supposed to go on it," she admitted. "Dad wrote this really long letter to the teacher about why I couldn't do certain stuff, but they must have forgotten or whatever. Bonnie was a total wimp." She smiled, picturing Bonnie up here on the platform, a silly little yellow helmet on, backing away against the tree. "She did it after I did, though." She felt an uncomfortable pang. If she didn't go back, she'd never see Bonnie again. She licked her lips, made herself keep talking. If she was talking, she'd stop thinking about that stuff. "I never told Dad I went on it."

"And your mum?"

Emery hesitated. "She didn't ask."

They left it at that.

The platform let out a musical creak as he sat down too, his longer legs swinging next to hers. If he was at all concerned about being high up, he didn't show it. But then why should he be worried? He was already dead too. Or was he? Presumably not, actually. But he wasn't alive, in any case.

"You're worried," he stated, his voice gentle.

"Yes." She saw no point in denying it—not with him, not in this place.

"About not going back."

"Yes." She shrugged. "Are you going to tell me that's normal?"

"I would, maybe, and it is, but—"

His words stalled as their surroundings shook. A tremor seemed to roll through her. She'd never experienced an earthquake, but she imagined it felt a little like this— a minor one, at least. "What was that?" She hated how frightened, how small her voice sounded. But he was smiling, and he leaned back on his palms, his posture relaxing. Around her, she could see the leaves that littered the forest floor, could smell a woody, piny sort of scent. And something else, too. A more citrusy fragrance, mixed with the salt and wind from the sea.

"I think it means we don't have long left here."

"What?" Emery's voice got higher in her panic. "Because I'm—"

"No," he said firmly. "Because you're going back. This happened last time."

She felt her chest loosen a little. "It did?"

"Yes."

She took a deep breath. "Well, that's good." Then she frowned. "How does it work, though? Because my heart can't *actually* have stopped for as long as I've been here, right? I've heard the doctors explaining it to Mum and Dad—they need to get it started again right away."

"Time works differently here," he said, like that was enough of an explanation.

"Hmm." She could press him, but she doubted she'd get anywhere. Maybe he didn't even know. So she swung her legs up and got to her feet. "Well, guess I better make the most of it while I'm here, then."

He tilted his head to look up at her. "And how are you going to do that?"

She reached for the harness, frowning a little as she fumbled to work out the straps. Then she fastened herself in and grinned at him. It was the only warning she gave before she took off, holding on to the bar above her as she sailed through the air.

She heard a surprised laugh behind her and let out a whoop. It echoed again and again through the air, no one there to hear it but them. She felt the laughter bubble out of her as she watched the trees zoom past, remembering the thrill of it from last time around so that it felt doubly good this time.

She ran to a stop when she reached the platform on the other side, just about managing to stop herself from falling over. She waited a moment for her breathing to calm before she shouted, "Come on! You've got to do it too!" She couldn't see him, but felt sure her voice would carry.

"No way!"

"Why not?"

"Because . . ." His voice trailed away.

"Come on, what else are you going to do? Stand there shouting at me until I return to the living?" It was bizarre how normal it felt to be shouting across a forest at some kind of angel-slash-guide-slash-ghost. "How are you supposed to *guide* me from there?"

She heard him swearing, suspected it was supposed to be quiet enough not to carry, and couldn't help the giggle that escaped. Then she saw the way the zip wire tightened and heard the whirring of the roller.

He looked far too big for it in a way that made her laugh—because it was designed for people much lighter than him, of course. She laughed again as he landed on all fours on the platform, shaking his head like a dog and giving her a dry look. But then *he* was laughing too, and neither of them could stop, and they were laughing so hard they couldn't breathe.

He managed to stop first, twisting into a cross-legged position. She hesitated, then sat opposite him.

She cocked her head. "If you're not supposed to guide me, then what am I doing here?"

"I'm going to pass on that one—your guess is as good as mine." He glanced away from her, his gaze flickering around the surroundings.

"What?" she asked sharply.

He looked back at her with a slight frown. "Can you see it too?"

She knew immediately what he meant—the haze that was creeping in around the woods, one that hadn't been there in real life. But no, was it creeping in or creeping *out*? Because now that she thought about it, it seemed to be coming from her, more than anything else. It should have felt scary, maybe, but instead it felt familiar, and she knew it meant she was going back—to Amber, to Bonnie, to her parents.

"I suppose this means goodbye?" she said. He nodded, offered her a small smile. "I'll, umm, see you soon?" She was very much hedging, but what were you supposed to say?

He gave her one last smile. It was a kind smile, she decided. Kind, and a little sad. "For your sake," he said softly, "let's hope you don't."

Chapter Five

The first thing Emery registered when she woke was the pain. Shooting pain in her chest, a tightness that made it feel like she couldn't breathe. But she gasped, and air flooded her lungs, and with that she registered the blood in her mouth. She turned her head to one side and spat it out, and the movement made her head throb painfully. She let out a small whimper.

"Emery? Can you open your eyes? Emery! Look at me!" It was her dad's voice, high and panicked and angry all at once. She forced her eyes open, but the onslaught of light made her snap them shut immediately. "Emery!"

"Give her a minute, James." Her mum's voice now, somewhere close.

"I'm just checking she's alive, for fuck's sake, Alice."

"I know that, but she's come round, she's okay, she just—"

"She's not okay! Jesus. We should have never let her go off on her own." Even in the state she was in, Emery recognized that her dad did not mean "we," and she felt the blame settle into the silence between her parents.

She coughed, and it hurt. But she forced herself to open her

47

eyes again. Her vision was a little blurry, but she could see her dad's face close to hers, his big hands across her chest, one on top of the other, his checked pajama bottoms covered in dirt from where he was kneeling next to her.

"Hey, love," he said, his voice gentle. "You're okay. You're okay now." But the words he'd just snapped echoed in her mind. *She's not okay! Jesus.*

She turned her head, looking up at the bright blue sky. "Mum?"

Immediately her mum's face was there, next to her dad's. "I'm here. How are you doing?"

"I'm…" Another cough wheezed through her. "I'm all right." She thought of where she'd been a moment ago, on a zip line in the forest, with no pain to accompany her. She thought of *him*, and how calm, how reassuring he'd been—compared to the waves of panic radiating off her parents. She took a cautious breath. This time, it hurt a little less.

"We need to get her to the hospital," her dad said. "Alice, the car keys are in the tent and Helen is on the phone to the ambulance."

There was the tiniest pause before her mum nodded and, after stroking Emery's head gently, she got to her feet. Amber crouched down to take her place. Her face was ashen, her eyes shining with tears from behind her stupid fringe.

"I'm sorry," she said, stifling a sob. She looked at their dad. "I'm sorry I didn't go with her."

"Don't be silly," Dad said gruffly. "It's not your fault." There was the tiniest inflection on the word *your*, though Emery wondered if Amber even noticed. Only then did he lift his hands away from Emery's chest. They were shaking. Her dad's big, steady hands were trembling as he pulled one of them across his stubbled jaw. He was still wearing his red bobble hat, she saw now, but it was nearly falling off, making his head look like a weird elongated egg. In any other circumstance, it might be funny.

"Come on then, Em," he said. "Let's go get you checked out." Emery started to push herself up, but her dad put his hand gently back on her chest to hold her in place. "No, I'll carry you."

"Dad!" Emery felt heat flood her cheeks. "Don't be silly."

"No arguments," he said, and she knew from his expression that she wouldn't win this one. She wasn't sure how he was strong enough to lift her up—he hadn't carried her around like this in years—but he got her off the ground, Amber bending to pick up his bobble hat when it eventually fell from his head.

Only when she was in his arms, being held like a baby, did Emery see that Bonnie and Colin were still there. They'd been hovering out of sight, watching the whole thing. Maureen was there too, her arm around Bonnie's shoulders, half her rollers still in so that she looked oddly lopsided. Bonnie and Colin were both pale, like Amber, with a matching waxy sheen. Bonnie had clearly been crying and Colin was standing stiff, his jaw tight.

Emery looked away, staring down at the ground, at where her bike was lying. Would she be allowed to keep it? Or would it be blamed for what had happened and get locked away in the shed or given to someone else? She felt a lump in her throat and tried to swallow it down. That wouldn't be fair—it wasn't the bike's fault; *it* shouldn't be punished.

She could feel eyes on her as her dad carried her back toward the tent. Her cheeks were flaming, her bottom lip trembling despite herself. She didn't want to cry—she couldn't bear everyone here watching her, and if she cried, it would only make things worse. She was trying desperately to make herself small, tucking her chin against her chest, curling her fingers under the sleeves of her coat. But she made the mistake of glancing up, just briefly, to see whether everyone was still looking at her. It was Colin she caught sight of first, and in the brief moment their gazes locked, she saw something flash in his eyes.

Guilt, she realized. That was guilt.

* *

Emery was sitting up in bed, pillow propped behind her, knees pulled to her chest. She'd wanted to go downstairs for a solid twenty minutes now, but the sound of her parents arguing kept her at bay, even as her stomach rumbled.

"Will you just stop! We're going round and round in circles, James."

"Because you're refusing to listen to me!"

They'd come home early from the New Forest yesterday, after spending the afternoon in the hospital. Emery hadn't been able to say goodbye to Bonnie because her mum had gone back to the campsite to pack up their things while the doctors ran all kinds of tests that her dad had insisted on. Afterward, he'd driven them all straight home. Holiday over, just like that.

Her bedroom door creaked open a fraction and she looked over to see Amber peering through the gap. "Can I come in?" Amber whispered. Emery nodded. It was a point of contention between them these days—Emery tended to barge in on Amber without asking, which quite often resulted in Amber slamming a textbook down on her desk and demanding she get out because she had *so much to do, Emery!* Amber, on the other hand, resolutely knocked politely before entering Emery's room, no matter how annoyed she was, as if to prove a point about how sisters should respect each other's privacy. But she wasn't proving a point right now. From the look on her face as she opened the door wider to step inside—uncertain, teeth gnawing her bottom lip—she wasn't sure if Emery would *want* her to come in.

In the brief moment before Amber shut the door behind her, the sound of their parents' voices swelled, stretching into every corner of Emery's small bedroom, around the single bed with its sea-themed bedspread, into the gap between the wall and the wonky dressing table passed down from Aunt Helen.

"This is the second time it's happened because you let her do something!"

"I didn't *let* her do something, James."

"You said she could go."

"Yes, I said she could go on a damned bike ride. The height of irresponsible parenting, is that what you're telling me? A thorn and a bike—they're the things that mark me as an unfit mother in your eyes, is that what you're saying?"

"I never said…"

Her dad's voice was muffled as Amber closed the door and padded over to sit on the corner of Emery's bed. She twisted her hands in her lap and Emery saw her nails were bitten down to the quick, the skin around them flaking off.

"You okay?" Amber asked.

Emery shrugged in a non-committal way. She supposed she *was* okay—she wasn't still hurting, anyway.

Amber looked down at her hands, still twisting in her lap. She was wearing her favorite high-waisted pale denim jeans, ones Emery had coveted when she'd first bought them, and a tie-dye top that Emery did *not* covet, given that it was completely shapeless. Amber's hair was scraped back into a ponytail, pulling her features tight, and there were dark circles under her eyes.

To Emery's alarm, those eyes started to well up. "I'm sorry," Amber whispered.

Emery frowned. "What do you mean?"

Amber took a breath, and Emery wondered if this was a conversation she had been gearing up to. Her sister tended to do that—think and think about something she wanted to say, stewing in her room for ages. Emery was the opposite; she often blurted things out without thinking, but at least it was all over and done with that way.

"I'm sorry I didn't go with you on the bikes." Amber hitched in a sobbing breath. Emery tightened her hold on her knees. She didn't know what to do—it was normally the other way around, with Amber there to comfort *her* if she was ever upset. Should she hug her? Pat her on the shoulder? "I'm sorry I didn't keep you safe."

Emery shook her head fiercely. "It's not your job to keep me safe," she said firmly. "I don't need..." But she couldn't finish, because she could taste the hypocrisy. She *did* need someone to keep her safe, didn't she? Or, more accurately, she needed someone to keep her *alive*. She'd always need that, she realized now, something hard and sharp pulsing in her stomach. It was the first time she'd understood. Unless they could find a cure for her condition, she would always be dependent on someone else to restart her heart.

"So you don't blame me?" Amber whispered.

Emery stared at her. Her voice sounded so small. Amber was only five years older than her, but she was *seventeen*, she would be leaving home for university in September. Amber was the big sister, something she pointed out at every opportunity, usually with a long-suffering sigh. But right now she sounded...young, Emery realized. Amber sounded young, and it was something of a revelation.

Uncertainly, Emery shifted into a kneeling position. Her knees had been grazed in the bike accident and they felt a little tender as she shuffled across the bed to sit next to her sister. "No," she said. "I don't blame you." She nearly put her arm around Amber to give her a reassuring hug, but that was too much of a role reversal for her to get her head around right now. Instead, she offered a small smile. "I would have been annoyed if you'd come. Cramping my style, you know."

Amber gave her a sly look. "Yeah. How would you have flirted with Colin without me there?"

Emery felt her cheeks flush even as she said, "I was *not* flirting with him."

Amber's lips twitched. "Tried to flirt with him, then."

Emery opened her mouth to retort, but her dad's voice rose again, cutting her off. "You're out at work all day, every bloody day, and *I'm* the one who has to watch out for her. Then you show up and allow her to do things and look what happens!"

"She's a child, for Christ's sake! She's supposed to be allowed to do things! And as for me being at work, you agreed to that! You were the one who wanted a second child, you were the one who said I wouldn't have to give up my career."

"Well that was before we knew what could happen if she's not supervised!"

Amber glanced at Emery. Emery's heart was racing, her stomach churning, making her feel a little sick. *You were the one who wanted a second child.* Did that mean her mum *hadn't* wanted her?

"She doesn't mean it," Amber said quietly. Emery pressed her lips together.

"I can't do this," her mum continued downstairs, oblivious, apparently, to the way her voice carried. "I can't tiptoe around while you act like she's a time bomb waiting to go off."

Whatever her dad said next, it was too quiet to make out.

"Maybe it won't happen again," Amber whispered. But it was a false comfort and they both knew it. Emery said nothing, only pressed her lips harder together. It was safer that way. After a beat, she felt her sister's arm come around her—Amber able to do what Emery had not. She tucked Emery against her side, and Emery felt relieved that it was back to normal, that she was the little sister again. She let her head drop against Amber's shoulder.

"They're just stressed," Amber said quietly. "It was…" She swallowed, whatever she was going to say clearly too horrible to articulate. She cleared her throat. "Do you…?" Again she broke off, but this time it was more of a quizzical tone, so Emery prompted her.

"Do I what?"

"Do you remember anything when it happens? Before or after or…" *Or in between.* Was that what she wanted to ask?

Emery thought about where she went, who she'd met, twice now. The fact that there was something there, a place to go to, someone to help you. Maybe it would comfort Amber—to know that Emery was okay, that she was looked after, whenever it happened. But maybe it would sound insane. Maybe Amber wouldn't believe her. An imaginary friend. It was a dim memory, but wasn't that what Amber had said the first time, all those years ago? She knew it sounded insane. But more than that, selfishly, there was a part of her that wanted to keep it—and him—to herself. Her secret, something no one else could touch or control or change.

"I remember falling," she said. "And I remember waking up." Not a lie, not exactly.

There was a beat of quiet between them. Then, "I think they've stopped arguing," Amber said. "Shall we go and get some lunch?"

Emery nodded and sat up as Amber took her arm away. She could go downstairs if Amber was with her—Amber could be the buffer. Besides, she didn't want to hear any more of her parents arguing—if she was downstairs, they couldn't talk *about* her.

You were the one who wanted a second child.

That was before we knew what could happen.

I can't do this.

That sharp feeling pricked her insides. She thought of Colin, his gaze locked onto hers, the guilt in his eyes as her dad carried her away. But he was wrong to feel like that. It wasn't *him* who should feel guilty.

It was her.

Chapter Six

Two years later (June 1993)

AGE 14

Emery peered around the kitchen door, saw her dad at the work-top chopping an onion with his back to her, still wearing the suit he wore to school. She pushed the door open wider—he usually pulled it mostly shut to stop the smell of cooking seeping into the rest of the house—and waited for him to notice her. The permission slip was clutched in her right hand. She'd had all week to get it signed, but it was now Thursday, and if she didn't hand it in tomorrow, she wouldn't be going to France on the history trip with Bonnie and the rest of her class. She'd been waiting because she'd been hoping that she would catch her mum in a quiet moment and get her to sign it without her dad around. Yes, he'd have been mad, but it would have been too late. But her mum hadn't been here all week, working late at the office as she always seemed to do these days. Her work was important, Emery was told whenever she complained about her not being there. There were people who needed her, it was why she became a lawyer in the first place.

So, what, some stranger is more important than your own daughter?

She'd got a look when she said that.

It was annoying, though—her mum was easier to talk to over dinner, and treated Emery as an adult, as someone who understood the world, whereas her dad still insisted on treating her like a child. They'd had a conversation about the levels of homelessness in the UK last week, and her mum had listened to what she had to say. Then her dad had come in, and when he'd heard what they were talking about he'd made a face and said, "That's a bit depressing for a Friday-night dinner. Can't we talk about something else?" And Emery and her mum had exchanged looks behind his back.

She also thought that if her mum was around more, it might stop the arguments—arguments Emery overheard at night when she was in her room and her parents assumed she was asleep.

"My work is important, James!"

"More important than mine, you mean?"

And then a silence that stretched on and on and made Emery's stomach curdle with anxiety. A silence she knew she was to blame for, because its very existence was down to the fact that *one* of them always had to be here, with her.

Her dad had still not noticed her standing in the doorway, so she padded over to him. The terra-cotta tiles were sticky under her bare feet, the back door flung wide open. The radio was on, but louder was the sound of Aunt Helen singing in the shower upstairs, having just come back from an exercise class. She always wore bright turquoise leggings, a purple top and a headband, like something out of a ridiculous eighties fitness video, but she seemed immune to how comical she looked and therefore pulled it off. "It's such fun," she'd told Emery when they'd collided at the front door as Emery had got home from school today. "You should come with me."

Before Emery could even answer, her dad had said, "I'm not sure that's the type of thing Emery should be doing." Which made no sense—surely exercise would make her heart stronger, not weaker? He'd tried to get her out of all PE classes too, and as assistant head teacher at the school she went to had set limits on which activities she was allowed to join in with, which was humiliating. She'd had to come up with ways to deflect attention or rebuff people who made fun of her for always sitting out, or being sent to the library when it was too cold to stand in the rain and watch her friends play netball. Which, admittedly, did not bode well for the piece of paper in her hand, crinkled and kind of sad-looking.

Helen's voice screeched tunelessly from the shower, the lyrics of the song indecipherable. Emery hadn't even known she was coming to stay; she wasn't sure if her parents had known either, or if Helen had just shown up unannounced, in between her trips abroad to research her book—though she wouldn't tell anyone what the book was about and hadn't, as far as anyone knew, written a word of it. Emery's mum always rolled her eyes whenever it was mentioned.

"Dad," Emery said, and he jolted in surprise, the knife slipping slightly between his fingers. He frowned at her. She was used to it by now, the quick scan up and down to check she was okay whenever she sounded like she might be about to tell him something. What would it be like to be able to open with *Dad* and not see the flicker as he wondered, quite literally, if you were about to drop dead? He masked it most of the time, so he must be picking up on something in her body language right now. She gave her shoulders a little roll, tried to cock one leg, appear relaxed.

"What are you making?" she asked, her tone faux-bright.

The look he gave her was skeptical—she never came into the kitchen to see what he was making, though she was often sent *out* of the kitchen for making toast before dinner. "Spaghetti bolognese."

Helen would no doubt complain, Emery thought. She was probably not eating meat or carbs or something right now. And she and Dad would snipe at one another about it the whole way through dinner. It never felt harmful, though, the way they bickered—there was always an undercurrent of affection.

"Yum," she said. "So I was just wondering…"

"Yes?" He lifted the chopping board, used the knife to slide the onion into the frying pan.

"You know the history trip?" She could've sworn he stilled, before measuring out a teaspoon of oil into the pan. Of course he knew about it, what with being assistant head and all. He'd *made* her go to his secondary school, even though Amber had been allowed to go to the other state school in the area, one where none of the teachers were related to her. *I need to be there if anything happens, Emery.* And it had been an argument she hadn't been able to win. She was just lucky that Bonnie had, loyally, picked the same school.

When he said nothing, she laid the permission slip on the counter, next to the chopping board. He glanced at it, and she saw the way his expression tightened, before he forced it into neutrality. Had he hoped she wouldn't want to go? Probably. It was a trip to see some castle or whatever, which would arguably be boring, but they would be in *France*, which was cool, and it was a whole three days just hanging out with Bonnie.

"It's not a good idea, Em. You know that."

It was the response she'd expected, but it still made her grit her teeth, made her want to fire up at him. But she and Bonnie had rehearsed this.

"The teachers are trained in first aid." He said nothing, neither confirming nor denying her theory. "And we'll be supervised all the time." She wasn't sure of that, either, but it seemed likely. "It's only seventy-two hours, and it's on a coach, so it's not high-stress flying, and—"

"I'm sorry, Emery. The answer's no."

She felt her nails bite her palms as she clenched her hands into fists. "So you're really not going to let me do anything, ever? That's bullshit."

"Emery!"

"Well it is!" He said nothing, and she folded her arms. "Maybe I'll move out, go to live with Aunt Helen." The sound of the shower running had stopped now, along with the singing. "*She'd* let me go to France."

"She can't—she's not your parent or guardian."

"I'll apply for emancipation, then."

"I doubt the court case will be concluded in the next three weeks."

Emery's blood heated. "You're not taking me seriously!"

Her dad sighed as he stirred the onion, the edges of it turning brown. "I'm sorry, Emery," he said again. "I know this may seem harsh, but it's what's best—"

"Does Mum think it's best, too?" Emery shot back at him.

"Emery." Her name was a warning growl.

"No, this is totally stupid." She felt tears prick her eyes, despite her promise to Bonnie that she'd stay calm and rational. "You cannot lock me away—I'm fourteen, I could get *married* in two years' time if I wanted to, and—"

"You're getting married, are you? Who's the lucky chap?"

"Dad!" She hitched in a breath, her throat tight and painful. It was infuriating that he was treating it all as a big joke. He glanced at her, and his expression changed.

"Love, I know it seems unfair, but—"

"Seems? It doesn't *seem* anything, it *is* unfair." She was trying to think of what she could say, trying to pull herself back from the urge to scream at him and storm out, to somehow rescue the situation, when she heard the sound of the front door opening. Seconds later, her mum appeared in the kitchen, barefoot like Emery, the backs of her ankles looking swollen and sore from the heels she wore (a concession to the patriarchy), slight sweat patches on her white blouse under her arms, her black skirt too tight around her waist. She smiled at Emery, but it was a little forced and she looked tired. When Emery didn't smile back, just shot her dad a scowl, her mum raised her eyebrows.

"All okay?" It was said tentatively—she clearly knew the answer.

"You're back early," her dad said, adding the beef to the onion and turning his back on his wife.

"Well the case wrapped up sooner than I…" She broke off as Emery swiped the permission slip off the counter and made to storm out of the kitchen. "Emery?" She put a hand on her arm to stop her from barging past. "What's going on here?"

The words burst from her, uncontrollable. "Dad won't let me go on the history trip." She was crying now—not because the trip meant so much to her, but because it was proof that things weren't going to get any better, that after the last episode, her dad was clearly never going to let her do anything.

"James." Her mum gave a tired sigh. "You're not going to be able to stop her going on every school trip for the next four years." *Four years.* How was she going to get through four years of this? Maybe she'd leave school at sixteen, find a job.

"There's a geography trip in Year 11. I'll be a chaperone, she can go on that one." *She.* Said like Emery wasn't even there. It reminded her of how the doctors talked to her parents about her at the check-ups, talked to *them* and not to *her*.

"I'm not even doing geography GCSE! And I don't want to go on a school trip when you're on it," she said, her voice vicious. For a moment he looked wounded, and an ugly part of her thought: *Good.*

"James," her mum began again. "I think we should let her go. We could speak to the teachers so that they're prepared if—"

"No." So final—as if he and only he had the right to decide.

"Maybe Alice has a point, James." Emery spun to see Helen

standing just outside the kitchen doorway, behind her mum. How much had she heard? Everything, probably—sound carried in this house.

"Stay out of this, Helen," her dad growled. Helen caught Emery's eye and gave a little shrug, as if to say, *Well, I tried.*

Emery pulled her arm away from her mum's grip and stormed out of the kitchen, past her aunt, who was standing there in nothing but a towel. Behind her, she heard her mum say in a voice that sounded almost devoid of emotion, "Are we really going to have this conversation again?"

And her dad's answer: "Apparently we are, because you refuse to listen."

So she'd done it again. Caused another argument—just by asking to go on a fucking history trip. She could feel her breathing getting faster and faster, her eyes stinging painfully.

Amber was in the hallway, her hair hanging loosely around her shoulders—that stupid fringe now grown out, thank God—wearing a white T-shirt under dungarees, all cool-looking while Emery was presumably red-faced, still in her school uniform, a crumpled piece of paper clutched in her fist.

"Come on," she said. "Let's go out."

Chapter Seven

"Dad will be cross we didn't tell him where we're going," Emery mumbled as they started walking down the hill toward Cambridge city center. It would take them forever to get there—they lived miles out—but there was nowhere else to walk to.

"Well, maybe Dad needs to loosen up."

"Yeah," agreed Emery. "He does."

Amber bumped shoulders with her as they walked. "So how are you, Little Em?" She'd only got back for her summer holidays a couple of days ago, and they hadn't really had a chance to catch up yet as Emery had been at school most of the time.

Emery gave a bitter little laugh in response to the question. She couldn't really explain how life felt more intense these days, with Amber mostly away at university in Cardiff. Now that it was only her and Mum and Dad, the house was too quiet and the watchful gaze that she had grown up with felt even stronger.

But while Emery missed her sister, so much, Amber seemed happier since moving away—more herself. And Emery didn't want to make her feel guilty for that happiness, though she hadn't realized that Amber had been *un*happy at home. She'd been trying to figure out what had been lacking, what had been making Amber small and stressed, rather than the somehow taller and *looser* person she'd turned into, seemingly overnight. Emery knew it must be a pain being the big sister to someone who was always the center of everyone's focus, everyone in the house holding their breath every time she tripped. She knew she'd always had attention thrust on her, whether she liked it or not, and she knew that probably meant that her parents were less inclined to ask Amber how *she* was doing. Had that been it? Amber had been so stressed during her A levels, but their dad had been on edge about Emery, and kept asking Amber to keep an eye on her if he had to do something, even if that something was just preparing a lesson in the next room, when Amber was supposed to be revising. She hadn't complained, and Emery knew it was because she'd felt guilty for what had happened when they went camping. Everyone so fucking guilty all the time.

"You know, that history trip will probably be really boring," Amber said conversationally. Emery glanced up at her but said nothing. "In my school, we had this trip to Germany, and we were literally only allowed off the coach for about three hours, tops, and someone threw up on the way back and they couldn't get rid of the smell the whole way home."

Emery wrinkled her nose. "You were allowed to go, though, weren't you?" But she felt the anger leaving her, giving way to tiredness. The sun was warm on her head, her curls pinned back with a headband, one she'd been told off for wearing at school today because it was too bright, apparently.

"How's Bonnie?" Amber asked.

"She's fine. How's uni—you learned how to fix people's wrists and stuff yet?"

Amber gave a snort of laughter. "Working on it. What about boys?" Emery made a face and Amber nudged her in the ribs. "When I left for uni, you had a crush on Colin."

"No, I was *contemplating* having a crush on him. There's a difference."

"And?"

"And I decided not to. What about you? Any men on the scene?" Amber flushed—she'd never been good at hiding things. "There is!" Emery exclaimed. "Please tell me he's better than Starey Stephen." Amber's one and only romance at school, as far as Emery could tell, had consisted of occasional hand-holding and games of Scrabble.

"He didn't *stare*, he listened."

"He did stare, it was shady. Shady Starey Stephen."

Amber pursed her lips, but said, "Well, they're nothing like Stephen."

"Good." Emery's pumps slapped against the hot tarmac as they walked, the back of her neck pricking with sweat underneath her hair.

"And I'm not even sure if it's anything yet," Amber carried on. "It's...Emery! What are you doing?" She grabbed Emery's upper arm, stopping her from stepping out into the road.

Emery looked pointedly at Amber's hand on her arm. "There are no cars, Ambs."

"Did you even check?" Amber's voice was high-pitched, on the verge of hysterical.

Emery rolled her eyes. "Yes, Mum, I did."

Amber ignored the tone. "Are you sure? You of all people should be careful when—"

"Me *of all people*? What, like getting hit by a car won't kill everyone, only me?"

The words hissed out through Amber's teeth. "Don't joke about this, Emery."

Emery gave her sister a long look, then heaved in a breath, the warm summer air doing little to cool her insides. "Right, I know. I'm sorry." She tried to keep her voice calm, but something was itching under her skin, the urge to scream building. *Be careful, Emery.* Always, always: *Be careful.* And—history trip perhaps excluded—she honestly was trying to be, to keep everyone happy, to stop her parents getting even more at each other's throats. But that didn't mean that it felt fair, that she should have to be more careful than everyone else, that people treated her like she was, to quote her mother, a time bomb waiting to go off, all because of something that was completely outside of her control.

She didn't *want* to be careful. She wanted to do something stupid, something *reckless*, just to show she could. She wanted to throw a full-blown tantrum and push her sister away from her, run out in front of the car she could see now coming down the road—a bright blue Fiat. She'd sprint to the other side, because she could, because she'd make it, because she wasn't a fucking idiot. Or maybe she'd stand there playing chicken, only jerking out of the way at the last minute. She pictured her mum giving her a look—a lawyer look, as she and Amber called it—and telling her she was *too old for that now*. She heard her dad's voice: *It's not a good idea, Em.* And she saw her sister's face, wide-eyed and panic-stricken, terrified of letting something happen to her. Thought again of the way Amber had crept into her bedroom after the bike accident, nervous that Emery somehow blamed her for what had happened.

She stepped back from the edge of the road and headed for the crossing at the traffic lights up ahead, pushing the button and waiting. There, nice and careful.

"So, looking forward to your GCSEs?" Amber asked, and Emery could hear the falsely bright tone. Her question wasn't helping. *What next, what are your plans, have you thought about your future?* One way or another, that was what everyone was always asking—all the adults. And her sister was not supposed to be one of them; she was supposed to be on *Emery's* side, them against the adults. And why the fuck was everyone asking *what next* anyway, when they were all so sure her heart might fail at any moment? She felt the bitterness swell and couldn't seem to do anything about it.

She said nothing in answer to Amber's question, because she didn't want to snap. Because she knew, deep down, that none of this was Amber's fault. She watched as the lights changed from green to yellow. Then to red. The beeping started, and Emery stepped out to cross the road, Amber with her.

They were nearly at the other side of the crossing when a car came around the corner, too fast for the speed limit. Emery sucked in a breath and jumped onto the pavement, heard Amber swear at the car as it hooted at them then shot through the crossing behind them before the lights even changed.

She heard, as if from far away, Amber muttering, "Where's the fucking fire?" But she'd already felt the jolt, her body reacting to the scream of the horn. She felt the whoosh of the wind in the car's wake, heard her sister's sharp intake of breath.

Her heart spasmed. And as she fell, in the moments before she lost consciousness, before her heart stopped entirely, all she could think was, *Oh for fuck's sake.*

* *

"I was being careful!" Emery shouted the moment she saw him. He held up his hands as if in surrender, and she tugged her hands through her curls, slightly dislodging the headband. He was watching her, probably waiting for her to calm down, and she straightened the headband, feeling suddenly self-conscious.

"I never said you weren't," he said, his voice calm, even.

She scowled at him, simply because he was the only one there to scowl at. And because she really *had* tried, this time, to be careful. She'd done the right thing, waited at the lights, looked both ways before crossing the street, the whole damn lot. She hadn't been doing something stupid, or reckless. Hadn't been doing something she'd been told not to—so, what, was she now just never supposed to cross a road in case a horn beeped at her?

"What are you thinking, Little Emery?"

She jolted, and it took her a moment to realize why. *Little Emery.* It was so similar to what Amber called her, and she never thought anything of it then, but . . . *Little.* For some reason, she didn't like the idea that he saw her as little. She glanced up at his face, at those gray-green eyes that she'd never quite been able to picture from last time around, even though she'd tried. She'd recently agreed with her group of school friends that Will Smith had *the* hottest eyes, but now she wasn't quite sure. She felt an uncomfortable heat rise in her chest and looked away.

"Nothing," she said. "I just . . ." She sat down on the grass. They were on the green near her house, where she and Bonnie often came after school to just hang out. It was warm, though thankfully a little cooler than it really was at the moment, and she was in the same outfit she'd been wearing when she'd collapsed onto the pavement. "I didn't want that to happen," she murmured, as he sat down next to her.

"I'm sure," he agreed.

"No, you don't get it," she said impatiently, her fingers tapping on her knee. "My dad, he . . ." But she couldn't really think of how to explain it—that this was going to send him over the edge. He'd probably find a way to blame her mum, and Emery felt a creeping dread, a certainty that it could be the final straw for the two of them. It was why she'd been so *good*. She hadn't wanted this to happen again, had thought that if she could *keep* it from happening, maybe her parents would eventually stop arguing—because there was nothing to argue about. "He won't like it," she finished lamely. "Neither will my mum."

"You can't help it," he said, his voice soft now.

"No," she said, though she couldn't quite bring herself to look at him. "I suppose not." And wasn't today evidence of that? That it didn't matter if she played by the rules or not, because it would just happen anyway? She sighed. "I wish we were somewhere better than the park, though."

He laughed, and the sound made her look at him again. "Well it's your party. Clearly, a part of you *likes* the park."

She wrinkled her nose because even though, yes, she *did* cherish those moments with Bonnie and her other friends when they all hung out here, the moments before she had to go home—earlier than everyone else—and go back to being the problem child, she still wished she could have taken him somewhere cooler.

A tremor ran through the park, and Emery swore the swings all the way on the other side shook with it. She felt her fingers digging into the grass next to her and forced herself to relax them, one by one. "I thought it took longer than that last time," she said quietly.

"I thought so too," he agreed. He smiled down at her. "Maybe each time will be different." *Will be.* It sounded like a promise, she thought, that they'd see each other again. And she found she quite liked that idea.

He was growing weirdly blurry now, his outline not quite distinct against the backdrop, his conker-brown hair merging with the bark of the trees in the distance. But when she glanced down at her hand, it stood out against the haze of green beneath it. She looked back at him, found his eyes and locked onto them. "Will you tell me your name now?"

She saw his lips move, but she didn't know if he answered her or told her again that it didn't matter what his name was—even if it did. It mattered now, even more for some reason. But she'd have to wait for next time, because she was being pulled back away from him, back to the pain she knew would be there when she woke.

**

Amber was bent over her, hair falling in front of her face, sobbing, still pumping her chest, not noticing that Emery had opened her eyes. Emery coughed like she had water in her lungs, even though it wasn't her lungs that were the problem.

"She's okay!" Amber's voice sounded blurry and out of focus, like Emery's brain hadn't quite moved from one place to another yet. It was such a contrast to *his* voice, and her surroundings felt too bright, too real. "Yes, she's breathing." It took Emery a moment to realize that Amber was not speaking to her, and only then did she notice her dad's phone on the pavement next to her. Amber didn't have a mobile phone—it was definitely their dad's. Which meant she must have taken it before leaving the house, just in case. Planning for something to go wrong.

Emery's vision moved in and out of focus as Amber snatched the phone off the street. "Yes, by the crossing. No, on Huntingdon. Okay." She let the phone drop to her lap, then brought a hand to rest on Emery's head, stroking her hair gently. Her fingers trembled on Emery's scalp. "Dad is on his way."

Emery closed her eyes briefly. Her head hurt. A lot. The back of her head, specifically.

She reached up to touch the sore spot, her arms feeling heavy. She winced as her fingers found something wet and sticky. She drew back her hand, saw blood. She must have hit her head when she fell.

She let out a little whimper, and Amber, still sobbing, moved to cradle her head in her lap. Across the road, two passersby looked at them but didn't come over. Did they think she was a drunken teenager? she wondered. What did they look like, sitting here? She didn't care, she realized. She didn't give a flying fuck what they thought.

"You're okay," Amber said. Over and over. *You're okay you're okay you're okay*.

But she wasn't, was she? She would never be. Seconds ago she'd been with *him*, and he'd looked at her with kindness and understanding. Here, there was no one with understanding, only panic.

"Mum?" she asked.

Amber paused for a second too long. "I think she's coming too." What had she heard, on the phone? Another argument, because of her? Emery's eyes fluttered closed.

"No!" The fear in Amber's tone made her open them again, even if she didn't want to, even if she'd rather sleep, and wake when the aftermath was done with and everyone had calmed down.

"Don't worry," she said, her voice sounding rusty. "I'm okay." She clasped her sister's hand, and Amber took it, even though her fingers were coated with blood. "It's okay." She repeated her sister's words back to her, even though it wasn't okay. Not really. And perhaps that was something she'd have to get used to.

Chapter Eight

Six years later (December 1999)

AGE 21

The music in the tiny house was loud enough that it vibrated under Emery's skin, making her want to move in time to the beat. It was freezing outside, but inside this stranger's living room she could feel sweat beading on her forehead and between the tops of her thighs, hidden under the tight black and silver dress she was wearing. Around her, bodies pressed into one another, now at the stage of the evening where personal space was more of a vague concept than a necessity, and the sound of laughter and chatter rose in waves over the music. The windows of the living room and the adjoining kitchen had steamed up completely, and someone had drawn a penis on one of them, proving that hitting your early twenties didn't heighten your sense of maturity. Emery conceded in that moment, lifting a glass of warm white wine to her lips, that she and Bonnie could probably have come up with a better way to welcome in the new millennium. But she hadn't been organized enough to make a plan, and while Bonnie had had about a million ideas, most of them had hinged on her boyfriend at university, who she'd now broken up with, so when Colin had invited them to his random school friend's party in Cambridge, it had seemed like the best option.

She helped herself to one of the few sad remaining chips in a paper bowl on the red-wine-stained coffee table. There were a few depressing attempts at Christmas decoration around the place—battered tinsel around the top of the windows, one single gold star hanging in the kitchen doorway. A student haunt through and through—though she liked to think that the house she shared with a couple of mates in Falmouth looked a little more loved than this one, and they were students too.

Bonnie fought her way back through the crowd clutching a bottle of Prosecco. It might be the one she and Emery had brought with them, or it could well be someone else's. At this point, who the fuck cared. She thrust it into Emery's hands, foam bubbling around the rim. "We have to have something to welcome in the new year!" She was swaying slightly where she stood, three inches taller than usual in lethal-looking heels, a bright blue dress—which she'd bought after she split with her boyfriend, to "show him what he's missing"—making her eyes look bluer than usual.

Emery swigged straight from the bottle, and Bonnie nodded in approval. Emery's phone beeped from inside the little clutch bag she'd spent far too much money on. She fished it out, and frowned when she opened the message.

Happy New Year, Emery. Xx

That was it. They were about to hit the year 2000, a defining moment in goddam history, and *Happy New Year* was all her mum could manage. It wasn't even midnight yet, but Emery always got these messages early, her mum being efficient and sending them before the network got clogged up.

This was what her relationship with her mum was limited to now—one-line texts on her birthday, Christmas and New Year's. Ever since Mum had walked out six years ago. Emery and Amber had tried spending the Christmas holiday with her the year after she left, but she'd been working the whole time and it was like she hadn't really wanted them there at all. Amber had tried to pretend it was all normal, filling the silences with mindless conversation, asking questions to try and keep things going. But Emery had felt jittery and anxious, and their mum had ended up driving them back to their dad's a day early—on Christmas Day itself.

And that had pretty much been that. Mum had moved to London after leaving them, presumably because it was easier for work, and though London was close enough to Cambridge that they could have theoretically still seen her, it had felt like too big a gap to bridge. And what was the point? She clearly didn't want to see them, no matter what Amber said. Although, a dark voice whispered in Emery's mind, the way it always did, maybe her mum didn't mind seeing Amber—maybe it was only Emery she had a problem with. And that was fine. Emery had decided that long ago. If her mum didn't want a relationship with her, then she didn't want one either. It was better, anyway, to feel like that, to feel *angry* about it, angry about this stupid New Year's message. Because if she didn't feel angry, she felt guilty, and that was worse.

She switched off her phone and dropped it back in her clutch bag. Out of sight, out of mind. Then she took another swig of Prosecco. She could feel it going straight to her head, on top of the wine already swirling there. She felt tipsy and a little reckless—and both of those were making her want to say something back to her mum. Something that wouldn't just be *Happy New Year.*

Bad idea, Emery.

"Are you okay?" Bonnie asked, and her concern was only partially marred by a slight hiccup.

Emery shrugged. "Just my mum."

Bonnie threw her arms around her. "Well *I* love you."

Emery snorted quietly and patted her on the back. "I love you too, mate."

"And I miss you!"

"How can you miss me? I'm right here."

"You know what I mean." Bonnie pulled back and pouted. And Emery did know—they'd headed to different universities, Bonnie studying history at Bristol, to "keep her options open," and Emery heading to Falmouth to study art, much to her dad's dismay, because she quite liked drawing. Although when she'd got there, she'd realized she wasn't nearly as passionate about it as most of the people on her course, and the fun had been taken out of it by studying it. Then again, she hadn't gone to university with some grand plan to be an artist—she'd gone because she'd wanted to make friends, go to parties, have fun, and postpone any sort of decision-making. And mission accomplished, on that front.

"Well, we'll be hanging out all the time soon," Emery said, handing the Prosecco back. "No doubt you'll be sick of me by the end of it." They were planning to go traveling around Australia after they finished their degrees, which suited Emery as it meant further postponing any decisions on what she was going to do about a job. They'd both been saving, though Bonnie had been far better at it than Emery and had a tendency to get annoyed that a) their funds didn't match, so they would have different amounts of money to spend, and b) Emery wasn't taking a more active role in planning the itinerary.

Right now, though, Bonnie shook her head seriously. "I would *never* get sick of you." Emery couldn't help laughing as her friend raised the Prosecco bottle to the ceiling. "We are going to have SO much fun this year. THIS YEAR. Can you believe it?"

The music was getting even louder, Emery was sure of it. She could feel the itching under her skin again, the need to both throw herself into the crowd and dance with her eyes closed, and also to escape entirely, be completely away from any and all people so that she could breathe. She compromised and closed her eyes briefly, took a breath.

"Looking good, Wilson."

She opened her eyes to see Colin there. She smiled and gestured down at herself. "Hours of work, I ought to." She and Bonnie had got ready in Bonnie's room at her parents' house, reminiscent of their school years, playing music loudly and going completely overboard with makeup. Because if you couldn't at New Year's, when could you? Colin looked good too, she noted. His blonde hair was messy, but in a deliberate sort of way, and he looked less tired than when she'd last seen him, when she and Bonnie had gone to visit him in London over the summer.

"Colin," Bonnie said seriously, pressing herself to Emery's side—whether deliberately or because she couldn't quite stand up, Emery wasn't sure—"I love you."

Colin raised his eyebrows at Emery, who grinned and gave a little shrug. He put his arm around Bonnie. "Love you too, sis."

Emery looked at Colin and Bonnie for a moment, two people who had been in her life for as long as she could remember, then made a snap decision. She turned toward the front door, fighting through the crowd and grabbing her coat off the back of the sofa.

"Where are you going?"

She glanced over her shoulder to see Colin following her, as she'd known he would, tugging Bonnie along with him.

"I need air," she said, and continued into the hallway. She saw Amber there, leaning against the banisters, wearing a long multicolored skirt and pumps, her brown hair swept off her face. She had come along at the last minute, apparently because she had nothing better to do, and had brought her friend Robin, whom she'd met six months ago. She showed no sign that she'd noticed Emery, too engrossed in a conversation with the blonde-haired and impressive-cheekboned Robin, who was now gesturing emphatically as Amber nodded along.

Emery barged past the remaining few people in the hallway and opened the front door, felt the whip of cold air across her face.

"Emery, what are you doing?" Bonnie exclaimed, still hanging off her brother's arm. "It's nearly midnight!"

"Let's go to the river," Emery said, shrugging on her coat. She needed to escape this claustrophobia. She thought of her mum, despite herself. What was she doing right now? Who was she spending New Year's Eve with? Would she think of them—her and Amber—or would she consider them ticked off, message sent, motherly obligation done?

"Yes!" Bonnie was immediately enthusiastic, and lurched from Colin to Emery, hooking her arm through Emery's elbow. "I LOVE the river." Emery felt her lips twitch—she really did love drunk Bonnie.

She turned back to Colin, who was hovering in the doorway. He glanced behind him, maybe searching for whoever had invited him to the party. Then he looked back at Emery, met her gaze. "Sure. Why not? I'll just grab our coats."

He reappeared moments later, helped Bonnie into her Little Red Riding Hood coat, his own no-nonsense black waterproof already zipped up. "Your friends won't mind?" Emery asked. He was, after all, back from London for the Christmas break and supposed to be catching up with everyone.

"Nah. They won't even notice."

They started walking down the hill toward town, toward the river. Bonnie grabbed Emery's arm. "Wait. Where's Amber?"

Emery patted her hand. "She'll be fine." She thought again

of the way Amber had been watching Robin, eyes intent on her and no one else. Robin was smart—studying for a PhD at Cambridge University—but Emery knew that wasn't the reason Amber was so engrossed, even if her sister wasn't ready to admit it yet, even if she still resolutely referred to Robin as a "friend." Better, really, that Emery hadn't dragged the two of them to the river too, otherwise she might have tried to cajole it out of them, given the state of mind she was in, and she'd vowed to be patient, to let Amber tell her when she was ready.

Over the top of Bonnie's head, Colin caught Emery's eye, gave her a little smile. Only a brief exchange, but Emery thought perhaps he was letting her know that he too had caught the vibe between Robin and Amber this evening, even if Bonnie hadn't quite cottoned on. It happened like that sometimes—Colin seemed so attuned to what Emery was thinking, a rhythm between the two of them that wasn't easy to find elsewhere. It was only in moments like this that she realized she sometimes missed it when he wasn't there.

The three of them walked down Huntingdon Road, past Fitzwilliam, with its ugly 1960s buildings. Emery could hear a bunch of students singing drunkenly at the tops of their voices somewhere up ahead of them. *Fitzwilliam till I die, Fitzwilliam till I die, I know I am, I'm sure I am . . .* Most of the students had gone home at this time of year, meaning the student bars were almost empty, but a few stragglers always lingered. Funny, really, that she had lived here most of her life, and she technically *was* a student, but she had no idea what it was like to be a student *here*.

Colin's little Nokia beeped. He slipped it out of his coat pocket to read the message, frowned, then sent a quick text back.

"Who was it?" Emery asked.

"Is it a *girl*friend?" Bonnie asked, laughing as if she'd come up with the most hilarious joke.

"No," Colin said, a little too quickly. As he glanced at Emery again, Bonnie snatched the phone from his hand. He made a grab to get it back. "Bon, come on, don't be a dick."

But she was already reading, coming to a stop as she did so—clearly deciphering a text and walking at the same time was beyond her limits right now. She frowned, looked up at Emery, letting Colin take the phone back. "It's from your dad," she said bluntly.

Emery felt her cheeks flush as she looked from Bonnie to Colin. "My *dad*?"

"No, look, it's not—"

"Not from my dad? Not from a James Wilson?" Colin said nothing—and he didn't have to, because Emery *knew*. "He's checking up on me, isn't he? For fuck's sake." She pulled a hand through her hair, even as Bonnie winced a little, no doubt regretting her decision to read the text. "That's why you're coming with us, is it? To make sure nothing happens?"

"No!" Colin reached for her hand, but she jerked it away. "No, Em, I swear."

She tried to take a calming breath, even as the itching—the *burning*—under her skin intensified. Her heart beat faster, egging her on. Urging her to do something, anything.

"How does he even have your number?" she asked.

"I don't know, the way everyone does." Irrelevant, she supposed—if her dad wanted to find a way to track her down, he would. And he thought the world of Colin—good, reliable, sensible Colin. He had gone through a phase of insisting that Colin accompany Bonnie and Emery when he himself couldn't, but she'd thought they'd long outgrown that.

"You replied," she stated.

"Yeah, because he'll worry if I don't. But that's not the reason I'm here, okay? I just wanted to hang out. I haven't seen you in ages."

She felt fire lick her insides, wanted to snatch the phone from him, to stamp on it. Wanted to take the bottle Bonnie was still clutching and down the whole lot—or smash it on the floor. She flexed her fingers, the tips turning numb with the cold. It wasn't Colin's fault. Her dad had probably texted her first, got all worried when she hadn't replied, because she'd switched her phone off.

Be careful, won't you, Emery? he'd said as she'd left the house to go to Bonnie's this evening. If only he knew some of the things she got up to at university, pushing the boundaries slowly, testing herself to see what she could get away with. After all, there was no point in being careful—last time she'd died because a car beeped at her, for fuck's sake. And then her mum had left, after her dad had gone off the deep end in protective fury. She hadn't been able to stop their family from breaking up. So what was the point in being careful?

Colin was still looking at her, waiting. She blew out a breath. "All right. Don't worry—I know what he's like."

He let his breath out on a whoosh too, and it made her wonder what, exactly, he'd expected her to do. Then he grinned and stepped between her and Bonnie, flung an arm around each of them. "My two girls!"

"We're not *your* girls," Bonnie insisted, but he kissed the top of her head noisily and it made her laugh. And then Emery was laughing too, and the three of them couldn't stop, cackling and swaying as they walked down the road, none of them sure what they were even laughing about.

They came to a stop on the bridge that crossed the Cam and all of them leaned against the balustrade, looking down into the dark river. It was cloudy above, but a sliver of moonlight escaped, bouncing off the water. Maybe they'd be able to see the fireworks from here.

"Is this the part where we're supposed to make resolutions?" Colin asked.

Emery raised an eyebrow at him. "What for? You've already got everything you want." It still baffled her that at fourteen, Colin had claimed he wanted to be a journalist, and now he was actually *doing* that, with a job in London on one of the national papers. Like finding a dream and following it was that easy.

"Not *everything*," he said, and though his tone was light, there was something hidden there—something that Emery thought it best not to delve too deeply into.

She shrugged instead. "I don't believe in resolutions. Better to keep living in the moment—if you plan your future, you won't enjoy what's happening now." To prove her point, she climbed up onto the concrete ledge of the bridge, holding her arms out to balance.

"Emery, don't." Bonnie sounded a bit more sober now, the walk having done her good. The Prosecco was balanced on the edge of the bridge too, waiting for a toast at midnight.

Emery looked down at her. "Come on. Live in the moment, Bon." There was that itching under her skin. *Do it, do it, do it.*

All around them, echoing from different places across the city, the countdown to New Year's had begun. A feeling of jubilance, of reckless excitement, rose within Emery.

Ten, nine...

She closed her eyes, a breeze whisking across her face. Her heart gave a little thump, reminding her it was still there, still beating.

"Emery, come on," Bonnie was saying. "Get down."

Eight, seven, six...

Emery felt a hand pat her leg, trying to get her to move. She opened her eyes, grinned down at Bonnie. "Wimp."

"Nutjob," Bonnie snapped back.

Five, four...

Emery laughed a little as Colin clambered up next to her, waterproof jacket already off.

"Live in the moment, right?"

"*Guys!*" Bonnie shouted. Emery took off her coat too, dumped it unceremoniously behind her, and shivered at the bite of the air.

Three, two...

"Well, Happy New Year, I guess," Colin said, with a one-sided grin.

One.

She jumped. She heard Colin whooping, presumed he'd jumped too. Heard Bonnie's *for fuck's sake* as if from far away.

There was a second of exhilaration, her heart leaping in her throat, that feeling of being on a roller coaster or driving too fast over a bump.

She only had an instant when she hit the river. An instant to register the icy water, the feeling of it surging around her, soaking her clothes and pulling her down. She felt the breath being sucked out of her. Then she tasted a metallic tang in her mouth, one she vaguely recognized.

And in the first second of the new millennium, Emery Wilson died again.

Chapter Nine

She was still cold, but not from the river. No, she was cold now because she was standing on the side of a fucking mountain, snow glistening in the bright sunlight all around her, pine trees topped with frosting to her left. To her right a chair lift moving silently with no one in it. The Alps. She was back in the bloody Alps.

Her heels were sinking into the snow, and she was still in her black and silver New Year's dress, which she tugged down, trying to make more of the material, her teeth chattering a little. Bare legs—why did she have to have bare legs? At least she wasn't wet, though, and really, all things considered, she should probably feel a hell of a lot colder.

She glanced around, not totally sure what she was looking for—until she saw him. A few strides away from her, wearing a more appropriate outfit—dark blue ski jacket, jeans and snow boots, a pair of sunglasses atop his conker-brown hair. She hadn't seen him in over six years, yet it seemed the most natural thing in the world right then to smile at him. "Well, hello there."

One corner of his mouth lifted. "Hello, Emery. Fancy seeing

you here." She laughed a little, shaking her head. Her breath clouded before merging into the air around her, clear and bright.

She cocked her head. "Not 'Little Emery' this time then?" She said it without thinking, then winced internally—should she be letting on how clearly she remembered their interactions?

But he just smiled. "You're not so little this time."

She huffed theatrically. "I'm still perfectly little, thanks very much." He laughed, and she felt a lightness at the sound of it. She let her gaze travel across his face. With each encounter, it was etched into her memory a little more, but each time, he still looked slightly different. His eyes were the same gray-green color, his hair the same brown. But he looked younger this time—though maybe that was because she was older. He smiled at her, and her stomach gave a little flip. He was *hot*. Yes, okay, she'd known he was attractive, but here in the mountains it really hit her, the sunlight catching his face as he looked down at her.

His smile dropped away a little and he gave her a questioning frown. "What is it?"

"Nothing," she said quickly, looking down at the snow as she felt heat creep into her cheeks. *Get a grip, Emery.* She could not go around thinking her angel of death was hot—there must be a psychiatrist somewhere who would have a field day with that. Not that she was going to actually tell anyone about it, of course. "You look a bit different, that's all." She lifted her gaze again, biting her lip. His *name*. She still wanted to know—

"Nick," he said, his voice barely a whisper. "My name's Nick." Her stomach jolted—at the fact that he had known what she was thinking, and at the sound of his name here where there was no one else to hear it. "I'm sorry I didn't get to tell you last time around." And the way he'd said it...it seemed like he hadn't said it out loud in a while. Like, maybe, he'd been on the verge of forgetting it. *Nick*. So ordinary.

She was still staring at him, trying to align the name with *him*, and he raised his eyebrows. She gave a little smile. "I suppose I was expecting Gabriel or something."

The green sparked in his eyes, lightening them, and she lifted her hand, held it out to him. "Well, it's nice to meet you, Nick."

He hesitated for a beat before clasping it, his hand dwarfing hers, his grip reassuringly firm. She let out a soft breath, relief sliding through her at the fact that she could actually touch him, that he was solid, real, like it was confirming that *she* was solid and real. But that didn't quite explain the tingle that ran up her arm and down the back of her neck at the feel of his hand on hers, or how she suddenly found that she could no longer make eye contact. A soft citrus scent washed over her, and something deeper, reminding her of salty sea air. Her stomach tightened in response.

Get a grip, Emery, she told herself again. *It's a fucking handshake.*

When he let go of her hand, she tucked a strand of hair behind her ear to cover the heat that had risen again to her face, even as she shivered, her fingers registering the lack of warmth.

"You know, you can change that if you like." He gestured

at her, and she frowned down at herself. "Your outfit. I've seen people do it before."

She pursed her lips. "How?" Then she sighed before he could answer. "Let me guess, you're not sure."

He smiled a little guiltily. Against the backdrop of the blue sky and the bright white snow, the gray in his eyes was somehow deeper. "It just sort of happens. But I guess it's when you're thinking about what you're wearing—like what you were wearing in the memory?"

Emery thought a little harder about being in the Alps, skiing with her family when she was eleven—the first and only time they'd been. The last family holiday where things had felt all right, before her mum had started to grow more distant, her dad more panicked, triggered by that damned bike accident in the New Forest.

She remembered the turquoise ski suit her parents had bought her, and even though it shouldn't fit her now, as she thought about it, there it was, made to measure. "Well," she said, slipping her hands into the pockets of the newly emerged jacket, "I suppose this is more appropriate." She looked out across the mountains again, then just sat down where she was, the snow fluffy and inviting. The chair lift continued to move slowly to her left, and there were zigzags in the snow made by skis, but the mountain was completely deserted. It could have been eerie, but instead it felt peaceful. All part of the magic of this place, she supposed.

After a second, Nick mimicked her, sitting down next to her, not quite close enough to touch. She could feel his gaze on the side of her face, though he said nothing.

Then, "Why did you do it?" His voice was soft, quiet.

She glanced at him. "Do what?" she asked, though she already knew.

"Jump into the river."

She gave a shrug full of a nonchalance she didn't quite feel. "For fun?" The sun was warm on her face, and though it made the tips of her fingers numb, she rested her palms on the ground behind her, feeling the satisfying crunch as the snow compacted.

He said nothing to that, only looked at her like he was trying to work her out.

"I didn't *mean* to . . . for it to happen. To come here," she insisted.

And she didn't know why this time, when she'd done other things—at university, and even here, on the skiing holiday—that might be considered risky or impulsive, it had made her heart stop. Her dad had initially refused to let her ski because of her condition, and she'd spent the first few days being bored and annoyed and wondering why the hell they'd come at all. Looking back, she thought it was probably a holiday to try and bind them all together—or maybe her dad trying to convince her mum to stay. Amber had been off skiing all the time—she was weirdly good at it, considering none of them had ever been before—her mum had been, surprise, surprise, working, and her dad had insisted that he and Emery go cross-country skiing, which was both hard work and incredibly boring. Eventually her mum had convinced her dad to let her have a lesson, and to her shock and annoyance, she had *not* been a natural like Amber, and so had fallen. Hard. Over one of the bump things. But she'd been fine—her heart had kept on beating.

Nick was still watching her, she noticed, waiting for something. "What?" she asked, feeling a touch defensive. It felt different with him, somehow, to last time. Last time, when she'd been fourteen and the world had felt like a different place—one with her mum in it.

"You didn't do it deliberately?" His voice was low, quiet. "To make your heart stop?"

His words caused an uncomfortable flash of heat to run up her spine, but she shook her head firmly. "No." In hindsight, it had been stupid. She just hadn't been expecting the water to be so *cold*. She was telling the truth, though—she hadn't meant to make her heart stop; she'd just wanted to do *something*. There had been a couple of times, right after her mum had left, when she'd pushed the boundaries—because maybe if it happened again, her mum might come back. It might be proof that the past incidents weren't because one parent was right and the other wrong; it was just one of those things that always might happen. And maybe her mum would have *wanted* to come back, to be there for her. Because whatever her faults might be, she was still her mum, and Emery had missed her.

But that wasn't the reason she'd jumped into the river—it was far too late for that. After a couple of years, Emery had come to the conclusion that her behavior probably wouldn't have made a difference in any case, because maybe her mum had been looking for a reason to leave, given that she had done so little to maintain a relationship with them afterward. Maybe, if Emery had died again, she'd have looked at it like it was proof that she couldn't handle a complicated daughter.

But now it *had* happened again. And only Colin and Bonnie were there, in the real world, to help her. They'd have to drag her out of the water and then try to restart her heart, and Jesus, she was a bit of a selfish bitch, doing that to them, wasn't she?

She felt a sudden surge of helplessness, at the fact that she was so dependent on other people. "What if they can't do it?" she asked out loud. "What if my heart doesn't start again?"

Nick's expression stayed carefully neutral. "I think you know the answer to that."

She did, on some level at least, but she'd been hoping for a more reassuring answer. More of the details of what, exactly, would happen. But maybe that would make her feel worse, so instead she asked, "Can I see what's happening to me right now? In the river, I mean? If you can see the moments before a death, can you show me the moments after?"

"I can't. I'm sorry."

Maybe that was for the best. Maybe she didn't want to see the panic as they tried to help her, because it would only make her feel more guilty. Easier to be here, with Nick, and pretend it wasn't really happening—the ultimate escape from her own skin. And indeed, that itching, burning feeling, the need to do something to prove to people that she didn't have to be so careful, had calmed since being here. She tilted her face up to the sun and closed her eyes.

"So, Nick. What have you been up to?" she asked flippantly. "Busy week?"

It got a surprised laugh out of him, and she smiled at the sound of it. "I don't really think in terms of weeks."

"But you've been seeing other people, right? *Guiding* them?"

"Yes," he said, and she could hear the smile in his voice, knew he remembered their conversation in the treetops all those years ago.

"Who?"

He hesitated. "I'm not sure I should say."

"Against the rules?"

"Well, I don't know if there are *rules*, so to speak—it's not like I get a performance review or anything." She snorted quietly at the idea of that. "It's just that the moment of someone's death, it feels kind of private."

She thought about that for a minute and decided he was right—she wasn't sure she'd want him telling others about her, about the memories she took him back to when she was at her most vulnerable. So she asked something else instead. "Do you ever get fed up, living in other people's versions of the world?" When he didn't immediately respond, she opened her eyes to check he'd heard, found him looking at her, his eyebrows pulled together. "What?"

He smoothed out his expression. "Nothing. It's just, no one has ever asked me that before. I guess I've never really thought about it like that. In some ways it's nice—seeing so *much* of the world." She sensed that he believed it—but maybe there was something else too, something he wasn't quite admitting to.

"How can you be sure they're seeing it the same way you are, though?" He gave her a questioning look. "I mean, it's brilliantly blue right now, and the snow is literally *sparkling*, but that might just be my perception of it, mightn't it?"

"I suppose so. But isn't that all life is? Someone's perception of it? So even if I'm only seeing it through the eyes of others, maybe I'm getting a wider view of it."

She nodded, then sniggered a little.

"What?" he asked.

"It's just... I'm here, in the Alps, having a philosophical debate with... well, you." She tried and failed to imagine having a similar conversation with Bonnie or any of her university friends and just couldn't. "Plus, I'm dead. Technically."

"There is that," he agreed, and there was a hint of dry humor in his voice, something she decided she liked hearing.

She shifted position so she was sitting cross-legged, angling her body toward him. "You said time is different here."

"Yes..." His voice was ever so slightly wary now, though she couldn't think why. Maybe he just didn't like answering questions about how it worked, given that he didn't actually seem to know all that much himself.

"So how long has it been for you since you last saw me?"

He stared into the distance, and was quiet for so long that she felt the need to break the silence. "If you can't tell me, I—"

"No, sorry, it's not that. I'm just thinking. It's like..." He tapped one finger on the snow. "It's like no time has passed and yet it also feels like an impossibly long time has gone by." He made a face. "Sorry. It's kind of hard to explain."

She nodded slowly. She realized that what she was really asking was how long ago in his mind she was a fourteen-year-old girl, but it was probably best not to go down that route.

"How come I always see you?" she asked. "I mean, you said there are others, so why . . . ?"

"I've wondered that too. I can't be sure, but I think it's like we're . . . *matched* to people. There must be a reason, I suppose," he mused.

"A reason you're able to help certain people?"

A pause, which made the resulting "yes" sound a little less confident.

"Do you think you *are* helping them?"

Another pause. "I hope so."

She let that sit for a moment. She'd assumed that he had *purpose*, that he was somehow part of the grand functioning of the universe and therefore totally understood his place in it—but the more she talked to him, the less credence she could give to that theory.

"So. You think there's a reason you were matched to me?" She couldn't quite meet his gaze as she asked, though she wasn't sure why. She saw him glance at her out of the corner of her eye.

"If my theory is right, then yes, I suppose so." A noncommittal answer if ever there was one.

She clapped her hands together, and the sound echoed around the mountains. "What's the spiel then?"

"The what?"

"You know, what do you usually say to people? Give me the speech."

He shot her a look. "Well, you're different." He said the word—*different*—like it was a good thing, something to be celebrated, and it sent a tiny jolt through her. Usually she heard that word used negatively—she couldn't do things other people could because she was *different*. The fear, barely concealed, in her dad's voice as he told her that.

It came then, the tremor that ran through the memory, one that might have caused an avalanche in the real world. Emery let out a slow breath, a weight lifting. She hadn't wanted to admit to herself that she'd been waiting for it—hadn't wanted to consider the alternative. She glanced at Nick, saw he looked relieved too. She nudged him in the ribs. "Hey, don't you want me to stay?" Oh God, was she *flirting* with him? *Bad Emery*.

He didn't look at her as he smiled, and the smile didn't reach his eyes. "I'd love you to stay, but that's not possible." He glanced at her. "You can't *stay* here, only pass through." She thought of how she'd once called his existence out as lonely. She didn't say it again, though—she didn't want to make him sad.

Instead, she looked around. "There must be skis here somewhere." Maybe she could give it another go, see whether she was as terrible as she remembered.

"You'd think, wouldn't you?" he mused.

She gave up looking and flopped back down on the snow, stretching out her arms and legs and moving them backward and forward.

"What are you doing?"

The utter incredulity in his voice made her laugh. "I'm making a snow angel!"

"Right."

She tutted at his tone. "We didn't get the white Christmas everyone was hoping for, so I'm making the most of the snow here."

There was a brief second, and then she felt him lie back on the snow next to her, and glanced over to see him making a snow angel of his own. She couldn't stop the laugh from bubbling over, and it bounced off the sides of the mountains around them.

She lay still with her arms above her head and blew out a breath, looking up at the clear blue sky. When she moved her hands back to her sides, her fingertips brushed past his. There was something intimate in the way they were just lying there, neither saying anything. The two of them, completely alone. She closed her eyes against the brightness of the sun.

"Are you okay?" he murmured.

She hesitated. She wasn't sure how to explain that while she wanted to go back, she was also dreading it a little. It was peaceful here, and she'd be returning to water in her lungs, and icy clothes stuck to her skin, and pain in her chest, and two very worried people hovering over her. And she'd have to deal with the guilt at putting them through it, and her own stupidity, and her dad's fear when he inevitably found out. But she also already felt defiant at the idea that she should have done anything differently, should have to try and predict when and where an episode might hit her. It felt too complicated to explain all that, though, so she just said, "Yeah. I'm okay."

She felt him sit up next to her and opened her eyes. She had to blink a few times to bring everything into focus because of the haze that had settled on them.

Nick got to his feet and held out a hand to her. She tried not to think too hard about the feel of his skin against hers, a slight roughness to his palms that she wouldn't have expected.

She bit her lip as he grew a little blurrier, seeming to dissolve as she became more solid. "Goodbye, Nick."

He reached out, brushing snow away from her temple, and the feel of his fingers sent a pleasant shiver down her spine. "Until next time, Emery."

Chapter Ten

Four years later (February 2004)

AGE 25

Emery reached out blindly for the glass of water on her bedside table, nearly knocking the lamp over in the process. She groaned as she bent her neck enough to take a sip, grimaced at the taste of the slightly stale water. One of her legs was caught in the thin sheet, and sweat was cooling on her back in the sticky heat. The fan was angled toward her, but it only gave off a pathetic limp breeze—she must be one of the only people in the whole of Australia who didn't have air conditioning. One of the many reasons she tried not to spend too long in her box of a room above the restaurant where she worked in Perth.

She listened to the sound of the shower running in the tiny adjoining bathroom, running her tongue along her teeth in lieu of a toothbrush. There was a throbbing behind her temples and her throat felt dry and scratchy. There was a faint smell of weed in the air, which made her empty stomach roll unpleasantly.

She sighed as she put the water back, reached for the phone instead. One new message.

Good night last night then?

She cringed automatically and immediately checked her outbox.

Colin. Co-lin! I'm walking along the sea right now and I'm thinking of going for a swim and I'm thinking of yooouuuuu and when we jumped in the Cam. When are you coming to visit again? I misssss youuuuuu.

Well, it could have been worse, she supposed. She tried not to text people from home too often—it cost loads, for everyone involved. But she and Colin had a habit of breaking that rule. With that thought came a rush of guilt—when did she last text Bonnie? They'd come out here together, but Bonnie had long since left, gone back to England for her sensible entry-level job, while Emery had stayed on, reveling in the freedom of moving from job to job, where no one knew her and she was allowed to be, well, whatever version of herself she felt like being.

Sorry, she texted back. *Apparently I was feeling overly sentimental.*

And now in the cold, harsh light of day?

Oh, I in no way ever think of you or miss you at all.

Good to know.

What time is it there?

6 p.m.

You waited all day to reply?

Things to do, Em, things to do.

Emery smiled to herself. Colin was now working at *The Times* and he liked to remind her of that one way or another as much as possible. Her phone vibrated in her hand.

Always glad to know you miss me, though.

She smiled but didn't reply. She did miss Colin—and Bonnie—more than she'd admit when she was sober, given that she consistently made a big deal about how she was living the dream out here. But it hadn't been him she was thinking of last night. She and Neil had been walking along the beach barefoot, the sea lapping their feet, and daring each other to skinny-dip. It had made her think of the Cam—the shock of the cold, that feeling of reckless abandon right before she'd hit the water.

No, she hadn't been thinking of Colin, who had been the one to perform CPR, getting her heart started again after he dragged her from the water. Nor of Bonnie, who had frozen, apparently. Who had told Emery afterward, crying, that she'd gone on a special first aid course so she could prepare herself for if it ever happened again, after witnessing the whole thing on the camping trip. It had left Emery with huge guilt and embarrassment, even as she'd hugged her friend and tried to put everything into that hug—how grateful she was, how stupid she felt, how very sorry she was for putting them through that.

Yes, they'd popped into her mind as she and Neil had stripped off and run into the water, but it had been Nick's face that had lingered as she'd replayed their last encounter and wondered if she'd ever see him again. But she obviously couldn't text Nick, couldn't even talk about him. So she'd messaged Colin instead.

A final message beeped through.

If you don't come home, I'll come out at Easter. X

She put her phone down, figuring she'd reply when her head was hurting less. Colin had been out to visit once before, when Bonnie had still been here. Would he bring Bonnie if he came out again? Or would he come alone? Her stomach rolled, and she couldn't figure out why—or whether the feeling was good or bad.

She heard the creak of the tap as the shower was switched off, and moments later, Neil appeared in the doorway, his broad shoulders taking up the entire space. He had a towel tied around his waist, his rusty hair was damp and tousled, and his feet left wet footprints on the stained beige carpet as he crossed to her bed, casting an eye around the room for his clothes. Emery took a moment to appreciate his body—sculpted and tanned from his obsession with morning runs on the beach. He'd told her he was a lifeguard when they'd first met a few weeks ago, at the bar she worked at downstairs, and then teased her for believing in the cliché. She'd made him work for it before she'd slept with him; not because she didn't want to—there had always been a kind of inevitability about it—but because she'd been a bit bored and it had been fun to see how hard he'd try.

She watched him dress, and he grinned at her as he pulled his T-shirt over his head, so bloody cocksure. Then he shuffled to the side of the bed, leaned over and kissed her cheek, smelling of her coconut shampoo. His eyes lingered on her bare chest, the one leg she had flung over the thin sheet in an effort to keep cool. "I'll see you later, babe. You working this arvo?"

"No." God, her voice sounded all croaky and horrible. "My sister's coming—Amber, remember? She's here for ten days, I've got some time off."

"Ah yeah, sure, I remember." A total lie, but she couldn't be bothered to call him out on it.

"So I might not be around that much," she prompted. She wasn't really sure what she wanted—for him to insist on meeting her sister, to say he'd miss her?

"Okay, babe. Just give me a text when you're free." That was it. Ah well. She'd known right off the bat that it would never be anything other than casual. And if she was being totally honest with herself, she knew why she'd been attracted to him in the first place. It had been the eyes—gray with a tinge of green. For one brief second, when she'd seen him across the bar, she'd mistaken him for someone else.

**

Emery shifted from foot to foot as she waited, glancing up at the arrivals board every now and then. The plane had definitely landed, so what the hell was taking so long? Around her, shoes squeaked on the shiny floor, and people hurried past dragging massive suitcases. Somewhere nearby, a toddler cried. She didn't blame them.

Her phone, hanging loosely in her hand, started to ring. She'd been checking it every few minutes, in case Amber had needed to get hold of her—but it wasn't her sister calling.

"I'm only answering in case of emergency," she said in lieu of "hello." "I've already spent far too much on credit this month."

"Well that's good, because—I'm engaged!!!!"

Emery nearly dropped her phone. "What! Oh my God! To Joe?"

Bonnie laughed. "No, to Humphrey."

"Who the hell is Humphrey?"

"No idea. I'm sure there are loads of Humphreys. Of course to Joe, you dolt."

"Oh my God. This is INCREDIBLE." People around the airport were casting her shifty looks, because she was full-on shouting down the phone like a lunatic.

"Calm down, we don't want your heart to go haywire."

She gave the obligatory snort of laughter at that. "I actually can't believe this," she said.

"Why, because I'm not the marriage type?"

"Well, no, I mean you absolutely *are* the marriage type—although actually, what do we think that really means?"

"Breadmaking?"

Emery gave a dramatic sigh. "Well I'm out then."

"So am I. Best tell Joe I've never made bread in my life."

"We did it in home ec at school one year, do you remember?"

"Hmm. I have a vague, traumatic memory of dough getting very out of hand."

"But Bonnie, we are so YOUNG." More looks from around the airport. One woman clasped her daughter's hand more tightly as they walked past, as if Emery was actually mental.

"I know, Em. But I love him." Emery could hear the smile in Bonnie's voice, and it made her smile too. "And it feels right."

"Well then." She let out a whoosh of breath. "Fucking fantastic, I say." Her best friend. Getting *married*. But Joe was actually pretty fucking perfect—Bonnie had met him in the canteen at work when she got back from traveling, a fellow employee at Cadbury.

"We're probably going to be engaged for ages anyway, so it'll be a few years before I'm *actually* married."

"Well that's good. More time to plan the bachelorette party." Married! Bonnie was getting married. Emery tried phrasing it in different ways inside her mind to make it seem real.

"Speaking of which...I think this goes without saying, but—"

"Bonnie Mistry, if you are going to ask me to be a bridesmaid, all I can say is that I look great in cobalt blue."

Bonnie laughed, and the sound was so joyous, it bizarrely made Emery feel like she was tearing up. "Cobalt specifically?"

"Yes. That and nothing else."

"Well, as maid of honor you'll get the swing vote, sooo..."

Emery let out a breathless laugh and squeezed her eyes shut. "I think I'm going to cry. No, wait, I am. I'm actually crying."

"You're not." She could *hear* the eye-roll in Bonnie's voice.

Emery opened her eyes, did a quick scan around the airport. Still no sign of Amber. "Well, okay, I'm not, but I feel like I *could*. Are you sure?"

"Of course I'm sure. Who else?"

"Okay. Okay. I'll be a great one, I promise."

"I know you will."

"So what do your parents say?"

"I haven't told them yet."

"What!"

"It only happened yesterday!"

"You're telling me first? Okay, a) I am totally and completely honored, and b) I think you should lie when you tell Maureen and say she's the first to know."

There was Amber, hair tied into a no-nonsense bun, coming through the barrier dragging a small, smart black suitcase behind her. And Robin, short blonde hair sticking up in tufts, clearly disheveled after the flight, dragging a much more appropriate *large* suitcase behind her.

"Argh, they're here. Talk about bad timing."

"What?"

"Amber's here—I'm at the airport. She and Robin have come to visit."

"Oh shit, I forgot that was today!"

"I want to talk to you, though," Emery said, speaking quickly as she moved to the front of the crowd and waved to get Amber's attention. "How did he do it? Did he get down on one knee? I bet he did, didn't he? Joe is *so* the type to get down on one knee. And where were you? Don't tell me, you're going to say something horribly corny like in the canteen where you first met or something."

"No." Bonnie gave a dramatic pause. "It was in Venice."

"Of *course* it fucking was."

Robin noticed Emery first and nudged Amber, and the two of them headed toward her. "Argh, Bon, I have to go."

"Yes, go! Tell Amber I say hi."

"I will, but please can we talk? They'll have to crash with jet lag at some point. I'll call you then, credit be damned."

"Yes! Any time. I'm too jacked up on adrenaline, I probably won't be able to sleep anyway."

Emery hung up as Robin and Amber approached. She smiled at both of them, hugging one after the other. Amber looked knackered, but Robin was perky as ever. Maybe she'd had enough practice at late-night coffee-fueled deadlines as an academic that a twenty-hour flight was nothing.

Emery beamed at both of them as she stepped back. Bonnie was engaged and happy, and now Amber was here. She felt a sudden rush of joy. "You made it!" she exclaimed. She took hold of Robin's massive suitcase, leaving Amber to deal with her tiny one. "Come on. Let's start having fun."

Chapter Eleven

Emery allowed Amber and Robin to dump their bags at their hotel before insisting on lunch at one of her favorite beach cafés. It was packed, as usual, but they got a good space outdoors under an umbrella. "It's so *hot*," Amber kept saying.

"Hot in summer in Australia?" Emery replied, incredulous. "That's *outrageous*."

"Where's our sunscreen?" Robin asked as they all sat down. "We forgot it, didn't we? Dammit. I was *sure* I'd got out the factor 50—we have to be careful, because the research shows that—"

"*You* might have forgotten it," Amber interrupted. "I, however, did not." She pulled a bottle of sunscreen out of her enormous handbag. A tiny suitcase but an enormous handbag, what was the point in that?

"I've also forgotten my toothbrush," Robin said to Emery, like a confession. "And I only packed one pair of socks. The ones I'm wearing."

Emery laughed. "I can take you to a shop after this. But in the meantime—mimosas, yes?" This earned a raised eyebrow from Amber, and Emery rolled her eyes. "You're on *holiday*.

Plus it's mostly orange juice. Plus it's practically bedtime for you anyway."

"I'm in," Robin declared, and that settled that.

She started fanning herself as they waited for the drinks to arrive, and Amber muttered, "See, it *is* hot."

"Only because we're not used to it," Robin said with a shrug. "It took ages for me to acclimatize when I was in New Zealand that summer."

"Ah yes," Amber said, "your year in New Zealand. I'd almost forgotten you even *did* that, you talk about it so little." Robin poked her in the ribs, and Amber laughed. Then they smiled at each other, and there was something so *intimate* about it, almost like they'd forgotten Emery was even there, that Emery felt the tiniest twinge of jealousy. She wasn't even sure why. She liked Robin—a lot. If someone's biggest flaw was that you sometimes couldn't understand them because they talked at speed about their research into a really specific bird in New Zealand, that was saying something. Plus Amber seemed happier than she'd ever been before—something that had not dimmed over the years they'd been together.

Amber had cried when she finally told Emery about Robin, apologizing for not having told her sooner, and Emery had hugged her and said she was happy for her, and it had been one of those scary moments when she'd felt like more than just the little sister—when she'd realized that Amber might need her as much as the other way around.

So yes, it was very much a good thing that Robin was in

Amber's life, and at moments like this, when they held their little conversations and just seemed to *settle* one another, Emery could see it, they way they fitted, completing each other's puzzle.

Maybe that was it. The news of Bonnie's engagement, then seeing these two together. She'd never even come close to anything like that. Hadn't actually tried, but still. She didn't know what it was like, to have her puzzle completed—wasn't sure she ever would.

"So, we have news," Amber said after the mimosas arrived.

"Don't tell me you're getting engaged too." The tiniest flinch crossed Robin's face, and Emery bit her lip. Stupid. Why did she have to say these things without thinking them through?

But Amber's voice was light. "No, well we can't, can we, but... Wait, who's got engaged?"

"Bonnie."

"*Bonnie?* But she's only your age!"

Emery laughed. "I know! Apparently some people get engaged at twenty-five. Anyway, what's your news?"

Amber took a breath. "We're moving to Edinburgh."

"*Edinburgh?*"

"It's where I'm from," Robin offered up. Even though, being all blonde and tall and moving in that fluid way of hers, she very much looked like she could be Australian, despite the fact that her skin was turning slightly pink in the heat. "I haven't been back for any length of time since I left for uni, and I kind of miss it—and a teaching position has opened up at the university there."

"And I've already applied for a physio job at a private clinic, which sounds great," Amber picked up. "I've got an interview when we get back."

Emery nodded, taking that in. It wasn't like she'd lived near her sister for ages, being on the other side of the world and all that. But she'd assumed she'd always be there in Cambridge when she eventually made it home. "How does Dad feel about it?"

"We-ell," Amber said, dragging out the word, "he might feel a whole lot better about the idea if you came home."

Emery sighed. "Don't."

"Sorry. Sorry! I just...He's worried about you."

"He's *always* worried about me, what else is new?"

Amber bit her lip. "I think, if you were doing something ...you know, well, *something*, it might make a bit more sense to him, but at the moment it feels like you're just staying away for the sake of it."

"I *am* doing something. I'm working, aren't I?"

"Oh Emery, you know what I mean." She was using her big-sister voice now, the one that made the edges of Emery's teeth grate. Robin made a show of picking up her mimosa and looking away toward the ocean, slipping her sunglasses over her eyes as if trying to hide.

Emery could feel the words she wanted to snap back rising inside her. But she didn't know Robin *that* well, and she hadn't seen Amber for two years. So she took a breath, tasting the sea air. "Amber, you just got here. Can we save the lecture for, I don't know, day three at least?"

Amber rolled her shoulders. "Sorry. Argh, you're right, I'm

sorry. I told Dad I'd bring it up, anyway, so now I have." She flashed a guilty smile, which Emery returned.

"How is he? Dad?"

"Oh, you know, the same. Keeps making noises about retiring." Emery knew that already. He insisted on weekly calls, mainly to ask how her health was, whether she was still going for her check-ups and when she was coming back. She *may* have told a tiny white lie and said that one of her friends was a nurse and was on hand if anything should go wrong, but she figured that if it reduced his stress levels, the deception was justified.

There was a beat that went on a touch too long to be casual. "Mum's fine too, in case you were wondering."

"I wasn't," Emery said, trying to keep her voice mild, disinterested. Amber looked like she might press the issue, but Emery spoke before she could. "So what do you guys want to do while you're here?"

Thankfully, Amber conceded and dropped the subject. No doubt she'd press it again when she'd had a wine or two, but right now she glanced at Robin, who rejoined the conversation, pushing her sunglasses to the top of her head. "I don't know—everything? We can see dolphins, right?"

"Yes, definitely."

"And we want to see where you work," Amber said.

Emery made a face as she tried to catch one of the waitresses' eyes to order food. "Eurgh, boring, let's not do that."

"Rottnest Island?" Robin suggested and Emery nodded. "Perfect. I've not actually done that yet."

Amber shook her head. "*How* have you not done that yet?"

"I've been busy with other more exciting things. Speaking of which, I've got a great activity planned for tomorrow."

"Emery…" Amber's voice held a warning tone.

"What?" Emery asked innocently.

"It isn't dangerous, is it? Not the type of thing Dad would kill us for?"

She put her hand on her heart. "Girl Guide's honor."

"You were a terrible Girl Guide."

Emery only grinned.

* *

Amber stared at the entrance to the building as the three of them got out of the taxi. "Skydiving? You want to go skydiving?" She shook her head. "You can't be serious."

"I want us *all* to go skydiving, and yes, I am very much serious." Emery put her hand on her sister's back, tried to chivvy her toward the entrance. It was early morning, and she'd dragged Robin and Amber out of bed, getting the hotel to issue them a wake-up call so they'd be here in time. It was something she'd wanted to try ever since she'd got to Australia, something she'd been saving up for.

"Emery, this is a terrible idea."

Robin said nothing, just eyed the entrance to the building curiously. It was about an hour outside of Perth and they'd driven down a dirt track to get here, and it had that brilliant feeling of being completely in the middle of nowhere.

"You say that about all my best ideas."

"That's because they're all terrible."

Before she could help it, Emery was snapping out words she'd promised herself she wouldn't say. "Did you ever think that the reason I'm still out here is because I'm fed up of being treated like a porcelain doll?" She winced as soon as it was out, because she knew what it had been like for Amber. Knew why she'd moved back to Cambridge after university.

"I'm sorry," she said quietly. Robin, sensibly, Emery thought, walked on ahead of them toward the reception area. Emery put her hand on her sister's arm, squeezed gently. "Ambs. When I was five, I died because a thorn got stuck in my foot."

A hitched breath. "I know. I remember."

"A *thorn*, Amber. So you know as well as I do that it could happen at any time. I just figure I should live, really *live*, while I can."

Amber scowled and glanced at her, taking her attention off Robin's back. "Don't say things like that."

Emery said nothing, only pulled her sister in for a hug, felt her return it. And she felt the comfort slide through her, the type that only a big sister could offer. She could smell the peppermint scent from Amber's favorite body lotion, something that was bizarrely soothing.

When they drew apart, Amber glanced at the sign above the building. *Skydive Geronimo*. She bit her lip. "I'm scared." Not really of the skydive, Emery knew—though it was certainly not something Amber would attempt unless someone forced her into it.

"Don't be," Emery said gently. "I'm not."

Amber sniffed. "I'm not sure if that makes it *more* scary." Emery rolled her eyes as the two of them headed to where Robin had disappeared.

"How did you know, with Robin?" Emery asked after a beat.

"That I was gay?"

"No. Well, I mean sure, if you want to talk about it."

Amber gave her a wry look. "I thought we were sort of done with the coming-out phase, to be honest."

"Right but how did you know she was the *one*?"

"Why?" Amber asked slowly. "Is there someone on the scene?"

"No. Definitely not." Emery sighed. "Forget about it. It's not important." She felt suddenly embarrassed for bringing it up.

"Em, what's—"

But Robin had reappeared from the reception area. "Okay, if we want to do this, we have to go in for the safety lecture." Amber swallowed audibly, and Robin laughed. "I, for one, am all for it."

Emery gave Amber's arm one final squeeze, and Amber took a deep breath. "Okay. Oh my God, okay. Let's do it." For her, Emery knew. Amber would do this for her.

* *

It wasn't the skydiving that did it. It wasn't being up in the plane, wind whipping in through the open door, staring down at the ground, which looked so very far away. It wasn't the instructor shouting behind her, "You ready? On three!" It wasn't the jump, the feeling of being in free fall, wind rushing past her face as her stomach lurched. Wasn't the adrenaline pumping through her veins or the jubilant whoop she'd let out just before the parachute jerked them back upward. That part had all been exactly as Emery had dreamed. Amber had even come up to her afterward, half laughing, her body shaking, and flung an arm around her shoulders. "Well, Little Em, maybe there's something to be said for this living-in-the-moment bollocks."

In the end, it had been getting into the taxi on the way back. Getting her finger trapped just as the door shut. Hot pain concentrated in her index finger, so bad that she wanted to swear at the top of her lungs. But she didn't even get the scream out before her heart gave up on her.

Chapter Twelve

"Skydiving, hey? Seems like you might nurture a love of dangerous activities."

Emery frowned at the sound of his voice behind her. "And seems like you might nurture a love of being annoying and cryptic." But she gave it a moment before she turned around, taking in her surroundings. She was by the sea, but a very different sea than the one she was currently living next to. The breeze was warm and gentle on her face, but it was not that sometimes oppressive Australian heat. The coastline was beautiful, the sky a bright blue that stretched for miles, and below where she sat on the edge of rocks that jutted out over the water, the coarse sandy beach was empty. Empty in a way it never would be in Falmouth in June, had this been the real world.

Nick didn't come around her into her line of vision. Didn't put a hand on her shoulder or force her to turn. Waiting for her to be ready, maybe. For her part, the reason she had to wait was because she knew that when she saw him, she wouldn't be able to deny it to herself. Wouldn't be able to pretend that she hadn't been wanting to see him. Worse—that she'd been *waiting* to see him.

Her stomach gave a pleasant little lurch as she finally turned. He was standing about a meter from her, the sun bright behind him so that he was partly obscured in shadow, light bouncing off his conker-brown hair. His sleeves were rolled up, showing arms she hadn't previously noticed were so muscled. She tipped her face up to meet those gray-green eyes and felt her nerves jumping along her skin in a way she knew was stupid. But she couldn't help it. He looked better than she'd imagined—better than what she'd been able to call into focus when she tried to remember the contours of his face. Was he supposed to be this attractive? It was unhelpful. Distracting. Plus, each time she saw him, she swore he looked younger, too.

"Why *is* that?" she asked out loud.

He raised his eyebrows. The next time Bonnie told her that one of the reasons she fell in love with Joe was because his eyebrows were sexy, she would not laugh. "You know, I'm not actually a mind-reader."

She pff'd. "Well that's ridiculous. How are you supposed to guide people if you can't read their minds?"

He gave a wry look in answer to that. "Why is what?" he prompted.

She shook her head. "Never mind." It probably had more to do with her than him, anyway. But... "How old *are* you?"

He frowned, clearly not expecting that line of questioning. "Thirty-five." He gave the answer so quickly, so *firmly*, that she stared at him for a moment. He cleared his throat, looking suddenly uncertain. "Well. Depending on how you count the years, I suppose."

"That's more like the Nick I know." It earned her a smile, though she had to look away, out to sea, to disguise the thrill, the *relief*, she felt at being able to say his name out loud at last.

She sat on the rocks, the sea spray crashing up to meet her bare legs. She was in a blue dress, the one she'd been wearing on the day of the memory, rather than the leggings and old T-shirt she'd worn skydiving. Above and behind her was one of her old favorite hangout spots, Hooked on the Rocks. Though the drinks were a bit too expensive for her student budget to allow her to spend as much time there as she would have liked.

"Where are we this time?" Nick asked as he sat next to her. She smiled a bit at the routine of it, at the fact that it was oddly comforting.

"Falmouth. In Cornwall. It's where I went to uni." She could see the lighthouse in the distance on the shoreline that curved round in an arc, and to her right, a big manor house nestled at the edge of the cliff, something that could be out of a du Maurier novel, especially on stormy winter days. "I suppose this could have been any number of times," she continued. "I came here a lot. But I think it's actually this one particular day." She glanced briefly down at her dress. "It was after exams, and I came here alone just to sit and be. Loads of people were celebrating the end of uni, and I joined them all later, but first I came here." She sighed. "There's something so brilliantly calming about the sea, don't you think?"

He looked out at it, leaning back on his elbows to take in the full view. "I'd have to agree with you there."

What she didn't say out loud was that although this moment, here on the rocks by the sea, was definitely a "happy place," she'd come here because she'd been trying to escape. Because amidst the champagne-popping and the laughter and the plans to go out later, there had been talk of the future and what next, after graduation. And while going traveling with Bonnie had been considered enough of a plan that she didn't have to elaborate too much, she was still subjected to a lot of discussion about *in five years*, and she always hated that sort of talk, because she lived with the fact that she might not *have* five years, if something went wrong.

She didn't really feel like voicing any of that out loud, but still, she could feel Nick's gaze on the side of her face in that way of his, like he was weighing her silence. She frowned at him. "Why are you looking at me like that?"

"Sorry," he said quickly, glancing away. "It's just, usually most of my interactions are spent calming people down or just..." he waved a hand in the air as he searched for the words, "being there, in whatever capacity." His accent held a pleasant Scottish lilt—a bit like Robin's, she realized, but with more of a burr. Was that because a Scottish accent was considered comforting? "People cry," he continued, "or they don't want to accept what's happening and they blame me, because they need to blame someone." She thought of that, of how it must feel. He caught sight of her expression, and it obviously showed more than she'd realized, because he spoke again quickly. "I don't mean it's all bad." A smile flickered across his face. "I played chess with an old man once. Or tried to. I'd never actually played chess, and he wasn't brilliant at explaining the rules. And there was a woman in her fifties, someone who had been struggling with illness for a long time, and she taught me to jive in this karaoke bar, which was both ridiculous and brilliant." He sighed. "But despite all that, with you..." He glanced at her again. "It's hard to believe that I get to see you again."

The words made her heart spasm a little—not exactly an unpleasant sensation. Like her heart *knew* it was the reason she was here and was glad about it. But she tossed her head back in a dramatic fashion. "It's hard for *you* to believe? What about me?"

She regretted the flippant words almost instantly—because he was being honest, and she was turning it into a joke. She bit her lip, studying his face, those sculpted cheekbones, as he looked out at the calm sea. "I'm sorry for calling it a lonely existence, all those years ago." His brow furrowed, and she wondered if he even remembered. She found herself flushing, at the fact that she *did* remember, each interaction firmly tattooed on her mind. "I mean, maybe you thought nothing of it, but it was a stupid thing to say," she continued hurriedly, trying to dig herself out of the hole. "I was only twelve, and—"

"I remember," he said quietly.

There was a pause in which they listened to the seagulls before Emery spoke again. "Is it? Lonely, I mean?"

"Sometimes," he admitted. Then he smiled at her. "Less so

with you here." He sighed again. "But it can be . . . sad to watch people in their last moments, over and over."

"How do you do it? How do you keep doing it, and not let it consume you?"

"I'm not sure it *doesn't* consume me." It wasn't the answer she'd expected. He always seemed so level to her. She supposed that showed how little she knew him. "But then maybe it's supposed to consume me. Maybe I wouldn't be doing my job properly if it didn't."

She wasn't sure how to respond to that, so they both fell quiet again. Then she murmured, "Do you ever wish it would all just stop?" She didn't really know what she was asking, because she didn't know if there was an option, somewhere to go *after* this.

He looked out at the sea for a long moment, his face tight. Then, "Sometimes." He frowned. "But when I think that, I remind myself I'm here because I'm supposed to be." The way he said it, though, it didn't sound like he was reveling in some higher purpose. It sounded like he was damning himself. She opened her mouth to press him, to ask what he meant, but he cut her off. "So, Australia, huh? What's that like?"

"Very . . . Australian. You know."

"No, can't say I do. I've never been to Australia. Never been abroad, actually, much as I wanted to."

"Never? No one has ever taken you there before?" She would have thought there would be lots of happy memories abroad. He was looking at her with a strange expression, and she realized she'd misunderstood something. "Or do you mean . . . ?"

"No." He said it quickly. "That's what I meant." He gave a shrug that would have looked casual if she wasn't watching him so closely. "Luck of the draw, I suppose."

"We were in the Alps," she pointed out.

"Oh yes. I forgot about that." But the lie was unconvincing. Still, she let it sit for a moment. In the meantime, she took a breath, closed her eyes and concentrated. She wasn't sure she actually could do it, but she tried anyway, focusing as hard as she could on an image in her mind. She felt the change in the air, that close stickiness, the heat on the back of her neck. And she knew, before he said anything, that it had worked.

"Whoa! What did you do?"

She smiled as she opened her eyes and gestured around. "*This* is Australia. Perth, to be exact."

He was staring at her. "You changed the memory? How?"

She shrugged. "Like I changed my clothes in the Alps."

He let out an incredulous laugh, and she got up from where she'd been sitting on the hot sand, putting her hands on her hips as she looked around. It was the beach where she spent almost every weekend, but again without the hordes of people. He was still staring up at her almost like he'd never seen her before. "I can't believe you just did that."

"Want to go swimming?" she said in reply.

He looked at the water in such a dubious way. "Are there sharks?"

She laughed, feeling light and buoyant—a feeling that was maybe at odds with how she *should* be feeling. But in this place, it was like she could forget everything else—the true definition of living in the moment. She rode that feeling and sprinted across the hot sand, changing into her bikini as she ran. The water was warm, as she'd known it would be, and she waded in, glancing over her shoulder to check Nick was following before setting off in a front crawl.

Nick was stronger, faster than her. That seemed unfair. Surely if it was *her* memory, her world, she should be the superior one. They came to a stop out beyond their depth, bobbing, watching one another. The power disparity between them that had always been intrinsically there seemed to evaporate out here—or maybe that was because she was now the one controlling things. Her hair was slick against her face as she trod water, and he... Well, his torso was bare, visible through the water, and was very impressive indeed. She tried not to gawk, but she couldn't quite help admiring the contours of his chest. Did he control what he looked like? If she was the one trapped in limbo, she'd make sure she had the perfect body.

Trapped. She'd thought it without question, but the way he'd talked about it, it seemed like the most appropriate word.

"What are you thinking?" he asked.

She bit her lip, tasted salt. "I'm thinking of you stuck here, and wishing I could do more," she admitted. "And I'm thinking that as much as I want to stay here, talking to you, I'm scared to find out what happens if I don't go back." She'd lied to Amber earlier—because although she tried not to be, she *was* scared. She was scared about what would happen if she died—truly died. Scared for herself, and for those she left behind. It was because of that fear that she pushed so hard, though it was something she'd never admit to anyone, because she didn't want to put even more of a burden on the people who cared about her.

"I know," he said softly, and the way he said it, it was like he'd heard everything she hadn't said out loud.

"I thought you weren't a mind-reader," she said wryly.

"I've got good at reading some things over the years. And I'm getting better at reading you."

It made her feel a little self-conscious, though not wholly in a bad way. "What are *you* thinking?"

He gave a mock sigh. "I'm thinking we might prune if we stay in the ocean much longer." She made a face and splashed him, and his laugh—his *laugh*—sounded out across the waves, a sound that made it impossible not to laugh along with him. She coughed as she nearly went completely under the water, her body giving up on her the way it always did when you laughed too hard. He reached out to pull her to the surface, keeping a hand lightly against her arm. She stopped laughing, all her attention going to that point of contact.

"I'm thinking," he continued quietly, "that I wish I knew how to stop you from being scared, even if that's impossible." She felt her breath catch. "And I'm thinking ... I'm thinking that I'm glad it was me you came to—for my sake, rather than yours."

Heat flashed through her body. His eyes were so green against the ocean, she thought now. Just the two of them, with the whole world right there. Still treading water, she moved a little closer to him, watching his expression. His eyes traced her movements.

She leaned in. She'd made it a rule to live her life caution-free, and now didn't seem like the time to break that rule. She could imagine what he'd taste like—salt and sea. And she wanted to know what he tasted like under that, too. Their breath twined for a moment, and his gaze dropped to her mouth.

But then he pulled back. "Emery." And with the sound of her name, the warning tremor shuddered through the landscape, matching the warning in his voice.

A different kind of heat flooded her now, and she jerked back, splashing as she pulled away from where his hand was still supporting her arm.

Stupid. *Stupid, Emery!* It wasn't the two of them and the whole world. The world was distant, far away, and he was trapped in the in-between while she . . .

She was swimming away from him, but he was keeping time with her easily. "Emery," he said again, and the placating way he spoke her name made her cheeks burn hotter still.

"It's fine," she said, her voice clipped, and slightly breathless from the swim. "I'm sorry. I shouldn't have done it."

"Emery, slow down."

She'd reached a shallower part now, and began to wade out of the water. She'd never really appreciated how difficult it was to wade gracefully. A heat haze had settled on the shoreline, bouncing off the bright sand. No, not a heat haze. She stumbled to a stop and looked down at her hand, its outline becoming sharper. She felt him come up alongside her, but couldn't face looking at him.

"Don't go back angry," he said, and his voice held the edge of an impatient huff.

"I'm not angry," she said, continuing to walk even though she obviously didn't need to—because she couldn't bear to stand still. And it was true—she wasn't angry, she was *embarrassed*. She wondered if anyone else had ever thrown themselves at him, wanting to feel something before death. She cringed at the idea. "I'm sorry," she said again.

"Don't be. *I'm* sorry."

She risked a tiny glance at him. "Why are *you* sorry?"

"For—"

"No, forget it." She wasn't sure there would be a good reply to that question.

The haze had well and truly settled in now, blurring the horizon. Thank God. A fail-safe way to get out of an awkward conversation.

It was only right at the end, the moment before she knew she was being pulled back, when she could feel her body calling to her, that she was able to look him in the eye. "Nick? You were alive, weren't you? Before you came to this place."

And in the grimace that flashed across his face, the way *he* wouldn't meet *her* eye in that final second, she had her answer.

Chapter Thirteen

"Honeybee, your dad told me to call you." Immediately, Emery regretted answering the phone to her aunt Helen. She grimaced as she slumped down on her bed, towel tied above her breasts, wet hair helping to make her feel cooler. There had been first-aiders on site at the skydiving center, and they'd taken care of everything after Robin had run for help, and even though they'd given her the okay to go home, it had taken a good two hours to convince Amber to leave her alone long enough to take a shower. Right now, she suspected the only reason her sister hadn't barged back into her tiny bedroom was because Robin was keeping her at bay.

"And why isn't he calling me himself?" she asked.

"You know perfectly well why." And Emery did—because her dad would know that either she wouldn't answer, or else it would turn into an argument, him panicking about her and her resenting him for that panic.

"I think you ought to come home, my darling."

"I'm fine, thanks for asking." Emery was aware her tone was petulant, but she couldn't quite help it.

Helen made a tutting sound. "Of course you're not fine, we all know that."

Emery felt heat flash across her bare chest. "Actually, I'm—"

"Yes, yes, you're fine, no big deal, just another heart attack."

"It's not a heart attack!"

"Well, anyway, darling, like I said, I think that's quite enough of Australia, don't you?"

Emery gritted her teeth. "Helen, that is not—"

"My place? Fair? I think we both know we're beyond that. It's my place because I care about you, as does your father, and it may or may not be fair, but life isn't fair at the best of times—and fairness is probably a subjective thing in any case. Now, I don't know the ins and outs of what you get up to over there, but I'm getting the general gist and I don't think it's wise."

Emery scowled, hoping that her aunt could somehow feel the vibrations of it. Then Helen added, in a tone she so rarely used, "He can't lose you too, my darling."

Emery closed her eyes, the scowl fading, a lump rising in her throat to take its place. *Lose her.* Like he lost his wife when she walked out—walked out because of Emery. Because she wasn't a normal girl and because her condition had put too much of a strain on the marriage. She didn't even know if they still spoke, had stopped asking because of the expression it would cause, the awkwardness that would ensue.

"He's not going to lose me," she said, though she was aware it was a false promise. She'd never be able to guarantee that, would she? Maybe no one could, but with her it felt finite—something *would* happen, it was just a matter of when.

Helen sighed. "You have a condition, Emery, there is no point denying it—you'd do better to accept it and learn to live with it."

"I am living with it!" That was the whole bloody point. "I'm living with it while the rest of you want me to be bundled in some kind of padded room or something."

Helen scoffed. Amber, Bonnie, Colin—even her dad, at times—had the grace to look contrite when she brought this up, but it never worked on Helen. "Don't be ridiculous. That's not at all what we're saying, and you'll get nowhere by exaggerating. But think of this—how would your dad feel if you were to die, really die, out there with no one to help you because you were off skydiving?" Emery swallowed, not wanting to admit that she'd been scared of that herself. And she still couldn't admit, not to Helen or any of her family, just how *much* it scared her. Yet she'd admitted it to Nick—why was that? But with the thought of Nick came the thought of the embarrassing near-kiss, and she shoved the image of his face aside. "Live your life, my darling," Helen was saying, "but do it a little closer to home, with some thought for the people who care about you."

"Right. Well, look, thanks for checking in and all that, but I've got to go—Amber's here." Emery paused. "Which you know, don't you?"

"What's that now? Did I tell you Amber brought Robin round for Sunday lunch last week? Lovely girl. Told me all about the plants I ought to be putting in my garden to attract the most diverse bird life. It got a bit technical, actually; there were numbers and diagrams and whatnot."

Despite herself, Emery relented a little. "I like your garden as it is." And she did—Helen now lived in Ely, not far from Cambridge, where she'd moved after Emery's mum left so that she could be nearer to them all, and she'd done absolutely *nothing* with the garden since then, so that it had grown wild and unmanageable. Yes, okay, some people would probably say it was full of weeds, but Emery liked the fact that it did its own thing.

"So do I, but don't tell Robin that. It was a bonding moment for us."

"How is it bonding if you weren't actually agreeing?"

"Oh, bonding is all about *pretending* to agree, honeybee."

Emery smiled to herself. "Bye, Aunt Helen."

"Bye, my darling. Bring me something Australian when you come back, won't you?"

Emery took her time getting dressed, then looked at herself in the mirror for a long moment before she went out into the tiny living space her flat offered. There wasn't even a kitchen—just a hob and a small fridge, chopping board propped on top, in the corner of the living room, which comprised of one sofa in about a square inch of floor space.

She folded her arms as Amber stood up off that sofa. "You told Dad."

Robin sprang up too. "I'll make us some tea, shall I? Emery, do you have a kettle?"

"No," Emery said, then grimaced, realizing she was being too short. "Sorry," she added.

"That's okay." Robin's tone was overly bright. "I'll go down to the pub, get us something, shall I?" And without giving either of them time to answer, she let herself out. Emery heard the sound of her footsteps creaking down the stairs.

"I couldn't not tell him," Amber said, a pleading note in her voice.

"It'll only make things worse, him knowing."

"Emery, you can't hide it!" Emery said nothing. That was exactly what she'd intended to do, should it happen out here. Fucking bad timing that it had to be when her sister was visiting. "And you shouldn't leave it to everyone else to tell him either—*you* should be the one to do it."

"Why?" Emery asked stubbornly. "Why, when it will only make him panic? Surely it's better for him *not* to know."

"Because you owe him the explanation, Emery! Just like you owe us..." Amber swore, and Emery could see that her big sister, who was usually so calm and collected, was struggling to rein it in.

Emery took a step closer to her. "No, go on, what were you going to say?"

Amber's eyes sparked when they met hers. "You owe it to us *all* to be a bit more careful." There was that word again, the one that sent a lick of fire across Emery's skin.

"It's *my*—"

"It's not, though, is it!" Amber threw her hands in the air. "It is *not* just *your* life, it's all of ours! Do you think *I* like being the one who is always reminding you not to do things? Do you think I want to be the one constantly telling you to be careful? I've had to do it my whole life, Emery. You could start looking out for yourself for once!"

Emery's heart kicked up a gear, and she felt the gut punch of her sister's words. Amber had never said anything like that before, in all these years. Sure, Emery had *guessed* she didn't like being constantly told to look after her, and she'd assumed it must be a pain to have a little sister who might drop dead at any moment, but Amber had never given voice to it. And now Emery wasn't sure what to do with it.

Amber closed her eyes. "I'm sorry. I didn't mean that."

"Yes you did," Emery said quietly.

Amber shook her head, and when she spoke again, her voice was quiet, soft. "We're all just *worried* about you, Little Em." Emery tried to take a calming breath. Like she didn't know that! Like everyone didn't tell her that all the fucking time. "What if...what if you don't come back next time?" Tears sparked in Amber's eyes now, the anger already long gone. "I couldn't bear it." And then, without warning, she was crying—and yet again, Emery was left with this awful pit of guilt in her stomach, for what she was doing to those around her, what she was putting them through. Didn't they get it? This was *why* she'd stayed out here. She didn't *want* this guilt, or their fear, or their blame— she'd just wanted to dump it all and run, leave it behind, and now it was following her.

She crossed the tiny room and fell onto the sofa, grabbing Amber's hand and pulling her down next to her. "Did you tell Mum?"

It was the second time it had happened since their mum had left. The first time, she'd called Emery to check she was okay, but the conversation had been stilted, awkward, a parent fulfilling a duty, nothing more. She'd suggested that Emery come to London, but it hadn't happened, and a few months later, after graduation—which her dad had come to alone—Emery had left for Australia.

Amber shook her head, managing to stem the tears. "Do you want me to?"

Emery hesitated for the briefest of seconds. "No."

"She might find out anyway. Dad might tell her." A pause. "Or Helen might." Emery snorted her agreement—Helen's disapproval of their mum's decision to leave was no secret, and she'd no doubt be happy to call her up and lecture her about needing to be there more for her daughters. Not that any of those lectures had worked so far.

"Well, she can call me herself if she wants to find out, can't she?" And then Emery could make up her own mind if she wanted to talk.

Amber glanced at her. "Do you forgive me?"

Emery scrubbed her hands over her face. "For what?"

"For calling Dad."

She huffed. "I'm not an idiot, Amber, I know why you called him." But Amber was still looking at her, all big-eyed. "Yes. I forgive you. But only if you forgive me."

Amber frowned. "For what?"

"For being me." And though she'd meant it as a joke, Emery felt her voice break. Amber's arms came around her, and as the tears arrived, Emery pressed her lips together to try and stem them.

"You should never apologize for being yourself. Never." Amber spoke fiercely, and Emery wondered if her sister was aware of the looks she sometimes got, hand in hand with Robin, looks Emery had noticed even on this holiday. If she ever had to fight to own a part of herself that some people refused to accept.

"You're right," she said, squeezing her sister's shoulder. "I'm sorry. Not for being me, but just for..." She left it unfinished and pulled back.

Amber bit her lip, looked at her in a careful way. "Would you consider a compromise? Like, would you consider carrying on living in the moment, or whatever, but doing it a bit closer to home?"

Emery hesitated. "Yeah. Maybe." For Amber, at least, she'd try.

There was a knock on the door. "Is it safe to come in?" Robin's accent was stronger when she was louder, Emery realized. And the Scottish lilt made her think again of Nick. He'd been *alive*. Nick had been a real person. She hadn't quite figured out how the hell she was supposed to process that just yet.

Amber went to let Robin in, while Emery got up and grabbed her CD player out of her bedroom. She pressed play, turned it up loud. Amber groaned. "Not this song!"

Emery nodded, then set the CD player down and held out her hand to her sister. Amber danced reluctantly at first, an awkward swish of her hips, a pathetic little bounce on her toes. And then the beat dropped, and Emery laughed and threw her arms in the air, spinning around. *Fuck it*, she thought. *Just fuck it.*

Without being made to, Robin joined in too, so the three of them were dancing and singing around Emery's tiny flat like total idiots, and Emery didn't care that she'd be told off by the restaurant manager later for making too much noise, because right now she was lost in the music with her sister and the woman her sister loved. And despite herself, a tiny part of her was recognizing that it wasn't always about the excitement of every little moment, but the people you shared those moments with—the same people she'd been trying to distance herself from out here.

So she'd try, she told herself, letting Amber pull her into a spin. She'd go back home, and she'd try.

Chapter Fourteen

Two years later (June 2006)

AGE 27

Emery hadn't been expecting to cry watching her best friend have her first dance with the love of her life. She'd expected it to be awkward and cringey, if she was being totally honest with herself. But standing at the side of the makeshift dance floor at one end of the beautiful barn that Bonnie and Joe had found on the outskirts of Cambridge—not yet with the "wedding venue" tag attached to it and therefore affordable—she could feel herself welling up. They were dancing to "Here Comes the Sun" by the Beatles, because one of Bonnie's favorite films was *The Parent Trap*, and she'd made Joe watch it with her on their third date. Bonnie looked so *happy*. Obviously, Emery thought to herself—it was her wedding day. But there was something about seeing the way they looked at each other, like they didn't care that there were a hundred people watching them, that made her realize how real it all was, as stupid as that sounded.

It was a late evening in June, and the weather had held. Now the sun was setting, and an orange glow filtered through the high windows in the barn, catching the edge of Bonnie's face. Her red hair was pinned up in curls with white flowers dotted throughout, the veil she'd worn for the ceremony having been put away somewhere. She wore a strappy dress and hadn't bothered trying to make her pale skin appear tanned, because *it just wouldn't look like me in the photos, Em.* Joe, tall, dark and handsome in the extreme, had taken dancing lessons, and it showed—he even picked her up and spun her around, making the crowd laugh along with her. They'd held the actual ceremony in a church nearby, because Joe's family were religious. Apparently Bonnie's mum, an atheist through and through, had grumbled about that, but she'd let it go when Bonnie had told her they could have the wedding in Cambridge. Joe was from further north, the edge of a Geordie accent sometimes creeping in when he let it, and his family had all made the trek down south.

Bonnie finally broke eye contact with her new husband and turned, eyes shining, to look at her audience. Her gaze found Emery, and she gave a jerk of her head. Emery smiled, and patted Colin, who was standing next to her, on the arm. "Think this is our cue."

Colin gave an exaggerated sigh. "If we must."

Emery ignored him, dragging him onto the dance floor at the same time as the band switched to Whitney Houston. "Come on," she said. "You know you want to *dance with somebody*." He groaned, and she flashed him a grin, then glanced over his shoulder to see that Bonnie had been encircled by a large group of Joe's cousins.

When she looked back at Colin, he was shuffling awkwardly from side to side, his hands pinned to his sides. "What are you doing?"

"I'm dancing."

"That's not dancing." She raised her arms above her head and did a dramatic, albeit slightly ungraceful twirl. "*This* is dancing." She continued to spin, making it bigger and bigger, while around her people shouted, *I wanna feel the HEAT with somebody*.

Colin sighed and did a ridiculous spin of his own, followed by an attempt at the chicken dance, which made Emery burst out laughing. "There you go, that's the spirit."

He grabbed her hand and spun her again. "Too bad whatshisname had to cancel. I'm sure he's a much better dancer than me."

"Ed," Emery said. "And he didn't have to cancel, I broke up with him, so it would have been slightly awkward if he'd turned up."

"Ah yes," Colin said, as if he hadn't already known that. "How long did that one last? Eight weeks?" She gave him a scathing look, but in all honesty, it hadn't been much longer than that. When they'd got past date four, she'd thought she should try and be a grown-up and invite him as her plus-one to Bonnie's wedding, but it had fizzled out pretty soon after that, which had annoyed Bonnie no end: *Look, I don't care either way, Emery, but do you* want *a plus-one or don't you?*

She blinked innocently up at Colin. He'd let his hair grow out a bit, so that it flopped into his blue eyes as he shifted from foot to foot. "Good thing I have you as my backup plus-one then, isn't it?"

"Ah, I think you'll find I was invited already, thanks very

much. What with me being a groomsman and brother-of-the-bride and all."

Emery's hand was too hot in his, and she pulled gently to extract it, pushing her curls back from her face. Bonnie had indeed gone with cobalt blue for the bridesmaid dresses—a strappy design to mimic her wedding dress, one that was a little too clingy for Emery's liking, but which she'd decided to own all the same. She sighed. "We'll have loads of weddings coming up now. Getting to that time, isn't it?"

"Guess so. Maybe next time we can go together." He said it casually, but she knew him well enough to read something deeper in the way he was looking at her.

She kept her voice deliberately light, giving a little laugh as she said, "What do you mean, we're here together now."

His voice was lower when he spoke again. "You know what I mean, Emery." It caused something to pull in her gut. Because she knew exactly what he meant, what he wanted.

The music shifted, a slower number, more awkward to dance to. She could feel heat crawling under her skin, knew she had to say something. This was Colin, after all. But she couldn't think of the right words, and the seconds were ticking by. "I'm going to go and get a drink," she blurted out. "Want anything?"

He shook his head, his expression not changing. "No thanks." He grabbed her hand as she turned to leave. "Emery?" She looked back, met those blue eyes. And tried not to wince at the expression there. "Just think about it. If you ever decide you want something more than a fling some day."

She scowled, pulled her hand away. His tone had been lingering on the edge of judgmental. "So what if I have flings? I'm having fun, enjoying life—that's allowed, isn't it?"

He leveled a look at her. "Seems to me more like you're *avoiding* life."

She took a breath, even as his words made her want to grind her teeth. She didn't want to argue—and this wasn't a conversation they should have right now.

"I'll be back in a bit," she said firmly. This time, when she walked away, he didn't try to stop her. Stupid, she told herself. It was probably her own damn fault. Joking and flirting with Colin had always felt fun, harmless—because for her they were friends. Good friends, but only ever friends. And fine, okay, maybe there had occasionally been the hint of something more between them, but even so... She'd been protected, she thought, by virtue of being his little sister's friend. But she should have been more careful. His words rolled around her mind again. *Seems to me more like you're avoiding life.*

Well, he was wrong, wasn't he? She felt the scowl that had returned to her face, tried to smooth it out. The maid of honor should not be scowling on the wedding day.

She found Amber at the bar—a makeshift one that had been put in specifically for the event, the owners of the barn trialing it to see if weddings were feasible. "Thought you weren't drinking," she said.

Amber jumped. Her brown hair, cut into a bob, had been neatly straightened, and she had a pair of small black studs in her ears. She was wearing a green dress with white flowers—something she'd bought especially for the occasion—but she'd been fidgeting throughout the ceremony, pulling it down her thighs, and Emery knew she wasn't comfortable in it, even if she'd never admit to it.

"This is for Robin," she said, holding up a gin and tonic. "But please don't draw attention to it." Her voice held a bit of a snap, and Emery raised her eyebrows. "Sorry. I just... I don't want people talking behind my back."

"They won't. You're trying to get pregnant, it's not that unusual."

Amber gave her a look, and Emery conceded with a small grimace. "Fine, okay. Maureen would probably talk. But only because she'd be trying to prove she's okay with it, so she'd want to tell *everyone* just how okay with it she is." She smiled to show she was joking, and Amber snorted quietly back. Emery wished she had more words of wisdom to offer—especially as, since she'd been living with Amber and Robin in Edinburgh for a few months now, she'd seen how much stress the whole thing was causing them.

She'd tried living with her dad after moving back to the UK, but had given up pretty quickly, unable to cope with the need to tell him where she was and what she was doing every hour of the day—a return to childhood in the extreme. So instead, she'd taken Amber up on the offer to sofa-surf. While she'd been in Scotland, she *might* have looked into a certain someone, who she was trying hard not to think about because it was all too confusing. But she'd found nothing—no evidence of who he might have been when he'd been alive. Which was hardly surprising, she supposed, given that she only had a first name to go on.

"What can I get you?" asked the bartender, a guy in his forties, maybe, who looked a little harassed, wiping a sheen of sweat from his brow.

"Just a Coke, thanks."

Amber gave her a look. "You not drinking either?"

Emery shrugged. She didn't really want to go into the reasons why—the fact that when she drank, she was more inclined to do stupid things, and as it was Bonnie's wedding, she did not want said stupidity to cause a problem with her heart and ruin her best friend's day.

Amber looked across the room to where Robin was standing, wearing a white shirt decorated with silver studs underneath a black blazer. She was talking earnestly to a guy in his twenties, gesturing emphatically as she did so, and the young man, although nodding, was looking ever so slightly scared. Emery couldn't help laughing quietly. "Who did she find to talk science with?"

Amber smiled, her whole expression softening. "Think he's one of Joe's many cousins. He made the mistake of telling Robin he's studying biology at university."

Emery shook her head mockingly. "Poor guy."

"Yeah, suppose I should go and rescue him." Amber picked up Robin's gin and tonic, then filled a glass with tap water from the jug on the bar before moving away.

"Ambs?" Amber looked back at her. "I know it'll happen for you guys." Because Emery knew it wasn't just worry over what people would say that was the problem. It was costing them money to try and get pregnant by artificial insemination. A gay tax, Robin called it—and this on top of not being able to have a wedding. They'd been through one round of IVF already, and Emery knew that Amber was being so careful. She wanted to be the one to carry the baby, and had been on a health kick, sticking to it even though they were in between rounds now.

Amber smiled. "Thanks, Little Em."

The bartender handed over Emery's drink, and she thanked him, then headed out to the courtyard. She'd just take a breather, get her vibe back, ready to dance the night away with her best friend. A guy in a tux was already out there, smoking. She'd only met him a couple of times, but knew this was Joe's brother, Alex. He looked at her as she shut the door behind her, her heels clacking on the paving stones. The warm smell of summer grass and hints of barbecue fell over her. Soon there would be a crêpe van, apparently, setting up outside to keep everyone going once the two-course dinner wore off, but for now it was quiet.

Alex held out a packet of cigarettes. Emery shrugged her thanks, took one. If she wasn't drinking, she might as well have a smoke. She placed it between her lips, and he lit it for her.

"It's Emery, right?" His voice was Geordie, just like Joe's.

She blew out smoke, fought the urge to cough—it had been a while since she'd smoked. "And you're Alex."

"Right." He flashed her another smile. "I think as best man and maid of honor it's obligatory that we have at least one drink together."

Emery cocked her head. "Bonnie warned me about you. Said you were a total charmer."

He put a hand on his heart. "You say that like it's a bad thing."

She laughed, but it turned into a groan when the next song came on. "*Dirty Dancing*, really?"

"Don't tell me you're the one woman on earth who doesn't like that film."

"Sorry, can't," she said with a sigh. "I just figure it's a little early in the night for it—I mean, where will we go from here?"

He grinned, and it was the type of grin that had *definitely* got him into trouble on more than one occasion. "You know, I can do the lift."

She laughed again. "You can *not*."

"I can." He dropped his cigarette, stamped it out. "Come on, I'll show you."

She shook her head. "You're joking."

That grin again. "Try me." She could see he wasn't quite sober—saw an empty glass of what might have been whisky on the paving stones by his feet. But the music was playing, and inside people were laughing and singing, and here she was, somehow separate from them all, at her best friend's wedding. And above it all, Colin's words were lingering in her mind. *Seems to me more like you're avoiding life*. It made her feel on edge, jumpy inside her own skin.

She stubbed out her own cigarette. "Okay. Why not?"

Alex laughed delightedly as she slipped off her heels, then

backed away, giving her space. And as the music changed, she ran, and she leapt.

And he caught her! He actually fucking caught her. And okay, it wasn't *exactly* graceful, and she wasn't actually over his head, and her legs were sort of flailing all over the place, but she was in the air! And then he stumbled, letting go of her so that she landed with a thump, losing her balance and toppling into him. They both fell, back onto the grass, thankfully, just off the paving stones, and she ended up sitting with her legs either side of his waist, her hands pressed into his chest, both of them laughing hysterically.

"What the hell are you doing?"

Emery stopped laughing first, looked over her shoulder to see Colin there, the door to the barn open behind him. She refused to blush. "What does it look like I'm doing?" At her tone, Alex fell silent and pushed himself awkwardly onto his elbows. She clambered off him, trying to make it as graceful as she could, and tugged down her dress.

"It's Bonnie's wedding," Colin said, the anger lacing his tone barely contained.

"I know that, thanks, as I am, in fact, the maid of honor."

"And yet you're still hell-bent on being the center of attention?"

"Ah..." Alex looked awkwardly between the two of them. "I'll just..." He gestured inside, then scurried off without another word.

Emery glared at Colin. "That's not what I'm doing."

"No? I saw the lift, Emery. Why are you pushing it?"

"Pushing *what*? It was a bit of fun!"

"And what were you planning on doing if that 'bit of fun' caused your heart to stop, hmm?" She shot him another glare. How dare he! She *was* being careful, she wasn't drinking, she was trying so fucking hard. But Colin didn't back down. "What if he'd dropped you? You want us all to come out and find you dead?"

She raised her chin, refusing to see the logic there, refusing to acknowledge that maybe she *shouldn't* have done it. "I would have been fine. I'm always fine."

"Only because there's always someone here to bring you back."

She tossed her curls. "Is that what this is really about, Colin?"

"What do you mean?"

"Oh, I think you know what I mean. I'm here talking to another guy, an *attractive* guy, no less, and you—"

He took a step closer to her, his fists clenched at his sides. "I what, Emery?"

She just gave him a look, then turned and stalked toward where she'd discarded her heels. He caught hold of her arm, pulled her back. "No, wait, we're going to talk about—" But she didn't hear the rest of it. Because as he'd grabbed her arm, it had wrenched a muscle in her somewhere, sending a pulse through her body. Enough, with her emotions already on edge, to make her jump, wince.

Enough, it seemed, to make her heart stop.

Chapter Fifteen

"Oh well, this is just great." Emery glared at Nick as everything settled around her. They were inside a restaurant with plush red booths and a sleek wooden floor, the candles that were flickering on each table almost eerie in the emptiness. Music was playing—a hum of violins that must have only been background noise at the time.

"Not happy to see me, I take it?" His voice was dry, and he was standing—she thought—a careful distance away from her. He wore a suit—unbuttoned shirt, sleek black jacket—almost looking like he'd dressed to match her wedding outfit, and was leaning against the wooden bar, an array of bottles lit up against the mirror behind it. Could they drink? Emery wondered. What would happen if she tried to get drunk in this place?

She scowled at him, trying to cover the flash of awkwardness she felt at seeing him again. His eyes, more gray than green today, were measured and careful as he watched her. She couldn't help but remember the last time she'd seen him, shirtless in the ocean.

Fucked up. This was so totally fucked up. *She* was so totally fucked up.

"I didn't mean to die," she said, her tone coming out more stubborn-child than she'd intended.

He raised his eyebrows. "And the other times you did?"

"You know what I mean," she said impatiently, tugging a hand through her hair. She was in the same cobalt-blue bridesmaid's dress, and for some reason she felt more exposed in it here, without a crowd of people to get lost in. "It's Bonnie's wedding."

"I know," he said quietly. "I'm sorry."

"It's not *your* fault." She flicked a glance at him, aware of the space between them—a space that was even more obvious when it was only the two of them in the entire restaurant, the smell of garlic and something charred still somehow lingering in the air. Then she closed her eyes and groaned. "This is not good. I can't be dead. Not now. I will *ruin* it for her." And she felt the hum of panic beneath her skin, fluttering inside her traitorous heart. She'd be okay. She'd *probably* be okay. But she thought of Colin accusing her of trying to be the center of attention. Unfair. Completely unfair and untrue. But still, now it had happened, hadn't it? Her best friend's big day—*of course* Emery would have to go and screw everything up.

"It's not your fault either," Nick said, with the infuriating air of someone pointing out the obvious.

She scowled again, then, in a snap decision, walked briskly around to the other side of the bar.

"What are you doing?" Nick asked.

She ignored him, opened one of the fridges and took out a bottle of champagne.

"Emery. What are you doing?"

"What does it look like I'm doing?" She glanced around, found champagne flutes and pulled down two. The champagne fizzed and frothed as she poured, and when she sipped, she could taste the bubbles on her tongue. She grabbed the other glass, stalked over to Nick and shoved it into his hand.

"I don't—"

"Oh shut up. Not drinking didn't seem to help me much in the real world, so I might as well toast Bonnie here."

He took a careful sip, then stared at the glass. "I don't know when the last time I tasted champagne was."

"Can't you just magic anything up here?"

He shook his head. "It's all dependent on what the other person wants, not me."

"Well, good. Because right now, I want champagne." She downed her glass, trying to drown the jumpiness under her skin that this time even dying had not been able to quell. She'd had champagne when she'd come here the first time, she remembered. The real *here*. Before she'd headed off to Australia, Amber had taken her out in London, a sisters' day out. Emery had wondered at the time whether the plan had been to meet up with their mum too, something that the empty seat next to them in the theater would strongly suggest, but if that *had* been the plan, only for their mum to cancel, Amber had never let on. They'd gone to see *The King and I* and then come for dinner in Covent Garden. Emery had loved it— loved the sheer number of people, the energy that rolled off the city. It had been gray and full of a misty rain, even in summer, but that hadn't diminished anything at all. London *suited* gray, she'd decided. It was different now, without all the people—you could still see the stalls, the open shopfronts, pop-up bars with outdoor seating—but there was no one here to enjoy it.

She refilled her champagne glass and could feel the weight of Nick's gaze on her back. "Don't judge," she snapped. "Isn't that, like, your whole ethos—not to judge?"

"I'm not judging," he said. And that mild tone only made the jumpiness worse. She felt her nerves twitching and realized right then that she couldn't *stand* his calmness, the way he was always so fucking level. She felt like she wanted an out—wanted to leave him in this empty restaurant full of her memories and return to Bonnie, to the wedding. She wanted an escape, when there was none.

"I'm missing out." Her tone was biting.

"You're not. If you go back, you'll—"

Something inside her snapped. "*If.* If, if, if!"

"Emery." There it was again—his voice was so patient, so *composed.* Why was he always doing that? "What's wrong?" he asked.

"What's *wrong*? What kind of a question is that? I'm here, aren't I? I'm back here, again—isn't that enough reason to be angry?" She couldn't put a finger on why it was making her feel like this now, only knew that she was fed up of it all. Fed up of having to be careful, fed up of the unpredictability, and fed up of Nick—of him acting like he had one emotion, and one emotion only. "For God's sake, Nick, do you think this is *easy* for me? Do you think I want to keep coming back here over and over again, wondering whether this time will be it, whether I won't go back, wondering how my family will deal with it, wondering if I've done enough to let my life go with no regrets?"

He flinched then, and she felt a horrible surge of triumph— at the fact that it was at least *something*. "I know it can't be easy," he said, and even if he was using that same patient tone, she could hear something behind it. A tension that hadn't been there before. "I know—"

"You don't *know*, though, do you? You said before that I'm the only one you ever see more than once, the only person like me, so how can you possibly know?"

"Well what do you want me to say?" And finally, there it was, a snap of some kind as he slammed his glass down on the bar, the liquid sloshing over the rim. "Jesus, Emery, you think it's easy for *me*? You say I don't know what it's like for you, but you have no idea—none—what it's like for me, either." He pulled a hand through his hair. "You don't understand how hard it can be, how trapped I feel sometimes, you don't—"

"Then tell me! You can't accuse me of not understanding when you don't even *try* to explain. You expect me to accept it, coming and going, and there's this whole part of my life here with you that I can never explain to anyone without sounding like a fucking lunatic, and yet you constantly try to keep everything back from me. So tell me! Tell me what it's like for you here. Or tell me about what happened to you. Tell me something real."

He stared at her for a long moment, and when he loosened

a breath, it sounded sharp. "Fine," he bit out. "Fine. My name is—was—Nick Ryemore. I was born in Inverness. I died a week after I turned thirty-five, on the night Margaret Thatcher came to power. I died in pain and scared for someone I loved."

Her heart stuttered, just a little. But she had wanted this—she had wanted real. "How did you die?" she whispered. And who? Who had he been scared for?

He shook his head, paling. And okay, maybe it was too much to ask him to go there. For now. "I'm sorry," she said. "For whatever happened to you."

"I'm sorry you keep getting dragged back here," he replied, his voice a little hoarse.

She sighed. "Maybe we should agree not to apologize to one another. It could get a bit repetitive." His lips twitched—the hint of a smile. But she had to look away as she took a sip of her champagne, glancing out of the window at the empty square. Because she'd only said what she'd said to cover up the lie—to herself, and to him. Because a part of her *had* wanted to be dragged back here. Because a part of her had wanted to see him again.

Her aunt Helen's words came back to her, loud, and a bit judgmental. *He can't lose you too.*

She set down her glass, braced her hands on the bar.

"What are you thinking?" he asked, as he'd done before.

She glanced at him. "I'm thinking how worried everyone will be, seeing me like this. And I'm thinking about how it will be when I go back."

He paused. "What *is* it like, when you go back?"

"It's..." She waved a hand in the air. "It's painful," she admitted. "Like my body has had to fight to bring me back, and even if that feeling fades, there's always a moment where it feels like I can't breathe, and like my chest has been hit by a moving car or something."

He grimaced. "Sounds fun."

"Oh, it's a barrel of laughs." She shook her head. "But really, it's other people that are the worst. Because they're scared, and there's nothing I can do to make that better. Because even though I'm back, they can't just forget it, and that means I can't either."

"Do you *want* to forget it?"

She looked at him, trying to figure out what he was asking. "Forget *you*, do you mean?"

He ran a hand across the back of his neck. "It can't be easy—remembering this. Knowing about it and having to pretend you don't."

She cocked her head. "How do you know I pretend? Maybe I've told everyone, given away the mystery of death."

"*Have* you?"

"No. But I *could*." She said nothing for a moment, knowing that he could hear the lie. Knowing that these moments between life and death would only ever exist for the two of them. "It's not that I want to forget this part," she said eventually. "It's more that I want everyone else to forget that it happened. Because otherwise they always look at me either like they're remembering the last time my heart stopped, or worrying about when it will happen again. It means that sometimes people forget to concentrate on the present me." She wrinkled her nose. "That sounds dumb."

"I don't think so." And maybe that was part of her attraction to this place—to him. Because he had no choice but to see her only and exactly as she was in any given moment in time.

They were both quiet, and over the background music, Emery felt something humming in the space between them. She tapped her fingers on the bar, nerves twitching again. "I should be dancing right now," she said, needing to fill the silence.

He nodded slowly. "Well, why don't we?"

She flashed a sharp look at him. "What, here?"

"Why not? It's not like there's anyone watching." He held out a hand toward her. After a moment, she took it, her palm fitting neatly into his. The humming beneath her skin intensified.

He led her out from behind the bar, found a space between the tables, then turned to face her. He put one hand on her waist, the other lightly on her back, and beneath her dress her skin heated. Her mind couldn't help zeroing in on the places he touched her, and she was aware of every inch of air between them. How easy it would be to move just a little closer, toward the heat of his body. He moved her in a neat circle, and as the tempo of the violins rose, he spun her away and back to him, catching her at the same moment as the crescendo broke. She laughed and saw the light that came into his eyes at the sound of it. "How did you get so good at this?" she asked.

He smiled. "There are some secrets I'll never tell."

It was a joke, but she bit her lip as she looked up into his face. "Will you tell me something about your life?" She felt the way his fingers tightened briefly on her back, a small spasm.

"What do you want to know?"

"Anything. A memory. A nice memory? Isn't that what this place is here for?"

"A memory." He said it slowly, and she wondered then how much he still remembered of his life. He'd died the night Margaret Thatcher came into power. She was a little hazy on dates, but that was a while ago. But then he spoke again, his voice low, careful. And even though he kept in time with the music, his gaze was distant, no longer concentrating on her. "One of my first memories is of being in a park near where I grew up, with my mum." He glanced down at her, and she realized she was holding her breath. "I was a war baby, born during World War Two." It gave her a jolt—the sheer impossibility of it. "My dad... After the war, he came back, but he wasn't the same." He shook his head. "I sometimes wonder if that will get lost, the impact of such destruction on a whole generation. Even I couldn't understand it, and I was only one step removed. Anyway. He died when I was eight, and I don't think my mum ever quite got over it—the fact that he died, but also the fact that he died a different person to the one she'd married. But before all that, I have this memory of being outside with her while Dad was at work, of being in the playground in the cold, and of her opening a thermos of hot chocolate and playing some game with me. I don't remember what game, exactly, but I have this clear vision of her laughing, and seeming so *happy*."

She noticed it before he did—the shift around them, the blurring of the edges as the deep reds and browns of the restaurant paled into faded blue and green. She felt it, too—a sort of ceding of power, like she was being pulled somewhere, a tug in her midriff, something she had no choice but to go with. And then they were there—wherever *there* was.

"Nick." She breathed his name and felt him still, his whole body turning rigid, his fingers tightening on her back, digging into her waist. And she knew, from the way he froze, unable to take a breath, that she was right.

This wasn't her memory anymore—it was his.

Chapter Sixteen

Nick took a shuddering breath and stepped away from her, the biting chill of the air coming in to take his place. He turned a full circle, his eyes wide, almost scared-looking. They were in a park—a vast green space spreading out before them with a path that wound its way through a mix of deciduous and evergreen trees. There was a lake up ahead, wisps of blue sky and weak sunlight bouncing off the surface. To their right was a playground—a wooden climbing frame, a metal tube slide.

"How is this possible?" he asked, his voice choked. But she knew it wasn't a real question. "God. I remember. This is where Mum used to bring me at weekends or after school. The one fail-safe activity, no matter the weather." He laughed, the sound incredulous, and pulled both hands through his hair, making it stick up in random places. "This is *impossible*. Is this what it's like for you?"

"Well, I suppose it's all subjective." But there were goosebumps rising on her bare arms—and not just from the sudden change of temperature, moving from inside a toasty restaurant to the open air of Scotland on a cloudy day. They'd been inside her memories plenty of times now, but there was something strangely intimate about visiting *his* memory. She supposed it made him fully real, in a way he hadn't been before. She wrapped her arms around herself, her blue dress feeling flimsy, and tried to imagine a young Nick. It seemed suddenly unfair that he'd known her her whole life, and she'd only had glimpses of him.

"Is this the memory you'd come back to, then?" she asked. "Your happy memory, if you were just moving through like the rest of them?" *Them.* She'd said it automatically, separating herself from all the other people who passed through this place. Because unlike them, she got to play at immortality—coming back to life over and over.

"I don't know. What I've noticed is that sometimes the memories surprise people—we're not always drawn back to where we think we would be." She thought about that, wondering what she'd pick as her one happy memory, if she was only allowed one. But she couldn't think of just one, and she supposed that was the problem—memories, and how you framed them, were constantly shifting.

"*Did* you have any memories in this place? Before you started helping other people, I mean." Was he here alone, at first? she wondered.

"One," he said quietly. "I was stuck in one memory. And it was not a happy one."

She watched him, the way he held his posture so stiffly, his gaze unfocused, body turned away from her. "How did you…get out?"

"I don't know. Certain knowledge settled on me about what would happen, what I was supposed to do. And then, well, you know the rest."

She scoffed. "Hardly." They were quiet for a moment, and Emery shuddered as the cool wind grazed her bare back. "Nick?" His gaze snapped to her, and he frowned, seeing her standing there on the verge of shivering. He closed the gap between them, shrugging out of his jacket. "What was your mum like?" She wanted to ask what *he* was like, but wasn't sure it would be an acceptable question.

He placed the jacket around her shoulders, and his citrusy sea smell enveloped her. "She was..." He glanced over at the playground, and she knew he'd be remembering. "Kind. Lovely. And sad, a lot of the time." He shook his head. "She pretended she wasn't, but I knew, even before Dad died, that she had this kind of sadness she carried around with her." He closed his eyes briefly. "I left her."

"What?"

"When I was old enough to leave home, when I got into a university down south, I took the chance and I bolted."

"Most teenagers do that," Emery said, keeping her voice careful.

"I didn't ever come back." He spat out the words like they were bitter on his tongue. "I escaped, because I couldn't bear to spend my whole life in one corner of Scotland, like she had done. I knew she didn't have anyone else, knew she hadn't got over what had happened with my dad, and I left anyway. I said it was because I needed to study, and then because I needed to work, but it wasn't the whole reason. I wanted to leave it behind, wanted bigger and better things—and she was a part of that." He stared into the distance, past the swings and to the trees beyond them.

"My mum left me," Emery said quietly, fixing her gaze on the lake. She felt Nick shift his attention to her, but didn't look at him. "I don't know if you already know that, but she left when I was fourteen—the day after I, well, died, I guess." *She left* because *I died.*

"I'm sorry, Emery," he said quietly, and she shook her head. It wasn't why she'd brought it up.

"I don't mean … I think, as the kid, you're *supposed* to leave the parent. I get why you might feel guilty, but isn't it, like, the natural progression of things or whatever?" It was what she told herself, whenever her dad tried to pull her back home. And it was different from her mum leaving her—a mother shouldn't abandon her children.

"I assumed at some point that I'd go back, at least for a bit," Nick said quietly. "But I never did. I was too selfish."

Emery bit her lip, not sure of what to say. She thought of the way she'd run to Falmouth, to Australia, and now to Edinburgh. Unable to stay with the people who loved her for any length of time, even though she knew what it did to them to have her so far away, knowing what might happen without someone there who was aware of her condition.

"I don't think you're selfish," she said. It was the best she could do.

He turned away from her. "Well, maybe you don't know

me as well as you assume." There was a trace of bitterness in his voice.

"And whose fault is that?" The words were out before she could think better of them. She shook her head. "It's okay if you're not perfect, you know. You don't have to pretend to be this serenely peaceful ghost man. You're not very good at it, anyway—you'll have to work on pretending you have all the answers if you want to go down that route."

"I think most people would disagree with you there," he said quietly. "They want perfection—or the illusion of it."

"How are you so sure? Do you ask them?" He was quiet. "I'm not saying you have to tell everyone everything—I'm not even saying you have to tell *me* everything. But wouldn't it be better to be more, I don't know, *you*?"

"No." It was blunt, no room for argument.

"Well, I disagree."

"Emery—"

"No, I'm not saying I know what you're like or *were* like or that I believe you're a beacon of good or whatever. Maybe you're not. Maybe you were *horrible*. But firstly, you're clearly not horrible now—or not wholly horrible—otherwise you wouldn't be able to do what you do, and secondly, maybe people don't want perfect in their final moments. Maybe they don't want all serene and level. Maybe they'd prefer something *real*."

He stared at the playground, and she wondered what he was seeing. "I have spent a long time," he said slowly, "building a version of myself that will survive in this place. There are things I am not proud of in my past, things I would do differently if I could. The person I was then is not the person people want to spend their final moments with."

Emery watched the side of his face, the echo of pain that was etched there. And she wondered what had happened, and why he'd ended up here. She wanted to go to him. Wanted to reach up, run her thumb along his frown lines to smooth them away. Instead she pulled his jacket closer to her.

"Did you ever think that maybe the reason you feel so trapped, though, is because you're pretending to be something you're not?"

He looked at her for a long moment. "Couldn't I say the same thing to you?"

"What do you mean?"

"Don't you pretend to your friends, your family, worried that they won't handle it if they know how frightened you really are? Isn't that why you keep moving around so much?"

Her heart spasmed uncomfortably. The haze was settling in. Not long now. "That's different."

"How?" She didn't answer, and he smiled, a little sadly, as he stepped in front of her. She tipped her head back to look at him, unable to stop herself. "I spent most of my life wanting more," he said, "and as a result I was never happy where I was."

She frowned. It wasn't an accusation, but there was something implied there. "I don't do that. I do the opposite, in fact." And she did, didn't she? She worked so hard to enjoy every moment, to live for *now* rather than some vague hope of what the future might be.

"I'm all for living in the moment," he said, with that uncanny ability to pick up on what she was thinking, mind-reader or no. She folded her arms. "I am," he insisted. "Trust me, I've seen enough people regret not doing just that."

"Well, then."

"But there's a balance, isn't there? Because if you're too caught up in living life in the moment, do you really settle long enough to enjoy anything?" She said nothing to that, and he sighed, and with the movement of his chest, he started to fade. "I don't think I'm pretending to be something I'm not. This version of me is still *me*, just as the version of you that you present to your family is still you. That's not the reason I'm here."

"Why, then?"

But he only gave a slight head-shake in answer. And now everything was fading around her as she grew more solid, and if she wanted an answer to that question, she'd have to wait until next time. So instead she said, "You told me once that you thought there was a reason you were matched to certain people. Maybe there's also a reason *I* was matched to *you*." It was only because she was going that she felt brave enough to say it. "Maybe I'm supposed to help *you* with something."

His face was a blur now, but she could hear the frown in his voice. "That's not how it works."

She spoke into the darkness, in that brief second before she was wrenched back to her body, the pain waiting for her there. "How do you know?"

Chapter Seventeen

Two years later (November 2008)

AGE 30

Bonnie grinned at Emery as they waited at the bar to order. "So? I told you this place was cool, right?" Someone jostled into them, vying for space at the bar, and behind Emery the queue pressed against her back.

"Very cool," Emery agreed—because she couldn't not. And actually, the bar *was* pretty cool. It was a new find of Bonnie's in Clapham, where she and Joe currently lived, and she had raved about it enough to convince Emery to have her thirtieth here. It had a 1920s art deco vibe, with a black-and-white patterned floor, plush booths around wooden tables, and a brightly lit gold bar, standing out against the dim candlelit vibe. The music was awesome—there was a live band that played jazz, the type of music you wanted to dance to, and before the place had become packed in the last half-hour, it had been exactly the right amount of buzzing.

When the guy behind the bar—hair gelled back and shirt opened two more buttons than was strictly necessary—slid over the two gin and tonics Bonnie had ordered, they grabbed the drinks and fought their way out of the queue. Emery was hot now, the effect of so many people packed into the same room, even though it was cold and dark outside—a true November evening. She was wearing jeans and her favorite high heels, black with silver stiletto spikes, and a bright green halter-neck. The ice clinked against the glass in her hand, condensation already beading on the outside. She wanted to press it against her forehead, her neck, but had spent ages on her hair and makeup. Because you only turned thirty once, right?

Bonnie headed back to their table—a large one in the corner that Emery had reserved ahead of time—but Emery was stopped halfway there by Amber, who grabbed hold of her arm, leaning in to speak over the chatter and laughter around them. "I'm sorry, Little Em, but I have to head." She nodded toward Robin, who was getting up from the table, baby bump clearly on show beneath a polo-neck sweater that she must have been boiling in.

Emery pulled back to scrutinize her sister. Amber was smiling, but she looked just as pale and drawn as she had when she'd arrived—face a little more hollowed out than usual, dark circles under her eyes. She'd not been herself the whole evening. Sure, she'd made a show of joining in the celebratory mood, chatting and laughing along with everyone else, but Emery had noticed that when she wasn't in a direct conversation, she fell silent, and her face would shut down. In those moments, she'd always reach for Robin's hand and the two of them would sit like that until they were drawn into a new conversation, talking and laughing again.

"Okay." Emery nodded. "I suppose having a pregnant girlfriend is a good enough excuse to bail." Four months pregnant—did you feel tired or anything at four months? She had no idea. Amber smiled, but it didn't reach her eyes. "Ambs—are you sure you're okay?"

There was the briefest of pauses, one Emery might not have noticed if she didn't know her sister so well. Then Amber nodded. "Absolutely, I'm fine, don't worry about me." Emery didn't quite believe it, but she didn't want to push the issue when she was several drinks down, standing in the middle of a crowded bar with all her friends looking on. Besides, she thought she knew what was wrong. Amber had wanted to carry the baby, after all. She was pretty sure both Amber *and* Robin had wanted that. But it hadn't worked out that way, after years of trying. And Robin was thirty-eight, past the "ideal" age to get pregnant, so there had been worry and drama over that at the hospital, Emery knew, doctors throwing out words like "geriatric" and causing even more stress.

"I'll see you at Dad's on Sunday?" Amber was saying.

"Yes, absolutely." Their dad was doing a big Sunday lunch on Emery's actual birthday, having claimed he was far too old to come all the way into London for a party in a bar.

"I'll give you your present there, then." Emery couldn't help smiling. Amber had always been strict about trying to give Emery her present on the day itself.

"Thanks so much for coming all this way." Amber and Robin had got a hotel for the night, having taken the train all the way from Scotland, though they were staying with Emery's dad after tonight.

Emery gave Amber a brief hug, said goodbye to Robin, then sat down again in the booth. Her university friends were on her left, in the middle of a conversation, and Bonnie was standing at the other end of the table, Joe's arm around her. She glanced around for Adam, saw his dark head of hair at the bar.

She was trying to catch up on her uni friends' conversation so that she could join in when Colin came over, having stopped to say something to Bonnie on the way. "I'm off too, Em." He bent down to give her an awkward one-armed hug. He'd grown a bit of stubble since the last time she'd seen him, and the blonde bristles rubbed briefly against her cheek.

"Okay." She looked up at him, feeling odd sitting down while he was standing. He'd barely spoken to her all evening, other than in a group chat scenario, and she'd expected him to be one of the last ones there, because he always used to stay out with her however late she wanted. But she wasn't sure she could voice that out loud. "Great to see you!" she said instead. Her voice sounded jovial and weird, and she pushed her curls away from her face like *that* would cover it up.

Colin raised a hand as if to squeeze her shoulder, then dropped it awkwardly to his side. "See you soon, yeah?" With that, he turned away, slouching off toward the cloakroom to retrieve his coat. She watched his retreating back, wondering whether she should have tried harder to speak to him tonight. But there had been so many people to talk to, and somehow she'd run out of time.

A G&T was put on the table in front of her, next to the G&T she already had. She looked up to see Adam grinning down at her. He kissed her on the top of her head—a gesture he tended to repeat more and more frequently the more drunk he got.

"Bonnie and Joe are ordering shots for the whole table," he told her. "Be warned." Sure enough, when Emery glanced over, Bonnie and Joe had moved over to the bar.

She shook her head in wonder. "She's on total form tonight."

Adam slid into the booth next to her. "You okay?"

"Yeah, course. Why?"

He shrugged. He had great shoulders, Adam, all broad and muscled. It was one of the first things she'd noticed about him when he'd asked her out, eighteen months ago. She'd been working at reception at a hotel in London, having finally decided to give life in the capital a go, and his sales company was hosting some kind of conference there. She'd since left the reception job and was currently working as an assistant at an advertising firm, trying to convince herself a) that she liked advertising because it was vaguely creative, and b) that she didn't care that she was an assistant when all her friends were now on much higher salaries and doing jobs that tended to have the word *manager* in the title in some way or another. And Adam, despite all this, had stuck.

"You look a bit sad, that's all," he said. "Considering it's your birthday. One year older—cause for celebration!" He lifted his beer, and she clinked glasses, rolling her eyes at him as she took a sip. It was true, though. She *should* be celebrating the fact she was another year older.

"I'm just worried about Amber."

Adam put an arm around her. "It's probably baby stress." He took another sip of his beer. "Hey, have you ever thought about that?" His voice was casual, but she could feel the way his arm had gone very still, holding her in place by his side.

"About what?"

"You know. Kids."

Her heart gave a painful thud and she reached for her gin again to chase away the chalky feeling in her mouth. "Ah..."

"Sorry!" He smiled down at her, a little guiltily. "Sorry, E." He was the only one to call her E—apparently it was a habit at work to call everyone by their first initial only—and she still hadn't figured out if she liked it or not. "Now's not the time."

She nodded vaguely. If he wasn't going to push it, she certainly wasn't going to discuss the topic voluntarily. It still felt bizarre enough that she had a long-term *boyfriend*, let alone anything else. They hadn't even moved in together yet; she wasn't sure they should be talking about children. Besides, she had no idea how to have that discussion. Because yes, she'd thought about it, but only ever in the context of not wanting them. She *couldn't* want children—it would be irresponsible when she couldn't even guarantee her own future. She was still being monitored, and the doctors had given her a defibrillator, though they hadn't figured out a way to make it fully portable, so it lived at home, in her cupboard, plugged in where no one could see it. She'd told Adam about her condition, explained the basics, and he'd claimed it didn't bother him at all—everyone had their quirks, he'd said, and this was just hers. But they hadn't really talked about what their future might look like, taking into account her heart.

Bonnie returned with shots at that point, and Emery took one, glad of the distraction. She made a face at the taste of the tequila, forced the wedge of lemon into her mouth and bit down. Then, when she saw Colin coming from the direction of the cloakroom, she got to her feet.

"Back in a min," she announced to the group at large, sidling out from behind the table and walking briskly after him, her stilettos clicking against the black-and-white floor.

She reached him as he was heading outside, caught the door before it shut and stepped out onto the pavement. The air was biting, and her breath misted in front of her against the dark, but after the sticky heat of inside, she welcomed it.

"Hey!" she said. Colin turned around and shrugged his hands into the pockets of his coat when he saw her. She wrapped her arms around herself as she walked up to him. The street lamps gave the night air a dull glow, and up ahead, a group of people walked along the pavement en masse, laughing and swaying as they stumbled on together. Colin was still looking at her, waiting for her to say something. "I . . ." She cleared her throat. "Thanks for coming."

"Of course. Wasn't going to miss your thirtieth, was I?"

She pulled a hand through her hair. "Will you tell Rachel I'm sorry she couldn't be here?" It wasn't exactly true—Rachel was boring and was always leaving everything early, dragging Colin with her. She worked shifts, and apparently she hadn't been able to get out of work to come this evening.

"Sure," Colin said, but the look he gave her said he knew

exactly what she was thinking. He rocked back on his heels. "Adam seems like a nice guy."

"He is."

"Good."

"Yes, it *is* good." He said nothing. Emery huffed out a breath. "Why are you being so weird?"

"I'm not being weird."

"You *are*." The words felt thick and heavy on her tongue, and she knew this wasn't a conversation she'd be having if she was sober, but she still couldn't stop herself. "You're the one who told me I should settle down, remember?"

He looked straight at her, blue eyes dark in the dim light. "Yeah. I remember."

She felt herself flush. Stupid. She was stupid to bring that up. "I miss you," she said quietly.

He gave another little shrug. "I'm right here."

"You know what I mean. I just..." She blew out another breath, watched it mist around her under the street lamps. "I miss *us*. Our..." She gestured in the air, trying to find the right word. "Rhythm." And it was true—since Bonnie's wedding, things had been off between them, and it felt like a part of her was always out of kilter as a result.

He gave her a look she couldn't quite interpret. "Rhythm doesn't come out of nowhere, Em." He said it lightly, but she could hear the tension under that tone. "You have to try to get it—you have to pay attention to the other person." She bit her lip. So did he mean he'd stopped trying? Or was he blaming her—because she'd never paid *him* enough attention? She rubbed her hands up and down her arms, bouncing slightly on her heels.

"You and Rachel should come round. To mine. With Adam. It'll be fun! I'll cook."

Colin gave her a hint of a smile then. "It definitely won't be fun if you cook."

Emery rolled her eyes. "Fine. I'll get Adam to cook. He does a great chili."

There was the briefest of pauses—was it Adam's name, hanging in the air? She cursed herself inwardly for making things worse. Then, "Okay, sounds good."

"Really?"

"Yeah. I like chili."

"Okay. Great!"

"Cool. Right, well, I better go—I've got to catch the last Tube."

Emery nodded. "I'll text you."

"Cool," he said again. He walked over to her, hesitated, then leaned in to give her a brief kiss on the cheek, leaving a warm tingle behind. "Happy birthday, Em."

She watched him walk away, something odd twisting in her stomach. Then she let out a shudder as the cold rolled through her.

She headed back inside, found everyone raising a shot glass to her when she reached the table—*more* tequila. They were down to the last ten people now, the final group, in it for the long haul. When she was about two steps away, everyone grabbed party poppers, holding them ready for her approach. Bonnie was smiling, but her eyebrows shot up as Emery looked at her, and Emery knew she'd seen her go after Colin. Because she wasn't sure how, exactly, Bonnie would take that, she looked away, to Adam, who grinned at her. She grinned back, feeling a rush of affection for him—for the fact that he'd thought about bringing along stupid little party poppers.

It was as she reached the table, her thigh almost touching it, that someone grabbed her, digging their fingers into her waist. She couldn't stop herself from jumping, violently, and she sucked in a sudden intake of breath, at the same time as the party poppers exploded in unison.

By the time she'd realized it was just Joe, drunkenly trying to scare her, it was too late.

Chapter Eighteen

They were in an airport this time. Heathrow airport. And being there with nobody around was a strange experience. The boards still showed arrival times, bright orange against a black screen, and fluorescent light bounced around the building, off the white floors and up to the too-bright ceilings. There was a Costa behind her, empty, of course, though the smell of coffee lingered, combining with that odd airport smell of cleaning liquid and old socks. She had the urge to shout, to see if it echoed.

"Do you know?" Nick said conversationally, "I think this is the first time someone has chosen the memory of an airport to come back to." She glanced over to where he'd come to stand next to her, hands in his pockets as he tilted his head back to look at the arrivals board.

"It was after Australia," she said, mimicking his posture. "I came back, because I couldn't not, and Colin was the one to pick me up. He's my friend," she added, not sure whether he already knew that, trying to remember which bits of her life he'd witnessed.

"Colin—he's the one who scared you?"

So he didn't know, then. "No. Why?"

"Just wondering. The way you said his name, it's... Nothing, forget it." But there had been something there, in his tone. Something she couldn't quite read.

"Anyway. He was waiting for me at the airport—here. I'd been worried about coming home and I hadn't actually told anyone when exactly I was arriving. I didn't want anyone to worry about me on the flight after... what had happened." She cleared her throat. "But I spoke to Colin just before I flew and let slip when I landed, and he came here to surprise me. And it was just so good to see him, and it felt like coming back might not be the most awful thing." She sighed. "I suppose, even though I'd tried not to tell anyone, I was glad to have someone there waiting for me."

She frowned slightly. Was it because she'd been thinking about Colin and wondering what to do, how to mend their friendship, that she'd been pulled back here now? And had she really been glad just to see *someone* waiting for her here—or had it been Colin, specifically, she'd wanted in that moment?

She pushed the thought away and turned, looked up at Nick. "Hi."

He smiled. "Hi. And happy birthday, I suppose." She made a face. "Sorry," he added quickly. "Maybe not the right thing to say."

She sighed and rolled her shoulders. She should feel panicked, upset that she'd had an episode on her birthday—her thirtieth, no less. She should want to get back to be with Bonnie. With Adam. Instead, she felt a sense of relief that she was here with Nick—that she could take a beat to be herself. But with that relief came guilt—because she knew she shouldn't be feeling like that.

She looked again at the boards, the destinations listed there. "Where would you go, if you could?"

"Not sure. I wanted to go everywhere, once."

She glanced at him, his face lit up by the bright lights around them. "Why didn't you ever go abroad?"

"I was planning to—saving money and all that. It was less of a thing then, I suppose. My mum had never been abroad, and that way of thinking just wasn't part of my childhood. And then, well…" He glanced at her, smiled. To show her he was okay, she thought. "It was going to be France or Spain first. I'm sure that sounds so boring to you."

"I went to Paris with Bonnie when we were sixteen. They served us wine with dinner and everything. I would definitely go back, climb the Eiffel Tower again." She scanned the cities in front of her. "I want to go to Mexico," she said. "It's next on my list, I hope." Would Adam go with her? she wondered. He'd been on about going to Venice together—of course.

"Sounds great," Nick said.

"We could learn to dive," Emery said with a smile. As long as she didn't tell anyone about her heart condition, maybe they'd let her do it. "And the food—I've heard the food is amazing."

"I always wanted to go to Africa," Nick admitted. "Botswana, maybe. Go on safari, stay in the bush. But it always felt like such a far-flung dream."

"Safari would be cool." In another world, another life—if they'd met as two ordinary people, at the right time, in the right place—would they have been able to plan adventures like these together?

"I've been trying not to think of you," she blurted out.

He nodded. "I can understand that."

She pulled her hand through her curls, feeling guilty—for saying it out loud when she knew he was stuck here, and for what she'd said last time she'd seen him. She'd said she would help him, or *implied* that she would, and then she'd met Adam and had tried to put Nick away in a corner of her mind. Not that she was sure how exactly she was intending to help him, but still. She hadn't even tried to figure out who he was since then, deciding that everyone was right—she needed to try to get a life. So she'd got a job and a boyfriend and tried really fucking hard not to think about him.

"Nick?" Her voice was quiet, a little hesitant.

"Hmm?"

"Just because I try not to think of you doesn't mean I don't."

There was a long pause, so long that Emery felt heat creep under her skin in embarrassment at having said it out loud. Then, "I think of you too. I can't help but think of you." His gaze locked on hers, and the heat that spread through her was different now. Even if she wondered whether he thought of her because she was the only person he saw more than once. Or because of something else.

She cocked her head, trying to keep it light. "Would you hear me if I talked to you?"

A small smile played over his lips. "Not God, remember?" His smile grew, into one she could imagine on a younger Nick, one without the weight of this place on his shoulders. It was a smile that made her heart stutter, just a little. "Why, have you *tried* to talk to me?"

She made a show of looking away, flapping a hand at him as if to tell him he was being ridiculous. And really, it would be embarrassing to admit just how often she'd wanted to talk to him, even as she told herself to get over it, even if those conversations only ever played out inside her own mind.

She took a breath of the slightly stale-tasting air. She'd been drunk a moment ago, several shots of tequila down. But now she felt sober, even if her head wasn't clear, exactly. She glanced up at him, caught him looking back at her. And felt the fizzing in the space between them.

She shifted her body away, trying to ease the tension. It was not a good idea to feel that fizzing. Then she closed her eyes and groaned. "I don't know what to do. I don't know how to stop this from happening." She puffed out a breath. "I am trying to settle, to be okay—but then *this* happens, and I . . ." She broke off helplessly.

"I wish I could tell you what to do," he said quietly.

She opened her eyes, and seeing him there, concern written across his features, gray eyes looking so *sad* for her, made her own eyes well up. She blinked, glanced down. Stupid. She'd get nowhere by crying. She wasn't even sure *why* she was crying.

She didn't notice Nick moving toward her, but then he was there, right in front of her, and his arms were coming around her. She felt the hesitation in his body, the way his arms tensed, just for a second, before he pulled her to him. She pressed her face against his chest, closing her eyes as she breathed in his scent. It was both a comfort and not, because her nerves were going haywire, too aware of every inch of her that was pressed against him. She allowed her own arms to come up, to wrap around his back, slowly, cautiously. And tried not to wonder what his skin would feel like, under the fabric between them.

"You've always gone back," he said softly. "I believe you will again."

She nodded against his chest. But... "I think that's the problem, though," she said, her voice a little muffled. "Because..." She swallowed. "Because a part of me doesn't *want* to go back." She didn't explain, but when she eased back, just a little, she saw the understanding flash in his eyes. "What are you thinking?" she whispered.

He took a breath, and she felt her body move in time with his. "I'm thinking that I don't know what to do. I'm thinking that I wish you could stay here, and that I'm not sure what kind of person that makes me, for wishing that. I'm thinking..." He leaned down and put his forehead against hers, and something in her sparked at the contact. "I'm thinking I wish our lives had been destined to meet in some other way, rather than this. Because I think we might have got on, you and me."

She wanted to say something jokey back, ask whether they didn't get on now, in that case, but she couldn't bring herself to. So instead she stood there, her forehead pressed against his, listening to the beat of his heart. And she didn't *feel* dead, didn't feel in between. She couldn't imagine right then that there was another version of her, lying on the bar floor, her friends panicked and gathered around her. Because this felt real, as much as that did—more, even.

"I have a boyfriend." She blurted the words out seemingly from nowhere, and they sounded odd out loud, like they didn't belong in this place.

He eased back, space settling between their bodies. "Okay." It made her feel stupid for telling him. Maybe he didn't care.

"I just..." She broke off, trying to think of something to justify it. "He's asking about kids. Which is ridiculous. I'm only just thirty and..." She thought of Bonnie, who was making noises about babies already, about a three-year plan to move out to one of the commuter towns.

"And you don't want children?"

"It's not that. Well, I mean it is, but..." She sighed. "Look at me." Irrelevant—he already *was* looking at her. Looking at her too much. She swallowed. "Look at us, here. How am I supposed to have children when I could be dead, just like that? How is that fair, or responsible?"

"Anyone could be dead, just like that." It was level and calm, but she heard the sadness there. For himself, she wondered, or for all the people he'd helped to move on?

"You know what I mean, though," she pressed. And she realized she wanted him to agree—because he was the only person she could really talk to about this, the only person who might have a shot at understanding.

"Maybe you should talk to *him* about it," Nick said, his tone pointed. "Maybe you should give him a proper chance."

She scowled and pulled out of his arms completely. "I didn't come here to be lectured." She muttered the words, because this was not the answer she wanted. Why couldn't he just *agree* with her? And there was a deeper annoyance, too—because she was trying. She'd thrown it back at Colin just now, out on the pavement—had pointed out that he'd encouraged her to settle down, even if she'd known full well that he'd meant for her to try with him. But really, it hadn't been Colin's words that had persuaded her to try with Adam. The reason she hadn't run at the first sign of commitment this time around was because of Nick—because of their last conversation, when they'd been inside his memory of Inverness. His idea that she'd been pretending had stuck with her, and she'd begun to think that maybe he was right; maybe she should stop moving and see what happened if she stayed still, with one person.

"You didn't choose to come here at all," he pointed out.

"No," she conceded, her voice on the verge of a bite. "And you didn't choose to have me here." *You didn't choose* me. It was childish and stupid, and she only just stopped herself from spitting it out. But it was true—she'd been forced on him, hadn't she, whether he liked it or not.

There was something careful about the way they watched each other then, the words hanging between them.

"Did *you* have kids?" she asked.

"No."

"Did you want them?"

"I don't know. Maybe."

"That's clear."

"Emery." He leveled her a look. "I am not the one with the opportunities ahead of me. It's okay for you not to be sure, but for you to make decisions because you're worried about what *might* happen seems kind of silly to—"

"*Silly?* It seems *silly?*"

The airport seemed to ripple, a soft earthquake that would have people scattering in the real world.

He was quiet for a beat. "I didn't mean that."

"Yes you did. Otherwise you wouldn't have said it. And let me tell you what's *silly*, Nick—it's you, stuck in this place by your own admission, just *existing* because you don't want to be yourself because you think you shouldn't and that you deserve to…" She trailed off, seeing the change in his expression, the tightness there, the trace of a grimace. "Wait—that's it, isn't it? You think you *deserve* to be here."

A ripple ran through the airport, and things clouded so that they were somewhere dark, and cool. Brick buildings towered above them to either side. An alleyway, maybe? There was the sound of someone screaming, an awful, painful scream, before Nick said, "No." And then they were back in the too-bright terminal.

"What…" Emery pressed her tongue against the roof of her dry mouth. "What was that?"

"Nothing," he said firmly. "It was nothing."

"Nick?" He didn't answer, and she felt a shudder run through her. For the first time, she looked at him with a different question in mind. She knew nothing about him. Had been assuming that he was fundamentally *good*, that he'd been put here to help people because he'd be good at it, like some sort of angel. But how did she know that? What if it was for another reason?

"If you think you deserve to be here," she said quietly, "does that mean you think you're being punished?"

The airport shuddered again, but the cold, dark alleyway did not return.

"I can't talk about this." His voice was firm, almost cold. But she knew guilt well enough, and she could see it there, even as he tried to shut it down.

"But what—"

"Let's talk about something else, shall we?" He looked down at her, brows pulling together. "Or not." She looked down too, at her hands, which were now growing sharper against a blurred background. Her heart was thudding. She didn't know what to do, what to think. She couldn't leave, not yet. She wanted answers.

"Next time," Nick promised, reading her mind again. "Go back and celebrate your birthday. Talk to your boyfriend. *Live.*" All commands, short and sharp. But then he leaned in and kissed her on the cheek. Soft and swift— just a whisper. And despite the fact that there were clearly things she didn't know about him, that there might be good reason not to trust him, she felt her body tighten in answer, a fizzing that shot through her, right to her core. She curled her hands into fists at her sides to keep from reaching for him, and the fact that she had to do so was enough to make her feel guilty, thinking of her real-life boyfriend, the one she was going back to. Because if she could, she knew she'd choose to stay here, with Nick, even just for a little longer.

His final words felt like they came to her across a chasm. "And Emery?" She found his eyes through the haze. "Just so you know . . . if I had a choice, I'd still choose you."

Chapter Nineteen

Adam kept looking at her as they walked up the path to the two-bedroom terraced house in Cambridge. Her dad had kept hold of their family home until Emery had made it clear she wouldn't be moving back, only then downgrading to something smaller, and cheaper. When he glanced at her for the third time as they stopped on the front step and rang the doorbell, she sighed.

"What is it?"

"Nothing," he said quickly. "Just...are you okay? Are you too cold, or...?"

"I'm fine." She was, in fact, too warm, bundled in her coat, because they'd walked from the train station, and even though it was November, the sun was strong today. But she knew Adam wasn't really worried about her being cold—he was worried about her heart suddenly faltering again.

"It's just...you seem a bit tense." But it wasn't her who was tense—it was him, starting every time she stumbled, wincing at every car horn on the way here. Like something might happen again to set her off. She supposed she couldn't blame him—it was the first time he'd seen what could happen first-hand. He was bound to be a bit worried, she told herself. But still, though she was trying to be understanding, she couldn't help wishing he wouldn't keep looking at her like she was a bomb. It came without really thinking, an echo of her mum's voice, all those years ago: *a time bomb waiting to go off*.

Her mum hadn't texted her today. It was her thirtieth birthday, and she had, apparently, forgotten. Emery was trying not to get upset about it. To tell herself that it didn't matter; it didn't make any difference to their relationship—or lack of one—anyway. It wasn't like she would have actually spoken to her mum, wasn't like they'd have gone out for a champagne lunch or anything. But still. There was a tiny part of her that felt hurt that she hadn't got one of those three messages a year, even though she told everyone she didn't want them in the first place.

She was the same age now as her mum had been when she'd given birth to her, she realized. Her mum had had Amber when she was only twenty-five, and maybe that was why she'd been so determined to make up for it, career-wise, afterward. She was speculating, of course—she'd never actually sat her mum down and *asked* her. Maybe it was something they would have talked about if she'd stuck around. Emery imagined her mum had been resentful of her—the second child who came along right as her career was taking off.

You were the one who wanted a second child.

Her dad had wanted a second child, not her mum. Before

they knew what would happen—before they knew that that child would be broken.

She scowled at herself as she rang the doorbell. *Stop it, Emery.*

Adam was still watching her, too carefully. She put a hand on his arm, worked up a smile for him. "Honestly, I'm fine. Now let's go and eat a massive lunch to celebrate my birthday again, shall we?"

Her dad answered the door with a grin that lit up his eyes. He was edging into his seventies now, but he looked more content than when she'd last seen him—retirement was suiting him. He'd loved teaching, she knew, but toward the end it had taken it out of him. Now there was color in his cheeks despite it being winter, and he looked fitter, like he might actually be going on those walks he always said he was planning to do. There was no denying his age, though—his once dark curly hair, like hers, was gray and thinning, more wisps than curls, and his gait was now a shuffling one, an old injury worsening with age.

He enveloped her in a hug. "It's so good to see you, Emery." Emery hugged him back, trying to shove down the rush of guilt that told her she should come to visit him more. He pulled back, gave her the familiar scan. She barely noticed it these days—perhaps it was only evident today because of Adam, because she didn't want him to get any ideas of how she needed to be looked after. "How have you been?"

"I'm good!" She stepped inside, shrugged off her coat and hung it on the old-fashioned hatstand her dad had bought when he'd moved house.

"And this must be Adam!" Emery turned to see her dad offer Adam a cringey wink. "She's finally letting me meet you, then!"

Adam smiled as he shook hands. "I've been pestering her about it for ages." There he was, the sure, confident Adam, the one she'd first met.

She gave an exaggerated eye-roll. "Yes, yes, okay, you two." She could hardly be blamed for putting it off—her dad would be studying Adam the whole time, trying to decide if he measured up, trying to decide if he could be trusted to keep her safe. He'd made no secret of the fact that he was thrilled she was in a relationship—he'd been on at her to find a partner for years. And Adam had wanted to meet her dad too, telling her it was about time. She thought again of the conversation he'd tried to start the other night, about kids, and pushed it away. No point thinking about that just yet. And this was exactly why she'd been putting it off—because it felt like a big deal to even be offering up this level of commitment.

There was a loud, unmistakable laugh coming from inside the house.

"Helen already here?" Emery asked.

"That she is."

"Good, I'm starving." She felt like the time on the train—the intensity of it, with Adam trying to pretend he wasn't watching her the whole time while she stared out of the window—had set her stomach churning, with the result that it now felt empty.

They made their way into the little kitchen, where everyone

was leaning against the counters. It wasn't really big enough for them to all stand there, but they managed it anyway. Her dad batted Helen out of the way of the oven, bent down to check something, and Helen immediately popped open a bottle of Prosecco, handed around glasses.

"Happy thirtieth, my darling! I just can't believe it, it's making me feel old."

Emery rolled her eyes, looked over at Amber, ready to exchange one of their shared wry looks about their aunt. But Amber wasn't paying attention, seemed to be staring very intently at the white tiles.

"And Adam!" Helen continued, lowering her glass, the rim now stained with red lipstick. "Well, I can't wait to hear all about you. Emery's told us practically nothing."

Adam gave Emery a meaningful look and she shot Helen a warning glare.

"Well, cheers!" Robin held up her flute of orange juice, and everyone copied, Emery's dad throwing the oven gloves over his shoulder. "I'm so jealous of you all right now," Robin said with a sigh, making a face at her juice before she sipped.

"How are you doing?" Emery asked.

"Oh, you know. Uncomfortable all the damn time and having to put up with some of my students looking at me like I'm contagious, but otherwise fine." Robin gave a rueful headshake. "I wish I could just lay an egg, sit on it for a while and be done with it."

Emery grinned as Adam gave a sort of politely incredulous

smile, and Amber came up beside Robin, squeezing her shoulder. Robin reached to cover her hand, their fingers lacing together briefly, a silent conversation.

"Right, well, let's all get out of the kitchen, shall we?" Dad said, gesturing at them. "I've got bruschetta for starters!"

"Wow, Dad," Emery said as she followed the others into the living-slash-dining room. "You really went all out."

"Well, I've got lots of time, haven't I? It's just poor old retired me all alone."

Emery put an arm around him and squeezed, and he smiled back at her, his eyes crinkling at the corners. No one had told him about her collapse the other night, thank God. She'd made Bonnie promise not to, and Bonnie was the only one there who had a direct route to her dad. Amber and Robin had left by then, so they didn't know either—Emery was just really hoping that Adam didn't bring it up. Or that he didn't imply it somehow, like with the way he was currently staring at the glass in her hand as if it was a danger to her. Jesus. She hadn't really thought about what it would be like, someone new having to adjust to it.

Her dad had put an enormous helium balloon with the number 30 on it in one corner of the room, and little foil 30s decorated the wooden table. Emery laughed. "Thought I'd forget how old I was?"

He tapped her gently on the head. "You only turn thirty once."

They all sat down while he went to get the starter. It was a small table, and there were only four chairs that actually matched, the other two having been pulled out of the bedrooms and put at each end. Behind the table were French doors that led to the little courtyard garden, which her dad had spent the summer months trying to make as wildlife-friendly as possible, with a fair amount of input from Robin. The dining area gave way to two sofas positioned around a TV, with another window overlooking the street outside

Adam pulled out a chair for her, a habit she'd taken a while to get used to, and she smiled at him. "Are you okay?" he whispered.

She grabbed his hand, pulled him into the seat next to her. "Adam, chill, okay?" she muttered. He immediately looked guilty, and then *she* felt guilty for making him feel like that. She blew out a quiet breath. She had to give him time, she knew that. It was a shock, seeing for the first time what happened to her. But she really, really didn't need another person treating her like she was breakable.

Helen caught her eye from her position at the end of the table, gave a not-so-subtle grimace and mouthed the word *men*. Well. Quite.

And actually, his expression just now, the guilt there, was making her think of a different man entirely.

Why? Why had Nick looked like that? What did he have to feel guilty about? What was he afraid she might find out?

No. Stop it, Emery. She had to focus on here, now. On Adam. Who was *alive*, and therefore more important.

As Amber and Robin sat down opposite, Emery noticed Robin

giving Amber a similar look to the ones Adam kept shooting at her. It made her frown—shouldn't it be the other way around, given that it was Robin who was pregnant?

Her dad came back in carrying plates of bruschetta with goat's cheese, which smelled amazing.

"So how was the other night, after we left?" Amber asked as they all tucked in. "Anything exciting to report?"

Adam shot Emery a quick glance. "Ah, well—"

"Bonnie ordered one too many shots for everyone," Emery said, shaking her head as if to say *classic Bonnie.* "And no one could take it anymore, so it all sort of disbanded." Not entirely a lie—Bonnie *had* ordered extra shots, and it *had* all disbanded very shortly after the last round, just not because of the shots. She could feel Adam's gaze on her, chose to ignore it.

"Bonnie didn't make everyone stay out and go to karaoke or something?" Robin asked.

"Nah, well, she's all sensible and married and boring now."

"Hear, hear," said Helen, who, after three divorces, was giving up and embracing the single life, or so she said.

Emery sensed another look from Adam, a touch of disapproval there, perhaps. But she'd meant it as a joke! It wasn't that she thought all married people were boring; she obviously didn't. And it was way too soon to even be thinking about that for them. Surely he was on the same page as her there? Though he had brought up children. She gulped her Prosecco as a distraction, thinking that it might have been a mistake to bring him. Maybe she should have lied, said she wasn't doing anything with her family for her birthday.

"So, Adam," her dad said, speaking through a mouthful of bruschetta, "Emery tells me you work in sales?"

Adam sat up a little straighter, like he was preparing for an interview. "Yes, that's right."

"I have to admit, I'm not really sure what that even involves—selling stuff, I presume?"

"Er…yes. Sort of." This time, Emery allowed herself to exchange glances with him. She'd told him bluntly when they'd first met that his job sounded incredibly boring, and she knew that was what he was thinking of now. They shared a small smile at the memory.

"What's your company like to work for?" her dad continued. "They treat you well?"

"Yeah, they're great. They do loads of stuff for the staff—like they're organizing this skydive for charity and we're all getting involved. Should be a great laugh."

"You doing it, are you?" Robin asked shrewdly. "Be warned—I was sick."

Amber let out a little laugh. "You were not."

Robin shrugged as she ate the last of her bruschetta. "I was in my mouth."

Emery's dad winced, Helen snorted, and Amber shushed her.

Adam looked like he wasn't sure whether to take Robin seriously or not, so after what looked like a moment of internal debate, he cleared his throat and looked at Emery. "You enjoyed it, didn't you, E?"

Emery nodded vigorously. "It was the best." Amber gave her a funny look, which she ignored. She refused to have the memory tainted by what had happened afterward.

"Any tips?" Adam asked, pushing his plate away and leaning back against his chair.

"Don't do it?" Amber suggested, earning herself a gentle elbow from Robin.

"Don't look down?" Robin said.

"*Do* look down," Emery countered. "It's the best part. No point without the adrenaline, right?" She shook her head. "It's so cool, being that high up and about to jump, I can't even explain it."

"Yes," her dad said, standing up and starting to collect their plates. "Well I think we can all agree that skydiving was perhaps not the best idea Emery has ever had." He said it mildly, but firmly enough that it ended the reminiscing. Emery handed her plate to him, though he didn't quite meet her eye as he took it and headed back to the kitchen. She tried not to let it get to her, though she suspected he'd never really forgiven her, for risking her life that way, or for being in Australia while she did it.

"Why, what happened?" Adam asked, dropping his voice.

"Nothing," Emery said quickly. "It's not important."

He frowned, but Helen came to the rescue just as Emery's dad returned with plates for the main course—Emery's favorite pea and ham risotto. "I was thinking I might go to that student protest in London next week. You know, the one about the fees and whatnot."

Emery took a sip of her drink. "Thinking of going to university, are you?"

But Robin was nodding, sitting up straighter. "You should

definitely go! They need support—the proposed changes in tuition fees are ridiculous. I'm still paying off my student loan. It's putting more and more people off going into academia, and it'll only get worse. And we need these new students—the other day in one of my supervisions, I was talking to Ellie, who's doing undergraduate zoology..." And she was off, and listening to her talk was soothing, requiring little to no input from anyone else as the risotto was served—complete with freshly grated Parmesan—and white wine was brought out to replace the Prosecco. Somehow the one-woman conversation turned from the terrible government plans to increase tuition fees to her research and the impact it would have on the conservation of the kiwi bird in New Zealand, though Emery was struggling to connect the dots.

"Knew you'd bring it back to that somehow," Amber said affectionately, patting Robin's hand.

At the end of the meal, her dad brought out a cake he'd had specially made in the shape of a 30. Emery grinned at him as she blew out the candles. "Really hammering the point home, aren't you, Dad?"

It was only once the cake was eaten that Amber cleared her throat in a deliberate sort of way. They all looked at her. "So, I've been thinking." She waited for a beat, and Emery picked up her wine glass, gestured for her to keep going. Amber took a breath. "I'd like us all to get together with Mum, maybe one day next week."

There was a physical reaction around the table. Her dad stilled, Helen did a funny little hiccup, and Emery felt her whole body tense. Adam was frowning, looking between all of them, and Robin placed a supportive hand on Amber's knee.

And in that palpable tension, Emery felt the weight of all the arguments over the years, could almost taste her sister's blame, even if Amber had never said it out loud, for her being the reason their mum had left.

"Where is this coming from?" she asked carefully.

"It's not coming from anywhere, it's always been here."

"Then why are you bringing it up now?" *On my birthday*, she wanted to add, but it felt too selfish.

"I'd just like us all to be together." Emery saw Amber clasp Robin's hand under the table—it was clearly something they'd discussed. Adam's gaze was darting between Emery and Amber now, obviously trying to figure it all out—he knew their mum had left, but not the ins and outs of it. God. She really shouldn't have brought him along.

"Well, I wouldn't like us to be," Emery said, trying to stay calm. She looked at Helen for support, but Helen grimaced.

"I'm not really sure it's my place to get involved in this." Emery fought the scowl. But it was the coward's way out— Helen always got herself involved. "I doubt Alice would want to see me in any case," Helen added.

"I've talked to her, and she's happy to see all of us," Amber said, her voice firm. "We can meet in a pub or something, so that it's..." *Neutral territory*, Emery thought. But that wasn't the bit that stuck with her.

"You've already talked to her? Without speaking to us?" *To me*.

"I had to start somewhere." Emery could see stubbornness setting in, from the tilt of Amber's chin, the setting of her shoulders. It was a stubbornness she hadn't really thought her sister possessed.

"But *why*?"

"I've told you why."

"Dad?" Emery said it as a demand, and looked over to where their dad was sitting very still, tight-lipped. She could tell from his expression that he didn't like this any more than she did. Amber might have forgiven their mum for walking out, but Emery felt sure that their dad, at least, had not.

"Amber," he said slowly, "of course you must see your mum if you'd like to, but I'm not sure that a 'family' meeting," he raised two fingers to do the air quotes, "is the best idea. It might make her feel ganged up on, for one."

"Right," Emery agreed immediately. "It *would* make her feel ganged up on, I'm sure."

"Not if we weren't ganging up on her."

Emery said nothing to that, but was sure her expression conveyed what she was thinking—that there was no way she could sit down and have a pint with her mum after all these years in a nice, amicable way, like Amber seemed to be suggesting.

Amber looked around the table once more, but when she did not find the support she was clearly hoping for, she got to her feet. Her chair wobbled but didn't fall. "Fine," she snapped, a sudden heat in her eyes, the amber glowing. "That's just…" But she couldn't finish. She simply stormed away, heading upstairs, her footsteps too loud in the silence that followed. Robin bit her lip, got to her feet and, with an explanatory wave to the stairs, headed after her.

"More wine, I think," Helen said, in a falsely bright tone.

"Right," Emery's dad agreed, clearing his throat. "Yes, and I've got a cheeseboard." Together he and Helen headed for the kitchen, leaving Adam and Emery alone.

Emery bent her head, massaged her temples.

"Um, is everything okay, E?"

She closed her eyes briefly, then forced a smile for him. "Yeah. Sorry." She took his hand, squeezed. "Just one of those family dramas, you know. She'll calm down in a bit." But she wasn't sure that was true—Amber didn't tend to lose her temper like this. She looked at the stairs. Should she follow? But knowing her, she'd only make it worse. God, she just wanted to go home.

She rolled her shoulders. Half an hour. She'd give it half an hour, try to make it up with her sister, then call it quits.

Chapter Twenty

Four months later (March 2009)

AGE 30

"So she's fine?" Adam pressed, looking down at the blood pressure monitor as if he might see something different from the doctor. "She's definitely fine?"

Dr. Holden—a woman in her fifties with a short blonde bob and a heart-shaped face—smiled up reassuringly to where Adam was hovering above Emery, one hand on the back of her chair. "It all looks normal to me, nothing to be overly concerned about." She slid the blood pressure band from Emery's arm, and Emery flexed her fingers automatically. Growing up, she'd always seen the same doctor at these yearly check-ups, a pediatrician who'd told her to call her Jo, and who had always had a smile and a wink for her. Now she'd been referred to the cardiology department, and though she still came back to Addenbrooke's Hospital in Cambridge for these check-ups, she didn't always see the same doctor.

"So there's no reason she should have another collapse any time soon?" Adam asked, and Emery glanced up at him, registering his almost aggressive tone. His attention was laser-focused on Dr. Holden, his body held stiffer than usual. He'd insisted on coming to the appointment today, even though Emery had assured him it was just routine.

"Well," Dr. Holden said, with a glance toward Emery, "Emery's episodes are irregular, and while there is ongoing research into her condition, we still don't have answers as to any meaningful patterns." She gave an apologetic smile, and Emery shrugged a little—she'd heard this all before. "In the future, there will hopefully be drugs that will be able to mitigate the symptoms, but they are a long way from being available and are only in the early stages of testing. Right now, all we can really do is monitor to see if there is any worsening of heart function or any abnormalities that might be cause for concern." She turned to her computer. "You said the last episode was four months ago?"

"Yes," Adam said, too quickly for Emery to get there first. She bit down her annoyance.

"And before that, it was two years, is that correct?"

Emery hesitated only briefly before confirming. She could feel Adam's gaze intent on her now. She'd never discussed the ins and outs of her episodes with him before, trying to make it sound like something that was so unlikely to happen, it was barely worth mentioning. A minor inconvenience, nothing more. He hadn't pressed her on it, and she'd thought she'd got away with it.

"All right," Dr. Holden said calmly, making a note on her computer. "Well, we'll just do the ECG next and see where we are." She gestured to the couch at the end of the room, and Emery got to her feet. Dr. Holden glanced at Adam. "As you know, Emery, you'll need to remove the top half of your clothing, so perhaps your friend would like to step outside?"

Adam glanced at Emery, and she met his gaze for a bit before shaking her head. "It's fine. He can stay." He'd worry more if he wasn't in the room, she suspected. She'd had countless electrocardiograms before, and they didn't tend to pick up any irregularities—which was part of what continually stumped the doctors. But it might be good for Adam to hear the word *normal* again.

She lay on top of the thin blue sheet, feeling it crinkle underneath her. The smell of antiseptic was stronger over this side of the room, and even though she knew the couch was cleaned between patients, she could have sworn a hint of sweat hung in the air. She waited while Dr. Holden attached the electrodes to her chest, ankles and wrists, smiling reassuringly at Adam while she was hooked up to the machine. He kept glancing at it like it was something to be deeply suspicious of.

"I know you know all this, Emery," Dr. Holden said, "but it's important that you lie still while we do the ECG so we can get an accurate recording." Emery nodded, and neither she nor Adam spoke for the next few minutes. She was used to these by now, didn't think anything of them. But it felt different, having Adam there.

"Okay, all done. I'm just going to have a quick look at the results, but from what I can tell, there's nothing to be concerned about."

"So there's nothing wrong? Specifically, I mean?" Adam asked as Emery shrugged her sweater back on. He was staring at the printout of the ECG like it might give him answers.

"No, it all looks normal," Dr. Holden said with a smile. "Of course, that doesn't mean there won't be a future episode, but it's reassuring to see a normal heart function."

"And you can't tell us when, exactly, that future episode might be?"

Again Dr. Holden glanced at Emery before answering. Asking her permission? Or wondering if Emery had fully explained the unpredictability of her condition? Emery looked away, making a fuss of straightening her hair after getting dressed. "I'm afraid not," the doctor said. "Now, Emery"—she gestured to the chair at her desk again—"let's just run through a few final things, shall we?"

Adam stayed quiet throughout the rest of the consultation, but Emery could feel the way his gaze kept flicking around, like the room itself might be able to offer some kind of insight. She told herself to give him a break. For all she knew, he might never have set foot in a hospital before. She should really ask him more about that, she thought with a slight frown. And it was a good thing, wasn't it, that he was concerned. It meant he cared about her, if he was worried.

But she couldn't help thinking of the way he'd looked almost disappointed when the doctor had said it was all normal. She knew that look—she remembered seeing it on her parents' faces, the first few years after her diagnosis. It was like he'd *wanted* there to be something wrong. Something, specifically, that could be fixed.

* *

Emery lay on the sofa, laptop propped on her lap, three cushions shoved behind her neck. She was hoping she had a good few hours until Beth—the girl she shared the two-bed flat with—came home, because she'd left all the washing-up from her dinner on the sideboard and hadn't wiped down the surfaces, and Beth was pretty strict about that sort of thing. Beth was also pretty strict on noise after 9 p.m. (she had a "no TV after 9" policy), the exact area of fridge space each of them was using, and the shower schedule. Luckily, she was also not around very much, choosing to spend the majority of her time at her boyfriend's flat on the other side of London, so Emery figured she'd actually lucked out, as far as random roommates went.

She was scrolling through Google, her favorite activity at the moment. She'd tried, honestly she had, to stay *present* and worry about things in the real world—like finding a job she actually liked, and committing to Adam—but she couldn't help it. She had to know more about him. Unfortunately, it turned out there were a fair number of Nick Ryemores in the world, and none of the photos she'd found online looked anything like *her* Nick. She'd expected it to be easier to get information about him—but then it wasn't like people had Facebook in the 1970s.

There was a knock at the door, and Emery jumped, slamming down the lid of her laptop and leaping to her feet, ready to run to the kitchen to look like she was in the midst of clearing up. But no, Beth wouldn't have to knock, would she?

She headed to the front door, assuming it would be Adam. He'd rung her earlier today to cancel their evening plans because he had to work late due to some incredibly boring-sounding sales meeting, but maybe he'd finished early, come to surprise her. But it wasn't Adam at the door—it was Amber.

Amber's hair was damp, her hands shoved in the pockets of her black coat. Emery stared at her. "What are you *doing* here?" Amber lived in Edinburgh. In *Edinburgh*. What the hell was she doing outside Emery's flat on a Wednesday evening?

Amber looked over Emery's shoulder, into the flat, then drew her hands out of her coat pockets, pushed back her hair. "You on your own, Little Em?"

"Er, yes…"

She nodded, then stepped inside.

"Ambs, not that this isn't a wonderful surprise and all, but what the hell are you—?"

"I've been trying to find a way to tell you this."

Emery shut the door, turned to look at her sister. "Tell me what?" She could feel the flare of her pulse against her wrists—a warning drum.

Amber took a breath as if gearing up for something, opened her mouth—and said nothing. They were still standing inside the front door, Amber's back to the coat rack, which was cluttered with about a million of Beth's coats—somehow the fifty-fifty split that applied to the rest of the place was not enforced here. She looked a pale yellow in the harsh light of the hallway, and dark half-moons sat under her eyes—she had never been one to cover up her lack of sleep with makeup. She was twisting her hands together. Something rolled in Emery's stomach—a kind of nausea.

"Amber"—she forced herself to stay calm, rational—"is everything okay? Did you and Robin…?" It would explain why she was here if something bad had happened between the two of them, though she couldn't imagine a situation where Robin would kick Amber out. Amber shook her head, her hair swishing with the movement. Emery blew out a breath. "Look, come and sit down."

Amber followed her into the small living room and sat down on the sofa, placing her hands in her lap and looking at Emery as she perched next to her. "Nothing happened with Robin," she said. "And she's fine." But there was something not quite right with how she was saying it—and there was still the fact that she was here completely out of the blue.

And then a different scenario occurred to Emery. She swallowed. "Has she…? Is the baby…?" Robin wasn't due for another month—if something had happened now, it couldn't be good.

"The baby's fine too." Tears sprang to Amber's eyes, but she jerked away when Emery moved to comfort her. "Robin stayed at the hotel because I wanted to speak to you alone. I thought…" She brushed her hair back from her face, her movements jerky. "Tomorrow we're going to Cambridge." She wetted her lips. "Actually, we're going to move back to Cambridge, we decided that last week."

"You're moving back? Now?" It didn't make sense—it all seemed too sudden. But Amber said nothing, just took another of those breaths, preparing herself for something. "Amber! You're freaking me out. What are you talking about? Why are you moving back? What's happened?"

Amber reached out, took hold of one of Emery's hands. And Emery felt that sense of balancing on the edge of something, could almost taste the metal on her tongue, the sensation she had just before dying—before she exchanged one world for another. Before everything changed. She almost drew back, almost shook her head, asked Amber not to say it—whatever it was.

Amber's hand, cold and clammy, squeezed Emery's. "I've got cancer, Little Em."

For a moment there was silence. No, not silence. A faint ringing, coming from far away. "No." Emery stated it bluntly, then shook her head. Amber's grip tightened on her hand. "No," she said again.

"Yes," Amber whispered. Tears were shining again in her eyes, and that, above all, was what got through to Emery.

"What...When? How?"

"It's ovarian cancer," Amber said, her tone brisk now. "I've known for about four months."

"Four *months*? Amber, what are you...?" Emery took a breath, felt the stale air of the flat hiss past her teeth. She couldn't process this. It didn't feel real. "Why didn't you say anything?"

"It was just before your birthday and I..."

She remembered now how Amber hadn't seemed right—both at her party and at the dinner. She remembered how Robin had watched her, ever so carefully. She closed her eyes, feeling the world tremble around her. *Cancer.*

"They think I'll be okay," Amber was saying. "I mean, they've got a treatment plan—I'll have to do chemo, the whole lot, but they think..." A slight hitch in her breathing. "There's a strong chance that I'll..." She trailed off, and only then did Emery realize she was just *sitting* there saying nothing when she should be comforting her sister. She opened her eyes, pulled Amber to her and wrapped her arms around her. Amber dropped her head onto her shoulder and Emery breathed in the warm honey smell of her sister. She felt Amber tremble, just a little.

"I'm so sorry," she whispered. She tried to think of what else to say. What *should* she say? This was her sister; surely she could find the right words. But none came—none felt right. Because there *was* nothing right about this. This was *Amber*. Her big sister. The *healthy* sister.

"I wanted to tell you," Amber said, her words muffled against Emery's shoulder, "but I didn't know how. Robin and I, we've been trying to work out what the best thing is, and how to tell everyone, but every time I picked up the phone to call you, I just couldn't. In the end, Robin booked us a train and, well, here I am."

Emery nodded. "And I'm here too, okay? Not just now. I'm here for you for anything, okay? We will get through this." She hesitated for a beat—but she had to know. "Have you told Dad?"

"Not yet. He's next on my list." Amber pulled back, scrubbed at her face. She was trying to keep it together, Emery could see. She wouldn't want to break down in front of her, so used to being the one that Emery relied on, not the other way around.

Emery bit her lip as something occurred to her. "This is why you wanted us to all meet up, isn't it? With Mum. You were going to tell us all together."

"Well, I wanted the option. I'm not sure I would have actually gone through with it."

Emery felt the guilt curdling in her stomach. "I'm sorry."

"Don't be. I should have told you sooner. I just didn't..." Amber didn't finish. Didn't know how to find the words? Didn't want people to look at her differently? Didn't want to make it real, by saying it out loud? Emery could relate to all of those, so there was no way she'd even *think* about giving her sister a hard time for keeping this from her. Even if she wished she'd known, wished she'd been able to be there for her over these last few months.

Instead she pulled her into another hug and tried to put all her emotion into that embrace. "It will be okay, Amber," she murmured. "You will get through this, and it will be okay." She was telling herself this as much as Amber. And she had no choice but to believe it, wholeheartedly. Because the alternative was too unbearable to contemplate.

Chapter Twenty-One

Emery sat in the café on her lunch break, stirring her latte mindlessly and staring into space as she waited for Adam. It was a café she'd been to once before, near Marylebone, closer to her office than Adam's. They didn't usually meet for lunch—it always ended up a somewhat rushed affair—but he had insisted, and she hadn't had the energy to argue. She'd gone through phases over the last few days, since Amber had told her about the cancer. There would be hours when she'd sit feeling numb and tired and like she didn't know what to do about anything, and then she'd be filled with a surge of adrenaline, the need to do something: find out more about ovarian cancer, plan trips to Cambridge so she could be there when Robin had the baby and take some strain off Amber, look into healthy meals she might be able to cook—anything to make herself feel useful.

She picked up the phone—Adam was a few minutes late. She stopped herself from sending a text to Amber. She wanted to be in touch constantly, check how she was doing, ask if she needed anything, but she didn't want to burden her.

The door to the café opened, and she watched as Adam

scanned the room, looking over the people hunched at laptops and the long queue waiting for lunch—this place was famous for its bagels, he had told her last time. He spotted her and headed over to her table immediately, his gait swift and determined.

"Emery." He said her name like he was trying it out, and she frowned up at him, trying to interpret the tone, as the sound of coffee beans grinding swelled. He seemed to hesitate before leaning down, kissing her cheek, his actions oddly formal. She caught a whiff of peppermint, layered over cigarette smoke—which was weird, because he'd told her he'd quit smoking just before they met, and she'd never noticed the smell of it on him before.

He pulled out the seat opposite her, chair legs squeaking against the wooden floor. "How are you doing?" he asked, still in that same slightly too formal tone. Or was that her? Was she the one being odd right now?

"I'm..." She gestured feebly in the air. She hadn't told him about Amber yet—hadn't been able to find the words. He'd been supposed to come over last night, but had called her from the office to say he'd had to stay late again, and she'd welcomed the excuse to cancel, unable to face either pretending to be okay or breaking down and crying on him. Because she knew that if she started, the fear would take hold and she wouldn't be able to stop. Right now, she was doing all she could to tell herself it would be fine. It would be fine because statistically you were more likely to survive ovarian cancer than not. It would be fine because Amber was tough, and she would get through this. It would be fine because it wasn't really happening. It wasn't really happening because Amber was the big sister, and this kind of stuff didn't happen to big sisters.

"Okay," she finished, because Adam was still waiting for an answer. "Just tired—couldn't really sleep last night." It was true. She hadn't been able to sleep properly for the last few days, waves of anxiety crashing into her every time she closed her eyes. She'd called in sick yesterday, but had just about dragged herself into the office this morning. Why was she even persevering with this stupid job? She didn't care about it, and actually, she knew for sure that she didn't want to go into advertising. What was she *doing* with her life?

"How are *you*?" she asked, knowing it was expected, trying to force herself into a normal conversation.

"Yeah, I'm..." But he broke off, pulled a hand through his hair. "Look, Emery." It wasn't her—his tone was *definitely* off. She frowned a little, tried to find clues on his face. But it looked the same—same pointed chin, same clean-shaven jaw, same slightly thin top lip. "I've been thinking, and I..." He cleared his throat, glanced around him, then dropped his voice ever so slightly. "I'm not sure that this is going to work out." This formal tone—was this what he was like in his sales meetings? she wondered.

He was looking at her. Waiting for a response, she realized. "This?" But slowly, it dawned on her. "Oh. Right. You mean us." He winced, then nodded. "Oh," she said again. But it didn't cut through—this didn't feel real either. There was the sound of coffee beans grinding again. On the table next to them, someone laughed loudly.

"I'm so sorry." She nodded, her body following autopilot. He was sorry, of course he was. He reached out, and she looked down at the table to see him place his hand over hers. It was too hot. She wanted to pull her hand back, but it didn't seem like the right thing to do. "I really like you, E. A lot. And I think..." He shook his head, doing a good impression of a sad, forlorn look. "If things were different, I really think we might be able to make a go of it."

She frowned. Everything he was saying was taking too long to register. And she was still waiting for the blow, for a rush of sadness or anger. "If what things were different?"

"No, sorry, I didn't mean...I just, I think we might be headed in different directions." But how did he know that? What direction was *she* moving in? Right now, she had no clue herself. "I know this sounds lame," he continued, "but I have quite a clear idea of what I want from life." The confidence was coming back into his voice now, the tone reminding her of when he'd asked her out, told her it would be a mistake for her to say no. "And I'm thirty-three now and I need to think...I mean, I have to be with someone who is headed down the same path as me, you know?"

Still nothing. She slid her hand out from under his. "Not really."

He picked up a napkin and started tearing bits off it. "It's just, with your, um, condition…" She stared at him. "And I mean," he added quickly, "you weren't even sure you wanted kids anyway. Right? I don't want this to end, I don't, but I've been thinking about it nonstop over the last couple of months, and I just think it will be more painful a year or two down the line."

"This is about me not talking properly about kids?" She felt like she was playing catch-up. Had she actually *said* she didn't want them? And surely she wasn't old enough to be having this conversation—was she? Had she somehow ended up being old enough without realizing it? It didn't matter. That was the key point here—she was trying, but none of this seemed to *matter* right now, because it was just paling in comparison. Amber had *cancer*. Nothing else was important.

She could tell Adam about that. Maybe he wouldn't break up with her; maybe he'd tell her he was sorry, offer some comfort.

"I hope you can understand." He'd torn the napkin into shreds now. She looked down at its remains, then studied him for a long moment. Something wasn't quite adding up. Her brain was on a go-slow, but she was sure there was something he wasn't saying. Could tell by the way he wouldn't quite meet her eye, even after delivering his little speech.

Her condition, he'd said. And the timeline—he'd been thinking about all this over the last few months. It was becoming clearer, slowly. He didn't want to be with her because she might drop dead at any moment.

"Emery?" His voice was hesitant.

217

"No, I get it," she said, and her voice sounded raspy, like she'd been shouting. "It wouldn't be fair for me to have kids, in any case."

He gave her a small, sympathetic smile, but didn't contradict her. And there it was—the real reason for breaking up with her. Because she couldn't be trusted to stay alive, because she was not a safe bet to plan a life with. And really, who could blame him?

Thankful for the numbness that had stayed with her, she got to her feet. Adam frowned up at her. "What are you doing?"

"I'm leaving."

"But..." Why was he trying to stop her? What did he want from her?

"It's okay. I get it, Adam. Honestly, I do." She'd been stupid, hadn't she, to assume she could have a normal, functioning relationship—it had to be only a matter of time for someone to see what could happen and be scared off.

She left without looking back, stepping out into the cold March air. Without thinking, she brought out her phone, scrolled through her contacts as she walked, and dialed.

"I'm so sorry," Colin said, the moment he answered. "I heard."

His voice cut through the numbness, and she felt a sob rack through her.

"Oh Em. I should have called. I wasn't sure whether you'd want to hear from me. Jesus. I'm so sorry. I'm here, okay? I'm coming round right now."

"I have to go back to work," Emery said, her voice thick with tears.

"Screw that. Go home, I'll meet you there—it'll take me an hour, okay?"

It took him fifty-two minutes, to be exact. Her eyes were swollen, her face no doubt blotchy and awful, when she opened the door to him. His face crumpled when he saw her. Then he immediately swept her into his arms, and she buried her face in his chest, sobbing. And it felt so natural to be in his arms, so comforting, that she knew he was the only one she would have wanted to see right now, the only one she could trust to be there while she broke down.

Well. Almost the only one. It was awful to think it, but in that moment she found herself wishing that something would happen, that something would scare her, or cause her pain, or whatever it was. Because, really, she didn't want to be here. She wanted to be *there*, away from reality, wanted to pretend none of this was happening.

And most of all, even though Colin—good, kind, lovely Colin—had come for her, it was Nick she wanted to see, Nick she wanted to talk to.

If I had a choice, I'd still choose you.

"I'm so sorry, Emery," Colin said, stroking her back. He didn't say it would be okay, didn't make her any promises. She wanted him to—maybe she'd believe him if he told her it would be all right. "Is there anything I can do?"

She started to shake her head automatically, the tears still wet on her cheeks, then hesitated, pulling back so she could look at him properly. He was a journalist. It hit her with full force as she stood there staring at him, her breathing steadying.

"Emery?"

She wiped her face with her sleeve. "Yes, there's something you can do."

He was nodding. "Anything."

"I need you to help me research someone." She heaved in a breath. "I need to find out who he really was."

Chapter Twenty-Two

Three years later (August 2012)

AGE 33

"So your sister's going to be all right?"

Emery glanced over to where Nick was leaning against the kitchen counter. *Her* kitchen counter—the one she remembered from her old family home. It was bizarre seeing him here, almost as bizarre as being back here again. It was a memory from before her mum left, an evening that shouldn't have meant much but had clearly stuck in her mind—the four of them eating dinner together, an occasion when her mum and dad were getting on, when her dad had attempted to cook something out of a new recipe book and ended up burning rice to the bottom of the pan, and her mum, back from work early for once, had ordered takeout. The smell of curry still lingered in the air, and the empty containers were on the counter behind Nick.

"She's in remission, which I keep being told is a good thing." Nick nodded, and glanced around the kitchen, seeming to take in the details of the terra-cotta tiles, the fridge covered in magnets alongside a photo of Amber and Emery—Emery with a wide, toothy grin—both of them clutching ice creams. For one brief moment she imagined him being in this kitchen in real life, in a world where he was alive and where her mum had not left. They would all be gathered around the round wooden table she was currently sitting at, Nick perhaps leading the small talk in an attempt to impress her mum and dad, Amber jumping in wherever possible to make things less awkward. It gave her a brief pang that there was no way they would ever have that.

Nick looked back at her, that gray-green gaze direct, almost assessing. "And how are you?"

"I'm . . ." But she trailed off, the word "okay" harder to force out of her mouth than usual. It was always harder to lie to him about that. She shook her head, felt her curls bounce against her back—her hair longer than it had been in years. "I don't know," she admitted. "I'm dealing, I guess." And she was. Yes, okay, her life had been on hold, waiting to see what happened with Amber, and yes, moving back to Cambridge hadn't been ideal, but she'd been near Amber and able to help with her niece and to run Amber to doctors' appointments when Robin couldn't. She wouldn't have changed any of that. And now Amber was better, and the doctors all seemed pleased and hopeful that she was in the clear. So figuring out what to do next was at the very top of Emery's list, because she certainly did not want to keep working at the boutique clothes shop for any longer than she absolutely had to, especially given that she'd been told off twice in the last two weeks for the fact that her smile was not welcoming enough.

Nick walked over to where she was sitting, pulled out the chair next to her, wooden chair legs scraping lightly across the tiles. Her eyes traced the contours of his face, the sharp jawline, slightly off-center nose. Very subtle lines around his eyes, lines you would only notice if you looked hard enough. And when those eyes found hers, she could not look away. She felt something rise in her throat, almost painful.

"I wanted to get to you," she whispered. His gaze did not falter, but there was a flash of something across his face, his lips turning downward into what looked like a grimace of pain— only briefly, though, before his expression evened out again. Emery swallowed. "When I found out about Amber, I wanted to get to you, I wanted to tell you about it. But I couldn't."

Nick reached out a hand as if it were automatic, stretching toward her. Then he faltered, and Emery thought he'd draw back. But he didn't. Without thinking, she flipped her own hand, linked her fingers with his. And felt something in her settle at the touch.

He looked down at their joined hands, then back at her face. And as she'd just done with him, she saw his gaze tracking across her features, taking in the details. Sparks of electricity danced along her skin wherever his eyes landed. And when they found hers again, she felt her heart thud against her ribs. "I wish I could have been there for you." It was a murmur, soft, but there was something deeper in the rasp of his voice. Something that caused her core to tighten.

She squeezed his hand gently, felt the pulse of his wrist thrum against hers. "You're here now." For a moment they just sat there, at her parents' old kitchen table, holding hands, the only two people in the world. But it hung between them—because it wasn't him that hadn't come. It was her, and though she was here now, it was only temporary.

Nick sat up straighter, drew his hand away from hers. She flexed her fingers, wishing he hadn't let go. "How's the boyfriend?" he asked, and though he was only speaking at normal volume, it sounded too loud in the small room.

Emery frowned. "Who? I'm not... Oh, Adam." She shook her head. "He's long gone."

"Oh." The beat of silence went on just a touch too long to be casual. "I'm sorry."

She shrugged. "It is what it is." She hadn't seen anyone since—she'd wanted to be there for her sister and hadn't been in the right frame of mind to be dating. Besides, what was the point? She'd given the long-term-relationship thing a go and had only been proven right—it wasn't for her. She was not a safe bet, as Adam had made perfectly clear.

"Emery, are you okay?"

She realized she'd been scowling down at her hands, now clasped together in her lap, and glanced up at him. She couldn't believe he was *here*, finally. She'd wanted to see him for so long, wanted to talk to him, to get to this place. In all the chaos and stress of the last two years, she'd craved a moment alone with him, a moment when she didn't have to pretend or be strong in front of her family, a moment when she could be with someone who understood all it was to be her, the only person in the world who shared this secret. And now here he was—two years too late.

"Emery?"

"Sorry. Yes. I'm okay." But the thing was, even though she hadn't been able to get to him, that hadn't stopped her digging. And as such, there was information she'd been sitting on for a while—things she and Colin had found out, things she had been waiting to ask him. So she took a breath, steeled herself. "Nick, who's Lisa?"

The effect of her name was instantaneous. Nick went very still, his shoulders immediately tense, the muscles in his face completely immobile. Like someone had pressed the freeze button. "What do you know about Lisa?"

She actually knew frustratingly little—though with a name, a place of birth and a date of death—the night Margaret Thatcher came to power—Colin had managed to find out who Nick was. Or who he *had* been. He'd studied at Oxford University, where he'd moved from Inverness when he was eighteen. He'd stayed on in the city afterward, from what they could gather, though it was hard to track down the ins and outs of someone's life from back then with just the archives to go on. His mother had died when he was in his early twenties, and there seemed to be no other family members to track down and ask about his life. They had, however, stumbled across a brief announcement in *The Oxford Times*. An announcement about two Oxford University graduates—Nick Ryemore and Lisa Hartington.

Emery straightened her back a little. "You were engaged, weren't you?" The piece had been more about Lisa than Nick—Lisa, who had come from a long line of Oxford graduates and who had been two years younger than Nick. Her family were generous donors to the university, and the article went on to list some of the charity work the Hartington family had done around Oxford. There was even a photo, Nick's arm around Lisa—younger than Emery knew him, but not by much, late twenties, perhaps, smiling broadly at the camera, looking almost cocky, so sure of his place in the world, not knowing that he would soon be dead, trapped forever in some kind of limbo. There was only the slightest hint of something behind his eyes, though Emery didn't know if she was imagining the tinge of sadness she saw there; if she'd stared at the photo for so long that she'd lost all sense of perspective. Lisa appeared to have been caught mid laugh, her head thrown back slightly, long hair—blonde, perhaps, though hard to be sure in black and white—caught in a windswept look. She was short, her head only reaching Nick's chest, even with heels on, and she had that kind of confidence on camera that only a few people did.

Nick closed his eyes, and Emery saw pain lance across his face. She felt something ugly writhe in her stomach—something she didn't want to admit to, something she wished she could shove aside, or not even feel in the first place. But it was there. Nick was hurting, and there was a part of her that was jealous. It wasn't fair of her—not at all. But that didn't stop it.

When he opened his eyes, there was a glint of steel in the gray. And when he spoke, his tone was cold. "You need to stop looking into me."

She tried not to feel hurt by his tone. "Why? Maybe it'll

help." She didn't say who, exactly, it would help. She wasn't entirely sure of the answer to that.

"It won't."

"How do you know?"

A ripple ran through their surroundings, her childhood kitchen blurring around them. And for a second, they were in an alleyway, the smell of something sour—rotten food, perhaps—replacing the smell of still-warm takeaway. A chill ran through the air. Emery remembered this; it was the memory she'd caught a glimpse of last time, the memory he hadn't wanted her to see. There was more this time—the noise of a nearby street swelled, the sound of a car horn echoing around the night sky. The air was damp, and cool enough to make Emery wrap her arms around herself, turning in a circle to see tall buildings, and bins stacked against the back doors of what might be restaurants.

"No." Nick's voice was low, and the sound of it wrenched something inside her, because he was pleading. When she looked at him, he stumbled back a step, shaking his head. He'd gone so white, his face was stark against the night sky, almost luminescent in this alley devoid of street lights.

Then an echo, vibrating across the memory. A bang. Something—or some*one*—hitting metal, the sound obscured in the distance by the noise of traffic. Then a woman's voice, begging.

Nick, please don't!

"No!" It was Nick's voice, this time, louder than the woman. He grabbed Emery's wrist, yanked at her as if he would pull her away from the alleyway.

The memory faded, and the kitchen came back into focus,

shimmering a little in the aftermath. Emery's mouth felt dry as she looked at Nick. They were both standing now, in the middle of the kitchen. Nick was still very white.

"Nick, what was...?" She took a shuddering breath. *Nick, please don't!* "Was that Lisa?" The sound of her voice, echoing.

"Leave it, Emery." He turned away, his back to her, looking out of the kitchen window to her childhood garden, complete with swing set.

Her head felt plugged with cotton wool, fuzzy and unable to think. What had she just seen? "Please, Nick, please tell me—"

"No." He bit the word out and she winced. For a moment they stood there in silence. She could feel her heart thudding against her ribs. How much longer? Surely she'd be sent back soon. He glanced over his shoulder at her, and his expression twisted. "I'm sorry." His voice was less cold now, though a long way from soft, reassuring murmurings.

"What aren't you telling me?" she whispered. He said nothing, only turned his head to look back out of the window. She stepped toward him, reached out and placed a hand on his shoulder. He flinched, and she drew it back. "I want to understand," she said, trying to keep her voice calm.

"This isn't okay," Nick muttered. "This isn't right."

"What isn't?" This time, there was more of a bite to her voice, and she felt her temper start to flare.

Perhaps sensing it, he turned around to face her. "You shouldn't be trying to find out about me. You shouldn't be thinking about me in between times. You should be living in the real world."

She frowned—this was not quite what she'd expected. "Can't I do both?" When he said nothing, she sighed. "You're part of my real world now, it's too late." He took half a step backward, a grimace twisting his lips, and she felt a rush of anger. "Could you just for one second stop pretending this is one-sided? Jesus, Nick. You're acting like I'm some kind of..." she waved a hand in the air, "silly little schoolgirl with a crush or something. For fuck's sake, don't you think we're past that? And what, you really want to tell me that you never think of *me* when I'm not here?"

His eyes hadn't left her face the whole time she'd been speaking, and now she felt her pulse flare against her wrist, waiting for his answer. *Stupid, Emery.* Stupid to say it, to put it out there like that.

"I have a job to do here," Nick said, his voice careful.

Emery folded her arms. "So I never cross your mind when I'm not here?" Her voice was a taunt, but inside, her heart had picked up speed, her stomach twisting as she watched his face for clues.

Half a beat of silence. Then, "Fine, I think about you." He was scowling as he said it. He lifted both hands, a kind of surrender. "Is that what you want to hear? I think about you so damn much, and the time between us becomes blurred so that I both feel like you are always here and yet I miss you every second when you're not."

A breath caught in her throat, trembled there. He was still scowling, like the admission had been dragged from him against his will, but he was also watching her, gauging her reaction. She stared at his face—a face that was becoming so familiar, it was starting to feel like a part of her. And she couldn't stop herself. She reached out, placed a hand on his cheek, her skin sparking at the contact, a thin layer of stubble rough against her palm. He lifted a hand to hers, resting it there for a bit. Then he gently drew it away, and she felt the sting of rejection.

"I can't let myself go any further," he said quietly. "I will be stuck here forever, and you will never be able to stay here. And it is already so damn hard every time you leave; it's hard thinking of you out there, having a life I will never be a part of. And that is *wrong* of me, Emery, don't you see that?"

She felt her heart tug at his expression. She wanted to wrap her arms around him, absorb some of his pain into her. It was so strong, the need to help him. And with it came a touch of fear, of what it might mean to do that. And what it meant that she couldn't recall feeling like this with anyone else before now.

"Do you understand, Emery?" he murmured. "I can't want you here with me, because then you would be dead for good. I could never want that. And even then, you could never stay." He shook his head. "There is no version of reality where I get to have you with me. So it's easier not to want it."

She could think of nothing to say, so she only looked at him. The space between them felt charged, like the air was vibrating. And there was a feeling like she was on the edge of something, standing on top of a cliff and looking down—like she was deciding whether to jump, or step back to safety.

Then the quake across the memory—the warning that their

time was nearly up. A warning of something else entirely, maybe.

Emery cleared her throat, trying to defuse some of the tension. "Well. That's quite the speech." But she didn't manage to pull off the easy tone she'd been shooting for.

His gaze ran across her face, and she found herself mimicking the action. How long would it be before she saw him again?

"What are you thinking?" Nick asked quietly.

She heaved in a breath. "I'm wondering if this can be real."

A hint of a smile crossed his face, softening his features. "I think maybe we're past—"

"No, I'm not talking on a metaphysical level. I mean... How much of you thinking about me is because I'm the only person you see more than once?"

He winced a little. "Ouch."

She bit her lip. "Sorry. But... well, I am the only one you see regularly, aren't I? So how much of it is because you're..." *Lonely.* She couldn't say it, though, couldn't hurt him like that. But it would be easy, wouldn't it, to want someone around more if they were the only person you ever got to see.

"If we're going down that road, how much of you thinking of me is because I'm the ultimate unavailable man?" He raised his eyebrows to make it teasing.

She huffed out a laugh. "Ouch."

"It wouldn't be that far off base, would it?"

She frowned. "What do you mean?"

"Don't forget, I know you." She opened her mouth to protest

at that, but he talked over her. "I know you avoid committing to people, avoid committing to any kind of future."

"Because I might not even have a future!" She gestured to the space between them. "This is kind of proof of that, isn't it?"

"That's just an excuse."

She felt a ripple of anger, shot him a glare. "Fuck that." She forced herself to take a calming breath. She would regret it, she knew she would, if she stormed away from him now. So instead she lifted her chin, nodded. "Fine. We agree then—this is all in our heads. We think about each other just because we can't have each other." Maybe it would be easier if she could put it all down to that. She wanted to know him simply because she couldn't. Nothing more.

He nodded slowly. "Agreed. It's all in our heads."

There was a long moment where they just looked at each other, neither of them wanting to be the first to back down. Emery felt her heart thumping against her ribs, felt the muscles in her body grow taut. Saw Nick's gaze drop to her mouth, just briefly, before returning to her eyes, and felt the whisper of a shiver down her spine.

She could feel it now, the way the memory was fading around her, could sense her body growing more solid in relation to it. Nick glanced around at the kitchen, noticing it too, then back at her. For one more second, they held each other's gaze.

Then, "Fuck it." He stepped toward her, and in one quick motion his hands were cupping her face. His thumb caressed her cheek—slightly callused and rough and so incredibly real— and she felt all her awareness go to that point of contact, heard her own sharp intake of breath. Then his mouth was on hers, hot and demanding, and she reached up, one hand digging into his shoulder, the other in his hair, pulling him closer to her.

Even as she became more solid and he started to fade, she clung to him, needing more of him, because he tasted every bit as good as she'd imagined and more, the citrusy sea scent overwhelming her, a hot need curdling in her stomach, over-powering everything else. And she knew he was wrong. They were *both* wrong. This was not in her head—this was the only real thing there was.

She was shoved back into her body with a suddenness she'd not felt before, like she had been wrenched from the memory, from Nick, and slammed into the real world. She gasped as the pain of it rippled through her, feeling like it might kill her all over again, and she welcomed the thought of it, because she wanted to get back to him, she wanted to be there, kissing him, wanted to feel his hands on her skin, wanted to see what more there was of him if she peeled the layers back.

Her eyes were closed but it still felt too bright, and she scrunched them tighter as she let out a whimper. Around her, there was shouting, and she was lying on something hard and a little sticky. Where was she? She didn't remember. She tasted blood in her mouth and felt panic stepping in to seize her. She didn't *remember* what had happened, what had caused her heart to stop—she had no idea where she was.

She forced her eyes to open, winced again at the bright light above her. Around her a group of people were peering down at her, one of them right there, practically on top of her, two fingers pressed against her wrist, checking for a pulse. She knew none of them. Strangers—these were all strangers.

"Has someone called an ambulance?"

"Oh my God, is she okay?"

"Someone get the manager!"

"Do you even know what you're doing?"

"Here, I've had first-aid training, let me—"

"I'm okay." Her voice was a wheeze, but the person closest to her heard her. He was a man in his forties, maybe, with the weathered look of someone who spent a lot of time outdoors. She was surrounded by shelves, she realized, and next to her was a basket, cheese, broccoli and orange juice scattered across the white floor. And blood. She felt a surge of panic, let out another whimper.

"Hey, you're okay," the man said, at the same time that she realized it wasn't blood, but red wine. The bottle had smashed around her. She flexed her fingers. Her left hand was cut, but tiny cuts, nothing serious. "What's your name, love?"

"Emery." She could barely get it out.

"Okay, Emery. You're going to be okay, do you hear me? An ambulance is already on the way. Do you want us to call anyone?" He was looking around for her phone, and clearly she must have dropped that too, because someone nearby handed it to him. She closed her eyes so she didn't have to see her audience.

"My sister," she whispered. "Amber Wilson."

"Okay, I'll do that right now. I'm calling your sister right now."

What had happened? She couldn't remember. She was in the supermarket, yes, and she remembered getting here, remembered picking out the bottle of Malbec. But she didn't remember what had set her heart off, what had caused her to collapse. And it was that, beyond anything else that had happened, beyond any revelation about Nick, that made her feel cold.

Chapter Twenty-Three

Emery stood on the balcony of Amber and Robin's flat, the French windows open as wide as possible, trying to tempt a non-existent breeze into the living room. Lily, her niece, was propped on her hip, little hands gripping her bare shoulders, her fingers occasionally wandering to the straps of her vest top. Emery's hair felt too heavy on her head, the back of her neck sweating.

"And that's the river over there," she said, pointing with her free hand in the general direction of the Cam. You couldn't see much from here, and she was running out of ways to keep this game interesting, but Lily had got bored of sitting in front of the TV watching the Olympics with everyone else.

Lily turned big brown eyes on her. "The ducks live there."

"Yes!" Emery realized that was a little *too* enthusiastic for the concept of ducks and laughed at herself, and Lily joined in. Emery knew it couldn't be possible, as it had been Amber's egg inside Robin, but she swore Lily looked like both of them. Robin's eyes, Amber's nose. Lily started fidgeting, bored already—she had an impatience that Emery couldn't help but appreciate.

From behind her, inside the flat, Emery could hear the commentator on the TV, and the sound of Helen demanding a top-up of Prosecco.

"Emery!" her dad shouted. "It's the rowing! You don't want to miss the rowing!"

"Call us when the sprints are on!" Emery looked down at Lily. "Do you want to watch people run really, really fast?" Lily stared at her, looking completely baffled. Emery bounced her niece to emphasize the point, but Lily looked unimpressed. Maybe Robin and Amber didn't talk to Lily as much about running as they did about ducks.

"Has anyone heard from my children?" Emery glanced into the living room to see Maureen, Bonnie and Colin's mum, heading back toward the sofa with the Prosecco, ready to top Helen up. Her lipstick was smudged a little, but her red hair was perfectly straight—the rollers she'd once sworn by now a thing of the past. "Why are they late?"

At that point, Amber came out onto the balcony, and Lily squirmed to be let down. "Mama!" She waddled over to her and held out her arms, and Amber bent down to scoop her up, handing Emery a glass of Prosecco before she did so. Emery's natural inclination was to tell her to be careful, but she bit her tongue. Amber hadn't been strong enough to hold Lily for a long time after she was born because of her treatment, and Emery knew how much it meant to her to be able to pick her up now.

"Can I have lolly?" Lily asked her mother hopefully.

"No, love, they're all gone."

"All gone?"

"All gone," Amber affirmed.

"Maybe later?" This was Lily's new favorite question, as far as Emery could gather.

"Maybe."

Emery smiled at her sister. "Given up on the rowing?"

"I thought it might be cooler out here," Amber said with half a sigh. They both glanced into the living room. Robin was leaning in toward the TV, shoveling popcorn into her mouth and looking very focused.

"I didn't know Robin was so into sport," Emery said.

"She isn't, she's just become obsessed with the Olympics." As evidenced by the fact that she had decorated the flat with the Olympic hoops hung up all over the place. "The other day she was lamenting the fact that she hadn't stuck to the hundred-meter sprint when she showed talent aged eleven."

Emery laughed and Lily wriggled to be put down again. Emery leaned back against the railing, enjoying the feel of the sun on her back, even if it was hot. Amber was looking healthier, she thought. Her hair hadn't properly grown back yet and was still a little tufty, almost child-like, like Lily's hair. But she'd been red and blotchy a lot of the time during treatment, and her skin tone was evening out now—and though she'd not put back on all the weight she'd lost, she definitely looked less frail.

She met Emery's assessing gaze, and Emery immediately

glanced away, caught in the act. She should know better—she'd caught people looking at her enough times like this, and she knew it was no fun.

"So how are you, Little Em?"

Emery looked back at her and laughed a little at her expression—all big-eyed concern.

Amber frowned. "What?"

"Just us." Amber raised her eyebrows in question, but Emery shook her head. She supposed she got it more now, the way her sister had always worried about her, the way she was clearly *still* worrying about her. But maybe it was best not to point that out. "I'm fine," she said instead. Amber said nothing. "Honestly, Ambs, I'm okay."

She was regretting getting that man to call Amber after she'd woken up in the supermarket a week ago. She hadn't been thinking straight, had been caught in the panic of coming to surrounded by strangers. But she'd worried her, and Amber didn't need to be worried right now. Which was also why Emery wouldn't tell her that the side effects had lingered for longer than usual this time around—she'd had sharp pains in her chest for days afterward, and she'd kept getting light-headed when walking to work, though that seemed to have eased off now. It was unnerving, yes, but there was no way she'd be telling her sister—or anyone else, for that matter. Her check-up was due soon, so she'd ask the doctor about it then, though she was sure they'd say the same as they always did: that research was ongoing, that her heart was, apart from its tendency to stop at random points, behaving quite normally, and that although there *were* drugs on the horizon that might help, they were still at clinical trial stage.

She thought again of waking up on the supermarket floor, the taste of blood in her mouth, the too-bright lights above her. Thought of what she'd been doing just before that. How it had felt to be wrenched away from Nick, slammed back into her body. And wondered, not for the first time, if these lingering side effects were her own fault. Because she hadn't wanted to leave him, had tried to cling on to him. Was it possible that she'd stayed there with him, in that place, longer than she should have?

"Amber, do you believe in soulmates?" She blurted it out without really thinking about it, and saw from her sister's expression that the weirdness of the question had not gone unnoticed.

Amber glanced back into the living room—toward where Robin sat, blonde hair cut right back to her scalp, something she'd said had nothing to do with Amber's treatment, but which everyone knew had been done in solidarity. "I'm not sure. Why?"

Emery shrugged, trying to look casual. "Just wondering."

Amber gave her a long look, a look that Emery had seen so many times before. It was what she thought of as Amber's big-sister look. "Well," she said eventually, "I think I believe you find people who make you... I don't know, better? Is that corny? People who you click with, people you're compatible with... People you're willing to work at it with, people you can imagine spending your life with. But I don't know if I buy into the whole 'there's that one perfect person and no one else' thing."

Emery said nothing, and Amber cocked her head. "Is that what you're waiting for—your soulmate?" Emery knew in part why she was pushing—she had been basically celibate since Adam, and the implication, under the question, was: *Is that why you haven't had a successful relationship yet? Is that why you're perpetually single?*

She took a sip of Prosecco to avoid answering right away—it was slightly too warm, none of them patient enough to let it chill properly. "What if you found your soulmate," she said slowly, "but you couldn't be together? Would it be possible, do you think, to ever be with someone else?"

Amber pursed her lips as she thought that one through, then her expression fell. "Oh Em—he's not married, is he?"

"What? No. No, it's no one specifically. I'm just wondering. Speculating, you know."

Amber tapped her fingers against the skirt of her floaty green summer dress. Then she said quietly, "I think you could drive yourself mad thinking there's only one person out there, wondering if you've found them."

Emery nodded, but didn't reply. She couldn't ask what she really wanted to ask, anyway. *What if you found your soulmate, but they'd been born at the wrong time?* "So how are you finding being back at work?" she said instead, aware that she needed to move the conversation onto safer territory. Amber had returned to work part-time as a physio recently, something Emery thought was unwise but which Robin, apparently, wholeheartedly supported. Emery suspected that Robin was just as worried as she was, but that she didn't want to stop Amber from having a life—and she could understand that.

"I'm enjoying it. It's nice to be using my brain again, and nice to be the one telling other people about their treatment options." She gave Emery a wry look. "I'm knackered, though—we both are." But she smiled over to where Lily was now sitting on Robin's knee, a smile that softened her face, a smile that made Emery feel more than a little emotional. She stepped over to her sister, put her arm around her and squeezed. She could smell the peppermint body lotion Amber used, layered over a hint of sweat that you could never escape in this kind of heat. Amber turned that smile on Emery, and Emery nodded—a silent conversation between the two of them.

"I just feel lucky, you know?" Amber said. Lucky that she'd had a child after all the problems they'd gone through. Lucky that she'd found Robin. Lucky that she was still here to be with them both, lucky that she'd got through the awfulness of the last few years. All of it, maybe. So many people would harbor resentment, the *why me* of it all, but not Amber.

"Anyway," she continued, "how are *you*—how's the job?"

Emery took another sip of Prosecco. Definitely too warm. "I, um, quit." Amber pursed her lips and nodded. "You don't look surprised."

"I wonder why that would be?"

"Well I wasn't exactly going to be a clothes saleswoman or whatever for the rest of my life, was I?"

Amber laughed. "What next then? Acrobat?"

"Oh my God, I wish—how cool would that be? Or a fire-fighter? I quite like the idea of being a detective, but I might have left it a bit too late."

"Chef?"

"Ballet dancer?"

"Tour guide? Oh wait, you've done that one." The two of them burst out laughing at the utter ridiculousness of Emery's career pattern. "What about something arty? Art teacher? I feel like there should be other art-related jobs, but I can't think of them right now."

Emery gave a non-committal shrug. It was what people always suggested, because of her degree, but she didn't have the passion to really go for it. Despite studying art, she'd never really considered making a career out of it, and that wasn't something she felt inclined to change.

"Maybe you should have a look for jobs outside Cambridge. Go back to London? Bonnie's still there, right?"

There was the sound of knocking at the front door, and Robin practically sprinted over to answer it, bestowing a very brief hello on the new arrivals before running back to the sofa, apparently desperate not to miss a single minute of the Games.

"I know, I know," Bonnie said, coming into the room with Colin close behind. "We're late, it's my fault, sorry."

Amber gave Emery a wide-eyed look. "You've got to be kidding me. I've got *summoning* powers!" They laughed again. "I feel like this proves my point—London with Bonnie?"

"Bonnie's actually in Tunbridge Wells, which is hardly London. But I'm not sure I want to go back there anyway."

"Abroad, then?"

"Ah, I seem to remember you dragging me home last time I went abroad."

But Amber didn't rise to that—instead she gave Emery's arm a little squeeze. "I know why you moved back to Cambridge, Little Em, and I'm grateful, honestly I am. And I love having you around. But I don't want you to put your life on hold for me, and now that I'm... well, now things are looking up, maybe you could think about *you* for a bit." But where would that lead? Emery wondered. Somehow, she was thirty-three and had nothing to show for it—no relationship, no career, no money. She'd spent so long convincing herself that she'd be stupid to plan for a future, and now it seemed she was already halfway into that future and it felt more by accident than design.

She turned to head off the balcony and back into the living room, where Maureen was now hugging her children and Lily had trotted over, interested in the new arrivals.

"Hello, little one," Emery heard Bonnie saying. "I got you a present!"

"Present!" Lily definitely knew that word.

"I invited Mum," Amber said, just before Emery crossed the threshold. Emery glanced back at her, trying to keep her expression neutral, despite the jolt.

"Oh, right."

"She's not coming."

Emery tried not to make the relief she felt too obvious. Not just for her, though—it would make the whole occasion awkward, and it was supposed to be a fun day, something they all needed.

Amber was looking at her, clearly waiting for some kind of reaction. "I've been trying!" Emery said. She realized she sounded too defensive and cleared her throat. "I texted her."

"Yeah, she said."

Emery frowned. She didn't like the idea of them talking about her like that. Their mum had been to visit Amber a few times since her diagnosis, but Emery had managed to avoid her so far. It might even have been deliberate scheduling on her sister's part—and that sent an uncomfortable wave of guilt through her, at the thought that Amber, even when ill, had felt the need to keep them separate. But it was good that their mum was making the effort. Even if, had it not been for Emery, Amber might have grown up having both her parents by her side for good. She caught herself in time to stop going further down that route. *It's the past, Emery. No point.*

She was about to ask Amber why she was bringing up the fact that she'd invited their mum—if she was going somewhere with it—when Bonnie appeared on the balcony, Lily following, chocolate around her mouth and clutching a new Olympic teddy bear.

Amber wrinkled her nose. "She'll go mental in a minute."

"Oh, sorry!" Bonnie said, bestowing a one-armed hug on Emery. "Robin said it was okay."

"Robin, believe it or not, is a soft touch."

Emery smiled at Bonnie. "It's so good to see you! Where's Joe?"

"Oh, he's coming, he's just parking the car—I made him drop me off outside."

"Quite right too. Come on, come inside, I'm going to get sunburned out here." Bonnie followed her toward the kitchen, which was separated from the living room by a line of wooden cabinets. "Prosecco? Might even be cold by now."

"Er, no."

"G&T?"

"No thanks. I'm, um, not drinking at the moment."

Emery stopped before the fridge, looked back at Bonnie. On the other side of the kitchen counter, Maureen was talking to Colin, while Helen, Emery's dad and Robin still sat on the sofa, staring at the screen. Bonnie started to turn a little red. And before she even said anything, Emery knew.

"Are you...?"

Bonnie nodded, sucking in a little breath. "I am."

"You're *pregnant*?" It came out a little louder than Emery had intended, and Bonnie's face developed a full flush. Emery winced. "Sorry."

"Well, at least it's out in the open now."

"Oh my *God*! This is amazing! Congratulations!" Bonnie had mentioned, the last time they'd met, that she and Joe were thinking about trying, but Emery hadn't realized quite how serious that thinking had become. "Wait—you are happy about it, right?"

Bonnie laughed. "Of course!"

"Boy or girl?" Emery demanded.

"Don't know. We're thinking we might be brave and not find out."

Amber came up behind the two of them, pulled Bonnie into a hug. "Couldn't help overhear," she said, with a wink at Emery. "Congratulations. This is the best news."

"Thank you! You'll have to give me some tips, I'm already panicking."

Amber smiled. "You'll be fine—and Robin's your go-to for all things pregnancy." It was said lightly enough that Emery thought Bonnie probably wouldn't notice the slight fragility in Amber's voice—the whisper of longing over not having been able to carry her own child.

And then Amber and Bonnie were off, talking about Robin's pregnancy and things to watch out for, and Bonnie was already coming up with stories and books she'd read, and Amber was explaining some of their decisions during pregnancy and afterward, and Emery found herself standing as if a little way out from the conversation—suddenly on a limb, unable to contribute, even though she smiled along.

Perhaps noticing this, Colin came over, breaking away from his mum, and gave her a hug.

Emery squeezed him back. "You're going to be an uncle!"

"I know! Look at us both, so grown up."

"Not as grown up as the parents." At least she had Colin. What would she do when *he* got married, had a family? She felt a slight spasm of panic at the thought. *No. Stop it.* It was selfish of her to even think like that. "No Rachel today?"

He shifted from foot to foot. "We actually broke up, a few months ago."

"What? Why didn't you tell me?"

He gave a little shrug. "I thought you had bigger things to worry about."

Emery bit her lip. "I'm sorry."

"Don't be. It wasn't meant to be." He didn't say why they'd broken up, and she didn't want to ask outright—though she could guess. Reading between the lines, from what Bonnie had let slip and the snippets of one-sided conversations she'd heard between Colin and Rachel, Rachel had not appreciated him being around for Emery as much as he had been over the past couple of years. "Does this mean we need a breakup night out? Tequila shots, the whole lot?"

"Yeah—why haven't we ever done that before?"

"No idea. Seems like we've missed a trick."

"We can make up for it. Although our numbers are dwindling." Both of them looked around the room—Amber and Robin, and now Bonnie, off tequila shots for the foreseeable. Colin gave a mock-sad head-shake. Then he grabbed Emery's forearm, pulled her slightly to one side. "On another note, are you still looking into that dead guy?"

Emery felt a nervous spasm run through her. "Why?" She'd not given Colin much of an explanation for why she'd wanted information on Nick, only saying that she thought he might be connected to her past. And when they'd started it all, she'd been a mess, so he hadn't pushed.

"I found out something about how he died."

Emery stilled. *I died a week after I turned thirty-five, on the night Margaret Thatcher came to power. I died in pain and scared for someone I loved.*

The alleyway that he had taken her back to, not once but twice now. The sound of a woman screaming.

"It was a mugging, apparently," Colin continued, apparently oblivious. "There's a small news article about it—we missed it last time."

Her palms felt clammy, the Prosecco shaky in her hand. "A mugging?" Her thoughts were circling widely, picturing his face, the way he'd shut her out when she tried to ask him about the alleyway,

Nick, please don't.

"Yeah. It was buried in a piece about unsafe streets, which is why we missed it."

Something fought through the chaos in her brain. "But you found it? You kept digging?"

"It sort of became a habit in my free time." For her. He'd kept digging for her. God, she didn't deserve him. "Anyway— it's only a short article, so I don't know the details. Just that he died of a knife wound at the scene. Does that help?"

Emery swallowed. "Yeah. Yeah, it helps." She held up her glass, gestured to his. "Top-up?" His glass was full, but she left anyway, heading back toward the fridge and hiding her face as she did so. She felt hot, her breath sticking in her throat.

Maybe I'm supposed to help you.

I will be stuck here forever.

Stuck here. A punishment.

Why? What had he done the night of the mugging?

I died in pain and scared for someone I loved.

What do you know about Lisa?

A punishment.

What did you do, Nick?

Nick, please don't.

Whatever he'd done, whatever he thought he needed to be punished for, she was sure it had something to do with Lisa.

Chapter Twenty-Four

One year later (July 2013)

AGE 34

Emery sat at a table on a street in Bordeaux, sipping an espresso in the early-morning sun. Around her, the city wasn't yet fully awake, but she'd taken to getting up before the shops opened, before her shift at the hotel started, and coming to her favorite café, near enough to the central fountain that she could hear the running water, under the watchful eye of the sand-colored stone buildings, the sunlight adding hues of gold and red. She'd always insisted she wasn't one for routine, but there was something peaceful about *this* routine: the walk through the city, the waiter who knew her name, who encouraged her to speak a little more French every day.

She'd moved out here six months ago, finding a job in hospitality and sticking with the *why not* attitude that had got her this far. Amber had encouraged her, insisting she needed to get out there, find what she wanted from life. Maybe *this* was what she wanted—the odd contentment of smiling at a familiar face every day, of having a group of friends she worked with in the hotel, the promise that she was manager material, according to her boss. And France was close enough that she could be home quickly if she was needed, and could still have a relationship with her friends, her family. Her dad hadn't even put up that much of a protest, and though she'd teased him, saying he was becoming compliant in his old age, she suspected that the real reason he'd not freaked out about it was because of Amber—both because Amber had warned him not to, and also because he'd just had to face his healthy daughter going through an awful crisis. It kind of put things in perspective.

She looked down at the sketch pad she'd brought with her. She'd started drawing again just after she'd moved out here—something about the beauty of the place, perhaps. Or something about being away from everyone she knew, which she'd always craved in her early twenties. She'd tried to capture the city, then faces she'd seen. She'd drawn Amber and Robin and Lily, intending to give the sketch to Amber next time she saw her—she'd love the fact that Emery was drawing again. But the face she'd been drawing today was the one she kept coming back to—the reason, if she was being honest with herself, that she'd picked up a pencil again. His eyes stared out of the page at her, though she could never capture the exact shade of them, the way the gray in the green seemed to lighten or darken depending on his mood. Nor could she capture the way he fought to keep his expression neutral, or the way those flashes of hurt or laughter could transform everything. And she certainly couldn't capture the way his lips had felt on hers, the tug that went through her at even the thought of it.

She looked at him for a moment more, then turned the pad over. She'd thought that coming to France would help her to stop thinking about him, stop obsessing over the way he'd died, stabbed in an alleyway, or why he thought he needed to be punished. If, in fact, there was any truth in that. She'd tried to find information on Lisa Hartington, but had so far come up blank—she couldn't find evidence of her death anywhere, and she'd decided not to ask Colin. He'd already given up so much for her, had lost his last relationship because he'd been there for her when she'd needed him. It wasn't fair on him. Besides, there was a tiny part of her, fighting against the rest of her, that didn't *want* to know. Because if it really *was* something awful, how would she face Nick again?

"*Encore un café, Emelie?*" Emery looked up, smiled at Matthieu. His skin was tanned leather, his eyes creased around the edges, and a tea towel was currently thrown over his shoulder. He'd struggled to get her name when she'd first met him, and after a couple of attempts she'd decided that Emelie was just easier.

She smiled. "*Oui, s'il vous plaît.*"

"*Nous avons aussi des croissants, si vous en voulez un?*"

Emery took a moment to digest the question, but the word "croissant" was pretty clear, so she nodded. "*Pourquoi pas?*"

As Matthieu went back inside, Emery's phone rang on the little plastic table. Amber.

"Hey!" she said as she answered. "So, I was just thinking about you, and I know I'm coming back to see you guys this week, but maybe you and Robin and Lily could come to France sometime soon? I can get you a discount at the hotel, and we could take Lily to the beach, and there's this cool place for wine-tasting where they go into the science of how the wine is made—a friend of mine said it was boring, but I'm sure Robin would love it."

Amber was silent at the other end, and Emery briefly brought her phone away from her ear to check she hadn't accidentally hung up. "Amber? Is the signal okay, did you hear me?"

There was a sharp intake of breath, and Emery felt her heart spasm in response. "Little Em—the cancer. It's back."

* *

The moment she saw Nick—despite the last year spent questioning what had happened in the alleyway, replaying the words of a fearful woman, despite wondering what he might have done to deserve being stuck in this place—Emery ran to him. His arms came round her immediately, strong and certain, his familiar scent cloaking her in comfort. She pressed her face to his chest, feeling the hard muscle under his shirt, and already the sobs were racking through her.

He didn't ask what was wrong, only tightened his arms around her. Because, of course, he already knew. It hadn't been a physical thing that had stopped her heart this time—not a noise or a slice of pain or the shock of cold water. It had been her sister's voice, and the implications of those four words. Now Amber would be on the other end of the phone, panicking that Emery had gone silent, but even though she should feel awful and desperate to get back to the land of the living, to reassure her sister and find out what it all meant, she was glad she was here. She *wanted* to be here, with him.

His hand was stroking her back, gentle and soothing, and his lips were kissing her hair as she sobbed. "Shh. It's okay. You're going to be okay. I've got you."

"My sister," she choked out.

"She fought it before. She can fight it again."

She became aware of how close they were, of the feel of his heart—beating despite all odds—of his hands still caressing her back. His shirt was wet from her tears, his cheek pressed against her hair. She managed to stifle the sobs and ease back, just slightly, so she could look into his eyes. No, her drawings didn't do him justice—maybe someone more talented would be able to, but she couldn't capture the essence of him, the contours of his face, the exact color of his eyes. His face was so close to hers—close enough to count his eyelashes if she wanted to. Her breathing slowed to match his, his rhythm calming hers. And for a tiny moment, she had that sensation of being totally in sync with someone, before a wave of grief and guilt threatened to overwhelm her and she closed her eyes against it.

"What will happen if she dies?"

He didn't tell her that she wouldn't—it wasn't his style to make false promises. "You know I don't know the answer to that."

"Will she come here, to you?" She could plan for that. She could tell him to give Amber a message, think of something to say. Already she could feel her heart picking up speed, heat coursing through her body at the pressure to think of the right words.

"I don't know."

"Well you're *useless* then." She pushed away from him, swiping at her tears and turning her back on him.

"She might not die, Emery," he said behind her.

Might. Might, might, *might.* She bit the inside of her lip to stop herself screaming at him and tried to shove the heat and the anger down. Tried to tell herself that Amber *would* be fine, because there was no alternative—it wouldn't matter what the odds said, because her sister was stronger than the odds. Look at Emery herself, after all—by rights she should have died for good when she was five.

"She'll come somewhere like this," Nick said, as if knowing that she didn't want to deal in mights and shoulds and what-ifs. "She'll have someone to help her, remember that. She won't be alone."

Emery felt her throat swell and the stinging start up in her eyes again. What form would this place take for Amber? What memory would she come back to? She looked around, only now taking stock of where they were. A garden with a pond at one end, surrounded by nettles. The smell of a barbecue, and freshly cut grass, and music coming from inside the kitchen, the doors throw open to the patio.

"I barely remember this. It was at my old house, but when?"

It was a rhetorical question, but he answered anyway. "It was before you died, the first time. You were playing in the garden, your mum and dad and sister all out here together. The radio was on, your dad putting sausages on the barbecue. Amber was reading a book and your mum was leafing through some kind of document, sipping rosé." She stared at him blankly, amazed at this level of detail. "It was the first time I met you," he said softly.

Before, she realized then; this was a memory from before everything started, before her condition, before her mum left. Was that why her brain was clawing her back here?

She took a deep breath, inhaling that summer garden smell. "Nick. What happened to Lisa?" Because she wanted to know—no point pretending otherwise. She wanted answers, so that maybe then she'd be able to move on from it. And maybe a vindictive part of her wanted to lash out at him, knowing he didn't want to talk about it, because he couldn't give her the *other* answers she needed.

"Emery." It was a warning tone.

"No—I want to know!" She sounded like a whiny child, one step away from stamping her foot. She stopped, breathed again. "Nick, I need to know. And maybe you need to talk about it, too." As she said it, she realized how right that was. Had he *ever* talked about it? Whatever *it* was? He could only ever form fleeting connections, only ever mold himself to someone else's needs. Surely that had to fuck with your head.

"You were mugged, weren't you?" she pressed. "You were mugged and stabbed. And Lisa...Was she with you? Or did you...?" But she couldn't quite bring herself to finish the sentence, because she didn't want it to be true. Didn't want the questions answered if they were not answers she could live with. *Did you do something to her? That night? Before that night? Was that why she was begging you—to get you to stop? Not to hurt her?*

He said nothing, keeping that poker face she now knew

so well, and she thought he wasn't going to tell her. Then his expression shifted, pain etching the lines of his face. He took a breath, and his whole body seemed to shudder. And with that, Emery's memory shuddered too, the scene shifting around them as she turned, trying to see what was happening.

They were in the alleyway again. Nick was standing with his back pressed against the wall, almost as if he was trying to retreat completely from the memory. Emery stood in the middle of the alley, her feet on worn concrete. It was cool and dark, a dampness in the air. Tall brick buildings towered above, and the smell of rotten food swelled around them. The traffic on the street at the end of the alleyway sounded very far away.

There was a second Nick looking into one of the bins. An alive Nick. It was dark, and she could only see the back of his neck, but she knew it was him from his build, his messy hair. He was wearing a leather jacket over jeans. "I don't see it." His Scottish accent was stronger here, in this echo of real life.

"I'm telling you, I must have dropped it in the restaurant." Emery jolted at hearing a second voice. It was a woman, standing a few meters from Nick, her arms folded. Lisa. Small and slim and blonde. Wearing a red skirt that flared out and a white shirt with a jean jacket over it. Tapping her foot—wedges—impatiently on the ground. "If they're insisting it's not there, then I'm sure they threw it out."

"It's a bright sparkly bracelet—there's no way they threw it out." There was a hint of impatience in Nick's voice—the echo of an earlier argument.

"You need to look harder."

"I can barely see anything—and I'm not rooting around in the bin."

"Nick, that bracelet cost—"

"I don't care what it cost! Why don't *you* look in the damn bin?"

He let the lid slam shut, turned to scowl at Lisa. His expression grew instantly wary, and he moved, angling his body so he stood in front of her.

"What are you—"

"Shh!"

A figure was coming toward them, the light from the street behind him, his face obscured in the shadows. Emery felt the warning shoot down her spine, looked to Nick—the real Nick—for confirmation. He wouldn't look back at her, his face a mask, though she saw in the depths of his eyes the horror of what was to come.

"I saw you two come down here," the man said, his voice a low growl, an accent she couldn't quite place. They were in Oxford, she knew—because Oxford was where Nick had died—but the accent came from somewhere else.

Nick grabbed Lisa's wrist—restraining her? Pulling her away from the man? She had frozen and didn't immediately respond.

"I'll just take your pretty purse," the man said to her, "and you, sir"—the *sir* was mocking—"you must have a tidbit or two."

Nick straightened, making himself big. He was taller than the man, but not by much. "We don't have anything to give you."

The man laughed—a hollow, hopeless sound. "I doubt that. Heard you talking about a sparkly bracelet. Cost a pretty penny too, you said."

"We've lost it," Lisa said, her voice a quaver. A horn sounded, but it was too far away. "You can look for it if you like—it's in the bin somewhere, I'm sure it is." *Smart girl*, Emery thought. Her heart was pounding despite herself. She wanted to urge Nick and Lisa to run, to dodge around the man. To somehow escape the inevitable.

"I'll do that, love." *Love.* So odd, the threat in that word, yet apologetic under it. There was a flash of silver, and Emery couldn't help herself—she gasped. Nick pulled Lisa toward the entrance to the alley, back toward the traffic, the bright street, the people laughing. But also toward the man, who was blocking their exit, holding the knife.

Lisa stumbled behind him. "Nick." Her voice was barely a whisper, and her shoulders were hunched, trying to make herself smaller. She couldn't have been older than late twenties.

"Get out of our way," Nick said, and there was a bravado there that made Emery's heart stutter. Did he think he could push past? Or did he genuinely think this man wouldn't hurt them? She glanced to the second Nick, but he gave nothing away, his face pale, fists clenched by his sides. "Come on now," said the memory Nick, "you're not scaring us." But their body language would suggest otherwise.

The man held the knife out, and his grip did not falter. "Your wallet, if you please."

Lisa handed her bag over, her hands shaking. "Here, take this."

"Thanks, love." As if she'd just handed him a cup of tea. The man looked at Nick, and Nick stared back. For a second, despite what she knew was coming, Emery thought it might be fine—she *hoped* it might be fine, that the man would let them go on their way. But then Nick's eyes dropped to the bag, a smart black one with a silver chain decorated with colored studs. His fists clenched and his eyes darkened. And Emery knew that Lisa had seen it too, the change.

"Nick, please don't." Her voice echoed around the alley, as though the memory stuttered on it. And Emery could hear how many times Nick must have replayed those words—an eternity to go over and over this moment.

He lunged and made to grab the bag, but the man was faster, and he slashed out, getting Nick right across his chest, ripping through the shirt underneath the leather jacket. Nick spun, made to punch the man, but his inexperience was obvious, while his attacker knew what he was doing—and was more desperate than Nick in the moment that counted.

It happened too quickly. A stab, then a pause before the man pulled back, blood coating the silver knife. Nick looked down at his stomach, almost surprised. Lisa screamed, and Nick fell, blood already soaking the shirt. And Emery could do nothing but watch, nothing but stand there frozen, as Lisa had been the whole time. Useless.

Then the man turned on Lisa.

"Please, no." She was backing away, but he was prowling toward her. Nick was crawling toward them too, blood smearing the concrete. The memory darkened, like someone had flicked a dimmer switch. Because Nick was dying, Emery realized. And not like how she'd died, with a sudden parting of the world, but with agonizing slowness. The scene grew dimmer still.

"Lisa." His voice barely audible, a husk, a plea.

The memory grew darker still, and Emery heard Lisa sobbing, then the sound of her smashing against the bins. One last glimpse of the scene—one last effort of Nick's to open his eyes—and she could see the man slashing at Lisa in panic, pushing her to the ground, her head cracking against asphalt. Then her eyes, dull and unfocused, looking into Nick's.

As the memory faded, they were back in the light and warmth of the garden, the smell of freshly cut grass replacing the stench of the alleyway. Emery's mouth was dry, her heartbeat in her throat. She wanted to offer some kind of comfort, but she was paralyzed by the horror of his death—of Lisa's death—and what it must have been doing to him all these years.

"Oh Nick." What did you say? *Sorry* just didn't seem big enough.

He was stiff, his muscles so taut they looked like they might snap. "It's my fault. It's my fault she died." An admission, choked out of him. How long had he been hanging on to those words?

"No," she said firmly—and she could at least offer him that. "It's *not* your fault. It's the man who—"

"It is!" He tugged at his hair, like he might pull it all from his head. And she understood it—the blame, the guilt. It wasn't the same, not by a long shot, but she still remembered, crystal clear, what her mum had said. *You were the one who wanted a second child. I can't do this. Time bomb waiting to go off.*

"When my mum left us," she said slowly, "I blamed myself. I still do, if I'm being totally honest—though I suppose I blame her more. I know it's not the same, but..." She wetted her lips as he watched her. "I know what that feels like, to think it's all your fault. But this is *not* your fault, Nick. You did not hurt Lisa. That man did."

"Your mum leaving was not your fault, Emery," he said quietly. "You were just a child."

"She couldn't handle it—couldn't handle my...condition."

"That's on her," he said firmly—so much more conviction than when he was talking about himself. "Not you."

"Well then," she said, bringing it back around to the point she was trying to make. "The same could be said of what happened to you."

He shook his head. "I could have just let it go. I could have let him have her bag—he might have let us walk away."

"*Might*, Nick. Life is full of mights." As was death, so it seemed.

"She died because of me." The words sounded dead, hopeless.

Emery could feel the stinging of her eyes again, the urge to cry for what had been done to him. And the guilt that meant he thought he deserved to be here, in this place, stuck forever between life and death. But crying would not help him now. So she went to him, took his hand.

"I didn't want to show you," he said, still in that same dead voice. "I didn't want to show you the worst of me."

She reached out, cupped his face. "Never be afraid of that. Never be afraid to show me all of you." There was the warning shake, the start of the timer counting down. There wasn't enough time to say everything they needed to.

She dropped her hand. "I thought we couldn't see people in memories." It wasn't the most important thing right now, but it was what came out.

"I don't know how I did it."

"Maybe you're more connected to that place than you thought." She tilted her face up to him, hoping for some change, for his eyes to grow less dull. *Not enough time.* "Nick, for what it's worth, I don't think you're here because you're being punished." She pressed a kiss to his cheek, heard the inhalation, felt the way his body went still—expectant. The way her own body tightened in response as their gazes locked, as a flicker of light danced in his eyes. He brought his hands to her hips, almost like he couldn't stop himself, and she lifted her hand to his neck, his skin warm and smooth there. His fingertips tightened their hold, digging in to keep her there, and she wanted to step closer, wanted to press the whole of herself against him. Wanted to forget about everything else, everything that had happened and everything that was to come, and just have him.

But they were out of time. She could see her hands growing more solid against his neck, could sense the memory dissipating around them. And she wouldn't fight to stay, because she had a sister who needed her. So she closed her eyes, pressed her forehead against his in goodbye.

"Emery." He said her name like a prayer. And she wasn't sure if she imagined his next words or if they were real, whispered through the fading memory. "Don't leave me."

Chapter Twenty-Five

Nine months later (April 2014)

AGE 35

Emery stood with her heels sinking into the grass underfoot, her breath misting out in front of her, the frosted air clinging to her bare cheeks. She should feel cold, she knew she should, but instead she only felt numb. She didn't know how she'd got through these last few hours. Didn't remember what she'd said when she'd got up in front of everyone to speak about her sister. She'd tried to think of the right words, words that encapsulated everything that was Amber, things that people should remember. She'd missed out too much. She didn't think she'd got across what a kind person Amber was—kind by nature, not because she had to try at it. How she was incredibly selfless, how she was always there for anyone who needed her, no matter what. How she'd put up with being the older sister to a sick child growing up, and never complained. How much she'd wanted children, and how happy she'd been when Lily had come along. How much she'd loved her career, because it was helping people and because she had a weird fascination with what pressure could do to muscles. How she'd handled her treatment with grace and dignity and never let on how much it was hurting her—how she'd held her head up until the end, because she'd wanted the people around her to be okay. How she'd revealed, just once, how angry she was, and how she'd bottled that up every day since, so that they'd all be able to function. How she'd been the best big sister, and mother, and girlfriend.

Wife. Amber had been a wife by the time she died. Robin and Amber had got married a few weeks ago, now that same-sex marriage was finally legalized in the UK. It had been a small ceremony, and Amber had been so weak, they'd had to make a concession to allow her to be seated. Nothing like the wedding she might have wanted—if she'd ever thought she could speculate on that. They'd done it for Lily, and for Robin, so that Amber would be theirs legally as well as in all the ways that counted.

Lily, who was now five years old, and who would barely remember the mother who had loved her so much.

There were a lot of people around her grave now, though Emery stood a little back, not wanting to be in the crowd, not willing to admit that this was really happening. There wasn't a headstone yet—that would come. Robin had already asked Emery for her opinion, and Emery had tried to function, to offer her thoughts, for Robin's sake. Because Robin, having been a rock for Amber throughout the whole process, had lost it entirely when she'd died. She'd not been eating, or sleeping, and little Lily didn't understand why one mummy wasn't coming back and the other one was broken. They were all trying to help, but Emery couldn't see how they'd get through it. Couldn't see an end to the way she felt—like everything she knew and loved had been ripped from her.

Robin was crying, up at the front of the crowd on this field of dead people, Lily holding her hand. And Emery couldn't make herself go to her to offer support and comfort. Couldn't make herself do anything other than stare. But Robin's mum was with her—and so were Emery's parents. Her dad *and* her mum. She was trying not to look at her mum, though she'd felt her gaze on her during the funeral. She'd spoken to her a few times, all about Amber, and she recognized the grief she saw in her mum's face—an older face than the one she remembered, the one she'd thought of whenever she'd wished for her over the years, or wished her away. Gray hair, lined skin, different glasses. She was in her mid sixties, but she looked older than Emery's dad. She'd left because she couldn't handle the fact that one daughter might die, and now the other daughter was dead. Amber was *dead*, in the ground. It wasn't fair. It should be Emery—she should have died long ago. It felt like the universe was evening things out, making up for her multiple chances at life by stripping Amber of hers.

Colin came up behind her, put a hand on her shoulder. She didn't even flinch. "Come on, I'll drive you home." He was in a black suit and tie, and his blue eyes looked red-rimmed and swollen.

"I don't have a home," she said numbly. She'd been staying with her dad, but she wasn't sure she could handle going back there—the two of them pulled apart by grief. Her mum was offering him comfort now, over by Amber's grave—one parent to another. Emery had offered to stay with Robin, but Robin had said no, and Emery hadn't pushed—maybe Robin needed to be alone, maybe she needed to break down with no one watching.

"You can come back to mine," Colin said. He steered her away, out of the graveyard and toward his car, and she let him, because what else was there to do?

* *

She woke in the middle of the night, and it took her a moment to realize where she was. In Colin's flat, in his room—he'd insisted she take the double bed and he have the sofa. It smelled a little musty. And over that, something distinctly him. She'd never really noticed his smell before—woody and musky and as familiar as her own. For a heartbeat, she was confused about why she was here. That was the way it had been for days now—the first seconds on waking blissfully blank, before the awfulness of what had happened settled in.

She crawled out of bed, feeling panicky. She wanted to leave—not the flat, but the world. She had been expecting to see Nick when Amber died. Hoping for it at the funeral—hoping something would shock her there to the one person she thought might have a chance at comforting her. He'd understand—he'd lost someone he loved. He was who she wanted to be with. It wasn't *fair* that she'd lost Amber, the one person she'd assumed would always be there, and now she couldn't get to the one person who never was.

She crept into the living room. Colin's flat was near Luton, right on the outskirts of London—he'd bought it, and it was all he could afford on a journalist's salary, even if it did mean a nightmare commute. He was awake on the sofa—whether he'd been unable to sleep or whether she'd woken him up by coming in, she didn't know. "Will you come and sleep next to me? I can't be alone."

He got to his feet without question and followed her back to the bedroom. He settled down next to her and she pressed against his side, her back to him. He put an arm around her, and that woody scent wrapped her up like a blanket. Neither of them said anything. He'd lost Amber too. Maybe not in the same way, but he'd known her practically his whole life. She'd been a constant for both of them. There was a comfort in that, in knowing that he might have an inkling of what she was going through. Enough that she turned, looked at him, their heads on the same pillow.

"Are you okay?" he whispered.

She shook her head. No, she was not okay. But more than that—no, she did not want to talk about it. So instead she shifted toward him and kissed him on the mouth, brief, but firm, gauging his reaction. He did nothing, just stayed perfectly still, so she reached out, ran a hand up his bare arm. She felt him stiffen, saw the way he was watching her.

"Emery." He spoke her name cautiously, a warning perhaps. She shook her head again and leaned into him. She needed this. She needed to feel something, needed the distraction. And this time, he kissed her back, hesitantly, and she felt his arm tighten around her. He loved her. She knew he loved her. And it was wrong and horrible and selfish of her, but right now she needed that love. She needed someone to comfort her. She wanted to feel real, to feel grounded, to feel anything other than this never-ending numbness. In that moment, she needed *him*.

He broke away. "Emery, I don't think you want—" But she ignored him and pushed him lightly onto his back. She bent down over him, her curls forming a curtain around their faces, and kissed him again, and now he kissed her back properly, his tongue in her mouth, his hands skimming down to her waist, tugging her toward him. His mouth moved to her neck, warm breath caressing her skin, her ear, and when she said his name, it was a plea.

He flipped her so she was under him and waited there, looking into her eyes. She met his gaze. Yes, this was what she wanted. Please, this was what she wanted. He bent his head to kiss the corner of her mouth, then down, toward her chest, his hands skimming under her pajamas, finding bare skin. She closed her eyes, lifted her hands above her head so he could tug off her top. Concentrated on the feel of him, of his hands caressing her breasts, then lower, dipping beneath her bottoms. Yes, this. Anything. Anything to take her away from herself, even if it was only fleeting.

Chapter Twenty-Six

Two months later (June 2014)

AGE 35

Emery stood outside the cream-colored building, thinking it looked more like a block of flats than anything else. There were tables and chairs on the neatly manicured front lawn, and big glass windows that glinted in the spring sunlight. The building was tall, a little imposing, and it almost seemed to frown down at her, like it knew why she was there and disapproved.

Her feet ached. She'd been walking round Oxford mindlessly for several hours, not really thinking, just wanting to get a sense of the city, of where Nick had lived. She'd tried to imagine him with her as she'd passed under historic archways, surrounded by the light golden buildings, or stared at the outside of the Bodleian Library, wondering if he had once sat inside it. She'd imagined him holding her hand, pointing out the best places to have a coffee or taking her to the river for punting. She'd thought of Amber too—there wasn't really a time when she didn't think of her. She'd seen a café-slash-bookshop and for an instant she'd caught a glance of long brown hair, the exact shade of Amber's, and her heart had stuttered. Before she'd crashed down with the realization that of course Amber wouldn't be here—she'd never even been to Oxford, as far as she knew—and that by the end, Amber's hair was far from long and silky, like that of the girl in the window. So yes, her feet felt exhausted, but the exhaustion went deeper than that, taking hold of every cell in her body. Two months. It had been two months since Amber's funeral, and she still felt like she was just going through the motions, like the numbness she felt would never end. Except for the nights when it *did* end and grief overwhelmed her and she sobbed and curled into a ball and wished that she would just fall asleep and never wake up, because that would be better, wouldn't it, than feeling like this. Than knowing there was no way out.

She took a steadying breath of the damp air. More rain was forecast over the next few days, and everyone was going on and on about how much rain they'd had this month, how it should be clearer and brighter than it was. Like it *mattered* whether it rained or not. Like anything fucking mattered.

She forced herself to move to the front door of the building in front of her, pushed it open and stepped through into a reception area. It was bright inside, with vases of flowers dotted all around—one on a round table in the middle of the room, one on the reception desk just behind, and one to the left, on a shelf between two light blue armchairs. She walked across the sleek wooden floor to the reception desk. There was classical music playing in the background, but it still seemed too quiet, and she felt conspicuous, like it was obvious she wasn't supposed to be here.

But she'd had to come. This was Lisa's last-known address—though the building had been listed under a different name, before the care home had set up shop. But even though the name had changed, perhaps they still knew what had happened to Lisa—where she'd been buried, maybe. And maybe she'd been buried with Nick.

She'd tracked the details down without Colin's help—Colin, who she'd put in a corner of her mind and decided it was best to leave him there. She'd barely spoken to him since the funeral, and on some level, she knew that made her a bad friend, maybe even a bad person, but she couldn't face the questions, couldn't face it if he were to look at her differently or want something that she couldn't give. She didn't know what to say to him, and she couldn't really work out her feelings, tangled and on mute as they currently were. So it was better to leave it until she was able to deal with all those things. Until she knew what she should say, what she *wanted* to say.

A nurse looked up at her from behind the reception desk, wearing a purple shirt over navy blue trousers, her dark blonde hair, graying at the roots, pulled into a bun. She took her glasses off, and they hung around her neck on a chain. "Hello, hun, are you here to see someone?"

"No, I…" Emery paused, trying to think of how to phrase it. Then she decided she didn't care what the nurse thought, didn't care that it might sound weird. "I wanted to find out about someone who used to live here. Lisa Hartington. This was the last address I could find for her, and…"

But the nurse was looking at her in a bemused sort of way, head at a tilt so that the glasses shifted to one side of her collarbone. "Lisa Hartington? She's still here, hun."

Emery stared at her, uncomprehending. "But she…" She swallowed. "Her address says Oakwood House."

"That's right. That's what this place used to be called, before it was bought by someone else. By us, I should say. It was before my time, but Lisa stayed—her parents didn't want to move her, see. Not got any family left now, poor love—her mum and dad died, and she never married. I think there was a fiancé once, but he's dead too, so I hear. Unless… You're not family, are you?"

"No, I'm…" But Emery was reeling, unable to process what she was hearing. "She's here? Lisa Hartington? She'd be in her sixties now, I think, or thereabouts. Blonde, quite petite." The description she gave was vague, and could quite possibly be wrong, based on a Lisa she'd seen in 1979. But this couldn't be right—Lisa had died, she'd seen it.

"Yes, hun, she's still here. You know her then, do you?"

"I…" Emery pressed her tongue against the roof of her dry mouth. "I know her fiancé's family." That didn't really make sense, because Nick's parents were long dead and he had no brothers or sisters, but the nurse nodded, pursing her lips slightly as she considered Emery in a new light. Her heart was beating fast, and the sensation of her body waking up after weeks in the "off" position was not pleasant.

"Would you like to see her? She never gets visitors. I just need you to sign in." And what else was there to do? She had to see, had to know. So Emery followed the nurse's instructions, the pen feeling slippery against her clammy palm, her pulse beating a warning drum against her wrist. Then the nurse led her through the glass doors of the reception area and down a corridor, past closed white doors, through a kitchen where someone was making a cup of tea, and to a bright open living space beyond. The residents of the care home were dotted around the room, some staring out of the big windows to the garden beyond, two people sitting opposite each other over a game of chess. Beyond them was a woman lying back on a recliner chair, facing the window.

The nurse glanced at Emery briefly, as if gauging her reaction, then led her toward the woman. She was unrecognizable from the Lisa Emery had seen in the alleyway. Her hair was short and white, falling in waves around her face—a face that was lined and somehow soft, the muscles slack. Her eyes were open, and they were a light blue—something Emery hadn't noticed in Nick's memory. Those eyes did not seem to register that there were two people standing over her.

"Lisa?" the nurse said, and Emery wondered why she was speaking so loudly. Maybe Lisa was deaf. She did not seem to have heard the nurse. Emery could only stare at her. Lisa was alive. She needed to tell Nick. All this blame he'd been holding on to—and here she was, alive. "Lisa, I've got a visitor for you." Nothing. Emery felt her stomach twist. This wasn't right. She could see now that it was only the reclining chair that was holding Lisa up, her head lolling back against it, her eyes fixed on the window without seeming to know what was out there.

"Lisa, follow my finger if you can hear me," the nurse said, a clear command. Lisa's eyes followed the nurse's index finger, back and forth before her face, and Emery sucked in a breath.

The nurse nodded at her. But to do what? It was clear that although Lisa was alive, she very much wasn't okay. Emery swallowed. She had to try. For Nick, she had to try. "Lisa? I'm..." *Oh God.* "I'm a friend of Nick's." No reaction.

"She responds to pressure on her hand sometimes," the nurse said, her voice gentle.

Emery took the older woman's frail, paper-like hand. It was soft; someone had clearly taken care to moisturize her skin regularly. Her own hand shook, even as she tried to control it. "Do you remember Nick, Lisa?" she asked in a whisper. "Squeeze my hand if you can hear me." She almost jumped, nearly dropped Lisa's hand. That had definitely been a squeeze. But Lisa's face stayed vacant, her eyes apparently unseeing.

Emery released her hand and stepped back. She looked at the nurse. "How...?"

"Maybe we should have a little chat."

**

Up on the bridge, the wind tugged through her hair. Emery stared down at the traffic below—everyone moving so fast, so determined to get somewhere. Where? Where was so important to get to? It seemed baffling to her in that moment—she had no desire to go anywhere at all.

She'd stopped a few miles out of Oxford, needing to get

out of the car, to breathe, to think. Lisa was alive. It was like a mantra in her mind. She needed to tell Nick. Even if...Yes, Lisa might be alive, but the cost...

It was raining. She was only just registering that now, light misty droplets coating her jacket, the tips of her fingers turning wet and cool. Wind caressed the back of her neck, and she shivered. She needed to get home, check on her dad. Needed to apply for more jobs, mindlessly, carelessly, as she'd been doing. Needed to answer Colin's latest message, stop being a terrible friend. Needed to call Robin, to visit Lily. It was overwhelming, the weight of all these needs—yet it all seemed abstract, separate from her. Right now, she felt rootless, like she could step off this bridge and gravity wouldn't even pull her down. And wasn't that the thing? She *was* rootless in so many ways—her whole life she'd been rootless, without the anchor to life most people had, aware that one mistake, one small shock, and that could be it. Yet she kept coming back—as close to immortal as one could get. But she didn't want to be immortal. She didn't want this to be endless.

She stared down off the bridge again, to the hard, unyielding tarmac below. It would be so easy to take a step. To claim a death that would not be temporary. To see Nick one last time—and be done.

She placed her hands on the ledge, the concrete rough against her palms. She pushed, her arms quivering a little with the effort, showing how weak she was right now. She'd just stand up on the edge of the bridge. Just stand up there and see how it felt.

"Um, excuse me?" She heard the voice behind her but didn't

turn, only pulled her other leg up onto the ledge, now kneeling there. The traffic sounded distant, but it couldn't be, it should be loud. Then she felt someone behind her grabbing her arm, pulling her back from the edge. And that was it. That was the shock she'd been waiting for.

Chapter Twenty-Seven

"What do you think you were *doing*?" Nick's voice was harsh, with none of the comfort that she'd been craving from him. He was walking toward her across a small bedroom with twin beds; she was standing at the other side, her back to the window, next to a small sink with two children's toothbrushes. He was looking at her intently, eyebrows pulled together, body stiff. Not the calm presence she was sure he was supposed to be in this place—that he had been so many times before. She thought of what he'd said when she'd last seen him, what she *thought* he'd said.

Don't leave me.

She'd thought he would be delighted to see her again, would scoop her into his arms, press a kiss to her hair. That was the reunion she wanted, and the lack of it made her defensive, so that her voice was a snap as she folded her arms. "I wasn't doing anything. You saw what happened—a stranger grabbed me and I—"

"That's not the whole story and you know it." He took another step toward her, forcing her to tilt her head to look up at him. "What were you doing on that bridge, Emery? What were you going to do?"

She didn't answer—because she wasn't actually sure she *knew* the answer. Instead, she looked around the small room. It was a B&B, you could tell by the decor. The twin beds had matching linen—blue and white striped duvet covers, pillows with blue and purple flowers. The wallpaper was a faded green, and there were bright paintings, abstract in style, with bold colors and shapes, opposite the beds. A faint smell of bacon hovered in the air. She felt a tug of recognition, which would make sense—it was her memory. And she could hear Amber's laugh. Not here, echoing through the landscape, but in her mind. A younger Amber, a childhood giggle.

"What were you going to do, Emery?" Nick repeated the question, but she kept her arms folded, staring him out. He rubbed one hand across his face, then dropped it and loosened a breath. "I know this has been hard for you—"

"You don't *know*, though, do you?" She gave him a scathing look, one designed to cut. "You haven't been there watching Amber getting sicker and sicker and being able to do nothing to help, while the doctors say they've done all they can. You weren't there at the funeral, having to listen to condolences, watching as everyone tried to accept that this could happen, hearing people talk all around about how *unfair* it was. You haven't had to face the aftermath for the last two months, haven't been there to help me try to pull my fucking life back together."

He had paled slightly, and his expression had changed,

his features no longer set in a frown. "Your sister?" His voice was soft, a little raspy.

"That's right. She's dead. Gone." And the stricken look on Nick's face made it worse somehow, because she'd been hoping... "She didn't come here? To you?"

"No. I'm sorry."

"Well then." She turned her back on him, not wanting him to see the disappointment and new grief etched there. She looked out of the window, to a small cottage-like garden, where insects would no doubt be humming around the flowers. Deep down she had been clinging on to the thought that maybe Nick would be able to pass on a message to her from Amber. That maybe she'd be able to cheat, be offered something no one else ever would be, because of her connection with this place, with him. But no. Losing that last hope was *crushing*; her insides caved in, something vital being scooped from her. She glanced over her shoulder at him. "Like I said, you don't know the first fucking *thing* about how hard this has been for me."

He was quiet for a moment. Then, "You're right, I don't know. I wish I did. I wish I could have been there for you. It's been driving me mad, not knowing. But that doesn't change the fact that..." She heard the swallow. "You need to try, Emery."

She turned to face him, gave a scornful laugh, felt something hot and bitter rise in her. "Who are you to talk about trying? You're punishing yourself—are you just going to be here eternally, holding on to that blame? What happened to you was shit—more than that. I don't have the words. But beating yourself up clearly isn't doing you any good, because why are you still here? *You're* not trying, are you? Not trying to move on, not trying to feel better, not trying to let go of the guilt you feel. So don't fucking lecture me, Nick."

He said nothing, and his expression shuttered, his poker face returning—the expression he reverted to whenever he was trying to cover up what he was really feeling. "I didn't mean to upset you."

"Well you did." She crossed to the sink, stared at the two toothbrushes—one bright blue (hers) and one red. Amber's. A holiday they'd taken, the four of them—and the first time she and Amber had shared a room. She felt her eyes sting as she reached out, picked up Amber's toothbrush. It felt small and ever so breakable. God, it *hurt*. She wanted to run from the room, sprint downstairs, find Amber in the kitchen, maybe eating a bacon sandwich. She wanted to be back here, where her biggest concern was Amber teasing her because she was snoring in the night, even when she was sure she wasn't. But she couldn't. This place was an echo of the past, and she couldn't go back there, much as she wished she could.

She put the toothbrush back in the holder, turned to lean on the sink. "She's alive, Nick."

He stared at her. "What?"

"Lisa. She's alive."

He went very still. "That's not possible. You saw what happened."

Emery took a breath. Then she started to explain—about tracking Lisa down, meeting her. About the fact that after she'd been in intensive care, she'd been moved by her parents to a place able to look after her. She explained what the nurse had told her—that Lisa had sustained severe brain trauma that night when she'd hit her head on the asphalt. She'd been in a coma, and though she'd woken up, started showing signs of recovery, that recovery had halted.

"A minimally conscious state?" Nick repeated, his voice flat.

"Yes." She explained what that meant—or as much as she understood from what she'd been told. A person who showed minimal or inconsistent awareness. Someone who might only be able to respond to commands, such as following the nurse's finger or squeezing Emery's hand.

Nick's own hands were clenched into fists by his sides and his face had grown paler. "Will she... Will she recover?"

She hesitated. She was sure he knew the answer, because of how long it had been. But she understood the need for it to be stated outright, like she had wanted to know what would happen to Amber when she died, like her dad had wanted the doctors to tell him exactly when and how many times Emery's heart would stop, so they could be prepared. It was the not knowing, sometimes, that was worse. "I don't think so," she said. "It sounds like sometimes people go through it after they come out of a coma and are on the route to recovery—but it's sometimes permanent. And I think—the *nurse* thinks—that after all this time..." She stepped toward Nick, her anger with him abating in the face of his pain. She took one of his hands in hers. "She didn't die that night, Nick."

He pulled his hand from hers, shaking his head and backing

away from her, nearly stumbling into one of the beds. "But this is worse! She's been stuck like that, *trapped*, all this time." He ran both hands through his hair. Then he dropped them, his body slumping in on itself. "That's why *I'm* trapped." His voice was a husk of itself—but it was certain.

"What? No, Nick, I—"

"It makes sense, doesn't it? That I'll be trapped as long as she is. I'm the reason it happened to her, aren't I? If I hadn't..." He swallowed, and the action looked painful. "She's been living between wakefulness and unconsciousness, and so am I, right?"

He was looking at her like he'd solved a puzzle, like he wanted her to agree. "I don't think that's right," she said slowly.

"It is!"

She threw her hands in the air. "Fine, then! Keep blaming yourself." The bitterness had risen in her again, and she wasn't entirely sure where it was coming from. At everything, she thought. Bitterness at everything.

A tremor ran through the B&B, like an earthquake shaking the building.

"No," Emery whispered. She folded her arms across her stomach. "No, I don't want to go back. I can't." She closed her eyes. "I can't face it."

"You can." His voice was as firm as it had been moments ago, but it was softer now.

"I can't."

She felt him draw nearer, opened her eyes to see he'd closed the gap between them. "You *can*, Emery. You have to. There is more out there for you, I know that." He reached out, ran his thumb along her cheekbone. "Death will come, sooner or later, but you don't have to chase it. You can try to make the most of life, you can be there for your niece, you can find something you love." He hesitated, then added, "Your sister would want you to."

She flinched back from his touch. "That's not fair."

He offered her a self-deprecating smile. "Life isn't fair. Neither is death."

"But I want to stay here. With you. I..." She took a breath, reached out to take both his hands. "I love you, Nick."

He pulled away from her grip, and she felt the lack of warmth like a shock. "You can't." His voice was harsh, almost as harsh as when she'd first got here. Pain ripped through her. She moved to the bed, needing to sit, and looked down at her knees to hide her face.

"Well I do." She'd never said it to anyone she'd dated before. Never *felt* it with anyone.

She could feel Nick's eyes on her but didn't want to look up. "You mustn't."

And there it was. Another person pulling away from her. Her mum, then Amber, even if it wasn't Amber's choice, and now Nick. She closed her eyes, tried to breathe through the pain. She felt the bed creak as he came to sit behind her. "Emery." He reached out for her hand, and she shifted away. Why? Why couldn't he just *lie*? Couldn't he see that was what she needed? "I don't want...You can't live for these moments with me. You can't want to be here more than you want to be where you belong."

"Who's to say where I belong?" she murmured, bringing her knees to her chest and resting her chin there, like she'd done when she was little.

"You're not immortal, Emery."

It was so close to what she'd been thinking on the bridge. And yet... "For fuck's sake, don't you think I know that? I'm constantly faced with my own mortality—isn't the fact that I'm here, again and again, proof of that?"

"But you keep going back, and that's a version of immortality, isn't it?" She scowled, but he carried on. He'd brushed it off. He'd just brushed off what she'd said to him, and now he was giving her a fucking lecture? "Sooner or later you *will* die, and when that happens, we won't get a happily-ever-after. You won't be able to stay here, with me. You will die—really die—and I don't want the next time I see you to be the end for you. I want more for you, Emery."

If they were anyone else, if they were both alive and allowed to be with one another, if they could spend time together without the sense of a ticking clock, without the knowledge that every moment here strained Emery's connection to her body, then maybe they could take their time with this. But as it was, they did not have that time—and Nick clearly knew it.

He took hold of her chin, angled her face toward him. Like a sullen child, she refused to meet his gaze. "Promise me? Promise me you'll try."

"I can't." Because the effort of even promising felt like too much. But as she thought that, she could feel her body calling her, her heart valiantly trying to restart. It would keep trying, even if she wouldn't.

"Look at me, Emery! You'll regret it if you don't try. I've seen enough to know. You'll regret it at the end."

She shook her head—as much as she could with him holding her chin. God, she felt tired. Even here, with him, she felt tired. "I didn't come here for this." The words were out before she could think better of them, hinting that it might have been a choice to come here. Was it? Would she have done it? She didn't know the answer to that. She powered on before he could notice. "I don't want to be told that I'll never forgive myself or whatever."

"Not just you," he whispered. The change in his tone of voice made her look at him, finally. His eyes were intense on hers, trying, perhaps, to look deeper into her. She shivered slightly. "*I'll* never forgive myself, Emery, if you die without trying to live."

She didn't know what to say to that—and the memory had started to fade, his hand less substantial on her face.

"I'll make you a deal," he said, speaking quickly now. "Maybe not today, maybe not tomorrow, but sometime, when you're ready, you pick yourself up and you try. Try to find something to hold on to, to put your guilt aside and live. And if you do that, I will try too. I will try to accept what happened. I will try to stop blaming myself. Okay? Okay, Emery?"

She felt the graze of his hand against hers, barely more than a whisper. But she was gone before she could answer.

**

"She's alive!"

"Oh Jesus. Oh God. I thought…"

There was a light being shone in her eyes, too bright. She tried to turn her head, felt it spin. Only then did she realize that she wasn't on the bridge. She wasn't outside. She blinked, trying to draw her surroundings into focus. There was a woman holding her hand—the woman who had tried to grab her, pull her back from the ledge? And a man in green was looking down at her, holding a defibrillator. There was a siren, and it was close. And she was on a stretcher.

"We're getting you to the hospital," the man in green said. "You're going to be okay."

But she nearly hadn't been okay. She'd been gone long enough to have woken up in an ambulance. How much longer would her body have coped without her heart before it was damaged irrevocably? Before her brain shut off?

As the man placed an emergency blanket over her, the woman next to her half sobbing, half crying, she thought of what Nick had said. *I'll make you a deal.* And they owed it to each other, didn't they?

She would, she promised herself. Promised him. She hadn't answered him when she was with him, but she answered him now.

I'll try, Nick.

And trying was all she could offer. Trying would have to be enough.

Chapter Twenty-Eight

Two years later (August 2016)

AGE 37

"The roast beef?"

"Yes, darling," Helen said. "That's the rare one, isn't it?"

"As rare as we could find, yes."

The waiter carried on handing round the plates of roast meat—and a filo asparagus tart for Emery—while Robin encouraged Lily to put her coloring to one side. Lily's tongue was poking out of the side of her mouth, and she seemed not to hear her mother, though whether that was on purpose or not it was hard to tell.

"Come on, Lily, you like roast lunch. And we got you extra gravy, look." The allure of extra gravy was enough to get Lily to comply, and she pushed her pencils out of the way and picked up her knife and fork. Seven years old. How was Lily already seven?

"What do you think?" Emery's mum asked, topping up Helen's glass of red wine. "Shall we get another bottle?"

"Oh, I should think so." For someone who had disapproved vocally of Alice leaving, Helen was being welcoming enough now as she caught the waiter, who was bringing over their sides, and asked for another bottle of Malbec. Emery's dad caught her eye and winked, and Emery smiled as she cut into her tart.

This was their second family lunch on Amber's birthday. The first one, last year, had been hard. It had seemed almost morbid celebrating Amber's birthday without her. It had been Robin who had suggested it, wanting to make sure that Lily still had contact with Amber's side of the family. And of course, Emery could hardly argue with that. It had felt right, too, to be around people who had known and loved Amber, and she'd come round to the idea a little after talking it through with Robin. Amber needed to be celebrated, Robin had insisted, and not forgotten—and she was right, wasn't she? So here they were, all doing their best to fumble through.

Helen held out the new bottle of wine the waiter had brought over and topped up Robin's glass, then moved to top up Emery's too, but Emery stopped her. "I can't, I'm driving."

"Oh, that sounds terribly boring—why?"

"I'm heading to Oxford after lunch."

"Why ever would you want to go to Oxford?" Said as if no one had ever heard of such a thing.

"I'm meeting someone there." Emery spoke vaguely, trying to prevent further questioning. In truth, she'd been to see Lisa a few times now, and this was the perfect opportunity to go again. The meal was being held in Derby, a point that was accessible enough for Robin to come down from Scotland, her dad and Helen from Cambridge, and Emery from Bristol, where she was settling in ready to start her course.

Because she'd kept her promise to Nick—she *was* trying. She had applied for—and got into—a master's in counseling and psychotherapy. Three years of part-time study, lots of work-based learning, and a fuck ton of money she'd have to dredge up from somewhere.

So she was killing two birds with one stone before she headed back to the south-west. Because since finding out that Lisa was still alive, she hadn't been able to forget about her. She felt she owed it to Lisa—she was the only living person who knew about her, it seemed, or at least the only person not to have given up on her. She was the only one who understood exactly what had happened that night. And she felt she owed it to Nick, too. He'd want to offer Lisa comfort if he could. Though having seen her a few times now, a part of Emery wondered if it would be kinder to let her go, given that she wasn't living in any true sense of the word. But she wasn't reliant on machines to keep her alive, so the law was tricky—and her parents hadn't conceded the idea of letting her die, apparently clinging on to hope that she might regain consciousness. And their instruction was the last one anyone had given.

"So, Robin," Helen asked, "how's Glasgow?"

"Rainy," Robin answered—the obligatory answer. "Did you know that it's the second rainiest city in Scotland?"

"The only surprise, my darling, is that it's not the rainiest."

"That would be Greenock," Robin replied, spearing a piece of broccoli. "Just down the road, with an average of 174.6 days of rainfall per year."

"Well, do remind me of that if I ever get the inclination to move to Greenock."

"But Lily likes her new school," Robin carried on, "don't you, Lily?"

Lily nodded her agreement, her mouth full of roast potato. What did she think, seeing her mum's family like this? How much did she remember of Amber? Robin had told Emery that they talked about her a lot, that she had photos of her up in Lily's room—that she was determined for Lily to know how much Amber had loved her. Robin was a braver woman than many, Emery had decided. There were some who would be unable to talk about it, to keep the memory alive, and she felt so incredibly lucky that Robin was not one of them. Amber had picked a good one in Robin—and there was a glimmer of happiness at that thought, under the wave of sadness.

Robin looked well, Emery thought. A little tired, perhaps, but well. Her hair had grown out a bit, though it was still short, a style only those with good cheekbones could pull off. Her Scottish accent had become stronger since moving back up there—Lily would no doubt pick up an accent too.

"How's the university?" Emery asked.

"Oh, it's great, actually. Better than I expected, if I'm totally honest." Emery knew it hadn't been easy, the decision to take up a new job, in a new city. Being a single parent was hard work, and even with everyone helping out, the burden would always fall on Robin. She knew it was part of why they'd moved back to Scotland, to be nearer to Robin's parents.

Once, Robin might have gone off on a little rant about

her research, but right now she went back to eating her roast. Maybe it would come back, that vibrancy, the love of what she did shining through. Maybe she'd get it again around other people, if not Amber's family. The thought tugged at Emery.

"How about you, Mum? How's London?"

Her mum jumped at Emery addressing her, nearly spilling gravy onto her lap. She was wearing a smart dress with a blazer over it, more suitable as office attire than for a pub lunch, in Emery's opinion. Her hair had grayed out completely, but Emery remembered that it used to be the exact shade of Amber's. They'd been told, growing up, that Amber looked more like their mum, Emery their dad. Was this what Amber would have looked like if she'd lived until her sixties? She forced herself to breathe through the flare of pain.

"Oh, it's, you know, London. Never a dull moment. Though I have to admit, I'm struggling now I don't have an office to go into. I've been thinking of taking up some consultancy work to fill the time."

Emery noticed how her dad was concentrating particularly hard on chewing. He too was abstaining from the wine so he could drive. It must be so weird for him, sitting at a table with his ex-wife. But he'd risen above the old resentment, better and sooner than Emery had—and she'd come to the conclusion that if he could do it, so could she.

The waiter came over at the end of the meal to clear their plates. "How was everything for you today?"

"Well, darling, the beef—"

But her dad talked over Helen. "It was wonderful, thank you."

"Anyone for dessert?"

"Lily, would you like ice cream?" Robin asked, brushing the vegetables that had managed to escape Lily's plate onto her own before handing it to the waiter.

"Vanilla!"

The waiter smiled. "Vanilla ice cream, coming up."

Emery smiled at Lily, then glanced at Robin. "That was Amber's favorite growing up, too."

"Really? She was always a strawberry girl to me—strawberry cheesecake swirl, if we could get it."

Emery felt the lump swell, swallowed it down. And saw it reflected in Robin's eyes. It would get easier, she told herself. Already, it was amazing that she could say her sister's name without breaking down. Someday, she knew, she would be able to reminisce and laugh about memories of Amber—and when that time came, she would need Robin.

"Here, Lily," she said, distracting herself and pulling over a sheet of Lily's paper, helping herself to a couple of coloring pencils. "I'll show you how to draw a cat."

Lily rolled her eyes. "I can already draw a cat, Auntie Em."

Emery laughed. She could laugh. That was something, wasn't it? "Okay. How about a manatee, then?"

"What's a manatee?"

"I'll show you."

When lunch was over, they all headed into the parking lot

together, hunching their shoulders against the slight drizzle. Emery turned to hug Robin goodbye before she and Lily got into their taxi to the station. "Don't be a stranger," Robin said.

"Never."

"You know you're welcome any time, right? As long as you don't mind a stay in the second rainiest city in the world."

"I thought it was only the second rainiest in Scotland?"

Robin waved a hand in the air. "Same thing, as far as I'm concerned."

"Not very scientific of you, is it?" Robin grinned, and it occurred to Emery how little she knew her, really. As her sister's partner, yes, but only as an addendum to Amber, not as a person in her own right. She'd change that, she promised herself, as she held out her arms to Lily for a hug. Lily jumped into them with the agility you only have when you're young, and Emery breathed in the smell of her. She knew she had to be imagining it, but she could have sworn she could smell Amber's peppermint scent.

"Miss you, little Lils." She squeezed her niece tight. But she understood why Robin had had to move. Cambridge would always be Amber's place—the place they'd met, the place they'd lived, the place Amber had died.

Emery put Lily down and Robin took her hand. "Come on, let's go and say bye to Grandad and Great-Auntie Helen."

Emery laughed. "She'll hate that—she only wants to be Auntie."

Robin grinned back at her. "That's why it's fun."

Emery found herself standing next to her mum. There was a

moment of awkwardness as a car engine started behind them. Should they hug? Neither of them seemed to be able to bridge that gap, and Emery wondered if it would ever stop being difficult between them. Probably not—it had already gone on too long.

Her mum fiddled with her glasses, slipping them down her nose then pushing them back up. "You'll let me know if you're ever in London?"

"I will." She didn't know much about her mum's London life—only snippets. That she'd retired, and was clearly already bored of that. She thought she might have a partner, but his name had only been mentioned once or twice, and she knew they weren't living together. Maybe one day Emery would meet him. It all felt fragile at the moment, and it was still hard not to feel resentful, not to remember the fact that she'd left—and why.

But now was not the time to say any of that. "It was good to see you, Mum."

Her mum smiled, perhaps sensing the half-truth. Emery's memories of her were only vague, really—sitting in the kitchen discussing homelessness. Her mum being late back from work and complaining of tiredness. Telling her dad to let her do things. Watching TV together and chatting about the ridiculousness of plot lines as a teenager. Easter egg hunts in the garden when she was little. Flashes of a life that she didn't fit into anymore. But she could try, she told herself. She would keep trying.

Her dad came to hug her goodbye as Helen and her mum

made a show of kissing each other on the cheek. "Safe drive, okay?"

"Oh, you know me, I'm always safe." It was an old joke between them, but he gave her a long look as she said it.

Then he sighed. "I'm sorry, you know."

Emery frowned. "What do you mean? Sorry for what?"

"I know I do that a lot. Tell you to be safe, to be careful."

"That's okay," Emery said slowly, not sure why this was coming up now. "You're a dad, it's kind of the thing, isn't it?"

"I know, but I..." He glanced over at her mum. It was her presence that was making him think of this, clearly. Echoes of old arguments over who was right, how they should manage a sick child who was only sick occasionally, and then violently, terrifyingly. "I shouldn't have tried to stop you doing things because I was worried."

Emery gave him a wry smile. "I hate to tell you this, but I did a lot of those things anyway, regardless of whether you told me not to."

"I know, but... Maybe if I hadn't tried to stop you, you wouldn't have felt the need to push yourself so much to do them."

Emery looked at him. At the lined face she knew so well, which had become suddenly, shockingly older over the last few years, like it had happened overnight.

"It's only because I love you, you know," he said quietly, and it brought a lump to her throat, though she didn't let herself cry. It still didn't take much to set her off, especially around the family. *Grief is circular*, she'd heard someone say once. And it was true—that circle might become bigger, but it always came back around.

But for now, she made herself smile and hug him. "I love you too, Dad."

* *

The drive to the care home in Oxford took less time than she'd expected—she was there in two and a half hours, ready for evening visiting. She smiled at the nurse as she entered the reception. The flowers in the vases were all white and purple today, though she didn't know enough about flowers to name them. She took a breath, geared herself up. It was a strange sort of torture, doing this over and over.

"Hi, I'm here to see—"

But the nurse's face fell before she'd even finished. "Oh hun. I wish you'd called."

Chapter Twenty-Nine

Emery swung her front door wide open, beamed at Colin and Bonnie. "You're here!" She ushered them both inside her tiny one-bedroom flat on the outskirts of Bristol. The kitchen was more a kitchenette, really, and the shower was small enough to make you feel claustrophobic—and in order to have both Bonnie and Colin to stay, she'd had to ask Colin to bring his airbed—but she'd pick this any day rather than going back to sharing a flat. Her master's didn't actually start until September, a few weeks from now, but she'd moved early in order to get to know the city, and Bonnie and Colin had come for the weekend to celebrate her step either into adulthood or back into twenty-somethingdom. Emery knew it was also to check up on her, and she was grateful.

Bonnie gave her a hug, then shoved a bottle of Prosecco at her. "For you. But also for me, because it's my first night away from Abi. Oh God, maybe I should call Joe. Colin, do you have my phone?"

Colin was putting down two overnight bags beside the front door. "Yes, I picked it up off the passenger seat, but why don't you give it a minute before you call him again? Not much will have changed in the last ten minutes, I'm sure Abi's fine."

"It's Joe I'm worried about. People aren't lying when they tell you how terrible the threes are."

Colin came over to give Emery a one-armed hug. "Hey, Em, how are you?"

"Oh, you know, living off temp jobs and *so* looking forward to student life again."

He grinned at her. "It'll be worth it."

She hoped she was doing the right thing, had picked the right path. Because it was okay to choose the wrong degree at eighteen, but not really as you approached forty. No, she stopped herself. She'd told herself she was going to stop questioning it. She'd applied, got in—God knew how—and was sticking with it. She'd decided on this subject for a reason, because she wanted to do something meaningful, and she had a strong idea, for the first time in her life, of what her future might look like, which direction she wanted to take after the course was finished. No point in second-guessing that now.

"Come on," Bonnie said, "let's have a glass of Prosecco. Or better yet, let's go to a pub. You know a good pub, right?"

Emery laughed. "It's Bristol, there are *plenty* of good pubs."

* *

"So, Emery, are you seeing anyone at the moment?"

Emery wrinkled her nose. She'd been hoping it would take

longer for this topic to come up, but they were a few pints down and Bonnie was a little tipsy, having told them regularly that it didn't take much to get her drunk these days. They'd exhausted the topic of Abi, and how Bonnie was finding being a mum, and how she'd gone down to part-time in her marketing job and was grateful for it, and how Colin had got a promotion and was now assistant editor of the whole bloody paper. And Emery had tried to ignore how ridiculous it felt that she was going back to study when her two oldest friends were proper adults. So now, it seemed, they were on to the dreaded topic of relationships.

"Er, no, not really."

"Not really, or no?" Bonnie pressed.

Without meaning to, her mind turned to Nick. She'd been coming back to him whenever she had a moment for days now, and he had been intruding on her thoughts even when she tried to concentrate on other things.

Oh hun, I wish you'd called. She passed away in the night.

He thought he'd been trapped there because Lisa was trapped. That both of them were stuck in a state of in-between. And really, it was as good a theory as any, wasn't it?

I'll make you a deal.

But if Lisa had moved on, and if Nick had kept his promise and tried to let go of the guilt he felt, did that mean he wouldn't be trapped anymore? Did that mean she wouldn't see him next time? Would there be someone else, someone who didn't know her, who didn't understand she'd been there before? The thought made her feel sick, even if she knew that maybe she should *want* that. If she cared about Nick, if she loved him, as she'd told him, then shouldn't she want him to find peace—if peace was, in fact, what was waiting for them after limbo?

"Emery?"

"What?" She felt Colin's eyes on her—he was waiting for her answer, too. "Oh, no. No, I'm not seeing anyone." She'd been sleeping with someone she'd met on Tinder for a few weeks after she'd got to Bristol, but as with all her other relationships, it had petered out. It was depressing, when she thought about it too hard, that her longest relationship had been with Adam—or Nick, if you wanted to count him, and she was pretty sure no one *would* count him. It was best not to think about it really, because if things continued down this route, soon she would be forty, and the pitying looks she'd get when she explained she was single and childless would be too much to bear.

"Well, you need to get out there," Bonnie declared. "Maybe there'll be someone on your course."

"Sure, if I want to be a cougar." She took a sip of her beer.

Bonnie pursed her lips. "Our aunt Isobel met the love of her life when she was in her fifties, you know—didn't she, Colin?" Colin gave a sort of nod-shrug in vague agreement.

"Well, good. So I've got plenty of time then."

"I'm going to get us more drinks," Bonnie announced, getting to her feet. "And chips! We definitely need chips."

"There's a kebab van just down the road, if you're hungry."

"Emery Wilson, I've come all the way here, my first night away since Abi was born—you are not taking me to a kebab shop."

"Noted. I'll think of something better."

"While I'm gone, tell her your news, Colin."

Emery looked at Colin as Bonnie headed for the crowded bar. Around them, chatter and laughter swelled, the smell of beer lingering in the air in a way Emery would only ever associate with an English pub. "You've got *more* news? More than the promotion? Which, by the way, I don't think I've fully said how proud I am of you for." She held her glass up in a toast, and he clinked his against it. For a moment, Emery had a flash of scrawny fourteen-year-old Colin declaring that he wanted to be a journalist, and with it came a rush of affection. She really *was* proud of him.

He cleared his throat. "Well, you know Natalie?"

"Your girlfriend? I do know her, yes." Colin had met her a year or so ago, and they'd moved in together at lightning speed. Natalie was a few years younger than him and ticked all the boxes: clever, as evidenced by her first class honors from UCL; interesting—her job involved something to do with the Ministry of Defense, though Emery was secretly convinced she might be a spy; and really quite stunning—the dark-haired, dark-eyed, sexy type. She might be a bit over-the-top for Emery's liking, but she'd seemed nice enough the two times she'd met her.

"Yeah, well, I . . . I think I'm going to propose to her."

"You *are*?" She said it so loudly, the people on the nearest table looked over at them. She never had quite mastered the art of keeping her voice down at moments like this. "Sorry," she said quickly, while he shook his head at her outburst, a small smile playing around his lips. "I mean, well. That's amazing, Colin." She tried to ignore the squirming in her gut, a squirming she didn't have a right to feel. She'd known it was serious—they lived together, after all—but she'd started to assume that maybe he would always just be *there*, in a way you couldn't be if you were married. Be there for *her*. She drained the last of her drink to cover up the selfish thought, aware of the way he was watching her and knowing that she should say something more congratulatory.

Bonnie came back before she could think of anything, plonking three more pints on the table then hooking out several packets of chips from under her arm. Impressive, Emery thought. Maybe being a mum and having to carry a small child around all the time made you better at juggling things. "So?" she asked as she sat down, immediately tearing into the chips, "Has he told you? He's getting married! Isn't that great?"

Emery couldn't help thinking there was a distinct difference between what Colin had said—*I think I'm going to propose*—and Bonnie's declaration. Colin seemed to notice too. "I haven't asked her yet, Bon."

"Oh, she'll definitely say yes. She's so in love with you, anyone can see that." Emery smiled her agreement but said nothing. She felt too hot. But then again, they were in a crowded pub in the middle of summer—of *course* she was too hot.

They finished the next round of drinks, and Bonnie, as she tended to do when drunk, held center stage, chatting about her recommendations for Colin's wedding, then telling them how much she just *loved* Natalie but not as much as she *loved* the two of them. At some point, Colin declared that he needed the loo and headed off toward the back of the pub. It was only after Emery had got another round in that Bonnie frowned. "Where *is* he? He's been gone ages. I want to finish these and go and get food. Fries! I want fries."

"I thought you told me I had to take you somewhere nice."

"Oh, I'm way too drunk for that now."

Emery laughed. "I'll go and find him—he might have gone outside."

She headed to the smoking area round the back of the pub and found Colin there as predicted. He was chatting to a group of guys, having clearly bummed a cigarette en route to the restroom. It was cold out here, but with her beer blanket, Emery hardly noticed it. She sidled up to him. "Mind if I have a puff of that?"

He jumped, then gave her a guilty look. She laughed. "Didn't know you still smoked."

He wrinkled his nose. "I don't. Sort of just...happened." He offered her the cigarette.

She shook her head. "Nah, haven't had one in years." She looked around as he took a drag, the cigarette nearly burned to the end. She hadn't actually been to this pub before, not really knowing the city, but she'd googled good places to go before Bonnie and Colin had arrived. It was packed out here, with picnic benches on the lawn beyond the patio where everyone was huddled together to smoke. She looked back at Colin. His blue eyes were tinged with red. "So," she said. "You're finally doing it—getting married."

"Finally?"

"No, sorry, I didn't mean..." There was the first hint of awkwardness in the air between them—the reminder of what had happened two years ago and was never talked about. Because she hadn't been able to find the words, hadn't wanted to risk saying the wrong thing—or promising something she wasn't sure she could give. And then he'd met Natalie, and that night had been put aside, for both of them. "Just, we're old, aren't we?" she finished, trying to make light of it.

He made a face. "I don't know about *old*. Just old*er*." He dropped the cigarette butt, stamped it out.

"So, shall we head back in?" she asked brightly. "Bonnie's demanding fries."

Colin rolled his eyes. "Course she is."

Emery began to lead him back inside, but he grabbed her sleeve. She turned and caught his eye, and she knew at once that he was going to bring it up. Just as she knew she couldn't stop him, even if they should have talked about it right away, before the years built up, before they'd had several pints of beer.

"Look, Em, I know we haven't really talked about what happened, you know, after..."

"Yeah, I know," she said quietly.

"And I know it was the wrong time and..." He blew out a breath and it misted in the night air, merging with the cigarette smoke. "I have mates who would kick me in the balls for even thinking this—I know that if you were interested, you would have let me know by now, believe me, I get it. But I... before I ask Natalie to spend the rest of her life with me, I just need to say it out loud. Because if I have a shot with you, Emery, if a part of you thinks that, I won't ask her to marry me."

She looked at him for a long moment, feeling her throat squeeze tight. His eyes—they were a little drunk right now, but she loved how earnest his eyes could get. How *kind* they were. Underneath the cigarette smoke and the smell of stale beer, she could smell his woody scent, and it made her feel comforted, and something more, something deeper. And in that moment, she knew that all it would take was a nod from her—a *maybe*. It was wrong and he deserved better than that, but she knew it. And with a lurch of her stomach, she realized how much she wanted to give him that maybe. How a part of her wanted to lean in right now and kiss him, and feel his arms come around her and know that he could be hers to keep. She wanted to think that she could commit to him, that it was an option, because Colin was one of the very few people who knew every part of her and still thought there was something worth loving. Her fingers flexed at her sides, and her stomach tightened as his gaze stayed locked on hers, waiting.

But it wouldn't be fair. She couldn't do it to him, couldn't be selfish with him. Couldn't make him give up everything for her *maybe*—not when he had another option.

So she took his hand, a hand so familiar, and squeezed it. "You're my friend, Colin." A part of her hated saying those words, hated knowing what she might be giving up. "And I want you to be happy." She took a breath, made herself look him right in the eye. "I think you should ask her to marry you."

He swallowed, and she caught it—the flicker of disappointment, of hurt, that flashed across his face. But he smiled. "All right." And he met her gaze too, neither of them faltering. "Thanks, Em."

Bonnie came out then, wrapping her arms around herself against the cold. "*There* you guys are! Have you just been out here chatting? What happened to fries?"

"Sorry, Bon," Colin said. "Let me just go for a piss, then we'll go."

"I thought that *was* where you'd gone."

"Got sidetracked."

He hurried inside under Bonnie's narrow-eyed look, which she turned on Emery when he was out of sight. "What were you two talking about?"

"Nothing," Emery said, a little too quickly.

Bonnie looked at Emery for a moment, then seemed to square up a little. "Look, I'm only going to say this once..."

Emery frowned. "Say what?"

Bonnie held up her hand. "I've never said anything before because I never knew what was going on between the two of you and I figured, well, if neither of you wanted to tell me then it's none of my business. And I'm a bit drunk, so don't blame me if this comes out wrong. But Emery, please don't do anything to ruin this for Colin."

Something hot flashed through her. "What! I'm not! I don't know—"

"You do. Maybe not deliberately, but you do. You know what he feels for you, and I think there's more that happened between the two of you than you're letting on. I know you need him, I get that. But he needs you to let him go."

Emery stared at her—at the friend she maybe didn't give enough credit for what she saw, what she noticed. Then she nodded. "I know. And I told him—I told him to marry her."

Bonnie blew out a breath. "Well, all right then. Come on. Fries. Do you think they have cheese too?"

Emery linked her arm through Bonnie's. "Oh, I reckon they could probably stretch to that."

And for the rest of the evening, she tried not to think of the man she'd just sent on his way to marry someone else—the man she'd always had waiting in the back of her mind, even when she'd known it was wrong to keep him there. She tried, too, not to think of the other man who might be lost to her. Because Nick had been right—she couldn't keep living for her moments with him. But that didn't mean it wasn't torture not knowing if he'd been right about something else. Not knowing if, the next time she died, he would still be waiting for her.

Chapter Thirty

Two years later (March 2018)

AGE 39

Emery lay on the floor of the office at the clinic, topless, her skirt pushed up around her waist, and exhaled slowly. She could feel the sting of carpet burn on the back of her thighs and her shoulders, and there was a slight rawness on her jaw from Luke's overgrown stubble. Next to her, Luke was panting hard. He propped himself on one elbow and grinned down at her before leaning in to peck her on the cheek, that stubble grazing her face again, then got to his feet, buttoning up his shirt. He had impressive pecs for a therapist, she thought. She knew he worked out—he'd told her that on several occasions, usually when the "exercise is good for mental health" topic came up. She had never been able to work out if that was a subtle dig at her to exercise more, do something about her slightly flabby stomach, something that had set in over recent months.

"Where's my...?" He looked around, spotted his tie and grabbed it off the corner of his desk—a proper professional's desk, all dark wood with folders on top.

Emery watched him get dressed, knowing she'd have to move in a minute. But it was pleasantly warm in his office, compared to the chill outside, and she was inclined to laziness right now. She'd met Luke this past year—he'd been one of her theory lecturers. Only for two lectures and only as a guest lecturer, he was keen to point out whenever she teased him about how they'd met. He was three years younger than her—something he also liked to point out—so the whole cliché of sleeping with your professor was hardly applicable here (his words). She'd gone up to ask some questions, and he'd asked her out for a drink. And she'd thought, why the hell not? He had been charismatic while lecturing, making everyone laugh, and he had nice coffee-colored eyes. Since then, they'd been seeing each other off and on, something she'd told herself was fine, given that he wasn't her teacher anymore, now she was in her second year.

He stood in front of the mirror opposite his desk to do up his tie—she still found it baffling that he had a mirror in his office. "I've been meaning to ask you," he said, looking at himself rather than her. "Do you want to go away this weekend?"

Emery pushed up on her hands, twisting her head to look at him properly. "With you?"

He laughed, finishing the tie. "Of course with me. This hotel in the Cotswolds has a last-minute deal on."

She shook her head. "I can't. One of my best friends is getting married."

"Oh." His lips pursed into a soft pout. He was sulky, she was starting to notice. Should a therapist, one who had written a successful book on the subject, be so sulky? She got to her feet, straightened her skirt and looked around for her top—which she saw had been flung onto the chair behind the desk. Maybe he wanted her to invite him to the wedding. Or maybe he was wondering why she hadn't already invited him. But she wouldn't have done even if the thought had crossed her mind. Because she didn't want company as she watched Colin getting married, of that she was sure.

She crossed to the chair, tugged on her top. He still hadn't said anything more, and she wondered if that was it, if it was over. She should care more about that. No, she should *try*. As she'd promised. So she glanced over to him. "We can go away another weekend, if you like?"

He crossed the room toward her, smiled down at her. "That would be great. I'll look up some deals." He loved a good deal. He planted a kiss on her neck, his hand moving to slip under her top. She laughed, swatted him away.

"You've got appointments." Maybe she shouldn't be so quick to assume that things were over.

Try. Her word of the fucking century. And she was. *I am trying, Nick. But are you still there, waiting for me to tell you about it?* As always, here was the lance of guilt at thinking that, at *wanting* it. But still the twitchiness set in, as it always did whenever she let herself dwell on it. She had to know, she needed to know, if she'd see him again. And yet her heart, her traitorous heart, kept beating on.

Chapter Thirty-One

The wedding took place in a country house in the middle of the Lake District—Natalie's choice, as far as Emery could gather. Although Emery had heard the words "spring wedding" bandied around too many times to count in the last few months, the weather was distinctly un-spring-like, all gray and misty rain and bloody freezing. With the outdoor option apparently—and thankfully—vetoed, they were currently sitting in what was, as far as she could gather, a massive glass conservatory. It was all white. Far *too* white, really. White chairs with white flowers on the end of each row, white ceiling, white table at the end where Colin was standing in his tux, looking a little nervous but laughing as his best man whispered something in his ear. Emery's heart tugged at the sight of him. And oh God, he was really doing it. He was really getting married.

The person next to her—an elderly woman who smelled of lavender—pushed into Emery, then scowled up the row, muttering under her breath. Emery tried to make herself a little smaller, shifting to the side of her chair. Having individual seats hadn't done much to make them feel less cramped—they were all rammed together in here. She hadn't realized Colin even *knew* so many people. Or were the majority of these people Natalie's friends and family? Either way, there was no chance she'd have so many people at *her* wedding. Not that she was ever going to have a wedding.

Stop it, Emery.

She'd regretted her decision to come alone when she'd first walked in, scanning the crowd for someone she recognized. Pretty much everyone seemed to be coupled up, though Natalie had instigated a "no children" rule. She'd had to make small talk with random strangers while she'd waited for them to be ushered to their seats, and she swore each and every one of them kept glancing behind her as if wondering if her partner was going to make a magical appearance and even everything up. Maureen had come over and given her a big hug—hair still as vibrantly red as Emery remembered from her childhood days, only now it took some work to keep it that way—but then disappeared off to talk to Natalie's parents.

Emery hadn't even managed to speak to Bonnie yet, because Natalie, ludicrously, had chosen her as a bridesmaid. Emery had let slip to Colin a few months ago how bizarre she found that, and Colin had just said it was because Natalie wanted Bonnie to feel included and she didn't have a sister of her own. Emery had agreed how *nice* that was, even though they'd both known she was lying. So now she was trying very hard not to feel like Natalie was taking away both her best friend and her...well, her other best friend. Something that was exacerbated by the fact that Natalie always treated her a little coldly, with a faint air of suspicion.

The music started and Emery stood along with everyone else. She watched as Bonnie came down the aisle, her pink dress clashing with her strawberry-blonde hair. Bonnie winked at Joe, who was standing up with Colin. No doubt the four of them had already had plenty of double dates, dinners that Emery would never have been invited to by virtue of being single.

She rolled her shoulders. Enough. She was being bitter—she'd promised herself she wouldn't be bitter.

But it didn't help that Natalie looked undeniably gorgeous. Of course she did—it was her wedding day. Her dark hair was pinned in a half-up half-down do, flowers—white, of course—giving an almost crown-like appearance. Her dress was sleek and showed off an impossibly slim figure, a goal Emery had long since given up on. She was smiling, no hint of nerves, and when Colin looked at her, he smiled too, his shoulders relaxing. Emery stared at him, at his bright blue eyes, the jawline she knew so well. He didn't look back at her. Not even a glance in her direction. Of course not. Why would he? She closed her eyes briefly as she sat down, as Colin and Natalie faced each other. And when she opened them, she pasted a smile to her face.

She made it through the ceremony, managed to force down the lump in her throat when they made their promises to each other. There were plenty of other people looking tearful or dabbing at their eyes—Natalie's mother was putting on quite the performance—but Emery was sure their tears were for entirely different reasons. She stood outside with everyone else waiting to throw confetti and swore to herself at the bloody *rainbow* that chose to come out in the weak sunlight as the newlyweds appeared, hand in hand. Seriously, world, a rainbow?

She muttered a vague excuse to no one in particular, headed for the bathroom. A plush one with low lighting and boxed tissues and brass sinks. She could feel the tears bubbling over, and she shut herself in one of the cubicles, put the toilet lid down, then sat and just *sobbed*. She tried to be silent, but she could hear the sobs escaping, tearing through her like they were cracking bone. She fought to control her breathing, fought to stop her lip from shaking. She hadn't expected it to hit her this hard. Yes, she'd been dreading it, in lots of ways—weddings were difficult when you got to her age and were still effectively single, and this was *Colin*. Despite the fact that she was the one who had closed the door, it didn't mean she wanted it rubbed in her face. But still, she hadn't expected the strength of emotion she was feeling—the *loss*.

He's gone, she told herself over and over. And in that moment, it really felt like she'd lost him, even though he was right out-side, waiting to cut the damn wedding cake. *But he's not yours anymore*, a dark voice in her mind whispered. He'd never been hers, though, she thought bitterly. Never been hers because she'd refused to let it happen. And now it was too late.

She put her hand on her heart, trying to steady herself. God, what she wouldn't give for it to stop right now. She'd told Nick she wouldn't live for moments with him—and she wasn't—but that didn't mean she didn't wish that her body would offer her an escape, didn't mean that she didn't wish, more than anything, that she could be with him right now, feel his arms around her.

She closed her eyes. *Are you still there, Nick?* And at that, the thought that he might not be, another sob racked through her.

There was the sound of the bathroom door opening, and she managed to steady her breath, hiccuped out one final sob. She waited as someone went into the cubicle next to her, heard the lock turn. Then she wiped under her eyes, shook back her hair. She couldn't stay hiding in here—what if someone got the wrong idea? So she stood up, flushed the toilet for good measure.

Her face was a wreck when she looked at herself in the mirror, even with the flatteringly low lighting. Her skin was starting to sag and her lipstick made her lips look too thin. There were smudges under her eyes and her cheeks were red and blotchy. Really attractive, Emery. She wetted a paper towel, tried to sort out some of the damage. She could not look like she'd been crying on Colin's wedding day.

A toilet flushed, the cubicle door opened. And Bonnie stepped out. Emery hitched in a breath. Unlike her, Bonnie looked all dewy, and in here, the clash between her hair and the pink dress was nowhere near as noticeable. They stared at one another in the mirror. For a moment, Emery thought Bonnie was going to tell her off or say something disapproving about how she had no right to feel like this, how she shouldn't be messing with Colin's emotions and what would he think if he saw her like this? But then her face softened, twisting into a grimace of sympathy.

"Oh Em." She came over, squeezed Emery's arm. And Emery had to press her lips together against another sob.

Bonnie ran her hand up and down Emery's arm, soothing.

She said nothing, but Emery could feel the years of friendship settling between them, the understanding. She thought of Bonnie's wedding, all those years ago now, when Colin had asked her out. That would have been the moment. If she'd been brave enough, that would have been the moment that could have changed everything. But when she closed her eyes, it was Nick's face there, as it always was. She inhaled slowly, breathing through the pain.

"It'll be okay, you know," Bonnie said, and Emery nodded. But what would she do if Colin drifted away from her? What would she do if Nick was gone? How could she keep going if she never got to say goodbye? "Come on. Let's go get you a drink."

Emery threw her paper towel in the bin. "Aren't you needed for bridesmaid duties?"

Bonnie shrugged. "Nah. I'm more of a token bridesmaid, I reckon. Besides, I'd rather hang out with you."

Emery let out a strangled laugh. "God, I love you so much, you know that, right?"

Bonnie grinned. "Why do you think I came to find you?"

She led Emery out of the bathroom. The door swung shut behind them. What would happen, Emery wondered, if she stuck her finger in there? Like the taxi door after skydiving, all those years ago? Would the pain of it be enough to shock her into death? But it was barely a breath of contemplation. She stepped away from the door. She couldn't do it to Colin, not deliberately.

So instead she'd drink and she'd dance and she'd laugh. She'd keep trying. Because she'd fucking promised.

Chapter Thirty-Two

One year later (March 2019)

AGE 40

When Emery finally did die again, she didn't even realize it was happening. She didn't remember being anywhere specifically, didn't remember anything other than being in bed with a book, trying to convince herself she was far too young to need reading glasses. She was still in her nightdress, and as she looked down at it, she frowned, wondering what had happened. It had been her fortieth birthday a few months ago, and though she'd not gone all out, she'd had a big group of people round to her two-bed terraced house just outside Bristol—the one that had finally got her on the property ladder, with help from her dad for the deposit. She'd thought that would be the moment her heart faltered again—like on her thirtieth. She'd thought someone would surprise her, or one of the children would jump on her from behind, not yet getting the memo to be careful around her. A part of her had hoped for it, because she'd wanted to come back to this place, wanted to quench the low-level nausea that felt like a constant companion as she wondered who she would see next time.

And now, finally, anticlimactically, she was here. There was a moment, as the scene seemed to shift around her, not quite taking form yet, when she couldn't see him. She turned around, feeling her heart step up its frantic beat, a sob building in her throat.

Then there was a figure, growing more solid as the memory around her started to settle. And she knew it was him—gray-green eyes coming into focus first as he stepped toward her. His mouth was crooked into a half-smile, and he scanned her face as she was now scanning his. She took a moment to stare at him, to reassure herself he was really here, that he hadn't gone. Then she ran to him, letting loose a sob as she did so.

"I thought..." But his arms came around her, and his familiar scent washed over her, and she didn't say the rest. Instead she tilted her face back, reached up her hand, trembling slightly, to brush her fingers over his cheek, the contours of his mouth. Then she was kissing him, as she'd wanted to for so long, and he was kissing her back, no hesitation on either of their parts. And she put it out of her mind, how he'd brushed her off last time, because he was *here* when she'd thought she might never see him again.

His hand was on her back, pressing her to him, and she was clutching at his shoulders, needing to feel the muscle underneath, needing the reassurance. He broke the kiss first, his eyes wholly focused as they looked into hers. His turn to reach out, trace her features. She felt lines of fire flare in the wake of his touch. "Emery." Her name was a prayer on his lips, as she'd heard it once before. He pressed his forehead against hers, his hand now rubbing soft circles on her back, as if he needed to keep touching, needed, just like her, to reassure himself that she was here. "I love you," he whispered.

She heard the truth in the words, felt it swell within her. In answer, she drew away, only far enough that she could kiss him again, softly first, just a whisper—an answer. It was he who broke the control, who deepened the kiss, making her groan, and with that groan his fingers flexed on her back, digging into her, before going to her waist. She felt that liquid pull in her, and as he moved to kiss her neck, she gasped, arching back.

"Fuck, Emery."

He pushed her against the walls of the memory, and she wrapped her arms around his neck as he kissed down the length of her throat. His hands traveled to her thighs, where her nightdress bunched as he grabbed it, his knuckles grazing her skin. She moved her hands to his shoulders again, pushing down to keep him in place as she brought her lips to his neck, needing to taste him there, everywhere, finally. She heard the sharp intake of breath and nipped him in response, felt his fingers tighten on her thighs. He lifted her nightdress, slowly, and she eased back to look at him, raising her arms over her head. He dropped the nightdress to one side and his gaze raked over her, taking in the lines of her body. And she felt no trace of embarrassment or self-consciousness as she might do with anyone else—not here, not with him.

His fingers skimmed the inside of her thighs until they could go no higher, his eyes watching their progress. And despite what her body was begging for, despite where she wanted him to go, she managed to cock her head, managed to gasp out, "Bit one-sided, this, isn't it?" He huffed out a laugh and she grinned in response as she ran her hands under his T-shirt, feeling muscle beneath. He tugged off his shirt, and she splayed her hands on his chest, feeling the beat of his heart—even if that heart had stopped beating long ago. His nose skated down hers, his lips kissed the corner of her mouth. Then there were no more hesitations, no more thoughts of caution as he lifted her, as she wrapped her legs around his waist, hands in his hair, his mouth on her breast.

He laid her down on the bed—a bed she hadn't even noticed before then—and there was the hiss of a belt buckle, the sound of a zip. Then he was on top of her, and flames were licking her skin everywhere he touched, his mouth following the path of his fingers and making her nerves crackle. Her insides pulsed at the feel of him over her, and her teeth caught his bottom lip, harder now. She ran her hands down the length of his chest, lower, until she could feel him, and he shifted, allowing her more room, and groaned softly against her neck.

"Nick." His name was a plea, her hips arching, whole body begging without subtlety. And then, finally, he was inside her, and she didn't even bother to stem the cry. He grasped her hands, linking his fingers with hers, and their gazes met, held. Both of them were trembling, his muscles held so taut above her she thought they might snap. Then he leaned down, kissed her, and she closed her eyes. This, she thought, was why it had never worked with anyone else. This—all she'd ever wanted was this.

Afterward, they lay face to face, tracing lazy circles over each other's skin, waiting for their breathing to settle. They were in her bedroom. She hadn't figured that out until afterward, but they were in her room in her terraced house, the mattress exactly the same—a mattress she'd spent a bloody fortune on—the lamp on the bedside table brilliantly out of place in its bold and tacky red, because it was the one Lily had given her for her fortieth birthday. Photos of Amber, Lily and Robin, Colin and Bonnie smiled at her from her dressing table, which was cluttered with various face creams and serums she'd been trying out. The walls were a light blue, though she was thinking about redecorating, when she could be bothered.

"So," Nick said, propping himself up on one elbow to look down at her. "What's new with you?"

She laughed. "Well . . . I'm actually training to be a counselor."

"Really?"

"I know, it's scary, right?"

"I don't know." He traced circles down her arm. "I think you've given me some pretty good advice in the past."

"I've got a few more months, then I'll be qualified." She'd just finished her research project, specializing in end-of-life counseling, and it had made her more convinced that that was what she wanted to do, helping people come to terms with their deaths. She wasn't sure whether to tell him about that, though, because effectively that was what *he* did, wasn't it? That was what had given her the idea, really. She felt she had a confidence on the subject, knowing what she knew and given her many brushes with death. It didn't make it any less scary or difficult, but every time she panicked, wondered if she was doing the right thing, she reminded herself that if she could help even one person with what was happening to them, it would be worth it. And that thought was grounding in a way she'd never really felt grounded before.

As part of the course, they'd also had to go through their own therapy—which made sense, she supposed, but which she had been dreading from the outset. So far, though, it had been more helpful than she would have guessed. Of course, she'd been unable to talk about Nick, which felt odd, given he was such a big part of her life, but talking about her mum had helped her work through some things she'd clearly been holding on to for a while. She'd known the theory behind it, of course—the fact that children very often blamed themselves, turning it inward, when a parent left, and that "leaving" could be anything from death to divorce to an emotional absence. But it was difficult applying that theory to herself, even with the help of someone else. She thought of what she and Nick had said to each other years ago. About Lisa, about her mum. *It's not your fault.*

He was watching her, his hand on her hip, and she realized she'd gone quiet. "Sorry," she said. "Anyway, that's my main update. I also tried and failed to date one of my lecturers, but it didn't work out."

"Your lecturer?"

She laughed at how scandalized he looked. Then she grew more serious and reached out to cup his face. "I can't believe you're still here." He said nothing, stroking a hand over her waist. "Nick..." She took a breath. She had to do this, she had to tell him. "Lisa died."

Pain flashed across his face, before his mouth set in a thin line. "I know."

Emery's heart stuttered. "You know?" she whispered.

"I saw her."

"She...she came here?"

"Yes." Emery was unable to imagine what that must have been like for him, and unsure whether to push, whether he'd want to talk about it. "Her as I knew her," he continued. He looked down to where his hand lay on her bare flesh and his fingers flexed there. "We were in her memory, back in Oxford. But not the alleyway," he added softly. She bit her lip, trying to stop herself from asking for more, trying to let him tell her only what he wanted to, even if she was desperate to know what exactly had happened, what they'd talked about.

Nick hesitated, then sat up, dropping his hand away from her. "This memory," he said, and the surroundings shifted around them. They were on a picnic blanket, on the edge of a river, the trees a strong leafy green, the sun warm. "It's where I asked Lisa to marry me," he added.

Emery shifted position on the blanket, completely naked and not caring. "You loved her." She kept her voice as soft as his—not an accusation, but an understanding.

"That version of me loved her, yes. And I'm so glad that I got to see her again. So glad I could be the one to help her in that moment. It made me realize..." He broke off and did not elaborate. "I've told you over and over that I was stuck—but I was wrong, I think. Because I realized, seeing her, that I'm not the same person I was. She knew that, and it was okay. And it made me understand that all this time I've been letting myself feel guilty for loving someone else, when I should have been thankful for it instead." He looked at her, and her heart swelled.

Her lips curved in a smile. "We're good at letting ourselves feel guilty, aren't we?"

He moved to her, resting his forehead against hers, a gesture that was becoming more and more familiar. "I love you, Emery."

She closed her eyes, breathed him in. But she couldn't stop herself from saying, "Maybe only this version of you loves me."

He shook his head. "Every version of me. Every version of me would love every version of you."

And she believed him, because she felt it too, that bone-deep connection, fate bringing them together when it should not be possible, because they lived different lives at different times.

He pulled back slightly. "I'm sorry I pushed you away, last time, when you said you..."

"Loved you?"

"Yes. I didn't want to give you a reason to want to come back here."

"I know. I get that." She didn't say it out loud, but she thought perhaps he'd been right—because she'd been at her lowest then, and if he'd told her he loved her, given her what she'd so desperately wanted, maybe she wouldn't have returned to her body at all. "Nick?"

"Hmm?"

"Why do you think you're still here?"

He hesitated, and she felt the nerves in her stomach pulsing.

Because she wanted him to answer with a certainty he'd never be able to give her that she would always have him.

"I think," he said slowly, "I think I could have gone. Left this place. After Lisa … it was like everything stopped—like I had a choice, to move on with her." Emery's heart was beating a little too fast.

"So do you think you *were* trapped?" She'd always fought against that notion, that he was here as a punishment. It would feel too morbid if that were the case.

"No, I don't. Do you know what, it's odd, because having that choice sort of made me realize I was wrong. It hasn't been a punishment, but more that I needed to understand something before I moved on—and maybe that's only happened because of what I do here, who I meet." He gave her a wry smile. "Maybe you were right all along—maybe you were matched to me to help me, not the other way around." He blew out a breath. "It's like this place has been waiting for me to come to terms with what happened to Lisa—and seeing her, I guess, was the last piece of that. But it was happening before, because I was trying, like I promised you, to stop blaming myself."

"So you chose *not* to move on? You chose to stay here?" The squirming in her stomach intensified. Was it because of her? Did he let go of his chance to move on because of her? She realized then that this was what he'd been feeling when she told him she loved him, when she stood on that bridge.

"I wanted to see you again," he said, in that mind-reading way of his. "I couldn't bear the thought that last time might be *the* last time, and I'd never be able to tell you what you mean to me."

She sucked in a breath. "Nick—"

But he held up a hand. "It wasn't just that, though. I'm *not* stuck." She frowned—because he'd just said that, and he laughed a little at the expression on her face. Lighter. He seemed somehow lighter than he'd ever been before. "For now, I want to be here. I'm good at what I do—there is a reason I was put here, and I don't think it's just for my sake. So for now, I'm going to keep doing what I'm doing—and I know that it's a choice."

She'd been waiting for the tremor through the memory—the warning bell. She only realized that when something else happened instead, and then only because of the shift in Nick's expression, horror coming in to replace the smile. Usually, before she left, she became solid as everything faded around her, but that was not happening. Instead, she could see that *she* was the one fading.

"Emery!" He reached out to take her hand, but his grip felt insubstantial. "Who is with you, Emery? Who is with you right now?"

"I . . ." She thought of her bed, her nightdress. "No one." And his panic was making her panic, so that she got to her feet, holding up her hand to see it fading still further, merging with the blues and greens and browns of the river landscape.

"No! This is not your time, it's not." He was on his feet too, his eyes darting around, tightening his grip on her hands as if to anchor her. And she was scared—because she didn't want to die. She wanted to go back, wanted to finish her degree, wanted to make a difference in some small way. The full force of that hit her. She didn't want to die.

Nick put a hand on her heart. And though she could see the fear dancing in his eyes, his voice was calm. "It's up to you now. Breathe, Emery. Fight!"

She felt herself gasp, felt the pain in her chest ricocheting through her body like shock waves—and then she was back in her bedroom, lying on the bed, drenched in sweat. Her heart had just stopped without warning in the night, and that had never happened before. She had no idea what had caused it, what she'd heard in her sleep or experienced in her dreams. It was beating now, but painfully, and she felt a retch rise in her body. She made herself get out of bed, walk to the bathroom. Every step felt like an enormous effort, and a shiver racked through her. She reached the toilet and was sick. Every muscle was aching. She closed her eyes, told herself to breathe.

You came back. She repeated it to herself, over and over. She'd come back—and proved one very important thing to herself: she wanted to be here. And she could do that. She could live here, fight for it. And she could settle for the brief moments with Nick, if moments were all that she could ever have.

Chapter Thirty-Three

Two years later (April 2021)

AGE 42

"Emery? Emery! Jesus Christ, open your eyes, will you?"

"Is she okay? Is Auntie Em dying?" It was Lily's voice that made Emery snap her eyes open, turning to one side and coughing up what felt like half her insides.

"No." Robin's voice was shaky. "No, Lils, she's all right. See?"

And this, Emery thought, a little bitterly, *is why Robin won't let me look after Lily on my own.* The crowd of people around them was now dispersing, Robin reassuring them that it was all okay, that Emery had just fainted. Emery, meanwhile, felt disoriented— half her mind was still with Nick, back in Dublin, in a hotel she and Bonnie had stayed at on a girls' weekend away. She blinked to focus on her immediate surroundings—they were in the middle of a brightly lit shopping mall, where Emery had promised to take Lily for her birthday so she could choose her own present. Lily, who was looking at her with wide, worried eyes, pressed against Robin's side in a way that made her seem younger than she'd been acting recently, full of excitement at turning twelve and desperate already to be a teenager.

"Don't worry, Lils," Emery said, forcing herself to get to her feet. "Remember, it's my superpower. I can come back from the dead." She did her best to put on a zombie face, and Lily giggled.

She could still feel the effects of coming round, her heart lurching and sending shooting pains across her chest, pinpricks of sweat running down the back of her neck. It was becoming harder each time to return to herself quickly and easily.

Lily was giving her a suspicious look. "It's not *really* your superpower, is it? People don't really come back from the dead."

"Only special people like me." It was clear Lily didn't believe her—she was old enough now to have lost that willingness to engage fully with the strange and fantastic—but Emery could see there was part of her that *wanted* to. Not quite all grown up yet. She kissed the top of her niece's head, smelling the peppermint scent she always associated with Amber. Lily was blonde, like Robin, though her hair was a shade darker; she was also lanky and tall, like Amber.

"It actually *is* scientifically possible to come back from a clinical death," Robin told Lily. "It's not a superpower, it's science."

Emery rolled her eyes. God, even that hurt. "Oh, take all the fun away, why don't you?" She looked around for her handbag, spotted it a meter or so away. Robin saw what she was looking for and bent to get it before Emery could.

"I think if I was going to have a superpower," Lily mused, "it would be to know the answer to every question. That way I wouldn't have to do any homework ever."

"That sounds like a great one," Emery agreed. "And brilliantly put."

Emery and Lily looked at Robin expectantly. Robin considered for a moment, passing Emery's handbag over to her. "Probably talking to plants."

"Talking to *plants*?" Lily was incredulous.

"Well, the research into animal behavior is so much further on, and I'm not sure I'd want to listen to animals' thoughts because of how so many of them are treated by humans, but we know very little about plants. I could facilitate the research in that area, and it would be so interesting to see if the early theories are right—that plants might be able to think and feel more than we've ever considered before."

Lily was frowning at her, and Emery huffed out a laugh. "Couldn't just go for flying, huh?"

"I had enough of that on our skydiving trip." The pang that would once have been intolerable was more of a sharp, brief stab. And when that faded, the memory made Emery smile, at how Amber hadn't wanted to do it but had tried anyway.

Robin took her arm, pulled her slightly away from Lily. "Are you sure you're okay?"

"I'm fine."

"You don't *look* fine."

"Well, coming back from a clinical death takes a bit of a toll, even if it's scientifically possible."

"I've seen you come around before. This time seemed ... worse."

"I'm fine, Robin, honestly. I've got a doctor's appointment in a couple of days anyway—I'll ask about it then." Not that it would do any good. Her check-ups were always the same conversations, over and over. "Right, let's get back to this shopping trip I so rudely interrupted."

"I want to go to John Lewis," Lily announced, clearly having been eavesdropping.

"You want to go to *John Lewis*?" She looked at Robin for confirmation.

Robin gave a shrug and a smile. "Her friend has a blanket from there and Lily loves it."

"Well you, Lils, are a girl of expensive taste. But all right. John Lewis it is." Emery linked arms with her niece and started to walk, ignoring the ache that was pounding at the back of her head—probably from collapsing on a hard shopping mall floor. "You know, Mama Amber used to have a pillow from there that she loved—she'd take it everywhere with her when we were little."

"She did?" Lily had called Amber "Mama" and Robin "Mummy" when she was little—perhaps too little for her to remember now. But Robin and Emery had kept the name alive by talking to her about Amber that way. "Was it blue? The pillow. Was it blue?"

"I, um, I don't remember." In truth, she did remember—it was green and silver—but she wasn't sure why Lily was asking with that determined little voice.

"I think it must have been blue," Lily said firmly. "She's wearing blue in the photo I have of her. I think blue must have been her favorite color."

Emery squeezed her arm, feeling a lump swelling in her throat. "Yes, I think you're right. I think it was blue." Because surely it was better to encourage Lily to talk about Amber this way, and anyway, despite the pillow, one of Amber's favorite colors *had* been blue.

As they walked into John Lewis, Robin and Emery exchanged a look over Lily's head and smiled at one another, and Emery knew this was what people had meant when they'd spoken to her, in the throes of grief, about things getting better, about the fact that there would be a time when it would hurt less—when she would be able to treasure the bits of Amber she was able to keep.

* *

"There's my favorite granddaughter!" Emery's dad pulled Lily into a hug as they all met around a table in PizzaExpress. Robin was making sure she did the rounds while she was down south—a holiday to see all of Amber's family. Her dad, Emery saw, had brought Karen, the woman he'd been dating. Karen was already talking to Robin earnestly, clearly trying to make a good impression, and Lily seemed pleased, as she'd landed one more present.

Emery saw her mum down the end of the table, with a smile fixed determinedly in place. She headed over to join her, helping herself to some water as she sat down. Her mum watched her drink with an attention Emery found a little unnerving.

When Emery gave her a look, she seemed to realize what she was doing and cleared her throat. "How are you?" she asked. "After earlier, I mean?"

Emery sighed—of course her news would have spread through the grapevine. "I'm fine." In truth, she felt tired, and her head was still hurting, but she'd learned what to do by now, how to reassure, how to save the worst for when she was alone. She caught her dad, too, looking at her down the table, and nodded reassuringly.

"Robin said you have a doctor's appointment in a few days?"

"Yeah."

"Do you...do you usually drive to those yourself?"

Emery raised her eyebrows. "Yes. Why?"

"I just..." Her mum swallowed. "If you ever need a lift or would like company at the appointments or..." Emery stared at her, and she flushed. "I don't mean...I'm not trying to intrude. I'm just..." She pursed her lips. "I should have been there. I should have been there, all the times it's happened to you."

Down the other end of the table, Lily was ripping into Karen's present. Emery opened her mouth, then shut it again. She didn't want to say the wrong thing. Didn't want to say that it was a bit late to go down this road now. But her mum was still watching her, waiting. She had to say *something*. "Well, Dad missed most of the episodes too, if it makes you feel any better. The last one I had before I left home was when I was fourteen. The one just before you..."

Her mum winced. "I remember." Her eyes fluttered closed, as if she were replaying some memory. Then she opened them, looked at Emery very directly. "I should have said this a long time ago, but I..." She blew out a breath. "I shouldn't have left. I should have stayed with you girls. And not doing so is something I'll regret for as long as I live."

Emery considered her for a moment. "Why *did* you leave?" She was finally asking that question—and perhaps only able to because of her career and the training she'd gone through. Aunt Helen had arrived now, her booming voice carrying down the table as she asked the waiter for sparkling water and a bottle of rosé, at the same time bestowing a present on Lily.

"I..." Her mum pulled a hand through her gray hair. "God, it was all just such a mess. I don't know if I'll ever be able to properly explain it, even to myself." She bit her lip, glanced away from Emery, picking up the napkin in front of her and folding it into quarters. "I suffered quite badly from depression after I had you."

Emery felt heat bloom around her collarbone. "I never knew," she said quietly.

"No, well. It's not something we talked about all that much. And I was fine, it got better. But I threw myself into my work— that much you remember, I'm sure."

"Yeah. Yeah, I remember."

"And I was worried that if I took too much time away from work, from my distraction, my mind would...Well. And then, with everything that was happening to you..."

"You couldn't handle it?" Emery tried to keep her voice neutral, tried not to sound like she was blaming her.

Even so, her mum winced again. "Maybe I couldn't. But

337

it was more that I felt I was being blamed." Emery remembered the arguments between her parents. Her dad, angry at her mum for letting Emery do things—things that any normal kid should have been able to do.

"I thought it was my fault," she said quietly. "That you left."

Her mum dropped the napkin she'd been folding and stared at her. "Why would you think that?" And maybe it was almost funny, the utter astonishment on her face—the idea that she hadn't even *considered* this.

"Because I heard you and Dad arguing about me. About my episodes. I was sure that if it wasn't for me being... well, you know, you wouldn't have left."

"Oh Emery." Her mum made as if to take her hand, but then drew back. Emery caught a faint whiff of something that smelled like lavender and thyme. It was a smell that made her think of her childhood. The smell of her mum's hand cream. "I'm so sorry. Your dad and me..." she glanced up the table to where he was smiling at Karen, "we weren't really right for each other. I loved him," she added quickly, "but as time went on, things just got more and more strained, and I... If you heard your name in our arguments, I can't apologize enough, but it was never about you. It was about me, and feeling like I was doing the wrong thing. I thought you'd be better without me there. You'd died—twice—because I'd not been careful enough. It was a constant argument between me and your dad, but when it happened again, when neither of us was there, I started thinking he was right—I was only putting you in harm's way. That's not to excuse any of it. I dealt with it all very badly." She sighed, looking tired in a way Emery hadn't really seen in her before.

Emery let it sit for a moment, watching as Helen waved over the waiter, ready to order food. "Thank you," she said after a beat. "For telling me. And as for the appointment—don't worry, Colin's coming with me."

"Okay." Her mum gave her a weak smile, perhaps appreciating the attempt to return to the practical. "Just know that even if I haven't been here for you before, I am now. And I understand if you don't want to let me back in, or if you can't, but if there's ever anything I can do..."

"I'll let you know, I promise." Emery smiled up at the waiter as he approached their end of the table. She ordered the goat's cheese salad, smiled a little more when her mum ordered the same. And when he took their menus and bustled away, she spoke again. "Mum? Don't regret it. Don't regret what happened or what you did." Regrets caused so much damage—she'd seen that with her patients. And with Nick. It wasn't always possible to let them go, but she could at least try. "Let's just see if we can find a way forward instead, okay?"

"Okay," her mum agreed. "I'd like that."

Chapter Thirty-Four

Emery sat opposite the doctor in his swivel chair, waiting for him to finish typing up something on his computer. To her left, Colin was standing reading one of the posters explaining the various parts of the heart with apparent interest. The office smelled of antiseptic, and the air tasted stuffy.

"So, Emery," Dr. Green said, pushing his glasses up his nose and looking at her in that direct, no-nonsense way of his. "Some bad news, I'm afraid." Her heart skipped a little, like it knew it was the topic of conversation. "Your heart is showing a deterioration in function. The ECG is indicating a degree of irregularity, which seems to have worsened since your last check-up, and your blood pressure is a little high."

"What does that mean?" Colin was by her side in an instant, and he sat down in the chair next to her.

Dr. Green continued to address Emery directly. "It means you could do with being careful, where possible. Avoid any high stress or unpredictable situations."

Emery only just managed not to snort. What ridiculous advice at this stage of her life, and given what they knew of her condition. Besides, life itself was stressful. She loved what she

340

did, but counseling wasn't always easy, and patients nearing death dealt with that in a number of different ways—some of which, obviously, could be on the traumatic side of things.

"Gentle exercise," Dr. Green continued, "nothing too strenuous, and watch your diet—you know, low salt, lots of fresh fruit and veg, whole grains, et cetera. That should hopefully help the blood pressure."

Emery sighed at the incredibly basic advice. "I can't do anything about the fact that my heart stops, though, can I?"

Colin shot her a glance before looking back at the doctor in expectation. Dr. Green considered them both for a moment, then took off his glasses, placing them on the desk and bridging his fingers in front of him. "Now, I don't want to offer you false hope, but there has been a clinical trial recently that has shown some very positive results. It was testing drugs that should be able to control the symptoms of your condition—and those drugs should, all being well, be on the market in the next few years. I can't promise you anything, of course, but I would be cautiously optimistic that it won't be long before I can write you a prescription and not just tell you to cut back on red meat." He said the last bit wryly, like he knew how ridiculous his advice about blood pressure had been.

"Oh my God!" Colin exclaimed. "That's amazing. Emery, isn't this amazing?"

Emery ignored him. "Control my symptoms how, exactly— what does that actually mean?"

"Well, if all goes to plan, taking the drugs continually should stop your heart from cutting out the way it does."

Emery said nothing, only nodded slowly, and Colin frowned at her. "Em, why aren't you more excited about this?"

She stood up. "Thank you, Dr. Green."

The doctor stood too, opened the door for them both. "Take care."

Emery headed out of the clinic and toward the parking lot, aware of Colin's eyes on the side of her face. "Emery—this is huge news. There might be a drug to—"

"Might," Emery said, and couldn't quite stop the snap. She didn't want to have this conversation, didn't want to start speculating. She'd come to terms with what happened to her, was trying to make the most of what she had, not by living in the moment to the extreme as she used to, but by throwing herself into her work, doing something worthwhile with her life. She didn't need the boat rocked now—all for a *might*, a might that would get everyone's hopes up when there was no guarantee it would even work. Sure, there had been talk of drugs before, but in a vague, nondescript future way—not as something that might feasibly be possible.

"Let's talk about something else, shall we? How's Natalie?"

"Yeah, she's all right." But she could hear it in his voice—something was *not* all right.

"Colin?"

He glanced at her. "She, er . . . she slept with someone else."

"*What?*"

"Emery, keep your voice down." He glanced around the parking lot, then ushered her the last few steps to his car, holding the door open for her before scurrying around to the driver's side. Emery rubbed her hands together in the cold, hunching in her big black coat. When would spring come? It was April—surely it should be warmer than this?

"When did this happen?" she asked, as soon as Colin was in the car.

He started the engine, turned up the heat. "A few months ago."

"A few *months*?"

"Yes, and Em, given that this is my marriage we're talking about and not yours, I'd appreciate you reining it in a bit."

"Right. You're right, I'm sorry. But why didn't you...?"

He checked his rearview mirror, put the car in reverse. "Tell you?"

She grimaced. "Sorry. I didn't mean that. I mean, I did, but I'm just surprised. And sorry. God, Colin, are you okay?"

He reversed out of the space, then shifted into first. "Yeah. I mean, I don't really know. It's not a lot of fun, your wife cheating on you, but I'm trying to, you know, get my head around it."

"Was it...?" She bit her lip.

He sighed. "Go on, ask."

"Was it a one-time thing?"

"No, it was definitely more than a one-time thing." He pulled out of the parking lot, and Emery saw the way he gripped the steering wheel a little too tightly. "She says it's not going on anymore. But she also says she's not been happy for a while. I can't work out if that's true, or if she's just putting the blame on me. I suppose things haven't been perfect, so maybe I should've noticed, done something about it sooner."

"She's the one who slept with someone else," Emery muttered. She felt a rush of anger that Natalie could do this to Colin, and flexed her fingers in her lap, trying to let it go. He was right—this was his relationship, not hers.

"Yeah, but there are two people in a marriage." Emery said nothing to that—she was hardly one to be handing out relationship advice. A beat of silence and then, "We're getting a divorce."

She let out a low whistle. "Jesus. Talk about burying the lead." She looked at him, saw his mouth set in a grim line, and felt her heart ache for him. "Is there anything I can do?"

"No, but thanks. Well, I mean you could convince me I'm not a failure for getting married and then divorced in the space of three years."

"Of *course* you're not a failure. This is life—shit happens."

"Is that your best advice as a therapist?" Emery let out a small laugh. "I just...I didn't think this would be me, you know? I thought I'd have it sorted by now—house in the suburbs, loving wife. Kids."

"Well, you've got the house in the suburbs," Emery pointed out. Although what would happen to that in the divorce? She didn't comment on the kids part, because she didn't know what advice she could give on that either. She'd never believed that children were an option for her—never thought it would be fair, with her condition. But seeing Robin—single parent but worth it, no matter how hard... She couldn't help wondering, if Amber had been diagnosed a year earlier, would they still have tried? That had led her to question, more than once, if she'd been hasty in her refusal to let her mind consider the possibility of children. But it seemed irrelevant now—she was forty-two, and she was single, and it was all too late. She had to be happy with everything else she had—her job, and her family and friends, and moments with Nick. It was a lot more than some.

"I'm so sorry, Colin," she said again. "You know, right, that if there *is* ever anything I can do..."

"Yeah. I know." He paused, frowning. "Actually. There is something."

"Anything."

"I want you to go on a date with me."

Her heart stuttered and the back of her neck pricked with heat. He'd said it so casually, but... "A *date*?"

"You said anything."

She fought the urge to laugh. "I know, but Colin..." She swallowed, trying to get her thoughts in order. "You've literally just decided to get divorced. And we're friends, and in our forties."

"Precisely. We are friends, Em. And I think there's a part of you that knows we could be something more." He said it confidently, no hint of embarrassment, even as her own cheeks flushed. "And yes, we're in our forties, and I'm about to be a divorcee and you're single, and really, we could do worse than each other, couldn't we?"

Emery felt her hands twisting together in her lap, forced them to be still. "Colin, this is...I don't think this is a conversation we should be having." Yes, okay, maybe there was a time or two that she'd thought about it, over the years. When she'd looked at him and wondered. But they'd not gone down that path for a reason—hadn't they?

"Well, I think it is." He shot her a glance. "I'm not saying now, but once my shit is all sorted, once the divorce is finalized, I'm going to call you up and ask you to dinner—and I mean it as a date. And if you're still single, I want you to say yes."

"Colin, I..."

"Just one date, Em. I think we owe it to ourselves—or at the very least, I think *you* owe it to *me*." She winced, and he wrinkled his nose. "Sorry. I don't mean...I just think that maybe we should try—even if it's only once. What have you got to lose?"

"You," she whispered. "I've got *you* to lose, Col." And that was it, wasn't it? When you boiled it all down, that was the heart of the matter. Because if she went there, if she really went there and she fucked it up, she would lose one of the few people she needed, really needed, in her life. And she didn't think she could stand that—she didn't think she could *survive* it, not again.

He took one hand off the steering wheel and reached over, squeezing hers gently. His touch lingered even after he drew his hand away. "You won't. I promise."

But he couldn't promise that, could he? She tried to sort out her mixed feelings, the way she'd felt when he'd got married, how she'd put it to one side. The way she'd felt so many years ago, after they'd slept together, lost in the depths of grief. But this was *Colin*—he was her friend. A friend who had been there no matter what. Who knew everything about her and had never shied away—and who she loved. She could admit that to herself. It was friendship love, sure, but then wasn't it different from how she felt about Bonnie? She hadn't felt the same sense of loss, after all, when she'd watched Bonnie walk down the aisle.

"Okay."

His fingertips jumped on the steering wheel. "Okay?"

She laughed, though it sounded slightly hysterical—and far too young. "Yes. Okay. If you still feel the same when your divorce is done and dusted, I'll go on a date with you. But it's just a date, okay?" she added quickly, concerned about his expectations, about what she was risking by agreeing to this. Already her nerves were pricking, wondering if she was making the right choice. And despite herself, Nick's face flashed into her mind. The sensation of his lips on hers, his hands on her bare skin. That feeling of peace she had when she was around him and didn't have to pretend. Could she really say yes to a date with Colin—even just one date—when she was thinking about Nick like this?

But Colin was smiling at her. And Colin was *here*, and she couldn't deny that the way he was looking at her sent a small, happy lurch through her stomach. "That's all I'm asking for," he said.

Chapter Thirty-Five

Six months later (October 2021)

AGE 42

Emery lay in Nick's arms, her bare back pressed against his chest, listening to the sound of him breathing. They were outside, under the sun, and she felt sleepy and peaceful. She'd asked him to show her one of *his* memories, and this was where he'd brought her. Somewhere in Scotland, in an open field, woods down the other end, a hedgerow behind them. She could smell grass and fresh strawberries in the distance somewhere. The sound of birds, heard but not seen, made up the background hum. It was so very hard, in these moments, to remind herself it was not actually real.

"What are you thinking?" His breath caressed her ear as he whispered, and a shiver ran down her spine as she arched her back into the feel of it.

"I'm thinking that I'm happy here, with you."

She felt the curve of his lips against her neck as he kissed her there. "I'm happy here with you too." He moved her hair to one side so he could kiss more of her neck, and she let out a hum of pleasure. Then he paused. She twisted to look at him.

"Something wrong?"

"No." He gave her back a reassuring rub. "It's just...I met one of your patients the other day."

Her body stilled as she processed that. "Who?" she asked after a beat.

"George."

There was a moment where Emery's heart gave a little lurch, remembering George's face. He'd been only fifty and diagnosed with a degenerative disease. She'd had to get good at putting her feelings to one side, at finding a compartment in which to store what she felt, watching her patients struggle as they approached the end of their life. She'd had to learn to see the good things, and to be there for people while not getting too attached. But George had had an easy smile and a sharp tongue and a wicked sense of humor. And he'd wormed his way under her skin, despite herself.

"Was he...okay?"

"Yeah." Nick kissed the top of her head. "I think he was. He talked about you. He said that you could have warned him about this."

Emery laughed a little. "Sounds like him. But like he would have believed me if I had."

"He said to tell you thank you," Nick murmured. Emery felt her throat clog as she blinked back tears and nodded.

Around them, the field trembled. "You know I love you, right?" she said.

He wrapped his arms around her, pulling her against him, and kissed her shoulder. "I have always loved you."

The meadow was fading now, the birdsong becoming more

distant. And somewhere equally distant, she swore she could hear Colin's voice calling her name. Colin, whose divorce had been finalized, who was coming to pick her up for their date.

"I wish I didn't have to leave you," she whispered. "I wish I didn't have to say goodbye."

"But that's the beauty of this. I will always be with you, even when I'm not."

Chapter Thirty-Six

Three years later (September 2024)

AGE 45

Emery stood in her bathroom, the windows flung wide open behind closed blinds, the late-summer evening light outside fading, and stared at the prescription in her hand. She had, in fact, been given two prescriptions at the doctor's. She'd gone in for HRT and come out with that—plus a drug for her heart. A drug that had now cleared clinical trials and was available to people like her. A drug that, if she took it, would mean she wouldn't have to worry about future episodes, wouldn't have to keep a defibrillator in her cupboard at home and one under her desk at work, wouldn't have to cover her office walls with instructions on how to perform CPR, just in case, or worry about being alone for too long.

A drug that, if she took it, would mean that she'd never see Nick again.

The doorbell rang. She turned from the mirror and headed downstairs, her bare feet padding on the carpet, her movements automatic. She opened the front door to see Colin, the top few buttons of his shirt undone, the backpack he'd recently taken to wearing to work slung over one shoulder, hair disheveled from the train from London to Bristol. He kissed her on the cheek, and she stepped aside to let him in. She still wasn't entirely sure what they were to one another. They didn't live together, but they accepted invitations to things as a couple, stayed around each other's houses at weekends and whenever they could during the week. They also had—really quite good—sex. Most people would consider that a done deal, maybe. She knew it was her, that there was a part of her unwilling to make that final commitment, scared of what it might mean.

"Hey, Em," he said, closing the door behind him. "Sorry I'm a bit late, got caught up at work." He held up a bottle of red wine. "Can you be bothered to cook? I can't—we could get takeout? Em?" Because she was just staring at him. He glanced at the prescription still clutched in her hand. "Hey, that's great, you got it."

"No, I…" Her voice sounded odd—strangely distant. "I mean, yes. But this, it's not…" *Words, Emery, use your words.* "Do you remember, a few years ago, when the doctor talked about a clinical trial, and a drug?"

"Yes, I will always remember that day as the day you finally decided to go out with me." He was grinning, teasing her. When she didn't return the grin or swat him away, his smile faltered. Then realization dawned on his face. "Are you telling me…?" His gaze dropped to her hand again.

"Yes."

"Oh my God!" He picked her up—actually lifted her off her feet—and spun her around. His brows pulled together as he set her down. "You don't look…happy."

Emery wetted her dry lips. "I don't know what I am."

"What do you mean? Emery?" He sounded worried now. "You can't tell me you're seriously considering *not* taking this."

"I . . . I don't know. I need to think about it."

"What on earth is there to think about?"

"I don't know," she said again, and her voice was more of a snap now. "Side effects."

"Side effects? But the alternative is *dying*, Emery. And the doctor said your heart might not be able to sustain many more—"

"I'm well aware of that, thanks."

He shook his head. He was still holding the bottle of wine. "I don't understand." No. How could he? "Don't you want to remove the risk that you might not be here? That you might not, I don't know, see Lily's eighteenth birthday, or watch Bonnie attempt to become a grandmother gracefully, or celebrate our ten-year anniversary?"

"Stop it, Colin." His words were cutting through her, and it felt like emotional blackmail.

"But I don't get it! What side effect could be bad enough to risk all that?"

I wouldn't see him. I wouldn't see him again. Her heart had picked up speed, a panicky feeling settling over her. "I need a minute," she managed to get out, and left him standing in the hallway with his wine, staring after her as she went upstairs. She headed back to the bathroom, set the prescription on the side of the sink and splashed water over her face, tried to take steadying breaths. But the prescription was glaring at her, and when she closed her eyes, all she could see was Nick's face. He wouldn't know. He wouldn't know what had happened to her, where she'd gone. If she took this drug, she wouldn't be able to see him to explain. She wouldn't be able to know for sure whether it was the right thing.

She shouldn't have told Colin. Fuck, she shouldn't have said anything. Because he only saw it as a good thing, and now he was going to make her take it and that would mean...

She heard the creak of the stairs underfoot, then the bathroom door was pushed gently open. "Em?" She looked over at him, her mouth dry, fingers gripping the side of the porcelain sink. "Look, I'm sorry, okay? I know this is a big deal for you." He was trying—trying to understand when there was no way he ever could, because she'd never told him, because there was a part of her she kept hidden, even from him. Her lovely, kind Colin was trying to understand why she wouldn't be happy about this—about the prospect of staying with him, no more heart defects, no more panic and chaos as they both wondered when it would happen next. And she didn't deserve that. The fact that she was questioning it, surely, meant she didn't deserve it.

She started to cry, and he moved toward her, his arms folding around her as the sobs came faster and faster. She wanted to scream, to bury her face in his chest, to take time to figure all this out. She wanted to say what she was really thinking.

I didn't get the chance to say goodbye.

It sent another horrible lurch through her. She couldn't do it. She couldn't *not* say goodbye. Surely she could just put it off—she could wait, take the drugs later, when she was ready. *If* she was ready.

And yet here was Colin, supporting her—sticking by her still, when she'd given him every reason not to. Who somehow found enough parts of her to love despite how much she'd hurt him in the past. Who she loved too. Maybe not in the bright-flare way that she loved Nick, but a love formed of memory, of connection, of intimacy. A love that was real and solid and made her feel safe. And if she loved Colin, if she *really* loved him, could she do that to him? Could she wait, risking her life as she did so, just so she could see Nick again? Could she risk *his* happiness like that?

"I hope you'll take it," he said, rubbing her back sooth-ingly. "I can't lie about that. Because I want a future with you, Emery." She hiccuped against his chest. A *future*. It was something she'd tried never to think about too hard, yet here it was, coming for her whether she liked it or not. "I know we haven't really talked about it, but that is what I want." He pulled back, grasped her chin gently and lifted it so she had to look him in the eye. His face shimmered in and out of focus through her tears. A face that she would hurt if she didn't take the drugs. A face that she might lose if the next time her heart stopped it didn't start again.

"But it is your decision," he said softly. "And I will support you whatever you choose."

A choice. That was what he was giving her. But how could she possibly do it? How could she take these drugs, keep taking them day in, day out, knowing that she'd never see Nick again? Knowing that he'd be *there*, waiting for her? And how could she *not* take them, knowing that she'd be risking her life day in, day out, knowing what the fear of that would do to the people she loved?

A breath shuddered through her, and she closed her eyes, laid her head on Colin's chest again and felt his woody smell wrap around her like a blanket, soothing her. She thought of the last time she'd seen Nick. *I will always be with you, even when I'm not.* She imagined him here now, imagined his arms around her, his voice in her ear. Another sob racked through her, and Colin's arms tightened their hold. But he said nothing more. He wouldn't push, she knew. Even if he didn't fully understand, he wouldn't push.

I will support you whatever you choose.

She kept her eyes closed, knowing that when she opened them, she'd have to make that choice. She stayed there breathing through her tears, and put off the decision that would change everything, one way or another.

Chapter Thirty-Seven

Forty years later

The last time Emery dies, she is eighty-five years old. She is in a hospital bed, her eyes closed, a machine next to her softly beeping. Her eyelids are slightly purple, her hair is white, though still falling in soft curls. The lines on her face are etched deep, her nose a little more crooked than I remember. Did she break it? It wouldn't surprise me if she had—she was probably doing something she shouldn't have at the time. Her hands are barely recognizable, lined and sun-spotted. Someone has painted her nails, though—a bright blue. Whoever it was hasn't been neat, and there are smudges set in the polish.

It's been over forty years since I last saw her, yet still I would know her anywhere. She is surrounded by a group of people. Colin is there, two years older than her, hair all but gone, blue eyes grave and shining with tears as he strokes the top of her head. There is a younger woman, maybe in her fifties, blonde, with warm brown eyes. That must be Lily. Her hand is on Colin's shoulder, a steady support, though I see the way her throat bobs as she takes a breath. In the corner of the room is a young teenager, nails painted the same color as Emery's, long blonde hair hanging around her face like she's trying to hide behind it, her teeth gnawing her bottom lip as she stares at the bed. Lily leaves Colin, crosses the room to put an arm around the teenager. "It'll be okay, my love," she whispers. Lily's daughter, maybe? Or even a granddaughter?

Colin leans closer to Emery, pushes her wispy curls back from her face. Emery's eyes stay shut, the machine beside her keeps on beeping. "You hear that, Em? It'll be okay. You were the one to tell me that, remember? And we're all here, we all love you." A doctor is there, hovering a respectable distance away. Colin takes a shuddering breath, then turns to the doctor, nods. He looks away immediately, as if he can't bear it.

I hear it, the last breath Emery takes, a few moments after the beeping of the machine flatlines. And I wish I could offer comfort to Colin, the man who has been by her side—I wish I could tell him that he is right, that she *will* be okay. That I've got her. But I can't. Because we are gone, Emery and I, away from the hospital room and the people left to grieve her, knowing that this time she will not come back.

As the surroundings shift, as we are pulled to the in-between, Emery turns to me, cocks her head and smiles. "Hello, you." My breath releases on a half-sob. Because here she is. And she is both the older Emery and the younger one, she is both an Emery who has grown, who was brave enough to choose to live life without me, and *my* Emery, the woman I fell in love with, the woman who gave me the courage to face my past—and made me realize I was wrong about my future.

She is crying, soft tears falling down her cheeks, and I feel the tears burning behind my own eyes as I take her in my arms, as I breathe in the smell of her, the spice and warmth.

"I knew I'd see you again," she whispers. "I always knew I'd see you again." I bury my head in her neck to stop myself from crying more—and in this place she does not feel old, or weak, or frail, as she seemed in the hospital bed, but vibrant and strong and *alive*. And I know that through it all, through all the people I have seen and got to know—got to know in a way that I never would have tried to before Emery—a part of me has always been waiting for her, for this moment.

She breaks away and tilts her head to look up at me, her gaze scanning my face in a way that is achingly familiar. "How long do we have?" she asks.

The corner of my mouth crooks up into a smile. "I don't know. I've always told you that." She laughs, and the sound sets me alight. Then she frowns as she looks around. "Where are we?"

I raise an eyebrow. "Don't you remember? This is your show."

She bites her lip as she takes in our surroundings. It isn't just one place, though, I notice. The memory is an amalgamation, something that has never happened before in all the time I've been here. There is a glimpse of a meadow in the corner, and to our left, what I'm sure is an airport terminal. There is a small twin bed—one I recognize from the B&B Emery took me to, twice. And here, where we are standing, is Emery's bed from the first house she bought.

"It's you," she says, looking back at me. "This is a memory of *this* place." She smiles at me. "It's you my brain wants to take me back to." Then the smile fades slightly as she looks over her shoulder, as if searching for someone. And I know, because I know her, what she is thinking.

"Colin?" I ask softly, and she nods.

"Do you think...Will he be okay?"

I hesitate, trying to choose the right words. "I think, if you chose to spend your life with him, he will have the strength to get through this, and find his own peace, when it comes."

She nods again, blinking back tears. "Yes," she says, her voice thick. "Yes, he will." She swipes at a tear that's managed to escape. Then she looks at me, and more tears start to fall. This time she does not brush them away. "I'm sorry. I'm sorry I didn't choose you."

I bring her hand to my mouth, kiss it gently. "I'd be sorry if you had."

She pulls me onto the bed with her, so that we are sitting side by side. Then she rests her head on my shoulder, a comforting weight. "Tell me," she says. "Tell me what has happened to you in all these years." So I do. I tell her about some of the people I met, tell her how, because of her, I have tried to find more connections to those people. Tell her how much I've missed her, and how proud I am of the fact that she chose life. And she tells me about that life—about marrying Colin, building a life with him. She tells me, because she knows she can, about how much she loved him, about how lucky she felt to have him and how she tried to make sure she was worthy of him. She tells me about watching her niece, Lily, get married in turn and have a baby. She gets choked up when she tells me how Bonnie is in a care home now, and about losing Robin, and how painful that was, and how she told Robin that she was sure Amber would be waiting for her. She tells me about her work, and about the ups and downs of that. And she tells me that each and every day, taking the drug was a choice—to stay there with the people she loved, and not to come to me.

And even if I'm sure it can't be possible, it seems that we have longer this time. Longer than I have with other people before they begin to fade. But the fading is inevitable—we both know that. We both have to accept that there is no going back now.

She notices it at the same time, and when she looks down at her hand, merging into the world around it, it is not with fear, or sadness, but acceptance. Those beautiful brown eyes look into mine. "Can you come with me?" she asks.

I place my forehead against hers, a goodbye that has played out so many times before. "I wish I could. But my place is here. It just took me a while to figure that out."

"Do you think there's something more out there?" Her tone is conversational. "Or is there nothing? I know, I know—you don't know." And there is enough of an echo here of the teenage Emery that it makes me smile. A different version of her—and one I love just as much. "But I'm about to die, for real this time—the least you could do is speculate with me. Clouds? Harps?"

I snort out a laugh, which ebbs as I see her fade even more. I take her hand, feel it already slipping from my grasp. I try not to panic, to grip it more tightly. Because that is not what she needs from me right now—and this woman, who has taught me so much, deserves to have an ending without panic, or fear. "I don't think there's nothing," I say, my voice firm, loud enough to carry to wherever she is going. "And whatever is out there, I believe our souls will find each other again one day."

She smiles, and I feel my throat tighten as I realize that this is the last time I will see that smile. "I'll hold you to that." Her voice is distant now, but still her very last words make it through to me, echoing around this place—a place forged of memories of us. "I love you, Nick Ryemore." My name—a name I'm not afraid to use now, because of her.

I force myself to smile, refuse to let her see the tears fall. "I have always loved you, Emery Wilson."

I hold myself together until the very last moment, and only then do I give in to the sobs, let the tears fall. But even as the last of her ebbs away, even as I feel the hold on my body break, I repeat my own words back to myself. *I believe our souls will find each other again.*

The world around me shimmers but does not dissolve into darkness yet, as though this place, *my* place, knows that I need a minute, that I am not quite ready to let go.

I believe our souls will find each other again.

And they will, I tell myself. Because how could they not?

Author's Note

Emery lives with a heart condition in this book—one that is thankfully purely fictitious. It is loosely based on reflex anoxic syndrome (RAS), which is a condition my niece, Lily, has. Reflex anoxic syndrome, or reflex anoxic seizures, can cause someone to stop breathing temporarily. It occurs mainly in young children, but can happen at any age. Unexpected stimulus such as pain, shock or fright can make the heart and breathing stop—though both return to normal soon after, and it is not fatal. However, while I got the idea for Emery's condition from this, it in no way resembles the lived experience of RAS or any other medical condition, and is purely a work of imagination.

Acknowledgements

The idea for this book has been playing around in my mind for several years now—it's a story I've wanted to write for a while but never thought I could! So many people have made this a reality—without whom this would still be a vague concept in my head.

Huge thanks to my agent Sarah Hornsley, who encouraged me to take the time to think this story through and who believed in the idea from my first rambling email about it. Her early advice on a partial first draft made me rethink a chunk of the story, and helped make it into the book it is now. Thank you for your boundless enthusiasm, patience and support. Thanks too to Cara Lee Simpson, for looking after me while Sarah was on maternity leave and supporting me both on this book and my previous novel, *One Moment*.

Thank you to my wonderful editor, Sarah Hodgson, for your genuine enthusiasm for this book and for smart editorial notes. Because this book felt like such a big idea to pull off I went through ups and downs writing it—and your support and encouragement after reading it made me feel it was worth it! Thank you to Kate Straker in Publicity and Sophie Walker and Felice McKeown in Marketing And I think covers for books like this have the potential to be really difficult, but Kimberly Glyder has so totally nailed it—huge thanks for creating a wonderful package!

Huge thanks to Emylia Hall at The Novelry for your creativity and encouragement—you are one of the most motivating people I know! There were so many people who supported my first novel, *One Moment*, but because of the way acknowledgements work I didn't get to thank them last time around. I'm so grateful to everyone who read and supported *One Moment*—which gave me motivation to write this book! Thank you to Georgina Moore and Catherine Jarvie for early support and brainstorming about this book! There are too many people to name, but special thank-you to authors Cathy Bramley, Jill Mansell, Veronica Henry, Holly Miller, Sheila O'Flanagan, Harriet Tyce, Elizabeth Buchan, Cressida McLaughlin and Fanny Blake for taking the time to read and quote for *One Moment*! And a huge, enormous thank-you to all the reviewers and bloggers who took the time to read and support *One Moment*—or, in advance, this book! There are too many people to name personally, but a special thank-you to Nina Pottell, Anne Cater, Jo Finney, Charlotte Heathcote, Claire Frost, Natasha Harding, Lisa Howells, Amy Rowland, Linda Hill and Deirde O'Brien.

Of course readers are the only reason authors ever get to write a book—so thank you, reader, if you have taken the time to read until the end! And an extra special thank-you to anyone who has reviewed or talked about either of my books in any way, shape or form—it means so much.

You Make My Heart Stop

Reading Group Guide

Dear Reader,

Thank you so much for picking up YOU MAKE MY HEART STOP. It means so much to be able to share it with you.

I've had the idea for this novel for a really long time but I just wasn't brave enough to write it. The idea felt too big, too complicated, and I wasn't sure I could pull it off. So it's such a special moment to be writing to you and to know that I did it—and that by the time you read this, it will be an actual book, in someone's hands!

For several years, I've loved the idea of writing about an angel of death, of sorts. Someone who has a rather lonely existence, who only ever meets people briefly as they pass away. And from there, what if this person falls in love with someone he is supposed to be helping to move on? It was a vague idea, but I loved the impossibility of it. For a while though, it was nothing more than that—an idea in the back of my mind, one that I loved but that I couldn't see my way through.

In 2020, during the pandemic, I was living with my sister, who has two daughters—Lily and Ella. At the time, Lily was six and Ella eight, and I was helping out, playing Auntie Becky and taking them to and from school (when they were allowed to go to school), cooking dinner, and helping with homework. Lily was quite ill with tonsillitis one day and stayed home from school. I went to pick Ella up, and I remember pulling back into the drive to see my sister in the front hallway, front door open, cradling Lily in her lap. She was in a complete panic because Lily had collapsed and stopped breathing. An ambulance was on its way.

Lily was fine—she came around before the ambulance arrived—but it was a long stay in the hospital and a stressful experience. We learned that Lily experiences something called reflex anoxic seizures, or RAS, where someone, most commonly a child, can literally stop breathing because of shock or pain, and sometimes, their heart can stop too. Quite often, apparently, children outgrow this, and the mechanics of what actually happens is something I don't quite understand. Nor, it seems, do the doctors have a complete understanding.

I didn't go on to write the novel immediately after this—and in my novel, Emery's heart condition is quite different from what Lily has gone through—but it did add to the kernel of the idea. The fact that someone could go through something that made their heart stop, and go through that more than once, made my vague idea feel just a little more possible. (Lily is very happy and healthy, and it's amazing how she bounces back after any episode, which thankfully hasn't happened in a while, and I named a character in the book after her, though she's still a bit young to understand the context of it all!)

When I finally sat down to write the novel—when I was finally feeling brave enough!—I realized that there was so much more to it than this basic idea. I had to dig deep into how this kind of experience would affect someone and how they might live if they thought that they might die at any given moment. And that's where it got interesting, when I started thinking about the characters.

I hope you enjoyed Emery's journey. It isn't always easy for her, and I don't know if she always makes the best decisions, but for me, those decisions felt real. And that was what I was always hoping for.

If you did read and enjoy, please feel free to get in touch on Instagram or X. Hearing from readers is the best thing ever.

With love and thanks,
Becky

Reading Group Questions

1. Over the course of the novel, Emery reacts to her heart condition by rebelling against the need to be careful, claiming that she's always living for the moment. Is that what she's doing, do you think? Can you understand her attitude?

2. How do you think you would respond to knowing that your heart could stop at any moment—do you think it would make you live life any differently?

3. Emery's parents struggle with the weight of having a daughter who has a heart condition, and each of them responds in a different way. Can you understand why the marriage fell apart? Do you think one or the other parent had a better attitude in how they interacted with Emery given her condition?

4. Emery struggles to form a long-term, meaningful romantic relationship for much of the novel. Can you understand why this is? Do you think you would behave differently if you were in Emery's shoes?

5. Arguably, Emery treats Colin quite badly at times. Why do you think this is? Could you forgive her for it? Could you understand why Colin was able to forgive her?

6. The sister relationship between Amber and Emery is a hugely important one throughout the novel. What do you think it must have been like for Amber, growing up as Emery's older sister, given Emery's heart condition? Do you think Emery ever fully appreciated that?

7. At the beginning of the novel, we learn that Nick feels as if he is trapped and being punished for something. Can you understand that feeling, once you found out about Lisa? Do you think only certain types of people might get stuck in a limbo like this one—and why?

8. Emery has a choice to make at the end of the novel—do you think she made the right one?

About the Author

Becky Hunter grew up in Berkshire, UK, and has loved reading since before she can remember. After studying social sciences at Cambridge University, this love of reading led her to a career in publishing, where she worked as a book publicist in London for several years before taking a career break and moving to Mozambique to volunteer with horses. It was here that she decided to give writing a proper go, though it was still a few years, a few more destinations, and a couple of more jobs before she had the idea that would become *One Moment*, her debut novel.

She currently splits her time between London, Bristol, and Falmouth and works as a freelance book publicist and editor alongside her own writing.

Find Becky on X (@Bookish_Becky) or Instagram (becky hunterbooks). She'd love to hear from you!